Praise for D...

"Emotional depth, romance and a mystery with twists and turns I never saw coming."

—*Cindy Gerard, New York Times Best-seller*

"With DEADLY RECALL Donnell Ann Bell has created another page turner and cemented her status as a suspense author on the rise."

—*Lois Winston, author of the critically acclaimed Anastasia Pollack Crafting Mysteries*

"Edgy characters, breathless pace, satisfying story . . . Deadly Recall is a real page-turner I didn't want to put down. For those who love suspense, Donnell Ann Bell is climbing to the top of her genre."

—*Bestselling medical romance author Dianne Drake*

Deadly Recall—2010 Golden Heart® Finalist

Other Bell Bridge Books titles by Donnell Ann Bell

The Past Came Hunting

Deadly Recall

by

Donnell Ann Bell

Bell Bridge Books

Bell Bridge Books
PO BOX 300921
Memphis, TN 38130
Print ISBN: 978-1-61194-244-6

Bell Bridge Books is an Imprint of BelleBooks, Inc.

We at BelleBooks enjoy hearing from readers.
Visit our websites – www.BelleBooks.com and www.BellBridgeBooks.com.

10 9 8 7 6 5 4 3 2 1

Cover design: Debra Dixon
Interior design: Hank Smith
Photo credits:
Photo (manipulated) © Susan Gottberg | Dreamstime.com

:Lrdf:01:

Dedication

In Loving Memory of Pamela Brown
Every once in a while you do meet an angel on earth.

Prologue

SISTER BEATRICE is in seclusion, children. She leaves us tonight. Please respect her privacy and keep her in your prayers.

Eden Moran raced along the blacktop. Tears streaming and haunted by the principal's words, she gasped when she fell. She landed hard and split open her knee. She wouldn't cry out. At any time, Mrs. Trevino would discover she'd left the playground.

Blood trickled, her knee stung, blond hair escaped her braid. Eden jumped to her feet and continued to run. Up the steps of St. Patrick's, she pulled on the heavy church doors and found them locked tight.

Please, please, please. She craned her neck.

The stained glass windows above the big wooden doors were open. She might as well climb a mountain.

If Sister Beatrice was inside, she would answer. Eden made a fist to pound then dropped it. If anyone else answered, she'd be in trouble. Mrs. Trevino would send her to the principal. Her parents would be furious.

It was a sin to disobey. But this time . . .

Nuns left. Even the *first* graders knew that. Still, to keep them prisoner? Not let them say goodbye? Her nose ran, her leg ached. Eden would never give up. Sister Beatrice understood—she'd saved Eden from the beak-nosed Sister Agnes, who called her a wild, undisciplined prodigy. Whatever *that* was!

Men's voices brought her back, and, for once, Eden was relieved to be her third-grade size and not big like her older sister Meghan. She squeezed into the cranny next to St. Patrick's front doors.

The voices turned out to be the school's creepy, always-staring janitor and the old grump who took up the collection. They moved beyond the church steps and rounded the building. Eden sucked in a breath and trailed after them. She paused at St. Patrick's side entrance, tried the knob, felt it turn, and slipped quietly into the church.

Glad she'd worn sneakers instead of her noisy Mary Janes, she crept along the hallway, inhaling the scent of candle wax and lemon polish as she strode. She could only imagine the stream of Hail Mary's she'd be saying if her pastor found her inside the church. Worse, she pictured how long she'd be grounded if he told her mother.

Mama *adored* Father Munroe.

Determined for neither to happen, Eden hid between the wall and the marble pillar and dared a peek around the column.

That was strange.

A lady knelt in the second pew. She looked like Sister Beatrice, but she wasn't dressed like a nun. She wore her dark hair back, but with her head bowed and her hands folded over her face, Eden couldn't be sure.

Then Father Munroe entered the sacristy and Eden stopped breathing. She scrunched even farther behind the pillar, but she needn't have worried. The only thing he seemed to care about was the lady. Crossing to where she knelt, he murmured, "Celeste."

Eden squeezed her eyes shut. Oh, no. It wasn't Sister Beatrice. She'd broken the rules for nothing.

"Robert." The visitor rose to her feet. "I was told you were on a pastoral retreat."

Was it?

"Forgive me, Celeste. I couldn't stay away. I had to see you."

The woman he called Celeste picked up a bag and tried to brush by him, but he blocked her exit.

"I catch my plane in a few hours. Won't you respect my wishes and leave me be?"

"I do respect you." His soft words carried throughout the empty church. "Celeste, I care for you deeply."

Stretching as far as her arms would go around the cool column, Eden strained to understand. Nuns and priests didn't talk like this. Yet, the more she listened, the more she was sure this was Sister Beatrice. So why was he calling her *Celeste?* And what was he *saying?*

"You have no right to feel that way. *I* had no right."

"That may be true, but God forgive me, I don't regret it. Think of the children, they love you. As for us, I always thought . . ." He reached for her.

She backed away.

"All right," he said stiffly. "I can see that you've made up your mind. If it's what you want, what happened between us will never happen again. You have my word."

"Your *word?*" She laughed, which confused Eden even more, because the lady wasn't happy. "After I put my life back together, I may become a lay teacher. But to belong to a religious order? Honestly, Robert, how can I preach chastity and abstinence when I can't honor my vows?"

"Only one man was perfect, Celeste."

"Don't you dare preach to me." She raised her voice in an angry whisper. "I have to know. How many women did you seduce before me?"

The priest's normally kind face darkened. "I won't dignify that with an answer."

"And I won't shame myself by standing in your presence any longer. I may be a sinner, Robert, but *you* are a predator." She dashed by him into the aisle.

He followed and forced her to face him. "What's gotten into you? Why would you call me that?"

"Let go of me, *Father* Munroe."

"Not until you listen to reason."

They'd gone beyond the pillar, so Eden snuck beyond it to see. It *was* Sister Beatrice. What's more, she was afraid. Trembling, Eden wanted to help her, but what could a little girl do?

She opened her mouth to beg them to stop. She was a second too late.

Sister Beatrice shoved him. Father Munroe staggered, but then he recovered and went toward her again. With his back was to Eden, she wasn't clear what happened next. All she knew was the thud that came afterward felt like a blow to her heart.

Eden froze as still as the column beside her.

Father Munroe dropped to his knees. "Celeste?" His voice sounded strange and high pitched as he cradled her in his arms. "Oh, dear God, no! Celeste, wake up . . ."

The noonday Angelus drowned out his wails.

Shocked back to the moment, Eden covered her ears. Toll after toll, the bells rang, misting like candle smoke into angry, gnarled fingers. Only they weren't pointing at Father. They swooshed down from the steeple and took aim at Eden.

Booming and hissing, they hounded her footsteps as she fought to get out of the evil place. *You disobeyed. You shouldn't be here . . . never would've happened . . . you left the playground . . .*

That's where they found her, flying high in a swing. When no one could coax her down, Mrs. Trevino yanked the chain and brought Eden to a wobbly stop. Puzzled by her teacher's red-faced glare, Eden shoved her unraveled braid from her eyes and glanced around for the other children. Finding them gone, she shrank back in the swing.

As grownups surrounded her, asking their very weird questions, Eden wanted to answer them. Truly. But she simply had no idea how she'd ripped a hole in her uniform, gashed her knee, or lost track of her classmates. So, grasping the chain, she looked up at them and told them the truth. She couldn't recall.

Chapter One

Seventeen years later

KEVIN DANCER negotiated the Northeast Heights construction site, stepping over rocks, scrap metal and two-by-fours. He paused as a man wearing a hard hat approached. The construction worker's frown appeared cemented on his face, and Kevin suspected the bronzed, cinderblock type was the welcoming committee.

"You with the cops?" the workman asked.

Albuquerque's finest hadn't made him a detective for nothing. He flashed his badge. "Kevin Dancer, APD."

"Walt Jackson, KLJ's area superintendent." He looked Kevin up and down. "You don't look Indian."

Kevin squinted behind his Ray-Bans. The super probably had formed that opinion from Kevin's sandy blond hair. He'd gotten the comment a few times since leaving Ohio, graduating from NMSU, and then deciding to stay. The Land of Enchantment was steeped in culture and tradition, among them its Native American dancers. "Could be," he said, "but I'm told Dancer's English. You got something to show me?"

"Yeah." The shorter man grimaced. "C'mon, we'll make a stop by the trailer."

Ignoring the workers milling about on the trailer steps, Jackson grabbed a hard hat marked *visitor* and commanded Kevin to put it on. The superintendent, it appeared, was used to giving orders.

Wordlessly, Kevin obliged. After all, he was a *quid pro quo* kind of guy. If nothing came of the sighting, it didn't do to shove his weight around too soon.

Stepping back into the Albuquerque scorcher, Jackson said, "This way. For your information, Detective, KLJ pulled permits, went through every bureaucratic hoop to build here. The Northeast Heights is in Albuquerque proper. We're not on reservation land, and there's not a known Indian burial ground for thirty miles. I got a penny-pinching owner breathing down my neck, and a timeline from hell. Now I got bones and the shook-up operator who disturbed them."

"Noted," Kevin said. Several tribes called New Mexico home, among them the Navajo, Apache and Ute. Given his knowledge of the tribal leaders and the meticulous records they kept, he doubted the construction workers had stumbled onto a burial site. He never said never, however, or speculated in front of a witness. *Never.*

The man in charge led him to a huge hole in the ground that had been dug for yet another shopping center to accommodate the city's half-million population. A sunning lizard appeared annoyed at their approach. It scurried from a rock into the shade of the landscape's ever-present prickly pear cactus.

The air was so thick with desert heat and kicked-up dust, Kevin tasted grit on his tongue. He literally saw waves of vapor rising from the soil. Orange mesh enclosed the area. Whether the site proved to be a crime scene or an undiscovered burial ground, if the bones proved human, the mesh would soon have yellow tape for company.

Beyond the immediate site sat an abandoned backhoe, and beside it a dump truck brimming with dirt. One worker leaned against the truck's grill, while another squatted next to the vehicle's tire and sketched the ground with a stick.

"Sammy, Ernesto," Jackson called. "This is Detective Dancer. He's come to see what you've found."

Kevin soon learned that Sammy, a long-haired scrawny kid, was the driver of the dump truck. Ernesto, the man doodling, was the operator of the tractor backhoe. Jackson explained that part of Sammy's responsibilities had been to secure the area from wandering personnel and to make sure most of the dirt made it into the bed of the truck. He also was the witness who saw the remains fall from the claws of the backhoe and called a frantic stop to the digging.

Using the large tire for footing, Kevin hoisted his frame over the edge and scanned the bed's contents. Finding bones, clothing or evidence intact now that digging had begun would prove a challenge. He donned gloves from his back jean pocket, then stifled a groan when he surveyed layer after layer of dirt.

He glanced down at the man scrawling in the sand. "Got a shovel some place?"

Ernesto came to his feet and hurled the stick away. "I'll get you one. Just tell me it ain't a kid."

Kevin shared a sympathetic shake of his head. "Can't tell you anything right now."

A few minutes later, shovel in hand, he returned to the job. Carefully turning accessible areas, he eventually struck something hard. He concentrated midway, siphoning the sandy mix to see what he'd come up with. About two feet into the dirt, a grayish white appendage appeared. Cops were taught the difference between animal and human remains, and while he was no expert on the body as a whole, he recognized a human femur.

He continued searching the vicinity with no luck, then moved to the rear quadrant of the truck. About two feet down, he hit another solid object. He turned the shovel on its side and uncovered what looked like a sternum. Traces of fabric were lodged in the fragile ribcage. Drawing it closer, he saw that the tattered blue garment still held the remnants of a silky sheen. Kevin's pulse quickened along with his hopes. If he had to make a guess, he'd say it came from a woman's blouse. If luck were on his side—a huge *if*—he might even stumble onto a tag or a label, which could break the case wide open. It would not only tell them the name of the manufacturer, it could lead right down to the store that had sold it.

Even so, who knew how long these bones had been in the ground? The fabric did provide one very important clue, though. The ancients didn't bury their dead in synthetic blends.

Securing his footing via the tire again, he jumped down. He focused on the sweating, akimbo-armed superintendent, who hadn't appeared to so much as twitch while Kevin was digging. The super's mouth barely moved. "Well?"

Kevin removed the gloves and hard hat and wiped his dripping brow. "I don't think you've invaded any type of burial ground."

Jackson breathed a sigh of relief. Unfortunately, it was premature.

"What I can tell you is you got yourself a suspicious death."

The super's bronze face paled. "How long before we know for sure?"

Kevin shook his head. "As long as it takes." He pulled out his cell and thumbed down the list of numbers until he reached Ike Krowtow, the Bernalillo County medical examiner. He gave Ike his location, then said, "You may want to call UNM in on this one. We'll need a forensic anthropologist."

The superintendent flipped his own phone open. "Close everything down and send everybody home."

As Kevin went in search of nearby shade and watched men walking away from their jobs, he derived little satisfaction in knowing the super had given his last order for a while.

Chapter Two

AFTER A PAINFULLY slow forensic investigation, Kevin Dancer knew the meaning of frustrated. The bones and dental remains found at KLJ's construction site had been identified as Celeste Lescano, aka Sister Beatrice of the Convent of St. Ursula. Yet the investigation had led Kevin and his partner, Sal Raez, in circles, ending up nowhere. It was said the two had a talent for making a dead lead walk, but a cold case this old was next to unsolvable. Give him a nun, who'd led a sheltered existence, with no remaining family, and you upped the chances to impossible.

And now the latest. His less-than-handy partner just couldn't hire a professional to patch his roof. Sal had fallen from the second story and broken his leg.

On his own for the time being, Kevin glanced at the name on the paper in hand and grabbed his jacket. If traffic held, Albuquerque's District Courthouse was a twenty-minute drive. According to her secretary, his newest lead should be there.

He pulled open the doors to the courtroom, grasping for any straw-like evidence he might have overlooked. Seventeen years could play hell on the memory, and potential witnesses regarding Sister Beatrice hadn't exactly been jumping out of the baptismal font. He moved his hand over the notes and the grade school photo in his pocket, as if their existence could prove he was onto something.

Eden Moran had been nine at the time of the nun's death, and one witness who remembered her described her as, "flakier than the crust of her mom's apple pie."

Determined to see for himself, Kevin bypassed a deputy and eased into a seat next to a woman resting her hands on a very pregnant belly. As he sat bouncing his leg, he realized he was hopeful. One, he hoped to catch Ms. Moran at the end of these proceedings, and two, he hoped the lady next to him wouldn't give birth.

Kevin's gaze wound past the spectators in the courtroom to the blonde representing a Hispanic defendant, and he leaned back for the show.

"Ms. Moran," the judge said.

She rose from the table, released her hair from a knot, and let her long hair fall free. Kevin resisted rolling his eyes. He'd become a cop for this very reason. Defense lawyers undid clean arrests and put the scum of the earth back on the street. Sure, she was only a court-appointed public defender, but she appeared to be learning fast. For her to use her valley girl looks to sway the jurors' votes turned his insides.

Still, even as he'd formed his opinion, she gathered her hair back up and did that thing women mysteriously knew how to do, securing it with God-knows-what. She shoved her hands into the pockets of a navy blazer, then acknowledged the prosecutor with a *you-had-your-turn* smile.

Kevin shifted in his chair.

Eden Moran might be manipulative. She was also stunning—the kind of woman who invited a man to look but don't cross.

"Wow," she said, surprising him further with her silky modulated tone. She approached the jury box and placed a hand over her heart. "Mr. Buhrmann just sold you a bill of goods back there. If I hadn't listened to Judge Estep's instructions, I might vote to convict my client, too.

The five-man seven-woman panel followed her every move, and Kevin acknowledged the finesse of a skilled attorney. Looking each one in the eye, she said, "No, Manuel Aguirre didn't live in the Ridgecrest neighborhood. No, he wasn't driving a car. And I have to agree with Mr. Buhrmann. If I passed my client on the street, I'd be afraid of him, too. Just look at his piercings and tattoos."

Pressing a thumb under her chin and a finger to her lips, she worked the jury. She narrowed her gaze, appearing in the height of concentration. "So because he was on foot, three of the homes he painted were burglarized, and he was in the vicinity when the police arrived, it's reasonable to believe the homeowner's assertions that it was Manuel who set up the crimes. *He* served as a lookout when Mr. Jacobs surprised the intruders who, in turn, severely beat him." She approached the defense table and pivoted again toward the jury. "Isn't it?"

She paused. "It is, if you fall prey to the DA's propaganda and don't consider the exhibits at trial." Picking up a voluminous folder, she said, "You must look closely at *all* the evidence. The sworn affidavits of the people Manuel worked for, the painting estimates he gave out the days of the burglaries, and the statement of the man who was repairing his truck.

"Manuel's vehicle might have been on the fritz, ladies and gentlemen, but that didn't mean *he* was. He couldn't afford to stay home." Eden glanced at the woman sitting next to Kevin. All eyes in the courtroom, including his, shifted. "His wife's expecting their first child.

"So what was Mr. Aguirre doing at the time of the burglaries? Not aiding and abetting, I assure you. He was drumming up business for when he *could* work.

"As for the piercings and tattoos? There's an old adage in this instance that seems appropriate." Removing her jacket, she stepped toward the judge. His Honor nodded emotionlessly, the courtroom erupted in murmurs and the prosecutor stiffened. "I believe we know it as, 'Never judge a book by its cover.'"

Like most of the people watching, Kevin leaned forward. Yeah, she was flaky all right. Flaky like a fox. She'd chosen closing arguments to pull this stunt where the judge was bound to grant her more leeway. Yet, facing the bench, she only seemed intent on flashing the judge, then, after he granted permission, the jury. As for Kevin, he would have given an entire paycheck to get a glimpse of what she'd shown that jury. Although by their raised brows and affirmative nods, it appeared she'd swayed their opinions.

Donning her jacket, she continued, "The prosecution contends Mr. Aguirre was an accomplice, and that whether he committed the actual burglaries or not, he was the instigator. "The men who stole the property and brutalized the homeowner have not been apprehended. Mr. Jacobs seeks justice. Everyone in this courtroom can understand that. But, ladies and gentlemen, you *cannot* convict a man for walking down the street.

"Not one witness has come forward to substantiate the homeowner's claim, and Mr. Aguirre himself insisted this case go to trial." She placed her hands on the jury box railing and lowered her voice. "This isn't about making a purchase and later suffering buyer's remorse. This is prison time for my client. What's more, this case is circumstantial. You have no cause to convict."

Along with everyone else in the courtroom, Kevin watched her return to the defendant's table, where she leaned in and conferred with her client.

HER ADRENALINE rush over, Eden sat with Manuel. Despite the deputies approaching to take him back to jail, she hesitated to smile. She wished she could guarantee him a favorable verdict. She couldn't. She'd done this too many times, when she expected a positive outcome and was totally blown away.

Manuel's tattoos snaked out from beneath the collar of the long-sleeved cotton shirt she'd insisted he wear, and without the multiple studs in his eyebrows, nose and ears, he simply looked wounded. She sighed. An IBM executive he wasn't. Nor was he a criminal. She'd represented too many who were, and she knew the difference.

"What happens now, Ms. Moran?"

She met his worried gaze. "We wait. We cross our fingers, we think positive and we wait."

He glanced over his shoulder to the place his wife had been sitting. "Lupe had to get back to work. I hope she's okay."

Eden grimaced. What could she say? Eight-and-half-months pregnant, Lupe worked in a hotel laundry. If this man was convicted, things didn't bode well for his family.

Signaling their impatience, the deputies directed Manuel to stand.

She ignored them, rose as well, and focused on her client. "You know what? I'm starving. I'll bet you are, too. There's a hotdog stand near the courthouse. What can I get you?"

Her client stared at her, aghast. "I'm a vegan, Ms. Moran."

Dropping into the chair as the deputies led him away, she propped her chin in her hand. A vegan. Of course he was. A painter by day, an artist by night, and a gentle spirit every step of the way.

In case of a hasty verdict, she ensured her cell phone was on, then left the courthouse. The scent of broiling franks made her mouth water. Several well-dressed men and women stood in line at Rudy's Fine Hotdog Cuisine, the area's most popular vendor. The little stand was a gold mine for Rudy and a godsend for anyone too busy for a sit-down lunch.

Manuel might have been a vegan, but Eden sure wasn't. She ordered her usual, a beef dog, with a smidge of catsup, extra mustard, banana peppers, and sauerkraut. Then, tearing off the wrapper, she prepared to take an unladylike bite and be in heaven.

"I'll have whatever she's having," a deep voice said close to her ear. Still chewing, she turned, almost to collide with a broad chest encased in a burgundy cotton shirt. Her gaze traveled upward passed some very nice shoulders to a guy in sunglasses. He wore an air of confidence as well as a decent smile. Lawyer maybe? If so, she'd never met him.

He stared down at her hotdog and his grin receded. "On second thought, make mine edible. One hotdog with mustard," he told the vendor, slipping Rudy a few bills. "Provided this pretty lady didn't use up all the condiments."

Before she could step back in protest, he took a napkin and dabbed the side of her mouth. Oh, yeah, he had the arrogance of a lawyer, but she quickly nixed the idea. Lawyers rarely wore jeans. Nor did they come stacked with abs or biceps like these. She'd been hit on by all kinds before, and if this clown thought he was charming, or that she embarrassed easily, he was about to find out otherwise. "Thanks. My mommy usually wipes my face in public, but since she's not here . . ." Eden started toward her favorite picnic table in the park across the street from the courthouse.

Her new friend with the monumental ego retrieved his hot dog and caught up to her. "Sorry about that. I just don't think yellow's your shade." He took his own good-sized bite of the dog, and her annoyance lessened.

"I saw your closing argument," he said. "You did a good job."

He'd been in the courtroom? How'd she miss *him*? He kept his dark blond hair shorter than she liked, but she loved dimples, and it didn't hurt that he wasn't obsessed with a razor. Based on his tanned, unlined face, she'd place him in his late twenties, early thirties. With those aviator sunglasses, it was hard to tell. She couldn't see his eyes. *Too bad.*

On the other hand, Eden never missed a chance for a critique. "So if you were in that jury room right now, how would you vote?"

"I only heard your side." He shrugged. "Besides, I come with a pretty strong bias." He pulled back his jacket, revealing the shield clipped to his belt.

A cop. Thus explaining his arrogance. She finished the last bite of the dog, tossed the wrapper in a nearby trashcan, then leaned down for a closer look at his ID. "Well, then, Detective . . . *Dancer.* As much as I appreciate the beauty tip, I don't think we—"

"I'd like to talk to you about St. Patrick's School."

As much as she willed it not to, her mind rewound seventeen years. She'd read the school was having financial woes and had formed a fundraising committee. Shading her eyes, she squinted up at him. Had he gone to St. Patrick's? "If you're alumni, you'll have to swing by my office. I don't keep my checkbook with—"

"Are you always this difficult to talk to?"

"Always." She blinked. "What part of 'swing by my office' confused you?"

"The part where I produce my credentials and you think I'm a solicitor." The detective pointed to the table. "Could we sit, please? I'm here on official business."

What he could have to say to her in any capacity was beyond comprehension. Still, it was warm outside, and she had a magnificent view of the foothills. She moved to a picnic table shaded by a poplar tree, stepped up on the bench and plopped down on the tabletop. "I think I should warn you, Detective, I didn't leave St. Patrick's on the best of terms."

"I heard."

"You *heard?*"

He opened a pocket notebook. "I talked to Mr. Edgars, the school's current principal. He went through old records and told me you'd been expelled."

"I prefer to think I was forcefully invited not to return. So did St. Patrick's burn to the ground and I'm your best suspect?" Frowning, she shook her head from side to side. "That's just sad."

"As far as I know, it's still standing." Kevin joined her on the tabletop. She liked that about him. He knew how to eat a hotdog, and he wasn't uptight.

"I was told when you attended school you were particularly close to one of its teachers."

A laugh escaped and she slapped her thigh. "I was *expelled*, Detective. They didn't make that part up. I wasn't tight with any of those cold-blooded penguins."

"Her religious name was Sister Beatrice," he said, undeterred.

As Eden mentally ticked off the names of her teachers, their names came easily to mind. Yet, at his use of this unfamiliar person, her stomach felt like she'd been afloat on the Red Sea at the time Moses had parted it. Eden pressed a hand to her stomach just as her cell phone rang.

Typical cop, Dancer didn't give space. She would have called him on his behavior if the party needed attorney/client confidentiality. But since all that was required was a simple, "good-bye," she saw no reason to challenge him.

She stood and flipped the phone shut. "Verdict's in. Gotta run."

He helped her from the bench, earning him yet another gold star and annoying her further.

She walked away. The tenacious man called after her, "Eden, you didn't answer my question. Sister Beatrice, do you remember her?"

Eden sighed and turned in his direction. No matter how much she liked the cop's looks, no way in hell was she reliving her days at St. Patrick's. "You seem like a nice guy, Detective. I wish I could help. Sorry," Eden said. "But that name doesn't strike a chord."

Chapter Three

"YOUR SISTER'S on line one," the department secretary called from the doorway.

Stretching across her desk, Eden waved to the harried woman who supported a department of twelve, then snatched up the phone. "You got my message?"

"You mean the sonic boom that pierced my eardrum?" Meghan asked. "Loud and clear. Remind me the next time I'm up on charges to call you."

"Thanks. It's a gift." Eden couldn't stop grinning.

From her boss on down, eight public defenders had squeezed into her shoebox of an office to congratulate her. Their gift of wilted daisies sat in a mason jar on the edge of her desk. Only the best for her, her boss, Dan Miller, had crowed. She'd laughed and threatened to share her caseload with the first lawyer who spilled water on the myriad files she'd yet to peruse.

As for her client, he'd literally grown in stature when the jury foreman announced, *not guilty*. Arm in arm, and very much relieved, Manuel and Lupe Aguirre had left the courthouse. *Free*.

Eden's heart swelled. She'd defended an innocent man, she was sure of it.

Broaching a subject not nearly as safe as her victorious court case, she asked her sister, "How's Steve?"

"Fine. Cory finally got leave. It looks like he'll be Steve's best man after all."

"Great." Eden manufactured her best upbeat tone. "I look forward to seeing him again." The when and the where she left unsaid.

Unfortunately, the connection wasn't weak enough to mask her older sister's sigh. Eden hated when either Meg or her mother sighed. They were so good at it. Eden tugged at her lower lip. No wonder she'd become a public defender. Between family, religious and societal expectations, she'd had enough guilt heaped on her to last a lifetime. "I'll be at the reception, Meg. I'm sorry. I don't do churches."

"What does that *mean*, you 'don't do churches?' That is the weirdest thing I've ever heard. You're one screwed-up human being, do you know that?"

Eden added her own sigh to the conversation. What *was* wrong with her? Was her mother right? Year after year when she'd refused to go to Mass, was it because she'd made an unknown pact with the devil? Her sister had been after Eden for a year to be her maid of honor. Why couldn't she do this one simple thing for her only sister?

"Relax," Meg said. "I'm through begging. You know Mom, it has to be family. She wants me to ask Darla."

Eden's heart sank. Just thinking about their allergy-ridden first cousin caused Eden's ankle to swell. Darla, who was Meghan's age, had hated it when the younger Eden tagged along. Darla had once checked Eden with her roller skate and denied doing it.

For Darla Barrett to be her sister's maid of honor . . . well, quite simply, Eden's demonic side sprouted horns. "What? Did they cancel roller derby that weekend?"

"*What?*"

"Nothing." She closed her eyes and breathed deeply. *Dammit, Eden, how can you tell her no?* Even after her mother could no longer tolerate Eden's *episodes* and shipped her off to live with Aunt Caroline, Meghan had called without fail. Where Joanna Moran had washed her proverbial hands, Meg had never stopped caring.

"It might be safer for your guests if I stood up with you, Meg."

It took a moment for the offer to register, but finally a gasp came from the other end. "Really, Eden?"

"Did you return my dress?"

"The shop where I bought it said all sales were final."

Eden pictured St. Patrick's and shook off the revulsion. Yep, she was the spawn of Satan, all right. "In that case, Meg, I'd love to be your maid of honor."

A few minutes later, Eden hung up and lowered her head to the desk. Tapping her forehead against the grain, she almost missed the knock on the door. She peered over the foot-high Pendaflex folders to see Detective Dancer in the doorway, then ducked in hopes he hadn't seen her.

Great. With so many positives in her professional life, why the sudden focus on St. Patrick's? Closing her eyes, Eden willed the church to explode and the cop to go away.

"KEEP THAT UP, you'll get a headache." Kevin leaned over the mountain of files and stared at the woman facedown on her desk. He hadn't waited for an invitation to enter. He suspected she'd have told him no. Judging from her desk, they appeared to have something in common after all. Leave it to one workaholic to recognize another.

She tilted her head and opened an eye.

"I knocked, but evidently we were in competition." He glanced around. "Nice closet."

"If you leave now," she said, "I'll bet you'll find someone double-parked outside. Hurry. It'll help you reach your quota."

At least she was fun to look at. Outside of the courtroom, she'd taken her hair down. With that platinum blond hair and model-smooth skin, she seemed more the type to glide down a runway than to defend the dregs of society. "I heard you won your case. You down in the dumps because you know he'll do it again?"

On that jab, she opened both eyes and sat up straight. "The government failed to prove its case, Detective. See that bookshelf to your left?"

He already had, along with every other detail surrounding the woman and her office—cheap furniture, crappy carpet. She had a window of sorts. Battered mini-blinds opened to a brick wall. Maybe the numerous scribbled-on Post-It notes stuck to the pane were meant to improve the view. They sure as hell hadn't hurt it.

She'd looped the jacket she'd worn at trial today over the back of her chair. Remembering the challenge she gave to the jury, Kevin's gaze shot to what she wore underneath. Unfortunately, the shimmering beige camisole hid way too much cleavage and her toned upper body. But at least he could die happy now. He discovered what she'd shown to the jury—a treble clef tattoo above her left breast.

Now wasn't *that* interesting? According to St. Patrick's admin files, Sister Beatrice, along with her other curriculum, had assisted in the school's music program.

As she'd directed earlier, Kevin acknowledged the bookcase. The volumes of constitutional law that lined the shelves weren't first-class editions or as comprehensive as the books J.T. kept in his library. Then again, there was no comparison between a public defender's office and his stepfather's criminal law practice.

Kevin's jovial mood disintegrated. "I've seen better-looking shelves at a garage sale, Ms. Moran. So spare me the defendant-has-rights lectures. I'm following up on our earlier discussion. I'm heading up a murder investigation."

"Who died?"

"The woman you denied knowing. Sister Beatrice from the Convent of Saint Ursula."

"Denied, and still do. I do not know anyone by that name." Eden reached into her desk and withdrew a roll of Lifesavers. "Peppermint?"

Calloused fingers met touchable skin. Popping the mint into his mouth, he ordered his mind back on track. "I find it remarkable that we interview two of your former classmates about this dead nun and both say talk to you."

"I won't even speculate." She glanced at her watch and twisted her hair into its typical knot. "What I do know is that I'm due at the detention center. And, Detective Dancer, if this woman *was* murdered, as much as I respect that you're trying to do your job, I, too, am an officer of the court. I frown on people killing each other. So from here on out, unless you want me to go over your head and cite harassment, I'd appreciate it if you'd take me at my word."

Her threats had zero impact on him; he also had zero proof that she was lying—unless he incorporated gut instinct and curiosity over a treble clef tattoo. Still, Eden Moran knew the system. If she went over his head, Kevin's commander would order him to back off.

She rose from her chair and reached for her jacket, which led Kevin to conclude that their interview was over. He turned and traversed the worn carpet.

"Detective."

He turned in the doorway.

"How did your victim die?"

"Sorry, Counselor. I'm not at liberty to say."

"Can you at least tell me when?"

He re-entered the office. He could be an asshole and punish her for not cooperating. All that would serve would be to prolong the animosity between them. Besides, now that he'd seen the tattoo, he wanted to gauge her reaction. "We place the time of death around seventeen years ago."

Her eyes widened. Eden Moran was smart enough to do the math. Sister Beatrice had died around the same time she'd attended St. Patrick's School.

"And you're just *now* investigating her death?"

"We found bones, Ms. Moran." To hell with his good intentions, his tone came out sharper than intended.

Her lawyerly mask slipped back into place. "I wish I could help. Good luck."

"Thanks. I knew you were a long shot, but I had to try."

"Have you tried speaking with the other nuns or the clergy who knew her?"

Had he *tried?* A visual of the push pins dotting the U.S. and International maps in his office came to mind. "They're either dead, in retirement homes or reassigned. My partner and I have spent months tracking them down and conducting interviews."

"I see." She shut the briefcase, then slowly came to stand beside him.

"You've considered that her killer might be, too, right?"

His jaw tightened at the injustice that had been done to the nun. "Yeah, and if that's the case, so be it. But someone has to speak for the dead."

"And on that, Detective, we're in complete agreement," she replied, sharing a sympathetic smile. "Something tells me if he's still out there, you'll be the one to find him."

"That's the plan—unless I'm ordered off the case for lack of evidence." He watched her closely. She gave nothing away.

"Where will you go from here?"

Kevin glanced toward her office window and the brick wall that obscured her view. He felt like he'd slammed into one. He shrugged. "Since no one seems to know her as Sister Beatrice, my next step is to see if anyone remembers her as Celeste."

CELESTE.

Long moments after Dancer left, Eden stood motionless. Along with a deep intake of oxygen, she drew her briefcase to her chest. She scanned her overtaxed brain, listing friends, relatives, coworkers, acquaintances, enemies, anyone with that particular name. No one came to mind. So what was with her stomach and these nonstop calisthenics?

She set her briefcase down and dashed for the middle drawer of her desk. Withdrawing the last of her Lifesavers, she chomped on the remaining two and checked her watch. A client charged with armed robbery awaited her at the jail.

She grabbed her briefcase. Let him stew a little longer. She'd read the facts of his case. He wasn't going anywhere. But Eden was taking a drive.

KEVIN SANK INTO the chair facing his partner's vacant desk as Sal hobbled toward him. His longtime associate hadn't quite gotten the hang of the crutches. Add carrying lunch to the mix, and the cop wore a three-day-old scowl.

From Sal's wife, Becky, Kevin had learned it wasn't wise to offer the proud man help, so Kevin ribbed his friend instead. "You want to hurry it up. It feels like I've been waiting an hour for you to make it across the room."

Sal set his McDonald's bag on his desk and gave Kevin the finger. "The only thing saving my ass from spreading is the fact I burn a zillion calories getting to a place that ordinarily takes me two seconds." Sal started to sit, then rolled his eyes. "I forgot my damn drink."

Chuckling, Kevin rose. He strode into the employee lounge across from the detective's division and returned a few seconds later with his partner's staple, a Diet Pepsi.

Sal flipped the tab. "How'd the interview with the little girl go?"

Little girl. From the reports they'd garnered, everyone still thought of Eden Moran as nine years old. "That little girl is some kind of woman now." Kevin whistled. "*Muy caliente*, partner."

"Are you kidding me? After all those old prunes I interviewed? I must not be living right." Staring down at his casted leg, Sal shook his head. "She tell you anything?"

Replaying his time with the public defender, Kevin said, "Yes and no. Get this. She's an attorney—for the dark side."

His partner's dark brown eyes widened. "Oh, man. And *you* went to talk to her? What a time for me to break my leg. What'd you do when you found out, rip her head off?"

Kevin acknowledged a new hire passing by. "Relax. I was cool."

"What do you mean 'yes and no'?"

"I mean I felt she was lying, and she was just as convincing that she wasn't."

Sal paused in opening the bag. The man who thought he could fix anything spread his big hands wide. "Will you listen to yourself? She's a lawyer, Kev. If her lips were moving, lying is automatic."

"She claimed she didn't know Sister Beatrice."

"There's no way you can believe that. All the reports—"

Kevin glanced at their boss's closed door. "We're this close to being taken off this case. Eden Moran has made it clear she'll file harassment charges if we pursue her. From what I saw, she's just the kind who'll do it."

"That's never stopped us before. We go around her—check with her family members. Corroborate her story."

"I thought of that, too. But she's not a suspect, and if we do—"

"Falls under harassment," Sal answered his own question while unwrapping his lunch. "So we do it quietly, without tipping her off."

"Why didn't I think of that?" Kevin said, sharing a smirk with his partner. "Any word on the priest who was there at the time?"

"*Nada.* These people protect their own, Kev. Know what I'm thinking?"

"With you? No tellin'."

"I'm wondering if he left the priesthood."

"If he left soon after the nun's murder, I'd be a little suspicious, wouldn't you?"

Sal fluttered his lashes. "You're *always* suspicious. I find that very attractive about you."

"Wiseass. So where do we go from here?"

The joker in Sal vanished and his scowl returned. "Since I'm chained to this desk, I run the priest through NCIC and break my mother's heart by hounding the diocese. You stay on the lady lawyer. Somebody's lying, and it can't be all of our witnesses."

Nodding, Kevin said, "Just wish she didn't have the power to make our lives miserable."

"Too late," Sal muttered. "Already there."

Kevin stood. "Think I'll check in with the Anthropology Department. Maybe it'd help potential witnesses if we had a composite of what Sister Beatrice looked like."

"Go for it. But don't expect to stumble on a looker like you did the pretty lawyer." Sal removed the tomatoes from his sandwich. "The nuns who taught me chased parked cars for a living."

Lifting a brow, Kevin suspected only Catholics could get away with insults like that. He walked in the opposite direction of the commander's door. One thing was for sure, until Kevin developed a firmer lead on this case, he was steering clear of the old man's office.

Chapter Four

EXECUTIVE DIOCESAN assistant Janice Charles prided herself on her professionalism and being the consummate representative of the Catholic Church. Today, however, she slammed the phone down, effectively cutting off the caller who once again identified himself as a Detective Salvatore Raez.

That was the third phone call from the Albuquerque Police Department she'd received this week, this one more insistent and threatening than the last. Instead of going through protocol and asking her his questions, he was demanding to talk to the bishop.

Of all the nerve. She reached for his calendar and counted the remaining dates until his return. The recently promoted monsignor never stopped. He'd earned this trip to the Vatican. She was *not* interrupting his spiritual journey to alert him that the diocese might have a potential problem. Janice had no qualms he would curtail his honorary celebration and return to New Mexico to deal with the police.

She massaged the left side of her neck, which constantly cramped during stressful times, and glanced down at her notes. Detective Raez wanted to talk to Father Robert Munroe about his time at St. Patrick's. Drumming her fingers on the desk, she slowly exhaled. Didn't they know?

No. Any contact she'd had with the diocesan legal counsel had been business as usual. If a crisis existed, the lawyers would be calling nonstop to establish damage control.

Three sharp raps on her office door interrupted her concentration. Marshall Knight, the business manager, entered, as always without permission, ready to exert his authority during the bishop's absence.

"By all means, Marshall, come in," Janice said, standing and placing a hand on her hip. "How may I *help* you?"

He tossed the files into her in-basket, then narrowed his gaze, obviously displeased at her lack of respect. "I asked Thomas to repair the garage gate three days ago. Any idea where he is?"

She held a sigh inward. "He was at Mass this morning. I'm sure he'll get to it as soon as he can. You need to be patient, Marshall. Thomas isn't a young man anymore. And yelling at him isn't helping."

The business manager curled a lip in disgust. "Don't give me that.

We're nearly the same age. If he'd do his job I wouldn't have to yell, now would I? We need to retire the old loon. For crying out loud, if he's not lurking, he's praying."

"What is the world coming to? Imagine, praying at a diocese." Janice reached for the top file in her in basket. "Happily, his retirement isn't your decision to make."

"It is while the bishop's away," Marshall warned. "Maybe I should make the hard choices the bishop won't and get rid of Thomas before he gets back."

Silently agreeing with Marshall, Janice pulled her hand away. Why the bishop tolerated the mentally erratic Thomas or the bad-tempered Marshall Knight was anyone's guess. But those were the facts she dealt with. "I promise you, the bishop won't take kindly to any ill treatment of Thomas. I'll make sure he fixes the gate by today's end."

"You do that," Marshall said. "Anything else?"

Janice opened the desk drawer and slid the detective's message inside. "I can't think of a thing."

Chapter Five

EDEN FOLDED her arms and stared up at St. Patrick's. Funny, years ago when she'd gone to church here, the structure had seemed enormous. Now it didn't appear much larger than a chapel. So why were her palms sweating, her hands shaking?

The door opened and a group of school children scurried out of the dimly lit building into the bright April day. One dark-haired boy held the door open for her. She stepped back and shook her head. A woman followed, giving Eden a curious stare. If she was a nun, she no longer wore a habit. To Eden's understanding, not many did these days.

A short, balding man exited next, and by his clerical collar, she gathered he was a priest. Withdrawing a loop of keys attached to his belt, he greeted her. "I was about to lock up, but if you want—"

"I don't. Thanks."

He lifted a brow. "Did you need something then? May I be of assistance?"

She glanced around the adobe structure. At the irony of where she was standing, she smiled. "No. I'm good."

His boyish grin widened. "My name's Father George Slater. I'm pastor of St. Patrick's. I don't believe I've seen you before."

"My name's Eden, Father. I attended school here a long time ago," she said, seeing no reason to explain the getting-expelled part.

"Ah." Light shone in his pale green eyes. "By your walker and innumerable wrinkles it must have been quite some time ago."

She laughed, tucking a flyaway strand behind her ear. "Good point. A long time is relative. I left when I was in third grade. Tell me, is the Convent of Saint Ursula still located on the church premises?"

He rocked back on his sturdy black shoes. "No, unfortunately. St. Patrick's is run by the diocese now. The convent closed its doors ten years ago, or so I was told."

That was a statement Eden faced with mixed emotions.

The priest glanced at his cell phone.

"I'm keeping you," she said.

"Not at all. I'm never too busy if someone needs me."

She wiped her hands on her linen skirt. "My sister's getting married here in two weeks."

"Her name?"

"Meghan Moran. She's marrying Stephen Sullivan."

"Ah, the Moran/Sullivan nuptials. You're Joanna and Edward's daughter. Wonderful family. I'm officiating at the event and look forward to meeting the entire clan."

Great. The priest liked her family. Should she share that she was the fallen-away member of the brood? "How long have you been here?"

"Three years. I came from Boston." His eyes twinkled as he emphasized his Bostonian accent. "I must tell you, New Mexico's been a culture shock."

"What part? The overabundance of desert or the lack of ocean?"

"Try lack of people, or for that matter, any part of a mass transportation system." He winked.

"That, too." Eden appreciated his easy going manner. Claiming a seat on the church's front steps, she relished the opportunity to be outside on such a warm spring day. "I moved back a year ago myself, only from the opposite direction. San Diego. I'm a lawyer for the Albuquerque Public Defender's office."

"Good for you." Father Slater joined her on the steps.

"A cop came to see me, a Detective Dancer."

"Ah, yes, he's been to see me as well. Terrible news about this Sister Beatrice, isn't it?"

Eden tilted her head to glance at him sideways. "Were you able to help him?"

"I'm afraid not. When the convent closed, the order took with it any remaining records. You say our upstanding detective came to see you?"

"He did." *Upstanding.* Eden nodded her head in agreement. She didn't know what Kevin did in his private life, but as a cop the adjective seemed apropos. "He's claiming witnesses say I knew this woman."

"Sister Beatrice? Did you?"

"No. And that's what concerns me. I've got a cop looking at me suspiciously because people say I did."

"Is it possible that you forgot?"

"I can tell you every single teacher I've had from first grade through college. To this day I can recite Supreme Court rulings I learned as a first-year law student." Eden tucked her palms beneath her thighs as she sat. "One of the things that got me through law school was my memory. So my question is why are people fixating on me?"

"Mistaken identification, perhaps? Ever listen to gossip, Eden?"

Rubbing the back of her neck, she lowered her head. "Me? Never."

He faced her with a sober expression. "You should. Just as a lesson, of course. If only as an example of how each version gets bigger and more exaggerated with every tale."

"You think that's what's happened?"

"If, as you say, you've this fantastic memory, I surmise that is the likely explanation. I look forward to celebrating your sister's wedding with you. Though, if you ever need to discuss your spiritual journey . . ."

"Organized religion's not my thing, Father."

"Ah then, that's an entirely different story."

She stiffened, wanting no part of a religious lecture.

"It's against policy to associate with nonbelievers."

"You're joking."

Father Slater smiled. "And you, my dear, got the punch line. I'd be out of a job if I held to that philosophy. This policeman bothers you by his questions?"

"Let's just say it's disconcerting to be told I know someone when I don't."

"This nun died several years ago, right?"

"Correct."

"My understanding is that your sister's wedding will be quite the affair. By the looks of things, your mother's invited the entire parish."

Eden sighed. "She has, and I'm not following where you're going with this."

"I would guess that a lot of old timers will be in attendance." An impish smile lit up his round face. "Perhaps if you invited Detective Dancer, he might pick up a new trail?"

Eden widened her gaze. "Why, Father Slater, you're devious. You think he might go with me?"

The priest rose from the steps. "Among my parishioners, I discourage gambling. But then, as you say, you're not one of the flock." Father Slater extended his hand. Eden took it and came to her feet. "If you ask Detective Dancer to escort you to your sister's wedding, and the bookies lay odds on his accepting, my advice is to stake your entire bankroll."

AS KEVIN STRODE the north campus of UNM's Health Sciences Center toward the Office of Medical Investigations, he viewed faces that looked familiar. They ought to, he thought. He'd been here often enough over the past few months to be enrolled. The OMI, located in the medical school's pathology department, primarily investigated current deaths, although it did have on staff highly trained anthropologists, who in this instance had determined both the identity and cause of death of Celeste Lescano.

But even though he'd walked the campus several times, once beyond the reception area, his comfort level disintegrated. He'd never gotten used to the smell. The Anthropology lab didn't come with the overpowering stench that accompanied a body at a crime scene; skeletons gave off a musty odor. It was the fact that to get to the bones, any remaining flesh and ligaments had to be *cooked* that gave him the creeps.

Shaking off what lay simmering in the stainless steel pots, he located technician Patty Freeburg at her desk near a window. Protective glasses and a white lab coat hid the brunette's pretty face and curvaceous figure.

They'd dated when he first joined the Albuquerque PD, but soon discovered they had little in common other than the crimes that brought them together. Fortunately, they'd remained friends.

She glanced up when he knocked twice on the door. "Hey you. Long time no talk to."

He approached her desk. "How's the bookworm?" He enjoyed reading, but Patty inhaled the stuff. She belonged to at least four book clubs that he knew of, ranging from commercial fiction to Greek tragedy. Forget hiking or going to a movie; her idea of a well-spent evening was sitting by a fire, drinking hot chocolate and reading.

"Getting smarter every day. Unlike someone I know." She removed her glasses. "Still up in the air?"

"Every chance I get." Kevin grinned. He'd gone in with two college buddies and was the proud part-owner of a hot air balloon. "Anytime you want to join me, the invitation's open. Only stipulation, you can't bring a book."

Patty shook her head. "You must've been in the neighborhood. Obering just left and said he planned to call you and Detective Raez."

Kevin checked his cell phone. "Nobody's called. What's up?"

Frowning, Patty leaned back in her chair. She placed her hands palms down and gradually met his gaze. "I don't know how to tell you this, but they're rethinking your victim's cause of death."

"I don't understand." Kevin stepped closer. "We've had the autopsy report for weeks. The report says blunt trauma to the head."

A slight flush appeared on Patty's pretty, heart-shaped face. "I know it'll sound like an excuse, but current caseload took priority. You gave us a cold case with a backhoe doing significant damage to the skeleton, and what we could only assume was an obvious cause of death."

"Go on," he said.

Patty rose from her desk. "Come with me." She led him to the morgue adjoining her office, opened a cadaver drawer and pulled a plastic storage container with a case number labeling the lid.

Kevin winced. What remained of Sister Beatrice fit inside a three-by-two-foot box. Partial skull, phalanges, femur, tibia, remnants of the pelvic girdle and sternum. Clenching his jaw, he thought of Eden and her adamant denial of ever knowing the dead woman. Well, hell, after tenuous leads and hours poured into this investigation, he'd thought he was onto something.

Patty tugged on latex gloves, picked up the skull and pointed to a small hairline crack. "Originally we thought a basal subarachnoid hemorrhage might have killed this woman."

Confusion mixed with the stress from a ticking clock was never a good combination. He glared at her. "English, Patty."

"The blow didn't kill her immediately," she explained. "The ME believes it might have caused a slow bleed."

"But the force would have still killed her, right?"

"Maybe, eventually," she said, returning the skull to the box and moving on to the sternum. "I'm not sure it would prove conclusive in court. Here's where it gets interesting."

"You mean I've been bored so far?"

She twisted her lips. "Pay attention, Dancer. Dr. Krotow and Dr. Obering usually agree on these things, so when they couldn't, several of us wanted to see what all the fuss was about." Patty took a pencil, and pointed with the eraser end to half-inch indentations down the sternum. Your backhoe really screwed up the evidence, Kevin."

Leaning forward he narrowed his gaze. "Those marks weren't caused by the claws?"

"That's where the argument ensued." Waving a hand over the box, Patty said, "If these notches were caused by the backhoe, where the majority of the skeleton was crushed and splintered, why are they only on the sternum and not on any of the other existing bones?"

"Holy shit," Kevin said.

"It gets better." Patty called his attention to the sternum again. "See this particular nick mark right here?"

As if he could focus on anything else. He nodded.

"Whoever struck your victim wanted to make sure the damage was permanent." Patty placed her right hand over her heart. "This woman was stabbed, Kevin, repeatedly, and in an area of the body where he made sure she wouldn't get up again."

A few minutes later, Kevin left the building, tugging his cell phone free of his belt. He'd asked for a recreation artist to be consulted, something Patty doubted would happen due to only the existence of a partial skull and budget constraints. His commander had pointed out several times that a head injury could have been accidental. But if that were true, why not report it—why dump the body?

His phone rang before he could punch speed dial. Recognizing Sal's number, Kevin answered, "Progress, partner."

"Commander wants to see us, Kev."

"Good. For once, I want to see him too. I think he'll be interested in what I have to say."

"You get a lead?" Hope sprang into Sal's voice.

"No. But I do have conclusive proof that Sister Beatrice was murdered."

There was a pause on the other end. "I'd get back as quick as you can."

Kevin didn't like the edge to Sal's voice. "Why? What's happened?"

"We're out of time," Sal explained. "Sorry, partner. Current caseload's climbing. Commander's shelving our cold case."

Chapter Six

GRITTING HIS TEETH, Kevin walked out of Albuquerque's Criminal Investigation Division while his frowning partner gimped alongside him on crutches.

"I'd pat you on the back," Sal said as they made their way down the building's steps. "But I don't see how falling on my face will do either one of us any good."

Kevin studied the ground. They'd been removed from Sister Beatrice's murder investigation. And it was *murder*. A point he'd stressed repeatedly to their commander. Benally had answered with one of his end-of-discussion stares, which left Kevin in no mood for Sal's ever-present quips.

"Tough crowd," Sal persisted. "Hey, come to dinner tonight. Becky loves it when I give her ten minutes' notice."

"Some other time," Kevin said. "Dammit, Sal, we knew this would happen."

They reached even pavement, and though Sal panted furiously, he did a helluva job keeping up with Kevin's rapid strides. "At the risk of pissing you off further, partner, Benally made some valid points."

"He usually does," Kevin admitted.

"And he didn't remove us from the case entirely."

True, but he might as well have. With the murder of a security guard, Benally had put them on the copper theft rings. The crime was not only statewide, it was a national epidemic. Kevin slid Sal a look. "Working a theft ring's like a yard full of dandelions. You pluck out a few, the next group pops up. Where the hell do you suggest we find this spare time? Just like Sister Beatrice, the case is *dead*."

With Sal's noncommittal shrug, Kevin's gut twisted. Didn't anyone care about this woman? Her body had been dumped, abandoned. She'd devoted her life to her religion. And what had she gotten as a reward? No one *remembered* her. She hadn't even earned a Christian burial, something Kevin suspected was incredibly important to her. That was the final insult burning in his craw.

Eden's mention that the murderer might be dead as well skittered through his brain. There was no question they had a better chance of finding the security guard's killer than whoever murdered Sister Beatrice. So why couldn't he let this case go? It wasn't the first case he'd been taken off, but it was by far the one he felt the most passionate about solving.

"Come to dinner," Sal repeated. "Since I can't toss Kenny and Taryn up in the air, you can to do it for me."

The thought of Sal's four-year-old twins lessened his scowl. Ordinarily, Kevin would accept. Not tonight. Tonight he wanted a cold beer, and to pore over the facts of the case one last time. Strange as it seemed, he felt as though Celeste Lescano was calling to him, urging him to find her killer, to lay her spirit to rest.

"As good as that sounds," he said, "I'd be lousy company." They entered the employee parking lot, and for the first time Kevin thought about something other than their unsolvable case. "You okay to drive?"

Sal pulled out his keys. "It's my left foot. Door's open, Kev. Swing by if you change your mind."

Five hours later, files spread over a card table he'd set up in his dining room, Kevin downed the last of his beer, caught the basketball score on the tube, switched it off and went into the bedroom to crash.

He was down to his boxers when the phone rang. He considered letting it go to voice mail, but it might be Dispatch. If it was, his commander had wasted no time in making the assignment switch. No doubt, now that a theft had resulted in murder, his superior officer was under pressure from the brass as well as from Albuquerque's business owners.

Kevin answered, "Dancer."

"Your name makes me curious. Are you any good?"

He studied the unknown caller ID. He hadn't been in a relationship for a while and wasn't crazy enough to guess. "Who's this?"

"You hound me all day and now you don't recognize me? I'm crushed."

He tried to contain his shock. "Eden?"

"You do remember."

You're kind of hard to forget. "What can I do for you?"

"Answer my question for one thing."

"Am I any good?" The question was way too loaded, and he pictured her beneath him. "If you're asking about dancing, sorry, I have two left feet. How about you? Do you like to dance?"

"On occasion. I thought maybe you took your wife out to the clubs every so often?"

"Fishing, Ms. Moran?"

She released a soft groan. "Pathetic, aren't I? You don't wear a wedding ring. But that doesn't mean much these days, and I like to know if a man's married before I ask him out."

"You're asking me out?" This time he didn't try to mask his surprise.

She'd done everything but run from him today, and when it came to Eden Moran, Kevin was sure men did the asking.

"As I said, as long as your significant other wouldn't mind."

"All the significant ones got away." He stretched out on the bed and leaned back on the pillow. Picturing her lithe body and provocative smile, he said, "I'm sure you've left a trail of broken hearts over the years."

"Not as many as I'd like." She laughed. "Law school's not exactly Match Dot com."

He shared in her chuckle. "I would guess not. All right, we've established I'm not married, so why are you calling? *Really?*"

"I told you. You seem like a nice guy and I need a date."

He glanced at the spare pillow beside him and smiled. "I'm not doing anything right now."

"I need a date, Detective, not a cheap tryst."

Well, he already knew nothing about her was easy. "Can't blame a guy for trying. And since we're getting to know each other, might as well call me Kevin. But as much as I'd like to go out with you, Eden, you're a potential witness in a murder investigation. I—"

"And as I told you today, there's nothing *potential* about me. I don't know your victim, which is why I've decided to do you an enormous favor. My sister's getting married the Saturday after next. As it turns out, in a place you seem particularly interested in—St. Patrick's."

He rose up on his elbows. What was she up to?

"My, my, I knew you were strong, but now you're the silent type? Still want to keep things professional, Kevin?"

He loved the sound of her voice, it was part of her charm, and if he wasn't so committed to this case, or turned off by what she did for a living, he might be taken with her. "You're a tease, Eden. I appreciate the invitation. When and what time?"

She told him. He hung up and thought of the files on the card table. The grim mood that had shadowed him since this afternoon became an afterthought. Maybe he could work this case on the side, after all. And if he enjoyed the view while doing it, he'd write it off as a perk of the job.

EDEN SWITCHED off the phone, returned it to the stand and perused the loft she'd purchased from her eccentric next-door neighbor. It was no more than a converted warehouse, but she'd fallen in love with the place the moment she'd set eyes on it.

The first ten years of her life had been spent living in a house that rivaled any of those found in *Architectural Digest*, complete with a stuffy don't-touch mentality. Later, when she'd been shipped off to live with her aunt, that environment had been more down to earth, but whether imagined or perceived, she'd always felt like an encroacher.

When she found a loft that bordered Albuquerque's Old Town, her hopes soared. It was close to her office on Marquette and came at a price a public defender could afford.

Now it was hers—all hers—mortgage payments and all.

She padded barefoot across her pecan floors, poured herself a glass of white wine, turned up the volume on the iPod and switched off the lights. If it weren't so late, she would have called Father Slater to thank him for the idea and tell him he'd won the wager. Kevin Dancer had said yes. As if when she'd mentioned St. Patrick's, the cop could refuse.

The remodeling hadn't successfully eliminated a draft. She pulled the afghan off the back of the couch and flopped onto it. Sipping her wine, she stared into the gas-lit flames. If the investigation revolved around anything besides her troubled past, and an unyielding cop doing the asking, she might try to learn more about the hunky detective. He certainly was fun to talk to, and when it came to conversation, Kevin gave as good as she delivered.

Still, she mustn't lose focus. The date was a ploy, one that would put him on to other witnesses who would help him solve his case, leaving her, a know-nothing bystander, out of the equation. And, Dancer *would* solve this case. Of this Eden was as certain as she was about not knowing the dead nun.

She closed her eyes. While she could effectively shut out the city lights mingling with stars, her mind circled back to today, to the poor woman who'd died and a cop desperate for answers. As a defense attorney, she empathized greatly. But something told her to step back—way back—and stay clear of this case that hadn't been assigned to her desk.

The music on the iPod switched to Chopin's Nocturne Op 9. The soothing music generally lulled her to sleep. Not tonight. As she listened to the classical thread, she gripped the wine glass and her eyes flew open. Each note carried with it a beat of unease. Eden pulled the afghan closer and she shuddered.

Chapter Seven

NO TREMORS, no headaches, no blackouts. So far, so good.

Surrounded by relatives and the beaming bride-to-be, Eden wriggled into a peach satin gown in a rear dressing room of St. Patrick's. She'd survived the rehearsal dinner and last night's practice inside the church. Deep breathing had helped, along with Father Slater's teasing and calming presence. The world hadn't exploded, and she began to believe she could be her sister's maid of honor after all.

Floral scents and perfume mists filled the air as Lilly, the groom's niece, scampered into the room carrying a bouquet of white rose buds. The tow-headed four-year-old looked priceless in a miniature peach dress that rustled when she walked.

Meg hadn't yet slipped into an exquisite off-the-shoulder wedding gown, complete with Basque waist and intricate embroidered bodice, and Eden couldn't wait to see her in it. Clad only in a slip and strapless bra, Meg stared at her image in the full-length mirror and asked, "How much time?"

Their cousin Darla sniffed and cast an impatient look at her watch. "Forty-five minutes. Lilly, will you *please* leave your flowers in the hall? All this pollen is clogging my sinuses."

Eden's Aunt Lorraine, Darla's ever doting mother, stood at once. "I'll get your inhaler, dear."

Lilly appeared crestfallen at having to give up the flowers. Eden took her hand and led her to a chair, while Aunt Caroline surreptitiously tiptoed behind Lilly to remove the offending bouquet.

"You know what, Lilly?" Eden said. "I don't know who's prettier, the flower girl or the bride."

The little girl beamed, none the wiser as Caroline set the flowers on a chest of drawers as far from Darla as possible. Eden shared a conspiratorial wink with the aunt who'd raised her from the age of ten. A lawyer herself, Caroline had been instrumental in Eden becoming one.

Family dynamics. She'd dealt with them forever. But even though Darla was high maintenance, she was a rank amateur compared to Eden's mother, who had yet to make an entrance. And there was no other way to put it—when Joanna Moran came on the scene, everybody knew it.

Someone knocked on the door. Meg pulled Eden close in the guise of a hug. "That'll be Mom. Keep it civil? For me?"

Protecting the jittery bride from any onlookers, Caroline held the door slightly ajar. "Eden? Your . . . date is here?"

Five sets of curious eyes zoned in on her, and Eden avoided what she was sure were their open-mouthed stares. She'd told no one that Kevin was coming. Why would she? He was hardly someone they'd get to know long-term. She left the bridal room, intent on putting *Operation Distraction* into action.

KEVIN SCRUBBED his clean-shaven jaw and nodded his sympathies to the groomsmen and ushers, who tugged at their own noose-like collars. The black suit he'd chosen for today was his favorite standby when jeans were out of the question.

Cops often attended functions following a crime, though most weren't seventeen years after the fact. A former lieutenant had told him once that cops were like artists. Up close, a crime's canvas didn't look like much. Step back and a broader picture emerged, one that might reveal how witnesses and suspects were connected.

"I told her you were here," the Hispanic, pony-tailed usher said upon his return. He stuck out his hand. "Jay Sandoval, longtime friend of the family. I'm also close to Eden."

So how come she's here with me and not you? Kevin returned Jay's handshake, which had the grip of a weightlifter on steroids. He introduced himself, without mentioning he was a cop or how he knew Eden. Today he wanted people to see him as a guest and talk to him in an unguarded, unpracticed setting.

Ignoring Jay's microscopic interest, Kevin focused on a statue in the entrance—a wild-haired crazy dude crushing a snake underfoot. Kevin didn't understand this faith or its icons. What he did know was that if the rock-hard guy on the pedestal was supposed to be St. Patrick, he made Indiana Jones look like a pansy.

But as Eden rounded the corner, thoughts of jealous ushers, kick-ass saints and Steven Spielberg went up like candle smoke. Kevin didn't need a genius IQ to know why she'd invited him. Even so, he'd have to be dead not to see she was all woman.

The clingy fabric of her strapless dress left little to his imagination, and because he knew he was here to look and not touch, he gave his mind permission to knock itself out. Her coloring set off her startling blue eyes, while her French braid was probably someone's creative suggestion to keep her from messing with her hair.

She smiled up at him, and those thoughts, too, went out of his head.

Suddenly, he was glad that Jay had been kicked to the curb, and sorry their date wasn't real.

"You made it," she said.

"Wouldn't miss it." He leaned down to kiss her cheek, an action that caused her to go ramrod straight, but he had to know. Yeah. She smelled as good as she looked.

Jay cleared his throat. "Eden. You want him on the groom's or the bride's side?"

Looking over her shoulder at the usher, she frowned. "The bride's, Jay, and in the reserved section, please."

"Yes, Jay." From behind Kevin came a woman's authoritative voice. "You may seat him with family. But give us a moment."

Eden went as stiff as bad-ass St. Patrick, and her smile froze into place.

Kevin turned to see who could derail someone irrepressible in her own right. An attractive older woman, the picture of Eden in thirty years, floated toward them in gold lamé.

She extended a jeweled-studded hand. "Joanna Moran. I'm Eden's mother."

"Kevin Dancer, Mrs. Moran. Thanks for having me."

"You're welcome. Edward and I are delighted you could come." Then, flashing her daughter a censorious look, she said, "Although it's unfortunate we couldn't have met you last night at the rehearsal dinner, or told the caterer you were coming in the first place."

"Mother . . ."

Joanna ignored her. "I assume you know Eden from work?"

"You could say that."

"You're a professional, then?"

"Mother." Eden stepped between them like a referee separating boxers. Unlike her mother, Eden lowered her voice. "I asked Kevin to come today because he's a friend. I'd like to keep it that way."

Her mom brought a hand to her throat, her icy blue eyes never leaving his. "Have I said anything to offend you, Mr. Dancer?"

"Not at all," he replied, somewhat amused. Joanna Moran knew exactly what she was doing, though if it was her plan to intimidate him, she should know more than a few suspects had complained that was his area of expertise.

"Good. I knew that about you the moment I laid eyes on you. I saw a man who could take care of himself. If I seemed shocked, it's because my daughter didn't mention she was bringing a date, that's all. But then why would she? We didn't know if she *herself* was coming until a few days ago."

Eden sighed. "All right, Mom. You've made your point."

"Have I? I'm so glad." Her mother smiled sweetly at Eden, and Kevin saw years of issues between these two—issues that, if they had anything to do with Sister Beatrice, he was more than happy to stick around to find out about.

Joanna moved to the church's entrance and threw open the front doors. Guests in the foyer waiting to be seated as well as members of the wedding party turned curious gazes in her direction. "Everyone? My daughter's not the only one who can keep secrets. Father Slater has graciously consented to be concelebrant at Meghan and Stephen's wedding."

Eden joined her mother by the doors. "What does that mean? What's a . . . concelebrant?"

"It means he'll be here to assist, while a very special guest will be officiating over the ceremony." Joanna waved to someone outside. Then, smiling broadly, she whirled to those present and clasped her hands. "We didn't know if he would make it back in time, but he has. Our wonderful friend and former pastor has just returned from his Vatican ordination. My dear friends and family, I give you *Bishop* Robert Munroe."

As applause and cheers echoed throughout St. Patrick's foyer, and the already-seated guests shifted in their pews to look back, Kevin wanted to dance a jig of his own. Cops had called Munroe a person of interest for weeks. What Kevin wanted to know was why members of the diocesan staff had failed to mention he was right under their proverbial noses the whole time.

Nearing six feet, with strands of silver threading his coal black hair, Munroe entered St. Patrick's like a celebrity coming on stage. As a mob of devoted followers set upon him, Kevin turned to thank his pretend date and tell her she was a genius for inviting him.

But with Robert Munroe's miraculous appearance, Eden Moran had gone missing.

DIGGING HER NAILS into her palms, Eden strode toward the bridal room, her mind on poor Father Slater. He'd been anticipating this event for months. And wasn't it just like her mother to make changes without telling a soul, or worse, to consider anyone else's feelings?

She was only a few feet away from Meghan's dressing room when a strong hand curled around her bicep. The next thing she knew, she was traveling in a different direction.

"Somebody yell fire and forget to tell the rest of us dopes?"

She stared down at Kevin's hand upon her arm. "Let go of me."

He eased up on his grip, but not entirely. "Why? What's happened?"

"My *mother* happened. This has nothing to do with you or the investigation. The wedding starts in ten minutes. I need to talk to my sister."

Releasing her, he didn't walk away, but merely matched her stride for stride.

Her face was on fire, she was so mortified. It wasn't that she particularly cared what Kevin thought of her; she wouldn't want anyone to witness one of her mother's legendary spectacles. Eden glanced at him sideways. "If you choose to stay at this circus, you should probably get seated."

"And miss the sideshow? Not a chance."

Traveling at a fast clip in four-inch stilettos when you're calm was foolhardy. Walking in them when you're angry bordered on suicidal. Her thoughts must have transferred to her feet. Eden stumbled. And wouldn't you know it, the good detective had hung around to witness. He reached out to steady her as Father Slater stepped out of the bridal room.

Wearing his clerical collar over black street clothes, the smiling priest shut the door behind him. "Eden, don't you look beautiful. I assume you've heard the good news?"

Catching her breath and striving for balance at the same time, she said, "Good news, Father?"

"About the bishop?"

She shared a confused glance with Kevin, then turned her dismay on the priest. "You're okay with it?"

"My friend and mentor here at St. Patrick's? I'm more than *okay*, I'm ecstatic."

Her throat felt as dry as unbuttered toast. "But you told me you'd been looking forward to this wedding for months."

"Indeed, I have." His smile faded. "Oh, dear. This is about me, isn't it? You thought I was being excluded. Eden, I assure you, I'll be right beside the bishop as Meghan and Steve say their vows. Imagine their joy when they tell their children they were married by a bishop."

With nowhere to stow her fury, it merely deflated. "Are you sure, Father? You've been the one to counsel them."

"Absolutely." He lowered his voice and his gaze softened. "Your dad's inside with your sister. You should join them. As for me, *I* better get a move on." He winked at Eden, then nodded to Kevin. "Nice to see you again, Detective."

"Father," Kevin said.

The good-natured man sailed off in the direction of the vesting room, leaving her alone with the annoyingly collected cop.

"Welcome to my world," she grumbled.

"Glad to be here. Slater's right, you know."

Still frowning after the priest, Eden sighed. "About what?"

"You do look beautiful."

A short time later, a soloist sang *Ave Maria*, the ushers escorted the stragglers to their places, and the wedding party took their positions in the foyer of the church. Eden's already-knotted stomach tightened to the point of painful as she glanced down the center aisle to the filled-to-capacity congregation.

The exquisite stained glass, the Stations of the Cross lining both sides of the pews, the statues, which led to the sacristy—these items were meant to lend comfort. So why was it she'd rather face a firing squad? She swallowed hard. Father Slater hadn't exaggerated. The entire parish had to be in attendance.

She urged herself not to take her mother's replacement of the priest as an omen of things to come. Joanna Moran controlled everything. Eden stood in the very place that had brought about a major family rift. Her refusal to go to Mass, to attend any function within St. Patrick's, had set in motion Eden's unwilling departure.

"Eden," Meg whispered. "What are you doing? You missed your cue."

She glanced over her shoulder at the glamorous bride on their father's arm. Bombarded by memories, she hadn't heard the wedding march's opening stanza.

She gripped her bridal bouquet and forced herself to take slow, even steps. Certainly the organist would play an additional chorus, if need be. But along with Meg's anxiety, Eden had gotten a glimpse of how hard it had to be on their dad to give away his eldest daughter.

Time had marked his age. Edward Moran was a CPA who'd spent his life building an investment firm. He'd been the consummate bread winner, and Eden and Meghan had never lacked for anything. He'd also given Joanna complete autonomy in raising his girls. He'd never intervened. Not even when she exiled their youngest daughter.

Back then, Eden had felt abandoned. Today she felt robbed.

Midway up the aisle, she glimpsed a woman focusing on her and whispering behind her hand. Self-preservation took over. It was the armor Eden adopted years ago when people judged her. She widened her smile. She was here for one reason: her sister.

At last, she reached the nave, where Steve and his best man, Cory, were waiting. In the presence of spectacular floral arrangements and accoutrements, she moved to the left, while the bride and groom assumed their places of honor.

Eden's plan had been to focus on Father Slater, but with him off to the side, she had no choice but to acknowledge the interloper who'd replaced him. There was nothing sinister-looking about the bishop, adorned in his rich white-and-gold vestments. Even so, a shiver shot up Eden's spine.

She had to get over her ill feelings about Bishop Munroe. It wasn't his purpose to slight Father Slater; he was simply honoring an old friend's request. But from the time he greeted the congregation, Eden grew edgy.

He commenced the Mass; she watched him uneasily. She'd known him when she was a child, of course. She recalled she'd even liked him. But as his voice rang out, with each uttered word, chills pricked her flesh.

How odd.

Every time he glanced her way, she looked elsewhere. Finally, she found she could relax when she focused on Kevin. Maybe it was because he was as much of an outsider as she. He sat at the end of the pew next to her Aunt Caroline. At one point, Bishop Munroe must have said something funny, because the congregation roared. Determined to give him the attention he deserved, Eden faced him. But again she had the overwhelming urge to turn away.

She looked toward the assembly. This time to her horror, the crowd had vanished and Eden saw only a dark-haired woman kneeling in the second row. Her heaving shoulders revealed her distress, and Eden felt compelled to go to her. But as she lifted the hem of her gown, the silky fabric changed in texture. She looked down to see her recent manicure had been bitten to the quick and her fingers were now the stubby digits of a child's. Instead of the gown, she wore the checkered green uniform of St. Patrick's. What's more, her knee was on fire and blood had soaked through a hole in the skirt.

Frustrated by this surreal mind game, she attempted to rally, to be there for her sister as promised. Yet the encompassing vision felt so real and off-kilter, it was like searching for a light switch in the dark.

She forced herself to home in on the bishop. Knowing he was flesh and blood, she breathed easier. Until the bells of St. Patrick's pealed, and before her eyes, he became a much younger version of himself. Leaving his position of prominence, he walked toward the woman in the second pew.

After that, Eden's mind shut down and her legs gave up the ability to support her.

SOME OF THE COPS in the division warned Kevin that masses were long, but he hadn't taken them too seriously. Now, shifting in his seat to get comfortable, he actually looked forward to standing or kneeling again. He'd spent the first fifteen minutes studying the crowd, but no one exactly stood out as the type who would bludgeon a nun to death.

He glanced at his watch. When he got married, he'd keep it short and sweet. He'd insist on "I do," and then concentrate on the part that *should* be drawn out—the honeymoon.

At least the view was good. Eden was a knockout, arguably prettier than the bride. As she walked down the aisle, appearing confident and relaxed, he was glad she had a good relationship with her sister. Maybe one day he'd be closer to his half-brothers. Who knew? He only wished they'd tried something on their own before breaking down and working for their old man.

Which brought him back to Eden. Given her occupation, he really should find things he didn't like about her. After today, he'd steer clear. Still, the beautiful defense lawyer had opened a door for him to find leads. He wouldn't forget the favor.

He refocused on Eden, who'd smiled at him earlier. He noticed now that her smile had waned. If anything, she seemed pale. It *was* warm inside the church, but the air conditioning had recently kicked on. Just the same, he didn't like what he saw. Was it his imagination or was she swaying?

Anticipating what was about to happen, he rose from the pew. And in a move that surprised even him, Kevin was out of the pew and rounding the corner.

Chapter Eight

"ARE YOU all right?" Kevin cut the Jeep's ignition, forced at last to address the intensely quiet passenger, who hadn't said a word since leaving the church. Eden, who made a striking silhouette against the property that made up the Paraiso Country Club, pulled away from the window. Behind the facility, which was built on a mesa, a setting sun backdrop cast the New Mexico desert into shadows.

"I fainted, Kevin. At my sister's wedding, on the most important day of her life." Eden lowered her head and released a small huff. "No, I'm not all right."

He didn't want to examine too closely how her sigh made him feel. "Technically, you didn't. You didn't hit the floor."

"You caught me!" Groaning, she pressed her fingers to her temples. "The second time today, I might add. I can't believe this. Meghan must hate me."

"That's not the way I saw it," he said, although he couldn't speak for Eden's mom. After the ceremony, while posing for pictures, Joanna had accused Eden of causing the scene on purpose. Kevin shook his head at that one. No one was that accomplished an actress. He'd seen the blood rush from her face. Either Eden's mother was an uncaring bitch, or they had some serious issues festering between them. Or both.

Eden appeared so down, he was tempted to touch her. But he'd given in twice today. He tightened his grip on the steering wheel and glanced toward the club. Most of the guests had already arrived, and late-comers were walking through the club's ornate Spanish-style doors. If he were to make headway on this straight-from-hell case, he needed to join them.

He couldn't. Not yet. Not when she seemed fragile enough to break.

"If it makes you feel better, it was so hot in that church, *I* thought about fainting."

Folding her arms, she raised an eyebrow. "Thought about?"

"You beat me to it."

She seemed to smile in spite of herself, and on Eden it looked good. If he was any judge of character, the episode wouldn't keep her down for long. "What do you say you shake this off, we make the rounds, and since I did save your pretty backside, you repay me with a dance?"

She leaned against the passenger side door. "What does dancing have to do with solving this case, Detective?"

Not a damn thing.

He was through lying to himself. He wanted to know, just once, how she'd feel in his arms. He pulled the keys from the ignition. "I'm doing this for Sister Beatrice. I'd be grateful if you'd help me put on a show."

KEVIN WANDERED the crowd while Eden joined her relatives in the receiving line. Her only request, before he turned everyone in the Paradise Room into a murder suspect, was that he bring her the stiffest drink the bartender had on his shelf.

He'd never had trouble drawing people into conversation. Even so, he was a stranger among lifelong friends. Thanks to Eden's episode in the church, however, people approached him. Morbid curiosity proved better than a line up.

Asking such questions as, "Friend of the bride?" or "Known the Morans long?" he quickly ascertained the identities of lifelong parishioners and those he wanted to talk to.

On his way to the bar, he bypassed drunks well on their way and waiters filling glasses for the sit-down dinner, and located the source of the vibrating floor—a talented band with the oxymoronic name of *Bad Music.* Then, planting his arms on the bar, he took the barkeep into his confidence. "Hey, buddy. My friend's in serious pain."

The bartender reached for the Absolut vodka. He mixed the drink and followed up with some pretty slick juggling moves. Sliding the glass toward Kevin, he said, "Don't try this at home, my friend. Vodka martini with a twist."

Kevin dropped five bucks into a tip jar, drawing his shoulders up when a woman's shrill laugh pierced his eardrums. When it happened again, he turned to see what banshee could produce such a cacophony and found a group of middle-aged women surrounding none other than Bishop Munroe.

The group was clearly enraptured by the clergyman's presence, and he seemed to be having a good time as well. He had charisma, Kevin gave him that much. Munroe had a way of singling out each admirer with what appeared to be his undivided attention. During the ceremony, Kevin had seen the man at work. What Kevin really wanted to witness was how the man played.

Kevin stole a sip of Eden's drink and slid back on the barstool to watch. He could drop by the diocese on Monday. For now, if Munroe had deliberately evaded police, he wasn't letting him out of his sight.

"Down, boy. I can hear those brain gears shifting from over here."

Kevin recognized Father Slater's strong Boston accent without even looking at him. He slid the priest a sidelong glance, "I'm that obvious?"

"To me, maybe, but then I know why you're here." Slater accepted a beer from the bartender, slipped him a few bills and joined Kevin on an adjacent barstool. "You're barking up the wrong tree if you think the bishop harmed that woman, Detective."

"Like it's never happened before," Kevin shot back. Then remembering who he was talking to, he added, "No offense, Father."

"None taken."

"Until I've heard his story, I can't form any definite conclusions anyway. But Munroe was at the parish at the same time as the nun. You know him well?"

"Well enough. He was one of my mentors upon my arrival at St. Patrick's three years ago." Father Slater took a long draw on his beer. "I also can tell you he abhors violence. I've seen him walk into the middle of a gang fight and break it up, with great risk to himself, I might add."

"I'll take that into account when I talk to him," Kevin said.

The priest smiled. "Looks like you may get your wish sooner than later."

Confused at Slater's meaning, Kevin turned to see the bishop headed their way.

"George," the bishop greeted the priest as he wandered close. Then, directing his attention to Kevin, he said, "Ah, just the young man I wanted to see. How's Eden?"

Kevin hopped off the stool to shake the man's hand. "Fine, Bishop. Embarrassed, but fine." As he'd done several times already, Kevin glanced toward the receiving line.

It wasn't difficult to imagine what lay beneath Eden's dress, and as Munroe's gaze followed and lingered, Kevin suppressed a surprising bout of jealousy. The cop inside him was happy at least. He'd witnessed firsthand that the bishop was an admirer of beautiful women.

"People faint more often than you think," Munroe was saying. "For some strange reason, when I'm talking." The bishop winked. "I'll have to tell Eden that."

"I'm sure she'd appreciate you saying so," Kevin said. "She feels terrible."

"She shouldn't. That was some feat you accomplished in the church. Are you some type of athlete, Mr . . .?"

"Kevin Dancer, sir." He and Father Slater shared a glance. "I'm in law enforcement."

If that information concerned the bishop, Kevin never saw it.

Munroe's practiced smile only widened. "Is that how you know Eden? Excellent. Joanna told me she was helping the unfortunates now."

Unfortunates? That was one way to look at the lowlifes Eden defended. What was this guy's story? Kevin needed a better read on Munroe. One moment he seemed phony as a three-dollar bill, the next completely sincere.

Should he broach the numerous times the police had contacted the diocese without a return phone call? Aware that the Albuquerque population was predominantly Catholic, and many were in this room, Kevin chose not to embarrass Eden or her family and decided for a more subtle approach. "I understand you've been overseas, Bishop. I'd appreciate a few minutes of your time to hear about your travels."

"A chance to talk about myself?" Munroe chuckled. "Consider it done. Why don't you and Eden join me at my table after dinner? I haven't seen her since she was a little girl. I'd love to catch up on old times. If you'll excuse me? Kevin? Father George? I see some old friends."

Once the bishop was out of earshot, Kevin murmured to the priest beside him, "You never mentioned anything about me or the investigation?"

Slater shook his head. "He's only been back a day or so. It never came up."

"He *is* your boss."

The priest raised his eyes skyward. "Not entirely."

"Meaning no disrespect, but why didn't you tell him?"

The priest took another swig of his beer. "Divided loyalties, perhaps? Did I ever tell you my family was disappointed when I entered the priesthood?"

"Really? Why is that?"

Slater shifted on the barstool and grinned. "I come from a long line of cops."

Kevin clinked his glass to his companion's beer bottle. "I owe you one, Father. Excuse me. I think Eden's waited long enough for her drink."

THOMAS WADED through the crowd of boisterous people, imitating their phony smiles, while the chattering around him and light from the blazing chandeliers tortured his soul. He'd been a member of St. Patrick's for twenty years, yet very few parishioners knew his real name. Not that any of these hypocrites mattered to him. The only person he cared about was the great man across the room, who as a young priest had called Thomas indispensable.

Indispensable. How he treasured the word.

Dressed in a thread-bare suit he'd purchased from a discount rack, he retraced the movements he'd made throughout the day. He'd attended the Moran/Sullivan wedding in an effort to get a good look at her. But without an invitation, he'd been afraid to arrive too early. As such, a rude usher had found no place to put him and shoved Thomas into the last available seat, naturally, in the very last row.

Then when the commotion hit and shocked murmurs erupted, he'd nearly jumped out of his skin. On tiptoe, he'd stood to see what happened, wanting to ask, yet he didn't dare. No one talked to *him*. Well, not unless a floor needed scrubbing or a toilet unclogged. That, it seemed, was the only thing Thomas was good for—cleaning up messes.

Which brought him to this reception, again, uninvited. For years, he'd carried the burden of wondering what the little girl saw—consumed with why she'd been running, as though for her very life, on the day he'd been called to the rectory.

True, that weight had lifted when she no longer came to Mass with her family, and when he later overheard she no longer lived with them, he thought his worries were over.

Until he discovered she'd returned and was some kind of lawyer now.

Thomas eased behind the final guest in the receiving line. It was time to find out why she fainted, exactly what she recalled. Sadly, if she recognized him, he would have another mess to clean up.

He glanced to where the bishop was standing. Father Munroe had risen to bishop! If that wasn't a sign, what was? Thomas would protect him at all costs. It was a calling he'd been reluctant to undertake all those years ago. But like Jonah in the belly of the whale, Thomas, too, was charged with doing God's will. And although Thomas would never become a great prophet, he would again become indispensable.

AS EDEN GREETED friends of the bride and groom as well as their extended families, she admitted this part of the evening hadn't been bad. She took a moment to consider what ached more, her swollen feet, her shaken hand or her constant smile.

But at least she was out of that church.

She felt the tap on her shoulder before she saw the absentee cop. Kevin stood behind her, glass in hand. Taking it from him, she murmured over her shoulder, "Next time I ask you to get me a drink, remind me to yell, STAT."

"Sorry," he murmured close to her ear. "I ran into some people."

"I saw. You're more popular than the bride." Eden took a sip and coughed. "Oh my God, what's in this stuff?"

"Vodka, vermouth, the kitchen sink. How are you doing?"

"Not bad," she replied, catching her mother's heat-seeking gaze and wondering how Joanna could smile, talk to old friends and still watch Eden's every move. "FYI," Eden continued, "Steve and Meg are brilliant. They're telling everyone they staged my collapse to hurry the ceremony along."

Kevin laughed, and Eden was drawn to his rich baritone voice. Laughing was something he did often and she liked hearing. Despite her mother's scrutiny and people moving in Eden's direction, she studied his mouth. Sexier lips on a man she couldn't recall. She tried another sip of her drink, which this time she tolerated. "I could get used to this stuff if it doesn't kill me first."

"So, being here . . ." he said, looking around. "Anything strike you as odd?"

"Nothing offhand." Remembering the incident during the ceremony, however, a chill fell over her. "Two of Steve's friends asked me out, Mr. Von Husen has the gout, and, oh, my third grade teacher is here, and she still hates me."

"Lila Trevino?" Kevin made a sweep of the room. "She doesn't hate you. I interviewed her. Any idea where she went?"

He'd talked to her third-grade teacher? Eden ground her back teeth together. They'd been through this already. She had no recollection of Sister Beatrice. Eden had brought the stubborn detective to tonight's event to make trouble for other people.

"Since you've already interviewed her, maybe it's time to move on to the other guests," Eden said. "This isn't about me, remember?"

He stopped his scan of the room and pinned her with a look that said otherwise.

"It *isn't*, Kevin." Some barrister she was, she croaked the last words.

He stepped close. "Whatever you say, Counselor. Oh, by the way, the bishop wants us to join him at his table after dinner."

Her mind flashed back to the church. What the hell was wrong with her? "He does?"

"Don't look so worried. I'm sure he just wants to reassure you he's not going to excommunicate you or something."

"As if I'd care." She hated feeling so out of control. She shook her head. "Kevin—"

"Don't sweat it. We eat, we dance, we talk to the man. What happened to that fearless lawyer I knew?"

"She's been sequestered." Eden eyed her mother, who'd all but turned purple. "Speaking of which, if you don't get out of here and let me visit with all these people I can't remember, I may get grounded."

"See you at dinner," he said.

He wandered off, leaving her to face the curious stares of her relatives and the last of the receiving line. Lifting the hem of her bridal gown, Meghan traded places with their aunt and sidled up next to Eden. In between handshakes and hugs, Meg said, "Are you deliberately trying to make our mother blow a gasket?"

Now that was an interesting visual. Eden's mouth twisted into a smirk. "Not intentionally, no."

"So talk," Meg said. "Tell me about Kevin Dancer. Where did he come from?"

"There's nothing to tell. He's my friend."

"Right. I have eyes. How'd the two of you meet?"

"He was in my courtroom the other day."

"Was he on trial or something?"

Laughing, Eden shook her head. Why did everyone expect her to bring home deviants? "No, Meg. Kevin brings people to trial." She lowered her voice. "He's a cop."

Oh, dear. Her big sister's burgeoning smile meant only one thing. Along with something borrowed and something blue, she'd tucked a matchmaking scheme in her garter. "There's nothing between us, and I'd appreciate it if you would keep his occupation between you and me, okay?"

Meg's smile faded. "Fine. You should let Jay know at least. Poor guy was broken-hearted when he discovered you'd brought a date."

"He'll live. He's in and out of relationships faster than he changes socks. Maybe you should tell him that Kevin and I are an item."

But Meg's gaze had traveled elsewhere and she wasn't listening. "Who invited *him*?"

"Who?"

"Keep your voice down. That creepy old janitor. What's his name?"

Eden leaned forward to glimpse the end of the line. "I don't know him." But even as she made the statement, her mind argued otherwise. His shaggy gray hair was plastered to his head, the suit he wore too big for his overly thin frame. But the one thing that struck her as familiar was his bulging gray eyes.

And then she remembered the rhyme.

Hail Mary, full of grace, keep me safe from old Timms' face.

She winced. Grade school girls jumping rope could be vicious. Eden hoped for his sake he'd never been on the playground to overhear their cruel jibes.

She said her hellos to the last guest before the custodian approached. In her line of work, she often met people who didn't fit in. Her job had taught her empathy, and that not everyone who resided in prison lived behind bars. If he had heard the awful chant, maybe now would be the time to repay him with kindness.

"Mr. Timms," Eden said. "How nice to see you. Thank you for coming."

His stare truly was discomfiting. "You remember me." It was a statement.

"Of course. How could I forget? Are you well? Still cleaning the church?"

He paused, and through those protruding gray eyes looked at her strangely. "I work in a different place now. You remember me." Again, it wasn't a question.

She nodded. "Certainly I do."

He never made it past Eden. He finished their odd little discourse, pivoted, and left the receiving line.

Unnerved, she watched him disappear into the crush of people. She thought about going after him. It was a thought that all but vanished as Meghan and Steve surrounded her. Meg latched onto her arm. "We're done here, little sister. Time to party!"

Chapter Nine

IT WASN'T THAT Kevin wasn't enjoying himself, but he hadn't agreed to come to this event to forward his social life. Amid raucous conversation and rock music, he glanced at his watch for the twenty-seventh time, then eyed the bishop across the room. He was more politician than clergy. And as more and more guests made their way to his table, it put him out of reach for Kevin, who wanted a private *tête-à-tête*.

Eden and the bride had disappeared into the ladies room, and with Eden his ticket to talk to the man, Kevin bounced his leg, impatient for her return.

The groom returned from the bar with two beers. "You looked like you could use one of these. You obviously didn't get the memo. The Moran women travel in packs and on their own timetables."

Kevin returned an obligatory laugh, far from sincere. He was twenty feet away from a witness. His chief worry was that Munroe would leave and force Kevin to take another approach. But as Eden and her sister returned to the table, his thoughts of the bishop were momentarily forgotten. She'd let her hair down, and the change from bridesmaid into goddess sent a solid jolt to his groin.

She plopped into the seat beside him. "Miss me?"

He clamped his mouth shut, lest it hang open. Her silvery blond hair was already a head turner. Add the waves created by the braid, it took everything he had not to reach out and touch the silky strands. He draped an arm around the back of her chair, taking in her face, then everything from the swell of the treble clef tattoo to the enticing valley between her breasts. "You went somewhere?"

She punched him and eyed his untouched sorbet. "Are you going to eat that?"

Wondering how she managed to keep her shape when she consumed the calories of a linebacker, he slid it toward her. She'd already devoured appetizers, a salad and a Cornish game hen main course. "By all means, I wouldn't want you to starve."

She shook her spoon at him. "I'll have you know, most days I live on yogurt."

He was seconds away from mentioning the first day they'd met she'd been wolfing down a Dachshund-sized hot dog, but in the recesses of his mind he pictured his mother mouthing, "Manners."

He did feel compelled to remind her though, "The bishop asked us to join him at his table, remember?"

Eden screwed up her face and set down her spoon. "Well, that certainly ruined my appetite." Her gaze traveled the room and she brightened. "But we can't talk to him if he isn't there."

"What?" Kevin's gut clenched as he located the empty spot where he'd last seen Munroe.

"He's dancing with my mother."

"He can do that?"

Eden polished off the rest of his sorbet. Tilting her head, her eyes narrowed and her expression turned pensive. "Apparently so. I think it's the Baptists who can't dance."

Shaking his head, Kevin stood and extended his hand. "C'mon. I think it's time you worked off some of that baby fat."

She laughed and rose to meet him. "I think I'm insulted."

PUT ON THE witness stand, Eden might have denied it, but the moment she'd been anticipating all evening finally arrived. With the band playing an old Johnny Rivers' tune, Kevin's warm grasp found hers. As he led her onto the dance floor, she couldn't stop grinning.

"The things I do for you, Dancer. See if you can get those big strong arms around me and all my *baby* fat."

"It'll be a chore," he said, returning her smile. "I'll do my best."

It was hardly an effort. She walked into his waiting arms. They fit. Physically that was.

After dinner, he'd taken off his suit coat, rolled up his sleeves and gotten rid of the tie. Unfortunately for Eden's pheromones, less was more on the cop. The removal of clothes revealed well-defined forearms sprinkled with blond hair, smooth, taut neck muscles, and a powerful chest she'd willingly curl up against. She knew better than to take this pretend fantasy further, but two vodka martinis and several toasts to the bride and groom later, her inhibitions had flown out the Paradise Room's window.

He'd been gallant, but also upfront. His focus was on the bishop and obtaining leads in this case. Even so, a huge part of Eden wanted him to forget about the job, for him to look at her as a woman and not just as a means to finding a killer.

Had he, she wondered? A couple of times she'd thought she'd seen admiration in his eyes. Swaying to the music, she lived out a fantasy and inhaled the man's woodsy cologne. She wrapped her arms around his neck.

"I think you like your job, Detective."

The look he returned was worthy of the silver screen. His hands fell to the small of her back, past the low-cut of her gown, connecting with skin, dispatching desire to her nerve endings. "What's not to like? I get to hold a beautiful woman and still get paid."

"Be serious," she said, struggling to find her voice. "You're a people person. You like your job."

"Parts of it." He twirled her around. "How about you? Do you like *your* job?"

"Parts of it," she said, annoyed at his evasion. "I find it rewarding. That case you sat in on a couple of weeks ago? My client was innocent."

"Uh-huh."

"What's that supposed to mean?"

"It means just that." He tucked a strand behind her ear and leaned close. "How does it feel to be the most beautiful woman in the room?"

That response doused Eden with a heavy dose of reality. He was playing her. As a cop, it was natural for him to fool the crowd in trying to solve his case. But not her. Eden averted her gaze. "Kevin, don't."

"I'm sorry? What?"

"Pretend. Try to distract me."

"Who's pretending?" He pulled her closer. "I don't have to be involved to state the obvious. Every other woman's in black and white next to you."

It took a moment for air to fill her lungs. Any other woman would be comatose by such flattery, especially coming from a guy like Kevin Dancer. Instead, it infused Eden with monumental distrust. He'd made no secret from the start that he despised her profession. Further, he knew so much more about her than she did about him. It was as though she was in the courtroom and the prosecution had hidden exculpatory evidence from discovery. She didn't want to see Kevin as an opponent. Yet, in a real sense, she did.

The song came to an end. She'd promised to see the night through, and she would. On her terms. "That was fun," she lied. "Give me a moment?"

"Absolutely." He frowned. "You okay?"

She gave him her best trial lawyer smile. "Perfect."

Eden walked off the floor casually, then beyond the Paradise Room she increased her strides. She pulled her hair up, recognized her chronic bad habit, and let it fall. Why was she angry? Because he wanted her life story, but wouldn't share his own?

Her tension ebbed when she reached the country club's plated glass doors. Beyond them, she saw Mr. Timms sitting on the cement bench outside and in the dark.

He hadn't left the reception after all. She watched him, an outcast who obviously felt safer on the outside looking in. Like her, she decided.

Did the janitor have anyone? Family? Friends?

She started to push open the door, when a deep voice behind her called out her name. Eden turned to see who it was and her night went straight to hell.

SMOOTH, DANCER, real smooth.

Kevin watched Eden walk off the floor, fully aware that he'd blown it. She'd been trying to draw him in, to talk about his job. Trouble was, he felt entirely too comfortable talking to her, and if he opened one avenue of communication, then what?

Once he revealed one fragment of his life history, she'd want to know more. And that was his problem. He'd left that baggage in Columbus. As a cop living in the Southwest, he'd formed his own identity. He shook his head, picturing how she might react if she found out. Perhaps she'd pity him. Or be so impressed, she'd want an introduction. Who knew?

He allowed his gaze to wander the room. Eden's mother danced with her husband. Kevin sought out the bishop. Terrific. Now he and Eden had both disappeared.

All at once Kevin needed air, too.

"BISHOP MUNROE." Eden stepped away from the door.

Wearing his charisma like a snake charmer, Robert Munroe advanced on her. "If I didn't know better, I'd say you've been avoiding me, young lady."

Only like the plague, Eden thought, hoping her mind didn't choose this inopportune moment to play one of its stupid pranks. She stared at him. How did one address a bishop? Accessing the catacombs of her short Catholic education, she located what she thought was the appropriate response and said, "Me, Your Excellency? Never. I simply didn't want to take you away from all your many admirers."

Speaking of whom, Eden thought, glancing around, where was an entourage when one needed one?

"Ah, a true lawyer at heart. Applying flattery *and* tact. I knew you'd do well in life."

Something about him rang false, and she found herself uttering the same words Mr. Timms had in the receiving line. "You remember me?"

"Remember you?" The bishop smiled. "Next to your parents, I was your biggest fan. You played a Chopin Prelude, I believe. I recall the day I was invited to hear you play. I'd been told you had talent." He shook his head. "Divine gift was a more apt description."

Eden stared at the man. Then, as though he'd ripped open a crypt, dead memories resurrected. Her thoughts turned to Sister Agnes and the last time Eden saw her.

"Enough of this nonsense, Eden. I don't know what's come over you. You will stop being difficult, you will read the music and stop playing by ear. You're cheating, child. You know what the Lord thinks of cheaters. Now mind me, young lady. Sit down."

Backing away from the old crone, she'd sobbed, "I'll never play for you. You're mean . . . you're ugly. I hate the piano. I hate you!"

And then in the principal's office the next day, sitting between her parents as if she weren't even in the room, or the topic of conversation. "Mr. and Mrs. Moran, we simply cannot tolerate this type of behavior."

"I can't tell you how disappointed I was to learn you no longer play," the bishop was saying.

Vaulted back to the here and now, Eden raised her head. Bitterness sharpened her tone. "I see my mother's kept you informed."

Concern creased his brow. "I asked, Eden. Joanna didn't bring you up. Yours wasn't a talent easily dismissed. What happened?"

"I don't know." Eden didn't trust her parents' longtime friend not to repeat everything she said. Even so, she was reluctant to be rude when it appeared he was trying to be kind. "Maybe I was too undisciplined," she said. "I tried to play a few years ago, but my heart wasn't in it. I still listen to classical, though. Bach got me through law school."

He opened his mouth as though he planned to say more when something beyond the plated glass windows distracted him. Frowning, he said, "I hope we can talk later. But I see someone I should speak to."

"Mr. Timms?"

The bishop stayed his hand on the door. "Why, yes. Do you know Thomas?"

"I did, a long time ago. You should ask him to join us."

Munroe stared out at the man seated all alone. "I will, Eden. But don't expect that to happen. The Lord's ways aren't always known." Glancing at her from over his shoulder, he pushed open the door. "To some, like you, He bestows talent. On others, like Thomas, He issues challenges."

NEAR MIDNIGHT, Kevin pulled into St. Patrick's parking lot, easing his Jeep a few spaces down from his passenger's white Honda Accord. His evening with Eden had ended much as it had begun—in silence. The only difference was, while her mood had improved, his had deteriorated.

Whatever had happened between them on the dance floor had caused a rift, and the exclusive attention she'd shown him before was a thing of the past.

Killing the engine, he tried to pinpoint when his normally stalwart emotions had vanished as well. When they'd danced and he'd held her, he'd wanted, well—her.

He sent that crazy notion packing. No matter how appealing he found Eden Moran, they stood on opposite sides of the spectrum. He wanted criminals on the inside of a cell; she did her damndest to make sure they were returned to the streets.

She had, however, been of tremendous help to him. He'd gotten precisely what he'd gone to the wedding for, an interview with a key witness in Sister Beatrice's murder investigation. Kevin owed her thanks, not attitude.

"Best non-date I've ever had. Thanks, Eden."

"Not a problem. I didn't want to go alone. It worked out for both of us."

She brushed her hair to one side, a movement he followed so closely it took him a moment to regain his focus. "Whether I came with you or not, you wouldn't have been alone for long. How many of those players did you dance with tonight?"

"I didn't know there'd be a test, so I didn't count. What time do you see the bishop on Monday?"

"Nine a.m."

"Well, then." She angled her head and he glimpsed her earlier impish behavior. "My work is done here. You've made a significant connection."

What was it about her that made him smile? Why couldn't she look like something that lived under a bridge, or be as interesting as cardboard? "You okay to drive?"

"Sober as a judge. I switched to ice water hours ago."

And she had. He'd paid attention. She met his gaze, level and sure, leaving little doubt she'd pass a sobriety check. He could insist on driving her home. Based on the way she'd pressed her body against him on the dance floor, she might even sleep with him.

Why start something, he'd live to regret? *Let it go, Dancer.*

"I'll walk you to your car."

"There's no need."

He reiterated, "I'll walk you to your car."

They reached her Accord. He requested her keys. Stalling for time, he checked under the chassis and behind the seats. Then out of excuses, he said, "All clear."

"Good to know." She wore a teasing glint in her eyes, as though she saw right through him. "Thanks."

Standing this close without kissing her required a new kind of restraint in him. Thoughts of other women vanished when he was around Eden Moran. "You gonna go out with any of those guys you danced with tonight?"

"Maybe." Her smile faded. "Not one voiced an objection to the way I earn my paycheck."

Kevin's throat tightened at the thought of Eden in someone else's arms. He also deserved whatever she threw at him. He still wasn't going there. He stared past her to the stucco wall separating the property from the interstate. Beyond the six-foot barrier, the late-night weekend traffic roared by. Locust hums filled the air. "Drive safe, Eden."

She leaned against the car and folded her arms. "Are we going to talk about this, Kevin?"

"No." He walked away. Fast.

"Fine," she hollered after him. "I mean, you don't owe me anything. I didn't do anything to help you."

Typical lawyerly tactic, she didn't fight fair. Kevin pivoted. "You ever need anything, you call me."

"I'm calling now." Eden lifted her chin. "What happened? I know cops near retirement age who aren't as jaded."

"You wouldn't understand."

"Oh, please. Is that the best you can do? Try again, Detective."

He'd seen her in action. If she wanted answers she could be relentless. Too damned bad. There wasn't a judge in sight to compel him to answer. *Keep walking, Dancer.*

"You know what's sad," she continued, drilling him as though he were on a witness stand. "Despite the fact you turned every question I asked back to me, you had fun tonight. I'd even wager you wouldn't mind doing it again. But you're too all-fired stubborn because of some pitiful thing that happened. So let's have it. Who'd you arrest? Who got him off and what awful incident occurred as a result?"

Kevin whirled to face her. "Nothing's wrong with your ego, Counselor. What awful incident? Try several. Ever heard of J.T. Garland?"

She hesitated and Kevin stepped close again. "Didn't law school teach you anything? Never ask a question to which you don't already know the answer."

"Jackson Terrence Garland?" she croaked.

"One and the same."

Eden went rigid, suddenly sick to her stomach. Kevin had encountered the grand manipulator in the course of his career? How was that possible? Turn on any high profile murder case on any major network, and there was a real chance the jurist's opinion was being solicited. J.T. Garland lived somewhere back East, if she recalled correctly. Why would an Albuquerque cop even cross paths with the man? Garland was notorious for gaining questionable acquittals for wealthy clients and celebrities. Along with her argument, some of the starch left her voice. "I'm familiar with his work."

"What do you know about him?"

Kevin's clenched, ready-to-snap jaw, unnerved her. She'd only observed ice-cool control in the cop. Seeing this side of him caused shards of uncertainty to pierce that conclusion. "He was required reading in my third-year Restorative Justice," she replied. Then, finding her backbone, she added, "J.T.'s brutal, ruthless, but if you're in trouble, I'd venture to say you'd want him on your side."

"You admire him." Kevin narrowed his gaze, making the statement as though he was throwing down a gauntlet.

Her heart picked up speed. Good grief. How should she answer this? For long moments tonight, she thought there could be something between them. But his hatred of her profession seemed almost virulent. "Actually, I do," she replied as tactfully as she could without sacrificing her integrity. "Defense lawyers serve a purpose, Kevin. I'll wager if you were ever fighting for your life, you might even call him."

"I wouldn't have to," Kevin said. "He'd be calling me. The unluckiest day of my life was the day Jack Garland married my mother."

Chapter Ten

WELL, THAT WAS that, Eden thought, as she pulled into her covered parking space next to the commercial building that housed her loft. Using the Honda's trunk for support, she tugged off her heels. It might take a day or two to regain her spirits, but she'd damned well relieve her aching feet now.

J.T. Garland. To learn he was Kevin's stepfather sent her already tumultuous emotions into overdrive. The only thing she'd gotten from the closed-mouth cop after he'd unleashed his demons was that he'd been twelve at the time of the union and that he had two younger half-brothers as a result.

Anything else she'd gathered was speculation. The fact that he'd never changed his name left her to wonder if Garland had merely tolerated Kevin's presence. Had he faced ridicule from his peers because of his notorious stepfather? What piqued her curiosity most was, if experienced legal professionals found Garland intimidating, what effect had he had on a boy about to enter his teens?

She used her key to access the compact entrance to her loft, then noted the upstairs light in the hallway was off. Mr. Lucero, the owner of the building, was a stickler for keeping it on. Considering the eccentric old man who lived in the unit next door to her, Eden sighed. She'd meant to bring him a piece of wedding cake, which, as much as she'd advise against it, he'd likely share with his cat.

She left the downstairs light on and trudged upstairs. She'd make him brownies come morning. Strike that. It *was* morning, and it was Sunday. All she wanted to do was climb into bed, forget that Kevin Dancer existed and sleep till noon.

That was until she reached the top landing and something crumbled between her toes. Thoughts of sleep disintegrated as Eden let out a squeak. Lifting her foot, she willed her heart to still and her eyes to adjust to the dim. Moonbeams drifting through a skylight helped identify what looked like blackened bread crumbs. Near her front door she discovered the source. Her antique terracotta planter and her recently planted pansies were scattered all over the wooden planked floor.

Whirling, she scanned the hallway and rafters in search of the culprit, then whispered, "Where are you, General?"

A hiss sounded overhead and she startled. With smooth, dark gray fur and eyes a penetrating shade of green, the gorgeous Russian blue was a pest, but normally a pussycat in every other way. She'd caught him recently swatting at her flowers. How he'd knocked over the heavy pot was anyone's guess, but before he tracked in any more dirt or woke up his owner, she'd keep him with her and let Mr. Lucero deal with the cat come daylight. Keeping her voice low, she murmured, "Here, kitty, kitty."

He sprang to another beam, out of reach, rounded his back and hissed again.

She frowned up at him. "What's with you?"

Her neighbor's door opened and the old man she'd been trying not to disturb stuck out his head. "Eden?"

"Mr. Lucero." She slumped in defeat. "I was trying not to wake you."

"That's all right." Dressed in a worn terry cloth robe, the old man yawned. "Sleep too much at my age, Father Time gets riled and doesn't wake you at all. What are you doing out here?"

She pointed to the rafters and the high-centered feline and waved an arm to indicate the damage.

Her neighbor stepped into the hall. "Ah, Eden, *lo siento.*" He glowered at his longtime companion. "What were you doing, you old dictator, digging in the Philippines again?"

She hid a smile. Mr. Lucero, who served under MacArthur, claimed the cat was the war hero's reincarnation. For several months now, his daughters had been trying to get the old man into assisted living. But Felix Lucero valued his independence. He took pride in his property, kept it maintained for the accountants downstairs, and except for this one idiosyncrasy appeared to possess all his faculties.

Although at times Eden wondered how the renowned general might have felt about coming back as a Russian blue.

Mr. Lucero reached between two overhead beams and pulled the protesting feline into his arms. "Now don't be difficult, sir. You've caused enough mischief for one night." He glanced at her. "Wow. *Muy guapa*, Eden. Did you get married tonight?"

"My sister did, remember?" Winking, she said, "Besides, who'd marry me?"

The man, well into his eighties, replied, "I would. If I were ten years younger . . ."

"I'm turning in, you old flirt. It's late."

"Same here. I'll clean up this mess tomorrow."

And he would. By tomorrow, the dirt would be swept away and order restored. Eden stepped over the broken flower pot, wishing she could say the same about life.

A short time later, she slid into bed. She considered for all of one second taking time to hang up the gown that lay on the dresser, or tossing her shoes into the closet. But in the next moment she closed her eyes.

To be back in school in the amphitheater of Armstrong Hall, surrounded by stressed out, overworked law students. Typically, Scott London, who sat in front of the class, prattled on, which Eden hoped he would continue so that Professor Erickson wouldn't call on her.

"Persuasive argument, Mr. London," the professor said, glancing over the rims of his bifocals, his hip perched on the edge of his desk. "Ms. Moran, care to counter? Tell us about Sister Beatrice, if you please."

Eden lifted her chin from her hand. "I'm sorry, Professor. What did you say?"

"You knew her. Witnesses said you did." But this time, the voice came from the row behind her. She twisted to meet Kevin's accusing glare.

"I told you I don't remember," she said, holding her anger in check and wishing he'd just go away. She faced the front of the lecture hall again.

"Perhaps a phone call to your parents will help you recall."

One step, two, and Armstrong Hall morphed into the previous evening and the Paradise Room's reception line. Clad in her lovely bridesmaid dress, she stood beside her sister while her former grade school teacher tugged at Eden's arm. Heat colored her cheeks as friends and family looked on.

She reached for her sister. "Meggie, don't let her take me."

Laughing, Meghan stepped back into the arms of her husband. "You ruined my wedding and now you want my help? Think again, little sister."

Naturally, her mother entered the ruckus. "She does that you know, drops bombshells on us. Answer your teacher, Eden. Why did you leave the playground?"

"I didn't." Suddenly, her knee was on fire and blood seeped through her gown. She scanned the crowd, horrified, encountering Kevin, Father Slater, the bishop . . . and not one sympathetic face among them. "I didn't!"

"You did," Mrs. Trevino said, advancing on her as she scowled. "I searched everywhere. Have you any idea what you put me through? Now, once and for all, Eden, tell the truth."

A painful sob lodged in her throat. Her mind was like contents under pressure as she struggled to think, to appease the grownup assault going round in her brain.

Then the angry voices transformed into ear-piercing yowls as grade school memories grappled to break free.

Springing upright in bed, Eden gasped. "I had to. She was going to leave me!" Disoriented, her heart racing, she threw back the covers. What a dream . . . that . . . unbearable racket . . . what had brought on such a *nightmare*? But even as the question swirled into the recesses of her memory, another round of wailing shattered the first traces of dawn.

General?

Eden yanked on a pair of sweat pants, ran through the loft and opened the door to the outer hallway. Just as she feared, it was Mr. Lucero's cat making the god-awful noise. She searched the overhead rafters, but saw no sign of him. Careful not to cut her foot on the fractured pot in the hallway, she scurried toward her neighbor's open front door. In the next instant, however, the caterwauling started up again, this time calling her attention to the stairs.

She raced toward them. And as she slid to a halt and grabbed the railing, her heart sank. Her neighbor lay in a heap at the bottom, his beloved Russian blue howling beside him.

MANY PEOPLE, when awakened from a dead sleep, turned to face a partner on the opposite pillow. Kevin's partner was a 9mm Glock, and beside it was his set-to-vibrate cell phone, which currently was jumping all over the bed. He reached for it, while checking the watch he rarely removed from his wrist. *Four friggin' a.m. on a Sunday morning.*

"Dancer," he said.

"Kev. It's Sal. I'm at the office."

Kevin lowered a forearm over his eyes and groaned. "*Why?*"

"Leg was throbbing and I couldn't sleep. I stopped in at Dispatch to shoot the breeze with my cousin. Your pretty lawyer just phoned in an emergency."

Kevin bolted upright. "Eden? She placed a 9-1-1 call?"

"She asked for an ambulance, man."

Kevin slid into his jeans. "You get an address?"

In record time, he was driving down San Mateo. Why would Eden need an ambulance? What had happened in the few short hours after they'd separated at St. Patrick's? Was there a break-in, an intruder? Or had the 9-1-1 call she placed had something to do with him?

That egocentric thought washed for all of five seconds. He'd seen many sides of Eden last night, but the one thing that struck him was that she knew who she was—at least professionally. It would take more than a cop's lowly viewpoint to shake that granite foundation.

Kevin decelerated around Central, squinted against the glare and picked up speed again. With no cars coming in any direction, he sped through a red light, still warring with speculation. *Get real, Dancer. Once you drove away tonight, you were no more than an unpleasant memory.* At that rationale, his pulse quickened. In his line of work, he was paid to picture the worst-case scenario.

He arrived at the address Sal gave him and did a quick rundown of nearby businesses. Albuquerque's Old Town lay in various stages of reconstruction, some buildings in better repair than others, many having undergone conversions to condos and lofts. The wooden two-story structure with the Superior ambulance and police unit out front appeared well maintained. Bypassing a large sign that read Old Town Certified Public Accountants, he entered an office foyer.

A uniformed police officer acknowledged Kevin, while two paramedics worked over a victim. Kevin stepped close, and at the realization it was someone else and not Eden, he breathed easier. But only slightly.

After receiving the patrolman's update, Kevin's relief wasn't complete until he saw her descend the stairs. Disheveled and dressed in track pants, her crystal blue eyes were void of their usual sparkle, the smudges beneath them dark with fatigue. She squeezed past the EMTs, and when she studied the old man on the stretcher, her lips tightened.

If she was surprised to see Kevin in the building's entryway, she didn't let on. "I've phoned his daughters," she informed the cop as she shot a worried glance toward the paramedics. "They'll be waiting at the hospital."

She finally acknowledged Kevin. "Don't you sleep?"

"About as much as you do." He turned to the patrolman. "Mind if I look around?"

The man who worked the night shift obviously wanted to call it a morning. "Fine by me. Looks pretty cut and dry, but I'll be outside completing my report if you want to talk to me."

"Thanks." Kevin turned to Eden. "Why don't you show me where and how you found the victim."

A look of utter defiance crossed her face, but perhaps because the patrolman was within earshot, she managed a civil response. "All right, but it'll have to be quick. I'm going to the hospital."

"Are you a friend of the family?" Kevin asked as he followed her up the wood stairs.

"We're neighbors. I take the role seriously."

Lucky neighbor, Kevin thought. Not many people did nowadays. He shook away another inconsistency between Eden and J.T. The only way his stepfather would come to another's aid was if a retainer were involved.

As they made their way to the second floor, Kevin noticed that even in baggy sweats the lady lawyer turned him on. Not a good thing. He forced his gaze from her shapely ass, then on the sixth step paused to survey the area. A narrow staircase, a dark corridor and an elderly man. When assigned to patrol, Kevin saw countless accidents involving senior citizens. So why did this one seem off?

Maybe because the stairway was so compact that an able-bodied person should have broken his fall by grabbing the handrail. The officer had mentioned Eden found the old man at the base of the stairs. Kevin pulled on the railing and found it anchored. Why had Lucero fallen so far? Had he misjudged? Or had a heart attack or stroke put him in a position to no longer care?

Eden waited on the top step. "Coming?"

The irritation in her voice urged him upward. "What kind of health was your neighbor in?"

"What are you, a mind reader? I was thinking the same thing. Mr. Lucero climbs up and down ladders and chases his cat twenty-four/seven. I keep wondering why he wasn't wearing his glasses."

"He wears them all the time?"

"They're part of him. He always said . . ." She shook her head. "He always *says* 'a bat sees better than me.'"

"Sounds like you like the old guy."

"He's the best." She squeezed her eyes closed. "He's just got to make it. Without his glasses and without any light, he didn't stand a chance."

Kevin glanced around. "It is dark up here."

"Burned-out bulb." Eden pointed to an antique light fixture to the right of the stairway.

He tried the switch. *Nothing.* Lack of glasses, an unlit hallway. Every nerve in Kevin twitched. He moved to the fixture.

"What are you doing?"

"Just being thorough." He reached up through the bell-shaped glass and prayed for a disintegrated filament.

The bulb turned in the socket. *So much for divine intervention.* "Try it now."

She flipped the switch and the light flickered on. "That's weird."

"That's what I was thinking," Kevin said. "Who's the mind reader now?"

Chapter Eleven

AS THE AMBULANCE drove off, Thomas stood in the shadows, reeling. He was like Abraham who'd been ordered to offer up his son as a sacrifice to prove his devotion.

And test him God had. Touching his stinging cheek, he found it was no longer bleeding, but his neck, face and back still bore the burning scratches from where the devil cat had launched its attack. Fighting it off had taken several pain-filled moments. Blindly, Thomas had lost his balance, tripping over and then crashing into the planter in the hallway that he'd deliberately darkened. For a time, he'd thought all was lost.

Until the key in the downstairs lock turned, and the Almighty had steered clear the way. Hurriedly, he'd broken into the storage unit adjacent to Eden's apartment. And there he'd stayed. Waiting. Watching. Praying.

This close to saving the Bishop, Thomas had very nearly jimmied the lock on her door, when her misguided neighbor discovered him.

Where Thomas had been tested and required to prove his faith yet again.

What had the old fool been thinking to challenge him, when right was so clearly on his side? He glanced down at the glasses he'd ripped from the old man's face. Thomas tucked the mangled frames in his breast pocket and slumped in fatigue.

So many trials. They'd gone on for too many years. He prayed Eden's neighbor would die. If not, another trial would be heaped upon his shoulders.

Chapter Twelve

THE HALLWAY flooding with light wasn't the only thing that came into focus as Kevin lowered his hand from the fixture. Eden reviewed the hours beforehand with startling clarity. Wincing, she replayed in her mind the events that had occurred since she'd walked in the door from the reception.

"I can't believe this," she said. Racing down the hallway, she stopped feet away from the shattered planter.

Kevin came up beside her. "What happened here?"

"When I came home last night, I thought Mr. Lucero's cat was responsible for this mess."

Kevin went down on one knee, picked up one of the terracotta pot's jagged edges and inspected the damage. He looked up at her. "What kind of cat is it, a mountain lion?"

Eden flushed. "Don't make me feel anymore foolish than I already do. It was late, I was tired. It never occurred to me that . . ."

That what? Her rational mind grappled with the impossible. That an intruder had been on the premises? Was that why the General had hissed? Craning her neck, she scanned the rafters. He'd been so out of sorts. She'd blamed him. When in reality, he must've been frightened, maybe even trying to warn her.

Kevin withdrew his phone and ordered law enforcement back to the scene. Then, waving a hand over the dirt-scattered hallway, he said, "Let's retrace your steps. When you came home you found . . . what exactly?"

Eden spent the next few minutes explaining about the General, his fondness for the rafters, how he'd hissed when she'd called him, her conversation with Mr. Lucero, and then finally saying good night.

"Which unit is yours?"

"That one." She pointed to the door behind him.

He nodded and made his way to her neighbor's. "And Lucero lives here?"

"That's right."

Kevin moved to the supply closet. "And behind this door?"

"Storage," she replied. "It's always locked though."

Kevin nudged the door with his foot. It creaked open. "Always?"

Eden's stomach lurched. "Always. Mr. Lucero keeps chemicals inside.

He wouldn't have left it unlocked. He worries constantly about the General."

"I think it's time I met this cat."

Leading Kevin into the unit identical to hers, Eden summoned the General, bewildered at the silence that followed.

She and Kevin separated in search of him, rendezvousing a short time later without success. "This isn't good," she said.

"Maybe he'll come out if I'm not around. Why don't you take a break and I'll check on the progress downstairs."

It was a suggestion she gladly accepted. Her eyes gritty from lack of sleep, she slumped onto her neighbor's faded blue couch and closed her eyes. When she opened them next, the cat, with an obvious limp, approached gingerly.

"Ah, baby, come here." It took him several seconds to reach her, but she didn't dare rush him. She might frighten him into hiding again. When he got close, Eden lifted him onto her lap and gathered the cat against her. Relieved by his purrs, she buried her face in his silky warmth and breathed in his musky scent.

This cat had to have faced Mr. Lucero's attacker. How she wished he could talk. What a witness he'd make. "Who did this, General?" she whispered.

Kevin returned a short time later. The cat stiffened in her arms and she tightened her hold. "No, no, baby, he's not going to hurt you."

Kevin closed the door and waited. Then slowly crossing the living room, he sat on the arm of the couch and gentled his baritone voice. "Well, hey, guy. Look at you. You really are a general."

LATER THAT morning, the consensus of the lead detective and cops on scene was that the attempt on the neighbor's life was a robbery gone bad. The pried locks were those of an amateur, the battered ceramic pot all but waving a banner announcing his presence. Fingerprints had been found; whether they belonged to anyone besides Eden or the old man remained to be seen.

Kevin wasn't sure why he felt such queasiness in the pit of his stomach as Eden slid behind the wheel of her car. Maybe it was because she held a job that pissed people off, and if the attack had been premeditated, most likely it was meant for her, not the neighbor. Kevin's pointing out this theory to the detective in front of Eden did little to repair his relationship with her, but he'd never been one to hold back critical information and wouldn't start now.

He looked past her to the backseat and the cat in the carrier they'd found on top of Lucero's dryer. "How's he doing?"

"His pupils are dilated. I'm scared. You don't think we hurt him more than he already is? He fought us tooth and nail not to get in this thing and now he's so quiet."

"He's a champ," Kevin said. "He'll get through this. You're going to the hospital after you drop him off at the vet's?"

She nodded and twisted her hair into its standard knot.

"I could go with you."

She slipped on her sunglasses and shook her head. "You've done enough. Thanks."

He wasn't sure he appreciated the double entendre.

"You should go home," she said after a moment. "One of us should get some sleep."

Like that was gonna happen. He removed his wallet and took out a business card. "You *think* you hear something, you call me."

The way she frowned at the card, it appeared she might argue. Instead, she took a deep breath, nodded and switched on the ignition. "See you around."

He watched the car until she stopped at a light then turned a corner. *See you around. Oh, yeah, you can count on it.*

Chapter Thirteen

EDEN ARRIVED home late that afternoon, exhausted and disbelieving. Felix Lucero lay in a coma, his loved ones holding a deathbed vigil by his hospital bed. They'd expressed their gratitude to her for coming, for taking care of the General, and then surrounded her with their earnest hugs and kisses. Her throat had been impossibly tight throughout the day. What would it be like to belong to such a family? To be accepted so unconditionally?

The fact was, she wasn't one of them. So, gradually, when she was sure she'd worn out her welcome, she'd eased toward the door and out of the ICU, not wanting to intrude on their sorrow any further.

With her weekend all but gone, she hoped to catch up on sleep before returning to work tomorrow. The majority of crimes were committed on weekends, and Mondays at the Albuquerque Public Defender's Office bordered between Bedlam and hell.

Leaving her covered parking space, she rounded the building, relieved that the detectives hadn't seen fit to outfit the building with crime scene tape. She, too, believed the attack was random, that her neighbor had surprised a burglar. She hadn't been with the APD long enough to make enemies as Kevin suggested. And, by all the evidence the inept culprit had left behind, he was probably already behind bars. Lord help him if she was the lawyer assigned to his case. She'd have to recuse herself, of course, but not before advising the DA to seek the maximum penalty the law would allow.

At the path to her loft, Eden froze. A pair of jean-clad legs blocked the entrance. Sidestepping the walkway into the rock, she fumbled inside her purse for her phone and her pepper spray. But before she pressed the button for emergency services, her brain clicked on. It was broad daylight. Not exactly the most sensible place for an attacker to come calling, or for a homeless person to take up residence.

Cell phone and pepper spray ready, Eden approached, only to recapture her breath as she sidled closer. She'd recognize those long legs anywhere. With his back propped against the wall, arms crossed, his baseball cap pulled low over his brow, Kevin sat under the building's overhang—*sleeping.*

She stared at the man, with his impossible attitudes and confusing contradictions. Then silently she crept to the step below him and sat down.

"Took you long enough," he grumbled.

Reaching up, she tipped his cap so she could see his eyes, immediately swept up in their deep brown depths. "For someone who doesn't like me, you sure hang around a lot."

"I never said I didn't like *you.*"

True, he hadn't. That didn't make his blunt rejection of her in St. Patrick's parking lot hurt any less, or resolve the issues between them. Even so, she'd take the comment and his presence as a positive. "Forget to pay your rent?"

"How'd you know?" He yawned. Then, stretching, he showed off some dangerously appealing biceps. "What do you think of my new set up?"

"I think I should call a cop. What are you doing here, Kevin?"

"Protecting you."

She laughed. "*What?*"

"With your attack cat out of commission, I figured I was the next best thing."

If only he knew. In truth, that's why she'd stayed at the hospital so long. The idea of an intruder on the premises wasn't exactly the best sleeping aid. She was infinitely grateful for his presence, not that it would do to tell him that. "I don't need a bodyguard," she said, her tone belying her thoughts. "Unless . . . did your guys find something?"

He tugged the cap back over his eyes. "No recognizable prints so far, no witnesses."

Eden blinked at the cop taking up space on her doorstep. How cavalier could he be? She was tempted to go about her business and leave him where he sat. But there were laws in this city and someone might trip on him. "So what's the plan, boy scout?"

Lifting the cap again, he returned an expression far from trustworthy. And trust him, she didn't. This man, with his chronic five o'clock shadow, appeared white-hat-hero material one minute, Casanova-hot the next. Her gaze left his face, only to fall upon his powerful-looking hands and the strong thighs that filled out his jeans.

Damned if her stomach didn't flip.

"Got anything to eat?" he asked.

Before her heated face gave her away, she rose from the steps. "Nope. Looks like you're out of luck."

He came to his feet as well. "That's okay, we'll order in."

THAT WAS TOO easy, Kevin thought, as he crossed the threshold of Eden's loft. She'd simply told him to make himself at home, she was going to bed. Then, closing the door behind her, she shut him out, much like she had the first time they'd met.

Well, if anything, she was consistent. And after the way things ended Saturday night, what did he expect, a five-course dinner?

Kevin ordered takeout from a nearby restaurant. Then, at the sound of running water, he hung up on the order-taker without a goodbye. He'd taken Eden at her word when she said she was going to bed. Ever the cop, he eased the door open, just in case. The clothes she'd been wearing snaked a trail to her bath.

The picture of Eden naked sent instant pain south. He'd told himself on the way over that this idea was terrible at best. But after the break-in last night, there was no way he was leaving her alone.

Jealous that she was making use of her shower when all he could think of was a cold one, he shut her bedroom door with a resounding click. In need of a distraction, he went outside to await the Chinese food.

Sal called the minute Kevin stepped outside. "We got a hit on those latent prints."

Kevin resumed his seat on the porch. "Somebody we know?"

"Somebody in the system."

"Good news for a change."

"Not necessarily. All it means is we got a name. Reuben Sharpe. Served time twenty-two years ago for third-degree sexual assault, got out of Southern New Mexico Correctional Facility, then fell off the face of earth."

"There's no record of where he went after he was paroled?"

"*Nada.* Sharpe was assigned to a work program. Six weeks later he walked off the job and was never heard from again."

"Well, he's back," Kevin said. "And I don't like where he's landed." Kevin calculated the distance of Lucero's storage closet and the distance to where the predator had lain in wait at Eden's front door. "Do you agree with the cops on scene that it was random?"

"Don't you?"

"If Eden had any other job, maybe. Now that we have a name, I'll check with Lucero's daughters to see if they've ever heard of this guy."

"Good plan. I got an extra ticket to the Lobos tonight. You in?"

Kevin took in the tree-lined street with its infrequent traffic. "Next time. Think I'll turn in early."

A skinny Asian dude in baggy jeans chose that moment to walk up the path. Carrying Kevin's order, he raised his head, scanned Eden's building and said, "Sweet crib, man. You live upstairs?"

"Hang on a sec." Before the gabby delivery guy gave him away any further, Kevin tucked the phone under his chin, flashed him an annoyed look and slipped him an exorbitant tip to get lost.

Gabby counted the money and gave him a thumb's up. "Thanks, man. Enjoy."

Gritting his teeth, Kevin set the food on the porch. What were the chances his partner had suddenly gone hard of hearing?

"What was that all about?" Sal asked.

"You heard?"

"Every. Single. Incriminating. Word."

Kevin shook his head. "All right. You got me. I'm at Eden's."

"Not one of your brighter moves, Kev."

Kevin couldn't agree with his partner more. That didn't mean he was leaving. "Someone attacked her neighbor. He might be after her. She's our one solid link to this case. Would you feel right about leaving her alone?"

"No. But I'd let patrol do their job. You're making it personal."

"I'm not." He said it more to reassure himself than to convince his partner. "Patrol's short staffed, and I keep getting hung up on the timing of all this. A break-in occurring at the same time I attend a reception with Eden?"

"As much as you want it tied to this case, stick with what we know. We've got an attractive, single woman who lives alone and prints of a known predator right outside her door. Plain and simple, Ms. Moran's neighbor surprised a bad guy."

"You're probably right, but—"

"I *am* right." There was no mistaking Sal's disgusted huff. "What? You think this Reuben Sharpe character was on the *guest* list?"

Kevin laughed. All at once he felt ridiculous. But just because he was red-faced didn't mean he was leaving. "Probably not."

"Now that we have a name, ask your pretty lawyer if she's ever heard of him."

"I will. By the way, you up for hobbling along with me to the diocese tomorrow?"

"What do you mean, hobbling? I'll race your ass there. What time?"

"Nine a.m. Bishop Munroe agreed to see me. It's not exactly kosher, he doesn't know the particulars, I mean. But at least I got us an in. I figure, you know . . . two against one?"

"I'm there. Besides, it'll give me a chance to pay my respects to the lying Ms. Janice Charles."

"Now that we know that Father Munroe and the bishop are one and the same," Kevin said, "it explains her motivation, don't you think?"

"Not enough to excuse her for obstruction of justice."

"Careful. I hate having the commander's boot up my ass."

Sal laughed. "Considering where you're standing right now, *amigo*, you have a funny way of showing it. Swing by and pick me up in the morning. I'll spring for breakfast burritos."

Upstairs, Kevin placed the takeout on the counter and went to tell Eden of its arrival. But when he eased the door open, he saw she was already down for the count. She slept on her stomach, childlike, an arm hanging off the bed, all that blond hair in her face.

Inching the door shut, he put his new list of questions on hold. Who the hell was Rueben Sharpe? Where had he been for twenty-two years, and why of all nights, while Kevin and Eden were at her sister's wedding, had he chosen to show up at her loft?

Sexual predators didn't go away. They were driven by unquenchable urges, and ninety-nine percent ended up back in the pen. So why hadn't Sharpe?

Kevin's thoughts turned to tomorrow's meeting. Would the bishop admit to knowing Sister Beatrice? Kevin wasn't optimistic. Munroe didn't act like a killer, but then very few waved I-did-it red flags. Had the bishop learned the police were on to him and asked someone to eliminate witnesses—someone like S*harpe?*

Filling his plate with Mongolian beef, Kevin admitted that Sal was right. This case had become an obsession. He was inventing conspiracy theories now.

So why couldn't he let it go? Carrying his meal to the sofa, Kevin sat down. He continued to sort through the events of last night. Munroe's frequent stares at Eden. His blatant attempts to draw her into conversation after she and Kevin joined him at his table. Finally, Kevin witnessing Munroe and Eden at the Parisio club's entrance.

Was Munroe a letch attracted to beautiful women? Or was he something more sinister?

Based on the introduction of a predator, dread worked its way up Kevin's spine. Was that the reason for the diocese's evasion? Was it possible that Eden herself had been a victim during her time at St. Patrick's? Model child, exemplary student turned rebel, expelled from Catholic school, she certainly fit the abuse profile.

Kevin finished his meal, barely tasting it, his thoughts consumed by the woman on the other side of the door. He should follow her example and hit the hay. He switched on the tube and caught the meteorologist's prediction for tomorrow's weather. Then, adjusting one of Eden's sofa pillows behind his head, he settled in for a long night. Maybe he should apply for a meteorologist position. He knew damned well sleep wasn't in his forecast.

EDEN BURIED her wet face in the pillow.

Mama was mad again because she wouldn't play the piano. She wanted to play, really she did, she'd simply forgotten how. The fact that nobody believed her made her miserable. But it was true. Where her fingers had once flown over the ivories, as if by themselves, these days they felt like bricks when she pressed down on the keys.

Maybe she could no longer play because so much had changed. She missed her friends, she missed St. Patrick's. She missed . . .

"You have a gift from God, Eden Marie Moran," her mother said, raising her voice. "How dare you squander it away?"

Eden sought out her father, who buried his face behind his paper. Meghan merely lowered her head and looked sad.

"All right. Be stubborn. After dinner you will go straight to your room." Her mother's low voice of frustration was worse than her yelling. "Help your sister set the table. Father Munroe will be here any time now."

Meghan handed Eden a plate, but she'd frozen in place. "Did you hear what Mama said, Eden? Help me," Meghan said quietly.

Her mother glanced up from slicing tomatoes. "What are you girls whispering about? Eden? What on earth? Edward."

"What is it now?"

"This is the last straw. Your daughter just wet into her shoes!"

Her dad lowered his evening paper and rose from the chair . . .

"Eden. Eden, wake up. You're dreaming."

Cringing from Daddy's shaking, her eyes flew open. But even as her mind registered that her father had never shaken her that way, and it was Kevin waking her, new waves of panic set in. From the moment she'd met him, she'd been set upon by vivid, unforgettable dreams. And yet, they weren't the disjointed messages of her subconscious; many were actual childhood memories—like this one.

She crushed her face to the pillow, mortified she'd been crying so hard that he'd felt the need to wake her. Her humiliation only deepened when the mattress shifted beneath his weight and she felt his warm presence beside her.

"You don't think I've ever had a nightmare?" he said softly.

Doubtless he had. That didn't mean she wanted to share hers with him. What she wanted was for him to *go away*.

"Were you dreaming about Mr. Lucero?"

She clutched the pillow tighter. Not even close. What did it say about her that long-ago memories surpassed a man on his deathbed. Kevin's assumption, however, had given her an out if she chose one. She lay motionless, trying to sort out her feelings.

He rose from the bed. "I'm here if you need me, Eden."

If you need me. What was he doing? How could he sound so disappointed when *he* was the one holding her at arm's length one moment, showing up on her doorstep the next? When they danced, he'd intoxicated her more than the vodka martinis, only to then rebuff her in the church parking lot? She didn't understand or appreciate his mixed messages.

She was no good at being thrown away. Thanks to her parents' rejection, she'd had a whole slew of first and second dates and one measly failed relationship. Her childhood had taught her to operate with her guard up.

She lowered her pillow to tell him as much when she discovered he'd already made it to the doorway. It sounded like a stranger's voice when she called him back. "Kevin."

But when he turned, and she saw the absolute concern on his face, her defenses shattered. "I guess . . . I would like to talk."

His gaze fell to her position on the bed and he frowned. "Good. I'll meet you in the living room."

KEVIN CURBED every impulse within him to interrupt, but now that he'd gotten Eden to open up, he wasn't willing to risk a single word. He chose a chair; she sat on the sofa. She told him about the nightmare she'd been having before Lucero's cat had brought her back to reality, and now about tonight's dream of a family unraveling.

He gave his instincts a mental high-five. Something *had* happened to Eden. Now his major concern was how to deal with it. She'd obviously blocked whatever it was out. As a cop, he had a duty to decipher this case. But as someone without the proper psychological credentials, did he have the right to pry into her psyche?

Still, Eden was a public defender. Surely, she'd seen cases that dealt with abuse. Perhaps she'd never looked closely at those that paralleled her own and made the connection.

She shook her head and laughed. "I can't believe I told you all that."

"That you wet your pants?" Kevin smiled back. "Big deal. I peed my pants once when Kenny Yokabitiz ran into a pole. The goof wasn't watching where he was going. It was Three Stooges funny and I lost it."

Giggling, she replied, "Was your mother as furious as mine?"

Kevin loved seeing this side of Eden. "She couldn't have cared less. She told me to go upstairs and change my clothes."

"Obviously your pastor wasn't coming to dinner and due to arrive at any minute."

"Can't say that he was," Kevin replied. "Did you and your mother always have issues?"

She tilted her head and screwed up her pretty features. "Not always. At one time, when everyone touted me as a prodigy, I was her pride and joy. The issues came when I wouldn't do as she expected. I think she got off on the praise more than I did, and when I quit, the adulation stopped."

Typical, Kevin thought. "Why did you quit?"

Eden emitted a sigh and closed her eyes.

He'd never seen such unadulterated sadness cross another's face. Torn between doing his job and his desire to pull her close, he curled his hands into fists and did nothing.

"I don't know. I just stopped. Haven't you ever gotten sick of something, people telling you that you have to do something one way when you can easily do it another? My instructor, Sister Agnes, never once praised me. Not once. Instead she said I lacked discipline. At one lesson, she asked me if I'd been practicing, and I told her I had. When she saw I wasn't reading the music, but playing by ear, she called me a liar. She sent me to confession, Kevin. A little kid forced to say she'd done something wrong, when she hadn't."

Eden's breathing intensified, while he held his. Watching the rapid rise and fall of her chest, again he was tempted to go to her. He couldn't. Something was happening.

"I guess that's the point when I'd had enough. What hurt most was my mother wouldn't stand up for me."

"That must've felt like a helluva lot of pressure to a little kid," he said.

Eden bounded from the couch. She moved to the loft's picture window and placed a palm against the pane. "Every time I was in a room with that old crone I felt like she was strangling me. I loved playing the piano my way. I wanted . . ." She turned to face him. Her eyes were glassy, darting back and forth as though the past was on rewind. "I asked my mother to let me change teachers. There was . . . I thought since Sister Agnes hated me so much, if I . . ."

This was it. Kevin rose from the sofa and approached her slowly, carefully. "If what, Eden?"

Her eyes continued their animated dance. "I thought it was so cool when I learned some of the other kids took lessons away from the convent. Sr. Agnes, she may have been a nun, but she was the *devil*. I thought if I could take lessons at the school like the others, I'd be okay.

"But my mother wouldn't hear of it. We couldn't dare hurt *Sister Agnes*. Never mind that she was killing me." Eden's shoulders slumped and her eyes filled. "So there you have it. I stopped playing out of self-defense. I couldn't bear that old bitch anymore."

Releasing his pent-up breath, Kevin moved to the living room window and took her in his arms. He'd have to have a heart of lead not to hold her. Even in an agitated state, she hadn't admitted to knowing Sister Beatrice.

Pulling Eden close, he ran his fingers through her hair, stroked her back and moved on to the next piece of the puzzle. "When Sister Agnes sent you to confession, did she send you to Father Munroe?"

Eden's tears soaked through his shirt. She nodded against his chest.

Inhaling deeply, Kevin asked, "What happened then?"

"I pretended to go, but I never made it inside the confessional."

Kevin tightened his jaw. "Why, Eden? Why didn't you go inside?"

She wiped her wet cheeks and she stiffened. "Because I was *nine years old*, Kevin, and I had nothing to confess. I went somewhere else instead."

Chapter Fourteen

BY THE END of the day, Thomas knew the layout of Mesa General Hospital by heart. At first he'd spent most of his time in the chapel, but after a time the chaplain, who came regularly to comfort family members, noticed him and eyed him strangely. The last time Thomas had gone inside to pray, the minister headed his way. But before he came near, Thomas rose from his knees and scurried out an opposite door.

Eden's neighbor had surprised the experts. In the last few hours, he'd been upgraded to stable and moved from the ICU onto the surgical floor. But while his family and doctors celebrated, the old man's improvement caused Thomas great concern. He couldn't allow the misguided fool to come out of it and identify him. Thomas might go by a different name now, but he still had the same old face.

In the basement, near the hospital's huge boiler and backup generator, he located the custodians' supply closet and changing area, where he slipped into an employee's light blue uniform and shoe coverings. Then, prying open a locker with a screwdriver, he ran his hands over a shelf and found a badge. Tyrone Washington weighed fifty pounds more than Thomas and he was black. Thomas simply removed the employee's laminated picture and left it blank. No one looked closely at Thomas. Perhaps that's why The Messenger had enlisted his help in the first place. He had no choice but to trust in the Lord. Like always, He would make Thomas invisible.

Thomas stocked the cleaning trays with supplies and then hid the package of empty syringes he'd stolen from General Supply. The things he'd learned in prison. Maybe his unjust confinement had been part of a greater plan. He trembled from the memory that had stripped him of who he once was and went back to the business at hand. He'd timed this assignment perfectly. Preoccupied hospital personnel were hurriedly changing shifts. The doctors and nurses who bypassed him never gave him a second glance. Thomas rolled the cart in the direction of room 526, an angel of death and completely invisible.

Chapter Fifteen

"YOU DIDN'T GO to confession, Eden, where did you go?" Sensing Eden's growing restlessness, Kevin tightened his hold. He stroked her back in smooth swirling motions and spoke in a low, even tone.

"I . . ." She lifted her gaze, and he saw in her a valiant struggle to remember. "What's wrong with me? It's like a chunk of my brain is gone."

Relief flooded through him. "Not your brain, sweetheart, your memory."

"What are you talking about?"

"Believe it or not, this is good news."

"*Good news?* My mind has drawn a complete blank and . . ." Shoving away from him, she faced him with a sardonic expression. "Oh, you're good, Detective. Terms of endearment, hanging around all hours of the day and night, making me think you're here to protect me. What a crock. Everything you've done from the moment we've met is about Sister Beatrice. You *still* think I knew her."

He didn't bother denying it. "At this point it doesn't matter what I think. This is the first time you've admitted to a memory lapse. Think about it. If you can tell me where you went after Sister Agnes sent you to confession, then my theory's all wet."

"I was nine years old," Eden said. "Do *you* remember every single place you went as a child?"

"In critical moments of my life? Yeah, I do." He wanted to shake those trapped memories free, it was so obvious to him what had happened. "You didn't want to talk to Father Munroe. You wanted to talk to someone else. Somebody you must've thought incredibly important. Who, Eden? Who was it?"

She swallowed visibly, then tossing her shoulders back, she drew herself up taller. "I understand your need to solve this case. I do. If I were fighting for my client, I'd be doing the same thing. But my past sucked, Kevin, and it's off limits—to you and everyone else. As far as I'm concerned, my life didn't begin until I moved to California to live with my aunt." Eden pointed to the door. "I think you should go."

"Eden."

"I want you to go. *Now.*"

Both jumped as his cell phone rang. Keeping his gaze fixed on Eden, Kevin answered, "Dancer." He listened dejectedly as Dispatch told him the next batch of sorry news. "I'm on my way."

"What's wrong?"

"There's been an attempt on Lucero's life."

"Oh my God. Give me two seconds to change. I'm coming with you."

"Damned right you are. Whoever tried to kill him got away."

Chapter Sixteen

EDEN GRIPPED the Jeep's armrest as Kevin sped through red lights and weaved in and out of late night Albuquerque traffic. Horns blared long and furious, yet he seemed oblivious. He was focused, maniacally so. Not that she wanted him to slow down. She wanted to get to Mesa General as quickly as he did, but would it be too much to ask to arrive in one piece? His flashing strobe light sat on his dash announcing his approach, but very few adhered to the rule to pull to the curb. Cars in front of them appeared to travel in slow motion. Gritting her teeth, she mentally urged them to *move, move, move*, as Kevin rarely lifted his foot from the gas. He left the drivers coming from either direction no choice—get out of the way or hope their airbags were intact.

In the horseshoe-shaped parking area that led to the hospital entrance, he skidded to a halt behind multiple cruisers. A uniformed cop jogged toward them and immediately demanded IDs. Kevin produced his shield, Eden her APD credentials.

He pulled to the curb, and as both exited his vehicle, Kevin demanded, "Come with me. And keep up."

She bit back a sarcastic remark but raced after him. Did he honestly think she would lag behind?

There were so many uniforms prowling the hospital's reception area, it looked like a cop convention. The elevators were shut down, while two guards maintained their stations near the stairs. His badge in plain sight, gun holstered to his shoulder, Kevin nodded to a uniformed patrolman. He held open the door to the stairway for Eden to enter, his tight lips and darting gaze signaling his impatience. Gone was the charmer who had held her on the dance floor, or the white knight who had treated her with such compassion tonight. Before her eyes, he'd transformed into a robotic-like man on a mission.

He took the stairs two at a time. Winded, Eden followed. She'd clearly become a desk jockey while Kevin kept in shape. He stopped at the fifth floor, she would later learn, not out of mercy, but because they'd reached Mr. Lucero's floor. This locale, too, contained a large contingent of law enforcement, as well as a team of doctors and nurses rushing about their chaotic business.

A group Eden assumed to be plainclothes detectives inhabited the corridor, one man on crutches particularly standing out from the rest. The four-man, one-woman contingent welcomed Kevin into their inner circle, while Eden was left to fend for herself. Irritated, and terrible at doing nothing, she strode to the nurses' station. Asserting her APD credentials to the woman behind the glass, and feigning authority she didn't have, she demanded to know where they'd moved her neighbor.

The lie worked. She'd taken a few steps toward his room, when Kevin closed in on her. "I thought I told you to stick with me."

"I'm not a novice, Detective. The nurse explained they're under lockdown. So how about you do your job and you leave me in peace?"

"Part of my job includes knowing where you are at all times."

"Or what?" She was through catering to this *user*.

The Hispanic cop on crutches sidled up between them. "Ms. Moran?"

"Yes, and you are?"

"Detective Sal Raez, Kevin's partner, ma'am. Sorry about your neighbor."

"That makes two of us. What happened?"

"Dolores, your neighbor's eldest, took a break from her father's bedside to get a bite to eat. When she returned, someone dressed like a hospital worker was standing over him with one of these." Balancing on one crutch, the detective held out an evidence bag filled with syringes.

Eden brought a hand to her throat as bile threatened to rise. "What's in them?"

"Nothing that we can tell. But we're sending them to the lab to make sure."

"I don't understand. They're empty?"

"Empty doesn't make them less lethal," Kevin said. "If he injected a syringe full of air into Lucero's IV—"

"His attacker wanted to cause an embolism," Eden finished for him.

"Would you like to sit down, Ms. Moran?" Detective Raez asked.

"No." Bracing for whatever came next, she said, "I want to see Mr. Lucero. And then I want to talk to his daughter."

"I'll take you to him," Kevin said. "As for Dolores, she was pretty shaken up. After a doctor looked her over, she asked to go to the hospital chapel. An officer escorted her to the first floor."

Eden addressed Kevin's partner. "How could this happen?"

"That's what we intend to find out." Sal's uncomfortable facial expressions mirrored the awkward movements of his crutches. "The good news is that this hospital has security cameras on every floor, stairwell and the surrounding perimeter. Techs are reviewing digital recordings."

"Speaking of which, it might be a good idea if you'd look at them,"

Kevin said. "See if you recognize anyone."

"Absolutely. Right after I see my neighbor and talk to Dolores," Eden replied. He'd asked her nicer this time, plus his request made total sense. Still, after all that had happened between them, Eden felt wholly churlish. "How about I meet you there?"

He leaned in close to her ear. "How about you cooperate with a police investigation?"

"I've done nothing *but* cooperate," she whispered back. "And look where it's gotten me."

"I was with you tonight because I care about you."

Part of her believed him. It was her insecure part that called him a liar. She rolled her eyes and started down the hall. They arrived at room 526, where a no-nonsense patrolman recorded her name on a clipboard, then stepped aside. Eden paused before entering and focused on the hovering Detective Dancer. "Go find out who did this. The cops outnumber the patients, for crying out loud."

His eyes narrowed and his jaw tensed. "Come back to the nurses' station when you're through and I'll take you downstairs."

She left him barking orders in the hallway.

Only a nightlight guided Eden as she entered the dark hospital room. The blinds were drawn, the overhead lights turned off. Moving to Felix Lucero's bedside, her throat closed. Careful to avoid his IV, she placed a cold hand over his, relieved to feel warmth.

The magnitude of someone entering an old man's room and trying to rob him of what was left of his life hit Eden with renewed clarity. She traced her hand over the sling that held his broken arm and studied the deep crevices in his placid face.

"You're not done here," she said, continuously stroking his hand. "Who's going to help me with my Spanish? Or take care of the General?" But the kind man who watched out for her never stirred. After a time, she sighed, released his hand, and then crossed the tiny room. When she reached the door, she turned back to him. "I'll find out who did this to you. I promise."

Outside in the hallway, she swallowed hard. The alone-time with Mr. Lucero had restored her priorities, and lessened her anger at Kevin. He was who he was, and he had a case to solve. She started in his direction, ready to check out the security tapes. That was, until she saw him at the nurses' station engaged in a conversation with an attractive redhead. Around them, staff and cops went about their business, yet Kevin seemed oblivious, focused only on the woman in green. Eden wasn't about to wait around while he garnered a conquest.

Deciding to stick with her earlier plan and talk to Dolores, Eden hugged the wall, this time willing him not to look her way. She needn't have worried. The redhead was smiling now and extending her business card.

Eden reached the exit, turned the knob and squeezed through the fifth-floor door. Negotiating the stairwell's concrete steps as fast as she dared, she anticipated Kevin's firm grip on her arm at any time. As she raced against time, she felt a keen sense of déjà vu. Skulking wasn't something she did on a regular basis, so why did it feel like she'd done this before?

On the first floor, she encountered another cop guarding the premises. She produced her badge and explained she had business in the chapel. He didn't even blink as he nodded and sent her on her way. Didn't speak well for hospital security, Eden thought. But the ID had served her purposes.

She entered the hospital's house of worship and waited for her eyes to adjust. Soft recessed lighting let in a smidgeon of light. Eight pews on either side separated the center aisle, and as Eden made her way into the inner sanctum, the hairs on the back of her neck started to rise.

Ordering her phobia *Not now*, Eden surveyed the room, locating Mr. Lucero's dark-haired daughter in the second row. Dolores prayed in Spanish, but Eden had no need of a translator. Grief and heartbreak sounded the same in any language.

As she had in the stairwell, Eden was struck by a premonition that this wasn't her first time in this chapel. But how could that be? She'd never set foot inside Mesa General before yesterday.

One step, two, she made her way up the aisle, while goose bumps danced their way up her arms. Intellectually, she was aware of what was happening; she was confusing her fear of churches with this simple hospital facility. Still, logic couldn't placate this particular horror. With every footfall the room spun faster and faster.

Chapter Seventeen

THOMAS HAD SOUGHT refuge inside the hospital chapel, this time not in one of the pews, but trapped in a stifling closet. Surrounded by push brooms, cleaning supplies and crumpled hymnals, he was careful not to bump against the wall or knock over any of the supplies. He stripped out of the janitor's garb, wadded it into a ball and stuffed it among the closet's considerable storage.

Sweat dripped from his brow. He'd barely made it off the fifth floor after the Hispanic woman surprised him. Her alarmed cry of "Who are you? And what do you think you're doing?" had shocked him so badly he'd dropped the syringes. As a result, he'd failed in his directive.

Amid hospital alarms and shouts of, "Stop that man!" he had known he'd never reach the elevators. Yet he'd managed to take the stairs. Even out of the janitor's uniform, it was a matter of time before the police found him. He'd tried to escape, cracking the door open now and then for visitors, but when the place wasn't occupied, the hallways were packed with cops and hospital personnel.

How ironic that he'd found his haven again in the chapel. Surely this wasn't where the Lord planned for Thomas to die? He removed the switchblade from his pocket and felt for his carotid artery. If the police found him, this was indeed where it would end.

Thomas turned the door handle ever so slowly. And what he saw made his heart rejoice. Eden was making her way up the aisle. Finally, he understood what God had in store. The Lord hadn't wanted Thomas to sacrifice the old man at all. Eden had been the divine plan all along. Thomas bowed his head and gave thanks. Gripping the blade as tightly as his earthly strength would allow, he murmured a heartfelt Act of Contrition. Then he burst out of the closet to fulfill his destiny.

Chapter Eighteen

KEVIN HEADED for Lucero's hospital room, the pretty intern's business card tucked inside his pocket. At least one woman would talk to him. But not *the* woman he wanted to talk to. What was taking Eden so long? What could she possibly be doing inside a comatose man's room? Reading him bedtime stories?

Enough already. He wanted her to look at the surveillance film. No matter how mad she was at him over his admitted machinations, he had a case to solve, and in his gut he knew the events that had led him to Mesa General were interconnected.

The uniformed guard at Lucero's door raised a quizzical brow at his approach. "Detective?"

"I need a quick word with the woman inside."

"Fine by me, but she's not in there. She left, I'd say nearly five minutes ago."

Shooting the guard a what-the-hell look, Kevin stepped back. He'd have noticed if Eden had taken the elevator. He located the stairwell. "If Detective Raez asks, tell him I've gone to the chapel."

"You got it," the guard replied.

MIDWAY DOWN the aisle, Eden paused to regain her balance. This was a hospital facility, she reiterated silently, not Saint Patrick's. A hospital chapel had nothing to do with her past. Even so, every time she looked Dolores's way, dizziness rocked her. With renewed determination, she continued down the aisle. If it was the last thing she did, she was going to find out what Dolores remembered about her father's attacker.

A row away from her objective, Eden glanced up to see the cross above the altar swaying. Back and forth, back and forth it gyrated, until the floor beneath her also started to buckle. Grasping the edge of the pew for support, she croaked, "Dolores."

When her cry for help went unanswered, Eden said louder, "Dolores!"

And this time the woman in the second pew turned to answer.

"Eden. Hello. There you are. Finally. I've been waiting."

"You have, Sister? For me?"

"*Of course.*" *The woman, too beautiful to be dressed in such ugly black, patted the piano bench beside her.*

Eden forgot about her new braces and smiled in delight. Tucking her school uniform beneath her, she scooted in close and breathed in Sister Beatrice's scent. Unlike Sister Agnes's gagging smell of Ben-gay, Sister Beatrice smelled of roses.

"*Does Sister Agnes know that you're here?*"

Eden lowered her head and played with her slipping braid.

As she often did when Eden came for a visit, Sister Beatrice tried to look stern. It never worked though. Sister Beatrice didn't have it in her to be mean. With a smile, she freed Eden's hair, separated it into three parts and styled a tighter braid. "Such beautiful hair. You know, my little ragamuffin, we discussed this. Sister Agnes must know where you are at all times, or you can't come anymore. She'll worry if you're continually late for her class. Understand?"

"*I wrote a song last night, Sister. Would you like to hear it?*"

The woman on the piano bench narrowed her gaze, then tweaked Eden's nose. "What do you think? I'd love to hear what you wrote. And then it's back to Sister Agnes. Do you understand, Eden? As much as I love seeing you, you mustn't come again without permission."

Relieved to be away from Sister Agnes, no matter how briefly, Eden placed her hands on the keys. The old crone's boring lectures of majors, minors, her stupid chords, scales and proper hand position ceased to exist. Music wasn't something you read like a book. It was something Eden heard in her soul. From there, it poured into her heart and glided into her fingers. There was no theory to it, Eden just played.

She completed the song, then glanced up hesitantly. Whenever she practiced her own music instead of concentrating on her lessons, Sister Agnes accused her of dawdling.

But the young teacher Eden admired so greatly didn't appear angry. If anything, she seemed concerned. She pressed a hand to her heart. "You wrote this, Eden? Truly? All by yourself?"

"*Yes, Sister, I did. Really.*"

"*I believe you. It's also very, very good.*" *Her pleased smile turned into a soulful sigh. "It seems we have an angel in our midst. I'll have to speak to Sister Agnes about you." Sister Beatrice touched her forehead as though she were trying to think. "No promises, you understand? I want you to be careful, Eden. I want you to look out.*"

"*Look out?*"

"*Yes, you must . . .*"

"Oh my God, Eden, look out!"

Eden's blurred vision and uncooperative brain refused to focus as Dolores lifted her arms. "Eden, that man. Behind you. Eden, look out!"

Still trapped in a warp between past and present, Eden's mind felt separate from her body. She could hear Dolores's high pitched scream, yet she couldn't react. She managed to spin just in time to see the flash of metal, but not before a razor sharpness plunged into her back.

The last face Eden saw before she fell was her beloved protector. Tears leaked from her eyes as she closed them. Sister Beatrice. Kevin had been right all along. Eden remembered.

KEVIN'S READY lecture for Eden disappeared the moment he heard the screams. Stepping out onto the first floor corridor, he paused to listen. They seemed to be coming from a nearby corridor. A uniformed cop snapped to attention as well. Kevin and the officer drew their weapons as they raced toward the chapel.

Medical personnel and hospital security converged from various corridors, looking like a MASH unit running toward incoming wounded.

"Stay back," Kevin yelled to a young doctor who rushed forward. "Everybody, stay back!"

As he burst through the chapel doors, his gaze flew to the center aisle. In stunned horror, he arrived in time to watch a gray-haired assailant stab Eden in the back.

"Drop your weapon!" Kevin roared, even as she went down. Either the bastard didn't hear, or he didn't care. He raised his knife to strike again.

Adrenaline pumping, heart ramming against his ribcage, a rage unlike any he'd ever known overtook him. Kevin bellowed one final warning, "I said drop it!"

And when Eden's attacker kept going, Kevin fired. The back of her assailant's skull disappeared, gray matter and blood spattered, and the rail-thin son of a bitch dropped to his knees. Then gravity did the rest, propelling him onto Eden's, prone, facedown body.

"*Now* get that doctor in here," Kevin roared. He tore down the aisle, kicked the blade out of reach even as he knew there was no point in checking for a pulse. Taking hold of the arms, Kevin dragged the no-longer recognizable corpse off of Eden.

Fear imploded within him as he lifted her blood-soaked hair from her back. "Stay with me, Eden. Eden." Afraid to touch her, afraid not to, he hated her pallor, hated that he could no longer breathe.

The young doctor who'd wanted to help in the first place rushed to Kevin's side. "My turn, Detective." The doc summoned two orderlies carrying a stretcher up the aisle.

Kevin stood aside as the medical professionals took over.

"Let's get her to the ER," the doctor said once the orderlies had strapped her to a stretcher.

Kevin followed on their heels until they rushed Eden into an exam room. Pacing outside of it, he almost ran into a nurse carrying equipment.

"You'll have to leave," the irate woman said, nodding toward the exit.

As he re-entered the waiting room, Kevin couldn't recall ever having such total control ripped from his grasp. Eden lay in a valley between life and death, and he'd blown a man's brains out tonight. What bothered him most was he felt nothing. He'd kept Eden safe and she was alive. Glancing down at the blood she'd left on his shirt and his hands, his heart seized. Yeah, she was alive. *For now.*

Chapter Nineteen

KEVIN STOOD outside the emergency room's pressurized doors after dispensing the news to Eden's parents. Their housekeeper explained the couple had taken their out-of-state wedding guests on a tour of Eastern New Mexico, but he'd managed to reach them by cell.

Unbelievable. Their daughter had been attacked at knifepoint, and they'd elected to wait until morning to return to Albuquerque.

His gaze flashed to the mounted television in the corner of the ER. A breaking news banner ran across the screen. At this very moment, his commander was holding a press conference outside the hospital entrance. How bizarre to be the focus of a tragic media event and to be reading the events on the screen. At any moment, Commander Benally would head Kevin's way to demand his shield and his gun. He swallowed the fury that had taken hold since he'd seen the bastard go after Eden with that knife.

Suspension. Administrative leave. Cops took a risk every day when they strapped on a gun. But a black mark on his otherwise impeccable record caused him to tighten his already clenched fists.

Nor could he get rid of the uncontrollable fear he'd felt at seeing Eden go down. That he might not have gotten the chance to tell her how he really felt about her—that she made him smile, she made him crazy, but most of all, she was the only woman, ever, who made him consider the possibilities.

The ER doors swung open, and Sal, with the aid of his crutches, joined him beneath the security lights. The black hair in his eyes and the dark stubble over his normally clean-shaven face magnified how long he'd been on the job. Maneuvering on his good leg had to be taking its toll.

As for Kevin, stress had settled between his shoulder blades. Screw slamming down aspirin; the only thing that could make his head feel better was a guillotine.

"I talked to Mr. Lucero's daughter and Officer Rowe. They corroborate your story to the letter." He conveyed the information to Kevin with a look of concern. "Lucky you got off that head shot, partner."

Recreating the scene in his mind's eye for the thousandth time, Kevin said, "I had no choice. If I had fired center mass, the bullet could have struck the victim. The head shot was my only option."

"You eliminated the threat and you saved Eden's life. Just to be on the safe side, though, don't talk to IA without a union rep."

His partner, who'd been on the job five years longer than Kevin, had never steered him wrong. Locked on a collision course with ramifications, he'd be facing intense scrutiny from Internal Affairs and the media. "Should I be worried?"

"*Nada*. You did your job."

Kevin pocketed his cell and followed his partner inside the ER.

The doctor who'd been Eden's attending physician stood at the circular admission counter. He glanced up from his writing. "Ah, Detective, there you are."

He braced for the outcome, but found he could breathe again when the doctor smiled. "It's all good. Ms. Moran's attacker hit soft tissue near the collar bone. Although it was fairly deep, my guess is she went down more from the shock. We've stitched her up. That doesn't mean it doesn't hurt like hell. We've given her something for the pain and doused her with antibiotics. I let her know we'd like to keep her overnight and she's agreed." The doc glanced around. "Is her family here?"

"They're out of town until tomorrow," Kevin said.

"Doctor Schroeder!" A Hispanic woman outfitted in scrubs called from the hallway. Schroeder exchanged a quick look with her and turned toward Kevin and Sal again. "Never a dull moment. Don't let me catch either one of you in here anytime soon, hear?"

Shortly afterward, an orderly appeared pushing Eden on a gurney. Kevin strode to her side. She reached for him, but her arm flopped uselessly. "Did . . . she . . . say yes?"

"I'm sorry, Eden. Who? Say yes to what?"

"Redhead," she slurred. "Pretty . . ."

Kevin brought her hand to his lips. "You're on drugs, Moran. I was conducting an investigation. Have you looked in a mirror lately?"

"Charmer." Smiling, she closed her eyes then winced. "Doctor . . . told . . . thank . . . Should've wait . . ."

To see the woman who never backed down from anything in such a frail state choked him. They'd garbed her in one of those miserable-looking hospital gowns and washed the blood out of her hair, but there wasn't an ounce of color in her cheeks. Kevin struggled to speak. "Go to sleep. I'll be here when you wake up."

They'd obviously drugged her with some heavy-duty stuff. Kevin doubted she'd heard his last words.

As the orderly wheeled her away, Sal placed a hand on his shoulder. "You heard the doc. She'll be fine, Kev."

Kevin watched the numbers light up above the elevator doors and memorized the floor where it stopped. "She looked so weak."

"And otherwise healthy," Sal said. "What I want to know is what's going on inside your screwed-up head right now."

"I'm thinking this is a helluva way to earn some time off."

"Look at it this way. While you're not on duty, you'll have time to check up on Eden."

True. But as much as the idea of spending time with Eden appealed to him, Kevin couldn't escape his obsession—to work this hard on a case only to be removed before its conclusion sucked big time. "You'll keep me informed?"

"What do you think? As a matter of fact, that's what I was coming to do before we were interrupted. Coroner allowed us to pull prints off the corpse. Turned out to be none other than our loft-lurking buddy, Reuben Sharpe."

Kevin rounded on Sal. "You're kidding me? Who is this guy? Why would he break into Eden's building, attack an old man, come to a hospital and go after them both?"

"I'll do my best to find out."

"And watch me go insane while you do it. Fuck this! What a time to be suspended."

As if he needed a reminder, their commander walked through the ER's double glass doors. Members of the press called after him. Cowboy hat at his side, the quiet Navajo held up a hand, indicating he was through with their questions. The electronic doors slid closed, blocking out their cacophony. "I hear you did good work tonight, Detective."

Reining in his fury, Kevin said, "Sorry it ended badly, sir."

His boss shook his head. "No harm done to an innocent civilian or to one of my men. I'd say it ended the way it was supposed to. But now procedure takes over and there's a whole new drill. Let's find us a place to chat, you and I. I'll need your side of things, then I'll fill you in on what's going to happen."

Kevin exchanged a look with Sal, who returned a supportive nod. He'd killed a man on hospital grounds. There would be lawsuits, media, background checks. There were too many unknown variables at present to relax. Kevin walked with his superior down the long, silent corridor.

SOMETIME IN THE early morning hours, Eden woke in a stark, dimly lit hospital room, her throat dry, her upper back on fire. Yet, all was right with the world. Kevin had promised to be here when she woke up. He hadn't disappointed.

Looking like a poster child for the uncomfortable, he slept in a chair, supporting his head in his hand. She suspected that even he'd agree he needed a shave. From where she lay, she could see every muscled inch of him, but her eyes continually drifted closed. What registered when her addled brain cooperated was that his shoulder holster was empty and the shield on his belt was gone. No doubt, he'd been suspended, and at that realization, her eyes welled.

The stupid tears were flowing now. After all her adamant denials, he'd been right. She'd known the murdered nun. Further, Eden must have admired her greatly. But how and why would she block out the memory of someone of such huge importance to her? The single memory of the two of them on the piano bench wound through her brain like a skipping CD. Was it the drugs? Why couldn't she remember beyond that point?

A sob tore from her throat, something Kevin must have heard, because he bolted upright.

"Eden? What's wrong? Are you in pain?"

She shook her head but he was already at her side. "I'll call a nurse."

"No nurse. I need to . . . tell you."

His gaze softened. Standing over her, he wiped away her tears with the pad of his thumb. "Okay. I'm right here. Tell me what?"

She had no right to ask, but suddenly she felt all alone in the world. "Do you think you could hold me?"

He looked from her face to the length of the bed. "Ah, honey. Bad idea. The stitches. I don't want to tear them open or hurt you."

"Please?"

He studied her face and she knew the precise moment she won him over.

Lowering the bedside rail, he shook his head. "I'll probably have some nurse kick me the hell out of here," he argued as he removed his holster and belt. Gingerly, he helped her slide over, propped himself against the pillow and slid his arm under her. His presence was more potent than the narcotics she'd swallowed, more comforting than a salve, and as his powerful arms wrapped round her, the pain seemed to lessen.

"You'll tell me if I hurt you," he said gruffly. "Now, what was it you wanted to say?"

The words were on her smiling lips, but she was already weaving in and out again. Even that slight amount of exertion had sapped her. The last thing she remembered was Kevin's hand stationed below her breast. It seemed natural there. Further, as Eden escaped once more into oblivion, the trauma of the past hours didn't weigh as heavily.

Chapter Twenty

DETECTIVE SAL RAEZ could make a mannequin smile, Eden decided as she rode with Kevin's partner to the Office of the Medical Examiner, or the OMI. Unlike Kevin's driven, to-the-point personality, a stand-up comedian existed behind his longtime-partner's façade. He'd been rambling about his wife and four-year-old twins when one comment finally registered. "Becky, she brings home these books on childrearing, I throw 'em out the window. I tell her our kids don't know how to read."

Half-listening, half-tuning him out, Eden wondered whose attention he was trying to divert, hers or his own. No doubt, Detective Raez had grave concerns for his partner. While Sal drove Eden to the morgue, Kevin faced a review board.

Still suffering the aftereffects of her pain meds and too little sleep, she also was caught up in the emotions barreling down on her. She had no idea what time Kevin had left this morning, but the kiss he'd planted on her forehead had left hospital workers entering and exiting her room all a twitter. Smiling at their romantic notions, Eden called her practical side to attention. With Kevin's baggage and his issues over her career, there was little chance for a happily ever after.

Now that she was coming down from the drugs, her mind drifted constantly to the vision she'd had in the chapel, followed by the song she'd played for Sister Beatrice. It was lovely, composed of simple chords, and the tune flowed through her like a gentle stream. How on earth had she ever forgotten it?

"You're quiet again, Ms. Moran," Sal said. "You know you don't have to do this. We could photograph Sharpe's body and see if you recognize him that way."

"It's Eden, Detective, and, yes, I do. I want to see who did this to me. Reuben Sharpe put Mr. Lucero in a coma, terrorized his daughter and attacked me. I may not know who he is, but it *is* personal."

"I see your point, and if I'm going to call you Eden, you better call me Sal. Or, if you prefer, my mother calls me Salvatore." He winked. "*Mi madre* knew what she was doing when she named me."

She thought of Mr. Lucero's infrequent tutorial sessions and did her best to recall her high school Spanish. Her scowl eased into a smile. "She must have taken one look at you and known you'd be a cop, Mr. *Savior*. Just the same, I think I'll call you Sal." Eden laughed. The slight jostle tugged at her stitches and she winced.

Oakley sunglasses covered Sal's eyes, but she sensed him watching her. "Painful?"

"Not bad. Provided I don't breathe."

They merged in and out of Monday morning commuter traffic on their way to the UNM campus, bypassing several cinder-blocked fences spray-painted with graffiti. Cottonwood trees, sagebrush and other blooming foliage dotted the terrain. It was a glorious spring day in the Southwest, with desert hues unfolding before her eyes. She'd come perilously close to missing this day, or any other, for that matter. Why had the man in the chapel come after her?

Had Kevin been right? Had she defended him and perhaps lost the case? It happened. Her thoughts turned to her already-high caseload and the docket that would have to be farmed out to other public defenders over the next couple of days. Her co-workers wouldn't be happy. That was all right; neither was she.

"Kevin told me he cancelled his appointment with the bishop," Eden said.

Sal cast her a sidelong glance. "He told you about that?"

She adjusted her own sunglasses. "When it comes to his murder investigation, we've been sort of in cahoots."

"Only about the case?" Sal lifted a brow.

"He's made no secret that he doesn't like public defenders much."

"So he's bullheaded. Give him time, he might come around," Sal replied.

"He told me about his stepfather," Eden said, hoping the remark would allow Kevin's closest confidant to open up. "Have you met his family?"

"His mom flies out every once in a while." He returned his eyes to the road. "We'll reschedule the appointment with the bishop. Won't be the first time we've had to switch priorities."

Partners, Eden thought. So much for shedding light on things.

Sal veered onto University Drive, passed several of the school's medical and research facilities on *Camina de Salud*, and parked near a huge tan adobe structure. Then, reaching into the backseat for his crutches, he turned to her. "What do you say the two of us walking wounded go identify us a body?"

Walking wounded, indeed. How apropos that he'd pulled into a handicapped parking space.

Sal greeted several of the staff by name and led her to the elevator, where they descended into the morgue. She hadn't had occasion to come here as part of her job yet, although public defenders were no stranger to death.

A technician in a white lab coat looked up from a metal desk when he saw them. Sal explained the purpose of the visit, and the tech emotionlessly led them to a refrigerated unit that housed the body.

As he withdrew the drawer that contained the deceased, Sal supported her elbow with his hand. "Ready?"

She nodded for the tech to proceed. But even as she steeled herself for what was to come, she breathed in through her nose, then out through her mouth and pressed a hand to her stomach.

He lowered the sheet that covered the dead man's face and Eden stared. Then slowly, she backed away from the table.

"Eden?" Sal asked.

She felt the blood rush from her head while the morgue's ghostly off-white walls closed in around her. "That's not Reuben Sharpe," she said. And with that pronouncement, Eden scrambled for the exit.

"DETECTIVE DANCER, one more question should get us through this preliminary interview," said the stocky man from the District Attorney's office. "Do you recall ever arresting Mr. Sharpe in the course of your work as an Albuquerque police officer?"

Kevin sat motionless beside his union rep, wearing the same dark suit he'd worn at Eden's sister's wedding, and answered the panel's questions. The interrogating team comprised two men and a woman and came complete with a stenographer, who recorded everything said. As he sat in City Hall, or Metro, as the panel kept calling it—he now understood the term *sweating bullets*. "No, sir," Kevin replied. "Not to my knowledge."

The panel in charge of his fate put their heads together and conferred out of earshot before acknowledging him once again. The blond female sergeant from Internal Affairs spoke next. "Last night after the shooting, Detective, you submitted to a blood test. We've received the results of the lab work. Let the record reflect that you've tested negative for narcotics or alcohol.

"We appreciate your willingness to come forward so quickly to get the process underway," she added. "Be advised that you will receive full pay and benefits pending a complete and final review of what happened at Mesa General Hospital on Sunday, 20, April. Until you're cleared for active duty, your shield will remain in the possession of your division commander. Your service weapon has been taken as evidence. The official ruling in this investigation could take as long as three months."

Kevin sat stiff, unblinking, not breathing. He'd put his fist through something later.

Commander Roland Pierce, a silver-haired legend on the force, was the last one to offer his input. "I can see the panic in your eyes, Detective Dancer, so let me lay it out straight. The investigation Sergeant Irwin's referring to will run parallel. And she's correct, it could take months. As for you, based on what we've witnessed today, you'll return to active duty in seventy-two hours."

The commander rose and picked up what looked like Kevin's confiscated Glock. Approaching Kevin, the commander said, "You may feel persecuted right now, son. Cops often do. But we have to get at the truth, without any appearance of impropriety or bias. You're a respected member of the Albuquerque Police Department. You'll use this substitute firearm until yours is returned."

Kevin accepted the gun, relieved that oxygen had found its way back into his lungs. "Thank you, sir."

As the commander's gray eyes bore into Kevin's, the commander said, "You *will* get counseling, Detective. No debate. You may think differently, but Mr. Sharpe wasn't the only casualty in this case. And watch your back. You'll be a bug under glass for some time. Based on your actions, and the man I see sitting before me, I think you'll survive it. That's it for now."

On that note, Kevin left the proceedings feeling less like a criminal and more like a cop. He said goodbye to the rep at the door and walked into the bright sunshine. Life all around him carried on as if nothing out of the ordinary had happened. He could live with the seventy-two- hour decision. It could have been worse. As for superiors and peers studying him under a glass, it had already begun. What was with everybody expecting him to snap? He'd already had his breakdown. Too bad they hadn't been in the chapel when he witnessed Sharpe go after Eden with that knife.

He'd been so lost in thought that he almost missed his cell vibrating against his belt. "Dancer," he answered.

"Hey, partner, how'd it go?" Sal asked.

"Pretty much like the boss said it would. Put me on administrative leave and told me to get counseling."

"Might want to see if the department shrink has room for two on that couch."

"Why's that?" Suddenly Sal's lack of levity had Kevin paying closer attention.

"Eden had a look at her attacker."

"Is she all right?"

"I think you better get over to the OMI."

Kevin started jogging. "Why? What happened?"

"She took one look at the body, denied it was Sharpe and then bolted."

"And you didn't stop her?" It didn't occur to him that he'd raised his voice until two pedestrians crossing the parking lot glanced his way.

"That would have been quite a feat with two good legs," Sal shot back.

"Ah, hell," Kevin said, breaking into a full-fledged sprint. "I'm on my way."

EDEN WAS a half mile away from the OMI before she stopped mid-stride and her panic subsided. Kevin had shot Mr. Timms? They thought Mr. Timms was Reuben Sharpe?

Out of breath, to the point of gasping, she glanced around the UNM campus. Surrounded by a mix of adobe architecture and modern buildings, the university was home to a dozen different colleges. She didn't know the grounds well, and already she'd lost her bearings. Before she got any more disoriented, she needed to focus. In her agitated state, she'd taken off without her purse. Without her cell phone, she couldn't even call Sal to tell him where she was. Good Lord, she was a head case. Blocked memories, dead bodies—what she wouldn't give for her plain old simple overworked life back.

A park bench sat a few feet away, and she made quick use of it. Slipping her hand between the collar of her shirt and her damp skin, she felt for the bandage covering the stitches. Her fingers came away dry. At least she hadn't busted them open.

Twisting her unwashed, stringy hair into a knot, she tried to think; she had to reason this out. The cops had prints, they had a body, and there was no denying she'd been stabbed in the back. She bent to clasp her hands. She'd known Mr. Timms from early childhood. He'd worked at St. Patrick's. Certainly he'd been strange, but he'd always been Mr. Timms. She recalled his constant stare, but there were other things, too. When he wasn't cleaning or pushing a broom, he broke up fights, bandaged bloodied knees. The sisters and lay teachers who'd worked at the school trusted him, relied on him. So had the bishop.

The bishop.

Eden lifted her head to study the campus, not really seeing her surroundings so much as the past. At the reception Saturday night, Bishop Munroe had left her to talk to the former school janitor, who waited outside. What's more, when she'd asked him to invite Mr. Timms inside, it was an idea the clergyman soundly rejected.

"Hey, chica, you don't look so hot. Need some help?"

Bolting upright, she whipped around, startled by a long-haired Hispanic male who approached. He wore a backpack and carried a textbook under one arm, resembling any one of the thousands of students on campus. But what did she know? Nothing was certain anymore.

"I'm okay," she said, watching him warily. "Thanks, anyway."

He moved around the park bench to face her. "You sure?"

He belongs here, Eden. Relax. "I'm sure."

When he walked away, she called after him, "Hey, you wouldn't know how I can get back to the OMI, would you?"

Following the young academic's directions, she was glad she'd asked, because none of the passing buildings or landscape looked familiar. She needed another pain pill, but until she made sense of this tragedy, she wasn't swallowing one more drug. Timms had said something the night of the reception. It had disturbed her then and she'd ignored it. *You remember me.*

Her attempt to be kind had put a man in a coma and a knife in her back.

No more.

Obviously, the safety of others and the crux of her mental stability revolved around her ability to recall. Suddenly, Eden had a new mission beyond getting well.

NOT TWENTY minutes later, Kevin arrived at the OMI to find Sal sitting on the building steps, one crutch beside him, the other propping up his chin. The ordinarily unflappable cop looked pissed.

"Any sign of her?" Kevin asked.

"*Nada.* And this ain't good, Kev. She's in pain and freaked out." Sal motioned to Eden's small purse beside him. "Took off without it. There's a couple of reporters inside, hence the reason I'm out here. I called University Security; they're out looking for your lady now."

Your lady. The jury was still out on that one. One minute Eden felt like a dream come true, the next she made him feel like he was doing time. "I'll make the rounds. If she comes back, give me a call." Kevin headed for his Jeep. But as he opened the driver-side door, a car with the UNM Campus Security logo pulled into the parking lot.

Eden exited the car.

Kevin walked toward her. He expected tears, or at least an emotional outburst. What he saw was fatigue and something else. "Are you all right?"

Lifting her chin, she replied, "Are you?"

"Couldn't be better." He held a hand up to Sal, signaling to his partner to give them a few minutes. Sal dutifully maintained his position on the steps. "What happened?" Kevin asked. "Who's the man on the slab?"

"I've always known him as Mr. Timms," Eden said, searching his face.

"But you know differently, don't you?"

"Prints don't lie. They confirm he's Rueben Sharpe. His prints were also found in the storage unit in your building. There's no mistake. So who's Mr. Timms?"

"I believe the bishop called him Thomas."

"Munroe knew the deceased?"

"Timms was the janitor at St. Patrick's during the time I went to school there." Shoving her hands in the back pockets of her jeans, Eden went on, "Not only did Bishop Munroe know him, the two of them had a little sidebar conversation the night of the reception."

"And you never mentioned it?"

Anger flashed in her eyes. "Believe me. I've been beating myself up for not recognizing the significance."

Kevin took hold of her arm. "I'm worried about you. Let's get you off your feet."

"Not yet. There's more." She paused in the middle of the parking lot. "All I ask is that you don't say, 'I told you so.'"

"Why would I do that?"

"Because I knew her, Kevin. You were right. Apparently I knew her better than most."

He grasped her shuddering body. "I take it we're talking about Sister Beatrice. You remember?"

"I'm starting to, in bits and pieces. But it's by no means a complete picture. I'm going to find out who killed her, Kevin. Will you help me?"

He pulled her close, inhaling the scent he'd come to associate with Eden. Didn't she know? With such an analytical mind, he was surprised. In her fragile state, he hesitated to tell her. Kevin shot a look toward the OMI and his partner. Sister Beatrice's killer likely lay on a slab in the building a few feet away. He'd give her time to decompress. "Whatever you say, Eden, I'll help you."

Chapter Twenty-One

KEVIN FOUND OUT quickly that he had a lot a lot to learn about Eden Moran. She did not ask for help easily. His first suggestion that she stay with her folks for a couple of days fell flatter than a dud missile. His second idea, not much better. She was *not* interrupting her sister on her honeymoon to ask if she could stay at Meg's place.

Eden simply instructed him to drop her off at the loft, which he thought was a very bad idea.

"Remember, the doctor said no driving while taking those pills," he said as he walked her to her door.

"No driving," she repeated. "Got it." She withdrew her keys from her purse and smiled at him, and then on tiptoe she gave him a peck on the cheek. "Thanks for everything, Detective Dancer. I literally wouldn't be here if not for you."

What was that old saying, if you saved someone's life, you were responsible for them? He stared into her earnest blue eyes and tried to read what she was thinking. On a scale of one to ten, the lady lawyer was off-the-chart beautiful, but after the last forty-eight hours, she had every right to look shell-shocked.

"You're sure you're okay to be alone?" He frowned. "I could take you out to lunch or something."

She shook her head. "I'm more than okay. I'm going to bed. I'll call you in a couple of days, how's that?"

How's that? In a couple of days he'd be certifiable. "Eden."

She slid her key into the lock. "Go home. You've been through as much as me." Tossing a glance back at him, she murmured a meaningful, *"Thank you again."*

She opened the door, stepped inside and closed it behind her. Emptiness hit him like a dull, hot wind, but she'd given him no choice but to walk away. It was sweltering inside the Jeep and he flipped the air conditioning to high. On the way from the morgue to her place, Eden had asked him to turn it off. The outside temperature gauge read eighty-three, yet Eden had claimed to be freezing.

Could be the drugs, Kevin thought as he drove through lunch-hour traffic. *Or not*, an inner voice chided. He was halfway home when he made

Donnell Ann Bell

an illegal U-turn and turned back.

He found her asleep in the reclined passenger seat of her car.

She jolted upright when he tapped on the glass.

"Let's go, Eden."

WELL, HE'D GOT her out of her car. Now what? Kevin mouthed his thanks to the waitress as she put Eden's enchilada plate in front of her. They sat at a table at *El Pinto Restaurant*, surrounded by busy wait staff and a packed-to-capacity crowd. She picked up a chip, dipped it in salsa, then set it uneaten on her plate.

He could have kicked himself for not reading the signs that she was afraid. No doubt Reuben Sharpe had inflicted a whole new set of issues on a woman already full of them.

As for Kevin, after taking a man's life, and the resulting suspension, he was pretty war-torn himself. It had been hours since he'd eaten. Eden might not be hungry, but he was starving, and the Mexican food's spicy aroma was doing a *merengue* on his stomach. "I'm not quite sure what to do here. Your lack of appetite is a first for me." He tried for a grin. "Mind if I dig in?"

"Help yourself." Her smile, too, was fleeting. "What happens next?"

Was she talking about the case, his suspension or their relationship? Having no ready answers for either, he quipped, "We find you a place you'll feel safe . . . other than your car."

"I told you," she said, shaking her head. "I needed something out of the glove box. By the time I found it, I was tired, so I leaned my head back for a moment and fell asleep."

"Uh-huh. Too bad you couldn't tell me what it was that you were looking for."

She flushed. "Would you stop being a cop and answer my question. What comes next in the investigation?"

"Since I'm suspended, it will be up to Sal to tie up all the loose ends. But the consensus around the office, mostly due to your confirmation of Sharpe and his alias, is that we've found Sister Beatrice's killer."

Eden jerked her head up. "What? Why jump to that conclusion?"

He swallowed the second bite of his meal and reluctantly lowered his fork. "Oh, I don't know, because it makes sense?"

"To someone on the outside, maybe. But I'd make darn sure you tie up *every* loose end before you label this case exceptionally cleared."

For a moment he'd forgotten who he was talking to; *exceptionally cleared* was an internal classification among police and legal agencies. When leads produced a suspect who went to trial and was thereafter convicted, the case was closed. If the suspect died before going to trial, the case was

99

exceptionally cleared.

"All right, Counselor. You want to connect the dots, how about this? Reuben Sharpe was convicted of class-three aggravated sexual assault. He worked under an assumed alias at a time and place Sister Beatrice was assigned to St. Patrick's School. He assaulted your neighbor, tried to murder him in his bed and came after you with a knife—the same MO, by the way, that killed Sister Beatrice."

Folding her arms, Eden said, "No doubt about it, you'd have enough to take to the grand jury for his *current* laundry list of crimes. As for Sister Beatrice's murder, I'm not so sure."

"Spoken like a true public defender. Too bad he's not here so you can represent him."

"Cute." Eden returned Kevin's smirk. "Did you talk to Father Slater?"

"Sal did. I'm not allowed any contact, remember? According to Slater, the man known as Thomas Timms retired from St. Patrick's years ago."

Frowning, Eden leaned back in her chair. "Then how did he know about the wedding? And where has he been all these years?"

"As to his present location, that's one of our loose ends. As for the wedding, it wasn't exactly a state secret. Maybe he caught it like I did . . . in the *Albuquerque Journal's Lifestyle* section." That remark did little to lessen her scowl, so Kevin added, "What's bothering you?"

"Why he did what he did. If he's a sexual predator, okay, that's a given. But why come after Mr. Lucero, why risk being caught in a populated, high-security hospital and try to kill me in front of witnesses?"

"People snap all the time, Eden."

"Timms was a janitor, Kevin, one of the meekest men I've ever known. I don't think he had it in him to do this alone."

"Careful. You're talking about the man who put a knife in your back."

Her food stayed untouched, but, hungry, Kevin dug in. She shifted in her seat and began drumming her fingers. He resisted reaching out and grabbing her hand.

"So you're convinced the bishop had nothing to do with Sister Beatrice's death?"

Ah, that's what she was going for. She wanted something on Munroe. "There's not a shred of evidence to prove otherwise. I can't arrest the guy because he gives you the creeps." Kevin lifted a brow. "Unless . . ."

"What?"

"Now that you're remembering Sister Beatrice, you're remembering other things, too?"

"No, but it's not for lack of trying. You forget I saw the bishop talking to Timms the night of the reception."

"I didn't forget. And as long as we're pointing fingers, *you* also talked to

Timms."

At the look of annoyance that crossed her face, he did take her hand, afraid she might bolt from the table the way she had the OMI. She tried to pull away, but Kevin held tight. "Let me ask you something. Do you think a man like Robert Munroe reaches the position of bishop by being stupid?"

"Of course not. Anyone can see that he's brilliant. I'm not challenging his IQ, just his ethics."

"Exactly. Munroe rose to the position of bishop by being shrewd *and* careful. I'd also guess that he'd surround himself with shrewd, like-minded people. Wouldn't you?"

"That makes sense."

"Good. Now, based on what we've seen of Rueben Sharpe, I'm willing to bet he belonged in a psych ward. What do you think?"

Her pursed lips remained fixed, she pulled back her hand, but she did acquiesce enough to say, "I'd have to agree."

Studying the woman who had to have been number one on her debate team, Kevin was thankful that at least she could be reasonable. Where in the hell had she developed such tenacity? Still, he had her dead to rights on this one. The idea that the bishop would trust a man like Sharpe to solve his problems didn't wash. It was an idea Kevin had struggled with, too, and one his commander had drilled into his thick skull last night in a secluded spot off the E.R.

"At one time you told me you thought the bishop was trying to evade the police. That no longer concerns you?" she asked.

"Not when he was out of the country and wasn't given the messages. Our background checks have produced nothing on Munroe. He has a spotless record, and he's an icon in this city." Kevin hesitated. "One thing I've been lectured on regarding this case is my objectivity. It's been a huge wake up call. Bring me proof, Eden, and I'll walk through fire to get the suspect. Until then, we have zilch, while the bishop has a whole list of lawyers on speed dial."

She lowered her head, clearly the culmination of recent events and exhaustion weighing her down. When she glanced up again, her eyes shimmered. "I know one person who's grateful you weren't entirely objective last night. I know I thanked you, but I'm so grateful you came after me."

As if he'd had a choice in the matter. Every time Kevin saw Sharpe's blade in his mind's eye, and thought of what would have happened if he hadn't intervened, his stomach roiled. Eden Moran was like quicksand. The harder he tried to pull free, the deeper she dragged him under. "That makes two of us."

"You were supposed to meet with the bishop today. Are you going to reschedule?"

"Suspension means no contact. Commander Benally agreed to get in touch with him. I'm sure if the bishop has his way I'll get a formal reprimand, if not more."

"Why would he do that if he's not guilty of something?"

"To make sure there's not a next time. You don't insult a diocese without consequences." Kevin shrugged. "Comes with the job. I have zero regrets. Besides, if I let anything happen to you, who would I argue with?"

"Knowing you, you'd find someone," she said dryly.

The waitress came with their check, and he stared at Eden's untouched plate. "Want to order a to-go bag for that?"

She winced. "Yes, please." Studying the food on her plate, she eventually acknowledged Kevin. "May I ask a favor?"

"Ask away."

"Take me back to the loft and wait while I pack a bag. I've decided to stay at a hotel for a couple of days."

"A hotel."

From behind Eden, the El Pinto's hostess carried a basket of long-stem red roses. Periodically, she stopped to sell them at tables. Catching her gaze, Kevin nodded toward Eden. The woman flashed him a wink and a smile, indicating she'd received his message.

"It's only temporary," Eden said, at last looking up at him. "I need sleep, and it's not going to happen at the loft." She raised her water glass and took a long swallow.

"Or you could stay with me." The words were out of his mouth before he could think them through.

She coughed, sputtering water everywhere. Grabbing her napkin, she quickly dabbed up the mess. "*With you?*"

Career-wise it wasn't one of his brighter moves, but now that he'd offered there was no taking them back. "Just so happens," he said, adding a trace of sarcasm, "I'm off for a couple of days, too."

She laughed, and the smile he'd been anxious to see broke free. Diners at nearby tables all but disappeared. Eden reached across the table and twined her fingers through his. Her touch was everything he'd expected, warm, vibrant, electric.

"You said it yourself, Kevin, the case is over. As much as I love the idea of not being alone, Sharpe's dead. You no longer have to protect me."

The woman carrying the rose made it to their table. He paid for it and handed the dewy bud to Eden. "At least stay with me until Sal gives us the all clear. No hotel, Eden. What do you say?"

Chapter Twenty-Two

ROBERT MUNROE picked up the morning paper again, stared at the front-page caption and the picture beneath it, and almost lost the contents of his breakfast. *Hospital shooting involves Albuquerque cop and confirmed sexual predator.* With every word, his heart picked up speed. The article caused him concerns on so many levels he didn't know where to stow his panic. Gripping the paper with both hands to steady the tremors, he continued to read. The article identified the dead man as convicted felon Reuben Sharpe. In addition, it listed Detective Kevin Dancer as the man who'd made the fatal shot.

He studied the dead man's likeness, which explained why none of his staff had barged into his office in hysterics and demanded damage control. The image was blurred and faded, as though it had been copied one too many times. Thankfully, nobody recognized Thomas or his given name. Robert had either been granted a stay of execution or a small miracle. That outcome remained undecided.

As he read on, he saw that Eden had been one of the intended victims.

And then he made the connection. Saturday night's reception. Dancer had been standing with Father George. He claimed he worked in law enforcement, and at the time, Robert had thought little of it. Even later in the evening, when Dancer asked if he could swing by on Monday morning to chat about the bishop's travels, Robert still saw nothing unusual in the detective's request.

But now Robert smelled a trap. A man in his position made enemies. The question was, why and by whom? What was going on here? And why in the name of all that was holy had Thomas gone after Eden? He should call Edward and Joanna to see how she was, but what if *they* had recognized Thomas?

His intercom buzzed and Janice came on the line. "Bishop Munroe, Bishop Delgado is on line one."

Robert picked up the phone and forced evenness into his voice. His enemies would not bring him down easily. "Janice, ask the bishop if I can get back to him. And hold my calls, please."

"Yes, Bishop. Are you—"

"I'm fine, Janice." Robert set down the phone. Fine? What an absurd word choice. He was numb and in shock. Even more shocked than he'd been to see Thomas at the Moran/Sullivan wedding reception. He'd seemed agreeable enough when Robert demanded he leave. To his knowledge Thomas had never disobeyed him. The poor miserable soul wouldn't have dared. So what then was the diocesan employee doing at Mesa General?

Dear God in Heaven. Diocesan employee.

Robert's gaze traveled to the window and the apartment over the garage, where he'd arranged for Thomas to live these many years.

This time Robert stood when he picked up the phone. "Janice, would you send Marshall into my office as soon as possible?"

"Of course, Bishop. May I—"

"Marshall, Janice. Please."

Robert ran the article through the shredder, realizing at once the futility. He couldn't very well buy up every paper in the city. He had to think, sort out his options. Should he come forward or plead ignorance? Approach the police, or wait until they came to him? Given Dancer's ruse on Saturday night, by all indications, they most definitely planned to approach him.

He'd done magnificent work over the years, penance for a past he assumed lay dead and buried.

A knock sounded and his business manager entered. "You wanted to see me, Excellency?"

"Close the door, Marsh, and take a seat."

"You're shaking, Bishop. What is it?"

Feeling the joy of his Vatican ordination and the authority he'd assumed slipping away, Robert gripped the back of his chair. "You helped me with a problem once, and I hate to involve you again. But I'm not sure where else to turn. The problem, you see, seems to have come home to roost. Can I trust you, Marsh?"

"With your life, Excellency."

Chapter Twenty-Three

EDEN STORED her uneaten Mexican meal in Kevin's refrigerator, then held the rose to her nose and smiled at his kind gesture. She certainly needed something to smile about. If there was a hell, the last few days had given her a glimpse of it. If her Aunt Caroline were here, she'd probably be quoting Nietzsche about now. "What doesn't kill you makes you stronger."

Feeling for the bandage that covered her upper back, Eden murmured, "Well, Herr Nietzche, if your words are true, I should be a fortress by now."

She placed the rose in one of Kevin's water glasses and leaned against his refrigerator. Why had she accepted his offer to stay with him? Was she trying to get her heart stomped on? Fatigue and pain were making her loopy, and she swallowed hard. Even as she knew she shouldn't be here, she justified the reasons she should.

With the case over with, she might never see him again. And at that lonely thought, she went in search of him. She found him stowing her overnight bag near the back hallway. Taking in his sterile white walls and the limited furnishings of his Albuquerque home, she asked, "Did you just move in?"

"A year ago. Why?"

She moved to a gray tweed couch with a faded design. Pivoting to face him, she ran her hand over it and glanced back at him. "Oh, I don't know, mindless curiosity, I guess." Directly opposite the sofa was the one luxury item she could see in the place—a big screen TV.

The dining room, too, might have had a decorator rolling up her sleeves. It could easily accommodate a formal dining room table and hutch. Kevin had seen fit to furnish it with a card table and a couple of folding chairs. Beside the table sat a stack of framed pictures on the floor. When she knelt to examine them, she feigned a German accent and said, "Did you know, my goot man, in some cultures people actually hang these on walls?"

Kevin lifted a brow and walked toward her. "Making fun of me, Eden?"

Smiling, she stood and suddenly everything about being here struck her as funny. She pressed her lips together and worked hard not to laugh. "Of course not. I think it's a great idea to leave everything just as is. That way when you move again, you're three-quarters there."

His mouth curved into its typical half smile. "I've been busy. And what do you mean move *again*? You don't like my house?"

"What's not to like? It's *empty*." That did it. She burst out laughing. In that moment, it was all she could do not to wrap her arms around him and bury her lips against his. She knew she could make him respond. Men didn't invite a woman to stay if they weren't attracted. But attraction only went so far. Just because he'd wanted to solve Sister Beatrice's case and saved Eden's life as a result didn't erase the issues between them.

And at that unpleasant thought, she sobered.

Kevin narrowed his gaze. "What's wrong? Is it the pain?"

"I'm fine."

"Liar." Taking her hand, he tugged her toward the hallway. "Let's get you to your room."

"Does it have furniture?" She slapped a palm over her mouth.

"You're hysterical, Moran."

Eden followed him past two closed doors, entering a room at the end of the hallway. Unlike the great room, this room was filled with heavy oak furniture, much more elaborate and cared for than the front of his home. Somehow she knew she hadn't entered a guest room. A closed laptop rested on an intricately-etched desk, while beside it, a bookshelf lined an entire wall, housing everything from nonfiction to classic novels.

Not only had she underestimated him, next to the pin-neat Kevin Dancer, Eden looked like a slob. Observing more pictures, she moved to a chest of drawers, these obviously treasured as they'd made it into his inner sanctum.

The first was of Kevin and a group of hot air ballooners toasting their champagne flutes to whoever stood behind the camera. The scene, overlooking a mesa, boasted one of Albuquerque's popular balloon festivals, and the photographer's lens must have captured at least fifty balloons filling the sky. "You're into ballooning," she said.

"Not as much as I'd like to these days." He stood so close his warm breath tickled her ear. Eden resisted melting in to him. Their conversations had always been one-sided, but she loved learning things about him. In the next picture, Kevin stood draped in a hospital gown, beaming at two newborns, one in the crook of each arm.

"I don't know who's cuter, you or these babies," she said.

"Sal's twins," he explained, brushing her hand with his as his fingers traced their tiny faces. "Do you know how many grandparents and aunts and uncles I had to fight off to get that shot? I was the first to hold them after their parents."

Breathless from his proximity, Eden nodded, sidestepping him to picture number three. Instantly, however, she felt him withdraw. This photograph, like the balloon shot, was taken outdoors. Four clowning boys, a teenaged Kevin on one side and a dark-headed kid on the other, had formed a human tower. On their hands and knees, they supported two preschoolers, the trust and adoration on their little boy faces evident.

"And these are?"

He'd fully retreated now and sat on the bed. "My brothers."

She set the picture down carefully, warring with confusion and disappointment. "But you said you had two brothers."

"The kid next to me was my stepbrother. He died a few years back."

More baggage. Still, she took it as a positive that, unlike the first time she'd asked about his family, he hadn't terminated the subject faster than a slamming door. It would be so easy to say *I'm sorry* and let the matter drop, but she was through walking on egg shells around him and she'd come this far. "Were you close?"

Kevin shrugged. "It was because of my friendship with Josh that our parents met in the first place."

She turned from the dresser. "May I ask *how* he died?"

Resting his elbows on his knees, Kevin stared down at clasped hands. "It happened during our first year of college." His blond brows knit together. "We were already going our separate ways. The old man was drumming law school into our heads. Josh was cool with it, but I wasn't biting. Anyway, the cops raided a party Josh was at—blood tests later revealed he was loaded. He tried to outrun the cops. Probably thought J.T. would kill him, since getting caught would end any chance of law school. Anyway, his car flipped and went over an embankment." Kevin squinted, as though picturing it all even now. "After that, I transferred to NMSU and came out here. And now you know the whole story."

She didn't, of course, but it was a start. Wishing events like these didn't scar those left behind, she walked toward him. When he didn't acknowledge her, she lowered herself to his eye level and placed her hand on his leg. "It means a lot that you told me."

He'd obviously erected the damned wall again, and caught in his stony gaze, she started to rise. But in the next second, he took a strand of her hair and twirled it around his finger. Her gaze swept over his hard jaw made softer by dimples, then set at odds again by his dark blond stubble. She settled on his lips and Kevin leaned toward her. And as she prepared for what she'd dreamt of for weeks, he said, "What do you think of your room?"

She sucked in a breath. She'd done it again. Whatever spell she thought was working between them dissolved. Eden shot to her feet. "*My* room? I thought this was the master."

"It is. Unfortunately my guest rooms are like the living room, filled with boxes. You'll take my bed."

Eden stared at the king-sized mattress, wanting nothing more then to drop down on it. But she was *not* taking his bed. "I can't let you do that."

"Sure you can." Kevin rose and strode to a walk-in closet, emerging a second later with a pillow and blanket. "With those stitches in your back, if you took the couch, you'd never get any rest. While me, I can sleep anywhere, and have." He paused in the doorway. "Bathroom's right through that door, Eden. Try not to miss sleeping in your car."

A FEW HOURS later, Kevin woke to a muted television, arm over his forehead, right leg propped on the back of the couch. *I can sleep anywhere.* Damn straight he could, that didn't mean he had to like it. He sat up slowly, realizing the sun was going down and he hadn't heard a peep from the other end of the house. *Good.* Eden was sleeping.

Leaving her alone in his bedroom when she went down on her knees had been a testament to his discipline. Did she have any idea how provocative she appeared at that moment? If he hadn't changed the subject right then, with the way she was looking at him, he would have had her flat on her back the next second. Fortunately, he'd been hyperaware of her injury, or it might have happened.

So he opted to get the hell out, which left *him* in pain.

He buried his head in his hands and scrubbed his face. What he wouldn't give for a shower and a shave, but all of his gear was in the master bathroom. Deciding to risk it, he stood, but at the sound of running water, he groaned. She'd obviously beat him to it. He'd use the spare shower, but first he needed a set of clean clothes.

Then it occurred to him, if Eden was in the shower, how was she handling her stitches?

He received his answer the moment he entered his bedroom. From behind the bathroom door, she let out a squeal and at the second one, he rapped on the door. "Eden?"

"What!"

"You okay?"

"What do you think?"

"Can I come in?"

"Why?"

A grin made it to his lips. "So I can help you?"

"Promise not to say a word?"

"On my mother's grave."

She hesitated all of two seconds before hollering back, "Your mother's not dead."

Exactly. He opened the door, semi-relieved to find her in her robe. On her knees, she leaned over the tub, her hair draped over her head. Unfortunately from the location of the toilet, she was unable to get her head completely under the running faucet.

"What are you trying to do?"

Still struggling, she retorted, "Well, gee, Kevin, *duh.*"

He smiled, bent down and patted her back. "There's a better way to do this, you know."

"Then show me, *Mister I can do anything.* I don't care if I get the stitches wet. I want a hot bath."

He lowered his hands to her waist. "Here, let me help you."

When you'd been raised in a houseful of boys, broken bones, gashes, scrapes and sprains were the norm, and you were lucky to have a nurse for a mom. Connie Dancer Garland constantly jerry-rigged fixes to allow the kids to sleep, bathe, what have you.

But Kevin wasn't his mom and none of his brothers had ever looked like Eden Moran. Even with that partially sopped hair and her exasperated frown, she turned him on. The blue of her robe matched the blue of her eyes, her scooped neckline showed off her tattoo and the tan line over her breasts, and a split in her gown gave him a glimpse of a mouth-watering thigh.

He'd been crazy to bring her here, and if he heard about it later, so be it. Last night's terror superseded the review board's taking issue with his behavior.

She placed a hand on her hip. "What do you want me to do?"

Stop asking me loaded questions for a start. "Give me a minute."

He returned with a box of Saran Wrap, amused when he shocked Eden into silence.

Her expression turned dubious as she occasionally turned to watch him. But she was a good patient, and following his instructions, she sat on the rim of the tub. Facing away from him, Kevin slipped the robe over shoulders. He then lowered it to her waist and fought to swallow. He planned to do what?

He'd been on the job for eight years, even delivered a baby in the back of a squad car once. Yet, during that time, no one had ever bewitched him like Eden. As his gaze fell over her, he felt like a rookie all over again. Her skin was so smooth it looked like a touched-up magazine ad.

But then he lifted her hair and caught sight of the four-by-six compress near her right shoulder. And at the thought of Sharpe plunging that knife into her, he wished the bastard alive again so he could tear him from limb to limb.

"You're frowning. Does it look bad?" Eden pressed a hand over his.

He shook away his outrage and struggled not to kiss her instead. "I haven't even removed the bandage yet. You might want to brace yourself, this is going to sting."

She jerked when he ripped, and instinctively his arms went round her. "Sorry, Eden, you okay?"

She returned a terse nod, but later, as he changed the bandage, he saw that gooseflesh had risen on her skin. He hurried his project along.

Eden assisted him by holding the strips of plastic. Then, using it as he would an adhesive wrap, he lifted her arm and circled her upper back and shoulder. And while the devil in him hoped to see her breasts, she modestly thwarted his efforts by keeping them covered.

Mission accomplished, he stepped from behind her to restart the water. Yet, at the rise and fall of her breasts, Kevin all but collapsed. He was a red-blooded male, not some kind of saint. So far, he'd managed to keep control, but with Eden's glossy lips, her dewy complexion, she had the look of a woman just royally . . .

Trapped in this too-close-for comfort sauna with a woman he lusted after body and spirit, it was time to get the hell out.

"You okay to take it from here?" he said hoarsely.

Her eyes blinked open. And as she clutched the lowered robe over her close-to-spilling breasts, she tormented him further. Running her fingers through the water, she returned a gaze that nearly killed him. She wet her lips and smiled back at him, "Oh, *Oui, monsieur, merci beaucoup.* You're better than room service."

Outside, in his bedroom, Kevin banged his head on the wall. *Room service. House guest. Friend.* Damn her for being beautiful. If he wasn't careful, he'd be adding her to his menu.

Chapter Twenty-Four

HALF AN HOUR LATER, Eden forced herself from the tub. She'd been careful not to submerge her shoulder, and thanks to Kevin's ingenious idea of plastic wrap, her bandage was dry to the touch.

During her soak, she'd obsessed over him for a while—his caring touch, the way he seemed to watch her every move. But near the end, her mind drifted to the hospital chapel and her vision of Sister Beatrice. Particularly the melody Eden had played as the two of them sat on the piano bench. She dried and braided her hair, humming what little she recalled of the tune. Sister Beatrice had seemed surprised that Eden had written it, and the grown-up Eden understood why. The stanzas were rich and complicated, and to this day she'd heard nothing like them.

Wouldn't it be amazing if she could recreate the composition from those long-ago memories? She immediately sent that thought into exile, the tune doomed to die an undiscovered death. Each time her mother insisted she sit at the piano and play, her stomach had convulsed and she'd shaken uncontrollably.

Slipping into pajama pants and a tank top, she also tried to remember her mentor. But those thoughts, too, were scattered, disjointed, and the attempt gave her a major headache. She could swallow a pill, but the pain in her shoulder was manageable and the truth was, a narcotic might dull the memories.

Patience, Eden. You can't force memories buried for seventeen years. *Patience?* Eden scoffed. Unfortunately, she'd never possessed that trait. Lord knew the man on the other side of the door was trying that nonexistent characteristic. After all of her promises to show some restraint, she'd gone back on her word. She'd been a tease to send him that flirty look before he left the bathroom. How could he wrap her in *plastic* and still not give in?

It was time to face facts—he wasn't interested in her romantically. Further, she was only hurting herself by engaging in this silly, besotted behavior.

After ten, she finally experienced the return of her appetite. Remembering her leftover Mexican meal, she went in search of her host to see if he wanted to share. But a quick search of the house revealed she was alone. When she finally found him on the back porch, she felt so relieved that she broke out in a smile.

A starlit evening awaited her as she stepped beneath the house's overhang. But it wasn't until after she ventured farther outside that she realized he was on the phone and she'd walked in on an intensely personal conversation.

He sat near the porch's balustrade with his back to her.

"I don't want him to fly out, Mom. No. Forget it. I'm fine. It's not necessary . . . Yeah, maybe. All I'll need is a head's up . . . Please, stop worrying . . . I love you, too."

Eden was already inside the house when she heard him flip the phone shut and say, "Where are you going?"

She stopped in the entryway. "To give you some privacy. Sorry, I didn't mean to—"

"You didn't. Come sit with me."

Disregarding her awkward feelings, she joined him on the step. He'd changed clothes, was barefoot and smelled amazing. As her gaze wound downward again, she noticed even his feet were sexy—long, lean and tanned. But why should that surprise her? Everything about Kevin Dancer was sexy. From the tight fit of his jeans, to the muscles bulging beneath his shirt, to the way he held the beer in his hand—*everything* about him turned her on.

He hadn't turned the porch light on yet, which left her to wonder how long he'd been out here. Maybe he'd come outside to veg and then received the phone call. It was a pleasant thought until Eden noticed the two uncapped bottles beside him.

Three beers did not make a staggering drunk. Still, it concerned her. She'd been so fixated on her own crisis that she hadn't considered what he was going through. He'd shot and killed a man last night, and the plain truth was she didn't know him well enough to know how he'd deal with that.

Should she talk to him? Leave him alone? Shoulder to shoulder, just the two of them in the secluded darkness, it was a perfect romantic setting. They even had a serenade of sorts—a chorus of crickets.

But thanks to that phone call, tension hovered like an unwelcome storm.

When the silence became unbearable, she reached for the beer in his hand and took a long draw.

He tilted his head and he frowned. "Should you be mixing alcohol with pain meds?"

Oops. She hadn't taken a pill since leaving the hospital. Not mentioning it, though, did seem a good way to segue into what she was thinking. "Probably not. Should you be drinking when you're depressed?"

"Who said I was depressed?"

"Oh, I don't know. Out here drinking all by yourself? I overheard the last part of your phone call. Your stepfather offered to help."

Kevin smirked. "No, Eden. He offered to come out here and shove his weight around. Big difference."

"Just the same, he *offered*. Sounds to me like your folks are concerned. My parents live in the same city, and I haven't heard from them since my stabbing."

What was the use? She handed him back his beer and started to rise, but he stopped her. Placing his hand on her knee, he said, "I'm sorry about your folks."

"Don't."

"I'm sorry? What?"

"Make this about me. For once, let's talk about you."

His jaw tightened, and even in the dark, she saw the spark in his eyes. "All right. How's this? The facts speak for themselves, and I don't need J.T. Garland to represent me."

"Understood. But, Kevin, review boards can go either way. If the APD is considering caving in to political pressure, you could make them rethink their decision by showing them that you have powerful backing, too."

"The day I force someone to keep me due to political pressure is the day I find a new line of work. I'm a good cop, Eden. I'm on my own out here and I like it that way. Besides, I don't need any reminders of the past."

Frozen, she sat on the step, watching as his large hand curled into a fist. God, what a pair they made. She would give anything to remember her long-ago history, while all he wanted was to forget about his. She told herself to back off. But when it came to Kevin Dancer, she had bricks where her brain should be. "And is your past the reason you're fighting being with me? My job makes me a reminder?"

He drained the rest of his beer. "At times like these? Yeah."

Feeling as though she'd been dropkicked in the stomach, Eden got to her feet. She couldn't get into the house fast enough to pack and call a taxi. But in the next moment he was behind her, prying her hand from the door and slamming it shut.

She whirled on him to voice her outrage. She never got the chance. He stood so close, he rendered her speechless. "Though I should tell you about the other times. Times like last night when your blood was all over me, and I thought I would lose you. Or today when you told me to go away and I thought I'd go mad."

His breath brushed her temple and tears sprang to her eyes. What was she, a yo-yo? How could she be furious one moment, sighing with relief the next?

"Let's not forget, too, the times you piss me off. Or make me laugh."

He curved his hand around the back of her neck and pulled her against him, all while traitorous tingles shot from her nerve endings. "And I can promise you one thing . . ."

Her heart nearly thudded out of her chest as his free hand found her breast. "You may share a profession with J.T. Garland, but I never once wanted to see him out of his clothes."

And then he kissed her. A beer-tinged, no-nonsense kiss that left her boneless, needy and craving. He touched her. *Everywhere.* As though his passion were a thoroughbred and someone had opened the starting gate. Powerful hands caressed her neck, breasts, her back, her stomach. And when he pulled her deeper into the shadows, she couldn't have resisted if she'd wanted to. Rather, she kissed him back, a willing accomplice. He sat on the balustrade, bringing her with him. Then, lifting her, he guided her to straddle him. She felt the tug of her shirt, confusion when cool air hit her skin, and shock when he pulled her top over her head and sent it flying.

He was hard and relentless, and when he freed her braid and ran his fingers through her hair, she nearly passed out from the pleasure. She was hot and achy and half naked on the porch of an Albuquerque cop. And when he reached for the drawstring of her pajama bottoms, half naked was a thing of the past.

How he could maneuver her as though she weighed nothing was the ultimate turn-on, and she couldn't get close enough. She was happily engaged in a tongue-dueling frenzy when she heard the click of his belt and the steel teeth of his zipper.

Want overruled common sense as he eased her on and over him. There was no going back. She was already climaxing when he drove into her. Nothing could have deterred her from leaning back and holding on. He shuddered, groaned, and clung to her at the same time her world ignited.

KEVIN PLACED his face between Eden's soft breasts and waited for his breathing to level. What the hell? One minute he was pissed as hell, the next he had her out of her clothes. Sometime during their lovemaking, he'd said to himself, "Okay, Dancer. Do it. Get her out of your system." Now the joke was on him. He was like a great white trolling the waters. Only it was Eden who'd dangled the bait, he'd bitten, and now *he* was dinner.

Her moans while they were kissing had made him half crazy, and thinking about it, he grew hard again. Between self-incriminations, it also occurred to him that she was speaking to him.

"Kevin, did you hear me?"

He lifted his head to gaze into a tormented sea of blue.

"I seem to be missing my clothes."

Ah, hell. So she was. He eased her off of him and set her down on the stone walkway. Finding her pants was a cinch. They remained at his feet where he'd dropped them. Retrieving them for her, he avoided her dazed look, and said, "Better go find your top."

He zipped his fly, scanned the night for a patch of yellow, and found it clinging to a spirea bush a few feet from the porch. Rolling his eyes, he took a deep breath. His back yard wasn't fenced. Good thing it was late. Most of the houses from his vantage point were dark.

By the time he trekked back up the steps, Eden had vanished. Not that he blamed her. He found her in the kitchen, wearing her robe and placing the beer bottles in the recycle bin.

Handing her the top, he tried for an ice breaker. "Looks like you don't need this anymore."

"Actually, I do. I'll call for a taxi. I know you didn't want this to happen."

He stepped farther into the kitchen. "I wanted it. I wanted *you*."

Her response to his honesty was to shake her head. He took her hand and led her to the couch. But when he sat, she remained standing. Turning from him, she slipped the robe off her shoulders and covered herself with the tank top. As if she needed to maintain her modesty and they hadn't just had sex on his porch. The image of her shapely back was an unkind reminder, though. He hoped their little tussle hadn't done any damage.

"Come here so I can check your stitches."

"I'm sure they're fine."

"Eden," he said, in a voice that brooked no argument.

Frowning, she dropped down beside him and faced away from him. He lifted her hair, relieved when he saw that the compress had held. But even though he meant to, he didn't let her hair fall back into place. He draped it over her shoulder instead. He'd known better than to touch her. Now he was addicted. Careful to avoid the bandage, he kissed her creamy shoulder and traced his lips up her neck.

"What are you doing?" she said at the same time a soft mew escaped her lips.

"What I wanted to do the whole time I was wrapping you in plastic. What I've wanted to do from the first day I met you. We didn't use a condom, Eden."

She hugged herself tightly and mumbled something about not using her brain. Then turning toward him, she squared her shoulders. "You have nothing to worry about. I'm not a teenager, I'm educated and I'm capable. I'd never hold you financially accountable."

Like hell. "I don't shirk my responsibilities either, just wanted to clear the air. We screwed up out there."

"I agree," she said stiffly. "Are we done here?"

He laughed. "No, we're not *done* here. We were having a pretty intense conversation before we . . ."

Her cheeks turned a becoming shade of red. "I should have minded my own business."

He nodded. Obviously not the action she wanted, because she crossed her arms over her chest and she looked away.

"I'm okay, Eden. From what I saw this morning, the panel sees the shooting as a justified kill."

"As well they should," she said. "But how do *you* feel about what happened?"

"Honestly?" Folding his own arms, he stretched out his legs. "I'm relieved, I'm angry, and there's not a damned thing I can do about it, so I cope. Given the circumstances, if I had to make the same decision again, nothing would change. Sharpe . . . Timms . . . whoever the hell he was, would be dead and you'd be alive.

"You used the word depressed. Not even close," Kevin continued. "I'm not going to start drinking to excess, and I'm not going to pull a Martin Riggs. Any other questions?"

"One," she said, studying him as if he'd grew a third eye. "Who's Martin Riggs?"

"Lethal Weapon? Pistol in the mouth?" Kevin winked at her. "Best cop movie ever made."

"You're really okay?"

"You're really off pain pills?"

She crossed her heart.

"Still want to leave?"

"I think I should."

"You think too much." He stood, pulled her to him and he kissed her again. When they drew apart, he looked deep into her eyes. "But there's been a change of plans. From now on, we're sharing the bed."

LONG AFTER KEVIN fell asleep, Eden lay awake in his arms, her head against his chest, listening to the mighty beat of his heart, happy to be breathing him in. They'd made love again, this time using a condom. Like always, she over-thought the significance. If they pursued this relationship, in addition to passion and lovemaking, they were in for turmoil and arguments. He hadn't exactly professed his feelings about what happened between them. It was way too soon and it wasn't his way.

After tomorrow, she'd go home. She was stronger now. Kevin wasn't the only one who could cope. For now, safe and alive was a great place to be.

Her eyes drifted shut, and the song she played for Sister Beatrice wound through her sated brain. Sighing, and on the cusp of sleep, she slipped out of his arms and back to her own pillow, determined to do more research on repressed memories tomorrow. Perhaps she would never recall the whole truth. Or perhaps a person only unblocked when they were good and ready.

Patience, Eden. You can't force memories buried for seventeen years. With one last final yawn, she drifted off to sleep.

For the night's recital, St. Patrick's gymnasium had been converted to an auditorium. The bleachers had been put away, the wood floor polished to perfection, and kids from various grades had gladly missed class to set up the gym with row after row of metal folding chairs.

Giddy from the excitement of her first formal recital, Eden stood with several music theory classmates behind the stage curtain. Jimmy Martinez pulled her hair twice and she stuck out her tongue and glared at him. She missed her braid, but Mama had said for tonight she should wear it down. She felt like a fairy princess in her blue velvet dress with lacy white neckline, matching blue ribbon, white hose and black patent leather shoes.

Her mother and father were seated in the second row. She'd already checked. Meghan was seated a few rows behind them, giggling with two of her girlfriends who'd come to cheer Eden on.

But what mattered most was Sister Beatrice. She'd promised to be here. Eden peeked through the curtain and scanned the room. With all the people and the auditorium filling, she saw no sign of her.

"Eden, come here, child."

She let the curtain drop, rolled her eyes, and turned to see Sister Agnes standing in the center of the group. "Now, let's go over the order in which you will play. Vanessa, you will be first, Jimmy, number two, Anthony, three . . ."

Eden held her breath, waiting to see where Sister Agnes would place her. If Sister Beatrice had to sit through too many pieces, she might not want to stay. Eden's daddy complained endlessly about how long Meg's recitals took. "It might help if they'd let me wear earplugs and bring a newspaper," he'd groused.

To Eden's misery, Sister placed her dead last. As the other children wandered off to take their spots, and the principal, Sister Joseph Marie, acted as MC, Eden started toward her friends.

"Eden, a word, please."

She stiffened and turned toward her music teacher. Eyes downcast she approached. "Yes, Sister?"

"Do you know why I saved you for last?"

Because you hate me. *Eden shook her head.*

"Because as much as I don't want to say this to you, you're the best."

Her music teacher didn't even bother to lower her voice. Feeling the other students' eyes on her, Eden's face grew hot. Vanessa Constantine would ignore her for weeks, thanks to the nun's careless comment. Sister Agnes went down on one knee, the smell of Bengay ever present. "You've done well with the Scarlatti sonata I assigned to you. I'm pleased. I warn you, though, if I hear that you've resorted to playing by ear, I will walk out on stage and stop the performance. In front of your parents and everyone. Do I make myself clear?"

Eden forced back burning tears. Sister Agnes would never see her cry. "I'll read the music, Sister."

"Good girl. I know you don't like me, Eden. But my job isn't for you to like me. You'll thank me one day. Discipline is crucial in life. With discipline and prayer, you will never go wrong." Her wrinkles lifted upward. The woman in the black habit really wasn't bad looking when she smiled. She just didn't do it often. "Oh, and Eden?"

Rolling her eyes a second time, she turned back to the nun. "I've asked Sister Beatrice not to come tonight. She's a distraction for you. In case you were hoping she would be here."

A gulp lodged in Eden's throat. She wanted to kick the old witch, wanted to bolt from the stage. Instead, she joined her classmates at the side of the stage. The recital began, and the night, along with Eden's misery, droned on.

When one performance remained ahead of her, Sister Agnes ordered her to get in line and the children who'd already performed to sit still. "Deep breaths. Just as we've done in class."

The curtain shifted and Father Munroe came back stage. "Hello, boys and girls," he said, and Sister Agnes's strict organization erupted in chaos as children scurried in his direction. "I'm so impressed with each and every one of you. God has blessed us, do you know that?"

Eden held back, but even some of her unhappiness eased. The handsome Father Munroe was such a nice man. It was hard to stay mad in his presence. He caught her gaze and he winked.

She returned a shy smile.

"Sister Agnes," Father Munroe said. "Would you mind?" He held the curtain for her as though he wanted her to go with him.

Sister Agnes wringed her hands. "I'm sorry, Father, we're in the middle of the children's recital."

"Yes, and you've done a marvelous job. But I need your advice."

"Now, Father?"

"Please. Sister Joseph Marie will help until we return. It's my mother," he said as he guided the old nun down the stage steps. "You see, she's fond of this particular song, and I for the life of me . . ."

Frowning, Eden thought that had to be the weirdest scene she'd ever witnessed, but at least she was spared Sister Agnes's awful presence for a while.

Sister Joseph Marie came through the curtain appearing as dazed and uncertain as Sister Agnes had been. "Eden, it's your turn, dear. Are you ready?"

"Yes, Sister." She took a deep breath and walked out onto center stage. The auditorium was packed, and her gaze fell on her mother, who was clutching her father's

arm, and her sister who was no longer giggling, but smiling, in the front rows.

Their presence should have been enough—they were her family after all. But Eden thought she just might break into tears. Somehow she managed to perform the required curtsy, and when she looked up, she saw her.

Sister Beatrice.

In the back near the door to the kitchen, the young nun lifted her hand in a gentle wave and beamed her encouragement.

Eden blinked. Her mouth fell open and her heart felt like it might dance out of her chest. Sister Beatrice had promised to be here and she'd kept her word.

Stage fright gone, Eden adjusted the bench, tucked her dress beneath her and studied the black and white keys. With no sign of Sister Agnes, she dismissed the difficult sheet music she'd practiced over and over and simply let the music flow from her heart. When she finished, she lowered her head, awaiting polite applause.

But there was none, not for entire seconds. Heat flooded her cheeks. She forced her gaze to look out toward the audience and discovered they'd come to their feet. As thunder erupted, Eden swallowed back tears of joy and relief.

Her gaze shifted to the wildly clapping Sister Beatrice, who smiled back at her. Then she blew Eden a kiss and disappeared through the kitchen door. As Eden stared after her, she knew. Sister Beatrice was a phantom, a miracle, or something in between.

Chapter Twenty-Five

TWO THINGS hit Kevin Tuesday morning as he set off on a run. One, if he wasn't careful, he could get used to waking up next to the woman he'd left asleep in his bed. Two, he still felt no guilt for killing Rueben Sharpe. Remorse, yes. Kevin had taken a life. No doubt, that sad fact would haunt him forever.

Eden had slept fitfully. He knew, because her cries had woken him. Whatever dream she was having affected her. It had nearly destroyed him to do nothing and see the tears slide from beneath her closed lids. But as much as he hated to see her cry, he held back. If her subconscious was trying to break through, his interference would only delay a process that needed to happen.

As for the suspension, in forty-eight hours he'd be back on the job. He'd already received an e-mail from his commander, telling him he was scheduled for a psych evaluation on Friday. If he wanted to keep his job, he'd go. But if he was supposed to undergo a Jekyll and Hyde metamorphosis, it hadn't happened yet, and those were the facts he'd relate to the department shrink.

He was less than a mile from his home in the foothills when his cell phone rang. Ten years on the force had taught him not to leave home without it or his weapon. He slowed to a walk, pulling the phone from his belly band, and saw that the caller was Sal. Kevin punched in *receive*.

"You out for a run?"

"Just wrapping it up. What's happening?"

"A whole mess of things. Based on Eden's ID of Sharpe, we ran the Thomas Timms' alias through the DMV."

"You sound optimistic."

"We located his street address."

"You going in?"

"Soon as the brass gets a warrant and figures out the best way to cover their asses."

"The brass?" Kevin pulled up his shirt to wipe his dripping face. "Why involve them?"

"Timms lived at a pretty exclusive address. Ever heard of Franciscan Post Drive?"

Kevin rarely had to resort to a street map anymore, but this street was unknown to him. "No."

"Me either. Like I said, it's a private drive. It's one of the side streets inside the Diocese of New Mexico's administrative property. Timms listed it as his place of residence on his driver's license."

"Holy shit."

"Funny, that's what I said."

"Sounds like closing this case was premature."

"Oh, we got the right guy," Sal pointed out. "But we do want to know if anyone aided and abetted. When Mesa General's administrators get wind of this, the lawsuits will fly. And, of course, our directive to treat the people at the diocese like they were holier than thou and above the law has the higher-ups shifting blame."

Kevin was having a hard time slowing his breathing, and it wasn't from his run. For half a second, he recalled Eden's suggestion that he call his stepfather. Not that he'd ever consider it, but, damn, her intuition was right on. "I take it my name came up?"

"Both our names," Sal said. "Particularly yours with the suspension. I was told to leave the room after that. I'm pretty sure Benally told the brass to go fuck themselves." Sal hesitated. "So, did you and Eden hook up?"

Kevin's sweaty collar grew even hotter as he grasped the significance of Sal's question. If the department wanted a fall guy, a suspended cop had a bullseye strapped to his chest. Not that he regretted what happened between him and Eden, but it would be foolhardy to broadcast that they were seeing each other. But this was Sal he was talking to so he admitted, "She stayed with me last night."

"Figured as much. I wouldn't go broadcasting your relationship. Keep a lid on things until we tie up the ends."

Kevin exhaled slowly. "Any idea when Benally will serve the warrant?"

"Today. So keep your head down."

"Consider me invisible."

EDEN PULLED her hair back into a functional ponytail, slipped into her bra and panties, and fastened her watch. Tilting her head from side to side, she inspected her rush makeup job. Not bad for a woman who'd almost met her maker two days before. With another dream gripping her, she'd lain in bed during the early morning hours until her brain shouted, "No more."

If the police were satisfied that Sharpe had acted alone, so be it. But if that was true, didn't it stand to reason her subconscious would recognize it and stop bombarding her with all the dreams? She couldn't go on night after night assaulted by memories she didn't understand.

Her mind cycled back to her recital. The dream proved that at one time she hadn't been afraid of Bishop Munroe, that she and the other children had all but worshipped him.

So what happened to change things between them?

There was only one way to find out. She wiggled into a beige camisole and reached for the skirt she'd packed at the last minute in case she was called into work. It was a high-waisted power-red pencil skirt that she often wore during closing arguments. That, along with the matching jacket, would be a perfect ensemble to meet the bishop.

Somewhere in the haze of her mind, it registered that Kevin had been tip-toeing around the bedroom this morning in workout gear. And with his Jeep still parked in the garage, she assumed he had to be somewhere in the vicinity.

It would be much easier to avoid an argument if she left him a note. She checked the time and frowned at the bathroom she'd left a disaster. The taxi was probably outside by now. Kevin might return at any moment. She had to move fast.

On one foot, she hobbled to locate a missing pump and scribbled a message on the legal pad near his laptop. She hoped he'd understand, but she wasn't about to be dissuaded. It was either find the answers she needed or spend the rest of her life on a psychiatrist's couch. Still, if one person had the power to change her mind, it was Kevin.

Well, that wasn't going to happen today. She opened her clutch purse and powered off her cell.

As she strode to the waiting taxi, the warm, sunny morning all but guaranteed she was making the right decision. She slid into the back seat and nodded to the mustachioed man behind the wheel. "Twenty Franciscan Post Drive. And driver, could you hurry?"

AFTER TRYING EDEN'S cell twice, Kevin crumpled the note in his hand and unclenched his gritting teeth. She wasn't trying to ruin his life. She was simply looking for answers. No way could she know she was interfering with a police investigation. She thought the case was over—he'd told her as much. These things Kevin told himself to stay calm.

He needed to get her out of the diocese before she talked to Munroe, or at the very least before the police served the warrant.

Screw calm. Sometimes panic was necessary. At all costs, he had to stop her. Two minutes later, he was in his Jeep and speeding toward the diocesan headquarters.

EDEN'S HEART REVVED a few notches as the cab driver drove through the diocesan gates. She'd purposely not phoned ahead. She wasn't about to be put off by an army of gatekeepers, be penciled in for later that week, or plied for information as to why she wanted to see the head honcho. Still, it had to be unseemly to pop in on a bishop unannounced.

She couldn't remember ever being here, but somewhere she recalled learning that the acreage had been donated to the diocese years before she'd been born. From the taxi's backseat window, she observed the administration's single-story building, which was housed between a forest of cottonwoods and an overgrown lawn.

She planned to avoid that building, however. Directing the driver to pull into the parking lot, she set her sights on the cathedral next door. As people filed out of eight o'clock Mass, her anticipation grew. She studied each and every face as they walked toward their cars, but had yet to make out the one individual she wanted to see.

Time stretched on and the driver fidgeted. "Meter's running, lady."

"I'm aware of that," she said as cars began emptying the parking lot. *Dammit.* She thought she'd been so clever. Saturday night, while the bishop had enthralled the guests at his table, she heard him say what he missed most while in Europe was not saying daily Mass.

At last she spotted him exiting the cathedral. He was walking with someone, and as Eden leaned forward to see who walked by his side, she gasped. It was a woman. He pulled her into his arms. If Eden hadn't known her all of her life, or known that Robert Munroe was ordained, she would have thought the two made a very handsome couple.

But she did know.

She asked the driver to wait, opened the car door and hurried across the parking lot and up the steps of the cathedral. Finding the two still locked in an embrace, Eden greeted them with a cool, "Hello, Bishop. Hello, Mother."

"Eden!" Joanna Moran jumped from the man's arms like a guilty teenager, while the bishop looked on with one of his beatific smiles.

"See there, Joanna. What did I tell you? She's fine. Eden, you've had us all worried."

Eden glared at the pair. "Really? I can't understand why. No one contacted *me*."

Her mother came forward. "The moment we reached Albuquerque, your father and I went straight to the hospital. You'd been released, so we drove to the loft."

"Did you ever think of trying my cell?"

Her mother stared at Eden. "Of course we did. I left a message on your voice mail and asked you to call me. Really, Eden, this is too much even from you."

"Joanna." The bishop touched her shoulder.

Remembering that she'd powered off her phone, Eden reached into her purse and turned it on. Scrolling past two missed calls from Kevin, she noticed the voice mail. She'd been so wiped out yesterday, she hadn't even thought of the phone in her purse. And it didn't make her feel any better that she'd accused her parents of not caring in front of Kevin.

"Where have you been?" her mother asked.

She set the phone on vibrate and dropped it in her bag. "I was at a friend's. I spent most of the day sleeping. I wasn't thinking, Mom. I was wrong to make you worry."

In a close-knit family, this might have been where they all tearfully embraced.

Joanna simply held her position by the bishop. "Your father and I are relieved that you're safe. As for Detective Dancer, we owe him everything for saving you from that madman."

"I'd say that's an adequate description of Reuben Sharpe," Eden said, studying the bishop through her peripheral vision and watching him pale. Then, focusing solely on her mother, she said, "If it's all right, I'd like to stop by this afternoon and tell you about it."

"You have to ask? Eden, we'd love that."

This wasn't exactly a Hallmark moment either. Still, it was the closest she'd ever come to one. "Great. For now, I dropped by because I really would like to talk to Bishop Munroe."

Her mother glanced from one to the other. "Robert?"

"It's fine, Joanna. I can certainly spare Eden a few minutes."

Interesting how he'd stressed the word *few*. She and the bishop maintained a stony silence until her mom reached her Lexus. Finally, Eden said, "Should we go to your office?"

"I haven't that much time." He extended his hand. "Let's talk in here."

Eden's gaze rose to the cathedral as she warded off a chill. Why was the universe determined to see her inside a church? She shuddered. "Perfect."

St. Francis of Assisi cathedral towered over St. Patrick's in size, yet when she entered the highly polished corridor, it was without her normally overwhelming sense of growing panic. Perhaps it was because sunlight drifted in through the stained glass windows and filled the space with ample light.

A full-immersion baptismal font occupied the marble atrium. Bishop Munroe dipped his hand into the holy water and made the sign of the cross, then quickly went to extinguish the candles he'd left burning after Mass.

Eden waited in the rear of the church, but as he traversed the sacristy, no amount of light could prevent the dizziness that set in or the goose bumps that rose on her arms. She gripped the pew, aware for the first time in hours of the bandage covering her stitches. Adding a new psychosis to her already screwed-up life, she glanced over her shoulder in fear of a crazy man wielding a knife.

Bishop Munroe snuffed out the last candle and strode down the center aisle. "I apologize, Eden," he said smiling. "But it looks bad for a man in my position to burn down a church. With Joanna so distressed, I felt I should talk to her immediately."

Still mulling over what she'd seen on the steps, Eden said, "She comes here often? St. Patrick's is closer."

"She goes to St. Patrick's on Sunday. I find it touching that she comes to St. Francis almost daily. Many of my former parishioners do. Joanna may not have said so, Eden, but she's thrilled to have you home."

She fought not to scoff in his presence. It had been Meghan who begged Eden to return after graduation. Her parents never said a word. "I feel like everyone went on without me," she said. "Did you continue to spend a lot of time with my family?"

"Not as much as I wanted to. I was transferred to several different parishes after my appointment to monsignor. But Joanna and Edward remained my close friends, which is why I know so much about your estrangement. I didn't like them sending you away, and I advised against it. Unfortunately, people are not required to take my advice."

He checked his watch, his demeanor very different from Saturday night, when he'd seemed so anxious to talk to her. It was also obvious that he was veering the conversation away from Thomas Timms. No wonder he'd risen to bishop, he was very good at manipulation. Little did he realize she was happy with the direction he was taking.

"In retrospect," the bishop continued. "Perhaps your mother knew what she was doing. Your aunt is a respected lawyer. Now look at you. You've followed in her very successful footsteps. Although, Eden, I worry about the faith element of your spiritual journey."

Eden smiled. Through everything, she'd never stopped believing. "Faith is a personal issue to me, Bishop. But you're right. I owe a lot to my aunt. I arrived on her doorstep a hellion, but she would have none of it. She said to me once, 'You think you've had it rough, I'll show you people with real problems.' And she did. My aunt may be agnostic. She's also a caring human being."

"Of that I have no doubt. As to faith, I'll leave that to the Ultimate Judge." Again, he looked at his watch. "I'm sorry, Eden. I have to go. I know you're here about Thomas, but my lawyers have said that under no circumstances am I to talk about him. I am relieved you weren't seriously hurt."

He was relieved? After all she'd been through to get here, there was no way he was simply dismissing her. "Answer one question and I'll leave. Did you know Thomas had assumed an alias?"

The bishop's handsome face soured. "Did I knowingly employ a sexual predator? No, I did not."

That wasn't what she'd asked, and if she were deposing him, she'd demand an answer. But this wasn't a deposition, and he was walking away. When he made it as far as the atrium, desperation rose in her chest. "Bishop Munroe," she called after him. "I didn't come about Thomas. I came about Sister Beatrice."

His broad shoulders stiffened, and she prepared for his outrage. But when he pivoted again, all signs of anger were gone, replaced by a look of utter astonishment on his face. With a newfound urgency in his step, he strode back to her. "Have you kept in touch with her, Eden? Do you know where she is?"

Stunned, she opened her mouth to reply at the same moment the phone in her purse started jumping. Then a sharp-featured man with thinning gray hair rushed in. "Excellency," he said. "You need to come at once. It's the police. They're here, and they have a warrant."

Chapter Twenty-Six

WHEN EDEN didn't answer her cell, Kevin circled diocesan headquarters several times to decide his next move. He could enter, try to locate her and run into his boss. Or he could enter, *not* locate her and run into his boss.

Neither option appealed to him. Cops were suspicious by nature. They would never see Eden's presence as a coincidence. They were trained to be judgmental, to think collusion. And, unfortunately, Kevin would look guilty by association. They would suspect he sent Eden to ask questions because he'd been suspended and ordered off the case.

He chose a park two blocks away, gripping and then easing up on the steering wheel. *Goddamn it.* He'd wanted to be the one to serve that warrant. Exiting the Jeep, he leaned against the driver side door and sent Eden another text message.

Leave now. Cops on way with warrant. Call me, damn it!

Had she seen the bishop? And if so, what had she given away that could jeopardize their investigation? If Eden had unintentionally given Munroe a tip that would help the diocese evade police, the target on Kevin's chest just got bigger.

His cell rang and he stabbed in *receive*. "Dancer."

"What's going on?" Eden whispered. "The police are here."

Shit. His heart went for a jog without him. "Where are you?"

"At the diocese in the backseat of a cab."

He raked a hand through his hair. Well, at least she wasn't openly visible. "I'm at Del Rio Park. Make an immediate left out when you exit the property, and head south. It's two blocks on your right. Get the hell out of there."

Her words were muffled as she said something to the cabby. "The driver knows where it is. I'm on my way."

"I'm parked between the basketball court and the playground." He snapped the phone shut and resisted slamming his fist against something while he waited for the taxi to appear. He settled for pacing.

The cab turned onto the park grounds a short time later.

Eden paid the driver and walked toward him. "A warrant?" she said when she came close enough to be heard. "But you said the case had been cleared."

"That was until we learned Rueben Sharpe's alias listed the diocese as his place of residence."

Her eyes widened. "No wonder the bishop called in the attack dogs."

"What do you mean?" Kevin didn't even try to hide the dread that crept into his voice.

"Lawyers," Eden replied. "He's represented to the teeth over this incident."

"You saw him?" Kevin pictured his career going down the toilet.

"I'd been with him about ten minutes when one of his staffers barged in to announce the cops."

He shook his head. "Who served the warrant?"

"No clue. Bishop Munroe and I were inside the cathedral. Too bad, too. I'd just gotten around to Sister Beatrice when the man rushed in. That's when the bishop left, I got your text, and here we are."

Unable to figure out how much actual damage she'd done, Kevin glanced away.

She stepped toward him and held out her hands. "How was I to know I was interfering?"

He turned to stare into her big blue eyes, realizing Eden was simply being Eden, seeking the answers she rightfully deserved. If the roles were reversed, he would have done the same thing—often had during his career as a cop. And if his job weren't on the line, he might even admire her tenacity.

But his job *was* on the line. "Why didn't you wait for me?"

"Would you have taken me to see him?"

Kevin had no answer to that, and she lifted a beautiful brow. "I thought as much."

He pulled her against him. "Next time, talk to me. I *can* be reasoned with."

Twining her arms around his neck, she angled closer. "Prove it."

He lowered his head to meet hers.

When they ended their kiss, she smiled up at him. "Aren't you going to ask?"

God, was she trying to kill him? "About?"

"My talk with the bishop."

Kevin narrowed his gaze. "How'd it go?"

"When I asked him about Sister Beatrice, he asked if I'd kept in touch with her."

Interesting response. If the bishop thought she was alive, Kevin could only conclude that Rueben Sharpe had acted alone.

"What are you thinking?" Eden asked. "You haven't stopped scowling since I got here."

"I'm not having an Einstein moment, that's for sure. Very little of this case made it into the papers. We deliberately kept it that way. Looks like we got our man."

"It must be awful not being there to see this thing through," she said.

"I'll live. Particularly with what you just told me about the bishop."

On their way back to the Jeep, she linked her arm through his. "What do you think normal people talk about when they're off work and don't have a dead body on their hands, or a case to try?"

"I don't know," he said, for the first time feeling a smile coming on. "Maybe we should try to find out."

He was already driving toward the exit when Eden slapped the dash. "Kevin. Stop!"

He slammed on the brakes. "What's wrong?"

She sat staring out the window at the playground, seemingly interested in a little Hispanic girl who ran toward the swings. A woman lagged behind, pushing a double stroller.

"Somebody you know?"

Eden didn't answer, merely remained engrossed in the kid for some reason. The little girl chose the middle swing and began pumping her legs back and forth.

Watching the swing's rise and fall, Kevin let the Jeep idle for a good minute before he said, "Eden?"

Sighing, she turned to him. "Sorry. Something seemed familiar."

He glanced toward the playground again. The little girl bounded from the swing and into the arms of her mother. "Are you remembering something?"

"Guess not. We should go before someone sees your Jeep."

"If something's triggering your memory, I'm willing to risk it."

"But I'm not. Must've been wishful thinking." She glanced at the family again, now making their way to the opposite side of the park. Nothing.

"Don't worry. If it's important," Eden said, "I'm sure it'll come to me."

Chapter Twenty-Seven

JANICE ROSE from her desk, startled by loud male voices in the outer lobby and the receptionist's cry of alarm. Shoving her arms through the sleeves of her navy blazer, she raced down a hallway lined with pictures of former bishops and pastors of New Mexico's ninety-plus parish seats.

At the sight of police officers and plainclothes detectives, she stopped abruptly. How dare these men barge in on the diocese? This was outrageous. She summoned all the authority she could muster, entered the foyer and said stiffly, "May I help you?"

A man who appeared to be Navajo pivoted in her direction. By the insignias he wore on his lapel, he was in charge. By his stance and the deference of those around him, he was the one she should reason with.

"I'm Commander Benally of the Albuquerque Police Department. We have a warrant to search the premises of one Reuben Sharpe, also known as Thomas Timms."

Janice's stomach dropped. Bishop Munroe had summoned the staff and told them late yesterday that Thomas had attacked two people and as a result he'd been shot and killed. Her only hope was that Thomas's madness hadn't touched the bishop or the Church.

She'd obviously been wrong.

When words failed her, Commander Benally said, "And you are?"

She drew back her shoulders. "Janice Charles. I'm executive assistant to Bishop Munroe." Addressing the diocese's recently hired receptionist, she said, "But the bishop's not in, isn't that right, Lindsey?"

"No, ma'am," she squeaked. "But Marshall went to get him."

Marshall again. Janice wanted to throttle the man. If he would stay out of the way, she could handle this mess.

A man in a walking cast sidled up next to the commander and the two held a private conversation.

Once they finished, the commander's dark eyes bore into hers. "My detective informs me that he's tried to speak with you several times, Ms. Charles. Unsuccessfully. I suggest we remedy that little misunderstanding right here and now."

"If you insist." Janice glanced through the plate glass doors to see the bishop and Marshall hurrying their way. She should have told him upon his return what she'd done, but with the bishop's harried itinerary, and now Thomas's death, there simply hadn't been time. Perhaps if she aligned herself with the commander, the bishop would never need to know. "If you'll come with me to my office, Commander, I'll get you a key to Thomas's apartment."

"No, ma'am. Detective Raez will have that honor. I'll speak to the bishop."

Detective Raez. Her mind revolving on what to do next, Janice moved down the hallway with the injured detective. The unsmiling man had yet to say one conversational word. Entering her pristine office, which she hoped he noticed, she moved to the utility box on the far right wall. How ironic that Thomas had been the one to install it. No matter what he'd been accused of, she was still finding the handyman's actions impossible to believe.

She removed the key labeled *Garage Apartment* and handed it to the detective. She doubted seriously that any explanation she gave would impress him, but she had to try. "Detective Raez."

"Ma'am?"

Opening the bottom drawer, she removed his messages from beneath her Bible and her holy cards. "I feel it's critical for you to know the bishop never received these."

He limped forward, and she wondered how he'd been hurt. His brusque, all-business manner prevented her from asking. He thrummed through the notes. "Any reason you wouldn't want him to talk to me, Ms. Charles?"

"It wasn't that I didn't want him to talk to you. He was at his Vatican ordination. Being the type of man he is, he would have come home."

"We could have done a phone interview," the detective said, unsmiling and piercing her with his cold gaze. "You realize this wasn't your decision to make, don't you?"

"I do now," she said. "However, from your calls, you indicated he was one of several people you were talking to. Bishop Munroe never takes time off, Detective. He deserved to spend his time away from the diocese without any major headaches. I took it upon myself to—"

"Usurp your authority."

The man had a heart of granite. She lowered her head. "I suppose that's true. The bishop only came home last Thursday, and with so much happening, I haven't had an opportunity to tell him about your phone calls."

"And you planned to?" the detective asked.

"Of course I did," she lied.

"So now you're worried about *your* job?"

"Wouldn't you be?"

"Frankly, ma'am, if I were in your shoes, I'd be petrified."

This man was no public servant, he was an uncaring *animal.* "You think you know everything, don't you? If you must know, the bishop would never fire me."

The intolerable man came toward her. "Pretty bold statement. I learned a long time ago, that nobody's irreplaceable. But I'll bite. Why's that?"

"If you knew anything about Bishop Munroe, you would know he has compassion for people. I told you the truth. I hid the messages because he deserved all the pomp and circumstance due a man of his stature being promoted. What concerns me is that our diocesan business manager has his ear, and depending on what mood he's in on any given day, he might very well use my actions against me."

"What's this man's name?"

"Marshall Knight. He and Thomas have been with the bishop forever."

"Define forever."

"His relationship with the bishop extends as far back as when the bishop was pastor at St. Patrick's."

"That would have been helpful to know three months ago, Ms. Charles. How long have you been here?"

"At the diocese? Five rewarding years. I came to work for Bishop Munroe when he was appointed monsignor. And because I've been here less time than Marshall, he reminds me of it constantly."

"You don't like your co-worker?"

"He's a bully. He bullied everyone, particularly Thomas."

"Did you talk to Thomas?"

"Very few *talked* to Thomas. I gave him assignments, but I'm afraid he lived in his own little world. May I ask you something?" she asked.

"You can ask," the detective replied.

"Do you think if I'd given the bishop those messages, any of this could have been prevented?"

Detective Raez's expression remained unreadable. "I don't deal in hypotheticals, Ms. Charles."

"I see. I truly am sorry, Detective. I give you my word, my actions were carried out with the very best of intentions."

"I'm sure," he said. "Let me ask you something. Would Marshall Knight have informed the bishop of my calls?"

"As you say, it's hypothetical, but if I had to guess, Marshall would have leapt at the chance."

"Then it's my guess the bishop chose the right man for the job. Even men of compassion don't appreciate people throwing suspicion on them during a murder investigation."

Dangerously close to tears, Janice swallowed hard and rounded the desk. "And as you've by now determined, he's not guilty of anything. So are you going to tell him, or not?"

The unfeeling man limped to the door. "I won't say a word. I'll leave that up to my commanding officer. I learned a long time ago it's never a good idea to usurp authority. I also learned never to elude a police investigation or to piss off a cop."

Chapter Twenty-Eight

KEVIN DISCONNECTED from his partner, grinning. Sal was on his way over. He wanted to share in person with Kevin the details of what had occurred at the Diocese. While carrying on their conversation, Kevin had glanced repeatedly at Eden—who was stretched out on his couch—noting how much she improved the view.

She was reading a mystery from his dad's collection, her eyes glued to the page. He approached to read the title, *A Caribbean Mystery*, by Agatha Christie, and nodded in appreciation.

There was nothing revealing about what Eden wore. She was decked out in capris and a baggy shirt, her long blond hair pinned up, and he found her sexy as hell.

With girly things spread out all over his bathroom, he should be counting the hours until she left. But the more he was around her, the more he enjoyed the scent of her myriad beauty products. He found it hard to believe their forced sabbatical was almost over, or that he'd gotten so used to her being here. But when he'd hinted about her staying a few more days, she'd dismissed that suggestion faster than a court order. She said she was going home and back to work tomorrow.

He propped a hip on the arm of the couch. "Want me to tell you who did it?"

"Want me to murder you where you stand?"

He moved to get closer; she turned on her side to make room. "Threatening a cop? That's a no-no."

"You're not a cop until tomorrow morning. No jury would convict me." She sighed. "I love Miss Marple. I wanted to be her when I grew up."

He held back a smile. The way she'd gone about contacting the bishop this morning, she was well on her way. "Sal's coming over. He's going to update me on the case and what they found at the apartment." Kevin glanced at the closed lid to the pizza box. "If you left any pizza, we'll offer him a slice."

She threw the book at him.

EDEN SMILED as Sal gimped through the door of Kevin's home in his recently acquired walking cast. His entire body, including his round face and puffy cheeks, appeared even leaner. Poor guy. Running around on crutches, now a cast—falling off a roof apparently agreed with him from a health perspective. Perhaps fitness experts should recommend that strategy in their next weight-loss market craze.

"Hey, Eden, you look great," he said.

She hugged him. "I was just thinking the same about you, Detective."

"It's Sal, remember?"

"Would you like some pizza?" She shot Kevin a dirty look. "There's plenty."

"Don't mind if I do."

Kevin's partner sat on the couch and launched into his revenge saga, and how he'd finally one-upped the bishop's evasive executive assistant, sparing no detail as to how he had the poor woman in tears by the time he left her.

Kevin had brought in a folding chair from the dining room. Straddling it, he rested his arms on the back. "So I assume the Commander told Bishop Munroe about her deception?"

Through a mouthful of pizza, Sal said, "Hell yeah, he did, without a 'she meant well' in sight."

"What was the bishop's reaction?" Kevin asked.

"He wasn't happy, but with the search of the deceased's apartment, he had other things on his mind." Sal glanced between Kevin and Eden. "Munroe didn't look like the cool cucumber you described to me, Kev. The guy was in shock. Learning his handyman was a psycho all these years and was suspected of killing a nun? Benally allowed Munroe to remain outside the apartment to answer questions during the search. By the time we were through, the good bishop looked like he'd aged twenty years."

Sitting beside Sal, her legs tucked beneath her, Eden kept quiet, hanging on every word. She supposed she should leave, but neither had asked her to.

"What did Munroe have to say about Sister Beatrice?" Kevin asked.

"He admitted they'd known one another, claimed she was a gifted woman, the kids loved her and stuff like that.'"

Remembering the woman who had gone to such enormous lengths to attend her music recital, Eden studied one of Kevin's blank walls. Kevin obviously noticed. Eyes narrowed, he asked, "You okay?"

She nodded and Kevin continued, "Harboring a sexual predator all these years spells big trouble for his diocese. Did Munroe ask for his lawyer?"

"Benally stressed repeatedly to Munroe that he was free to call one. Or that he wasn't required to stay during the search. Munroe refused. He wanted to be present as much as we did. I got the impression he wasn't only in shock, he was angry."

"Did the commander ever allow the bishop inside?" Eden asked.

Sal shook his head. "No way. Cramped, stifling space, lots of crime scene techs moving in and out. I'll say one thing for Janice Charles. She pegged Marshall Knight right. That man's a pain in the ass. He's the diocesan business manager, and it appears the bishop's got two power mongers working side by side. If one of them ends up dead, I'm charging the other."

"What about the alias and his hiring of Timms?"

"Both Knight and the bishop claimed they had no idea. Back then, of course, he said these people weren't slid under microscopes the way they are now. He said Timms came with excellent references and he did a good job."

"Any idea how Sharpe came up with the alias?" Kevin asked.

"*Nada.* And no identification in the apartment that said he was anyone other than Thomas Timms."

"What else did you find?"

"Religious paraphernalia, plus a direct link tying Sharpe's interest to Eden."

Glad they'd allowed her to stay, Eden leaned forward. "Really? How so?"

"Several newspaper clippings that referenced your sister's wedding, highlighting the time and place of the event, including the reception."

"So how did he know where I lived? I'm not a member of any parish, and my phone number's unlisted. Did Sharpe have a computer?"

Sal glanced at Kevin. "Is she after my job?"

Kevin nodded to the Agatha Christie novel on the table. "She thinks she's Jane Marple."

Eden screwed up her face at both of them. "Don't take your show on the road, boys. I'm waiting."

"No computer." Sal sobered. "We think he'd been following you, Eden. We found an Old Town map with your address blocked out. In my professional opinion, I don't think Timms ever heard of Google or MapQuest."

"So everyone's still convinced he acted alone?" Kevin said.

"Unless forensics shows differently. Our dead guy was a religious fanatic and a lunatic rolled into one. Oh, did I mention this guy cornered the market on candles?"

Kevin's head shot up. "Why was that?"

"The ME says the deceased had numerous burn marks on his body.

We think Timms was into self-mutilation."

"Why automatically assume it was self-inflicted," Eden said. "Couldn't he have been abused?"

"We considered abuse," Sal replied. "Then disregarded it from the amount of wax on the table and floor. ME also claimed some of the burn marks were recent."

"This is too much." She buried her head in her hands. Thomas had to have been one tormented soul.

"Maybe he burned himself to fend off his urges." Kevin suggested.

"That's what we're thinking, too."

"Or paying a penance," Eden added, looking up. "If he was a true believer who couldn't control his demons, knowing that he killed a Bride of Christ, he had a nonrefundable ticket to hell for sure."

"She *is* after my job," Sal said.

Suddenly, any sense of levity evaporated and Eden felt sick to her stomach. The evidence rapidly pointed to Thomas as Sister Beatrice's killer. Eden wanted to lash out at life's unfairness, to go back in time and undo what he had done. A beautiful woman inside and out had been taken much too young.

Sal studied his watch and stood. "Well, this party's definitely fizzled. I'm out of here." He snapped his fingers. "Oh, you'll read the reports tomorrow, but the dude had a ton of bibles with highlighted passages. What we really thought was weird were the holy cards."

"Is that important? Holy cards are popular among Catholics," Eden said.

"I'm Catholic, and ordinarily I'd agree," Sal admitted. "The big deal is he didn't have a collection, he had one specific card. Five of them spread throughout the apartment of the Angel Gabriel, each with a biblical verse that was signed, 'The Messenger.'"

LATER THAT NIGHT in Kevin's master bath, Eden slipped into Kevin's pinstriped dress shirt just for fun. It swallowed her, but she liked how she looked in it and loved being surrounded by his spicy scent.

Tonight was her last night as his house guest, and a trace of melancholy set in. What a wild, lovely two days. Love making, investigating a murder, falling in . . .

Looping a towel on the rack, she shook her head. *Cool it, Eden.* No matter how much the man in the other room set her heart on fire, or seemed to care about her, they were at the pretend stage. Permanency happened to other people.

Resolution in check, she opened the bathroom door and said resolve booked a flight out the window. Wearing nothing but boxers, looking better than a male model for Calvin Klein, the ripped Kevin Dancer lay on his stomach. He was staring at his laptop, his head facing the foot of the bed.

She'd hoped he might notice the dress shirt she'd confiscated, and that it might lead to something interesting. The frown on his face probably nixed that idea, as he was absorbed by something onscreen. Perhaps he was focused on tomorrow and the fact he would once more be a cop.

Bummer. She'd finished the Agatha Christie book, but she might have to reach for another. Sliding beneath the covers, she asked, "What are you looking at?"

"Holy cards."

That sounded interesting, so she plopped down on her stomach beside him. "Having a religious experience, are we?"

A smile tugged at the corner of his mouth. "Something like that. There's a bunch of these suckers."

"They're called saints. And, yes, there are quite a few. Will the forensics team dust the holy cards for fingerprints?"

He had yet to notice she was wearing his shirt, which annoyed her, but she was definitely interested in his response to the question. As his obsessed gaze darted back and forth over the images on the monitor, he said, "They'll check everything they bagged for prints. If you were there, they'd even dust you for stealing my shirt."

It took a moment for the comment to register. "You big jerk. You didn't even look at me. How . . .?"

He closed the laptop and lowered it to the floor beside the bed. Flipping onto his side his eyes took on a smoky, interested gleam. "Know what bothers me?"

"What's that?"

"You look better in it than I do."

She lifted a brow. "Want me to take it off?"

"Uh-uh." His fingers moved to the top button. "That's my job."

Later, after they'd made love, she turned away from him, lest he know how tight her throat had gotten, how badly she needed him, and how much she dreaded tomorrow. It was too soon to have this depth of feeling for a man. But she did, and her heart hurt.

He rose up on an elbow, twisted a strand of her hair around his finger and kissed her. "Anyone ever tell you you're amazing? Beautiful, sexy, fun?"

"Flatterer." She smiled. "I care about you, too, Kevin."

"Sure you're ready to go home? As you can see, I have plenty of room . . . and books."

Eden snuggled deeper into her pillow, the owner of a sated grin and a lonely heart. "Goodnight, Kevin."

She was vaguely aware of his continued sweet murmurings, but her mind had traveled elsewhere, focused on the unbelievable tragedies seventeen years in the making. How odd that her introduction to Kevin had activated these triggers in her brain. From the moment he'd unwittingly defied her to remember, she'd met his challenge and more. Due to his persistence, she remembered her mentor. Little by little, she was recreating the events from the past.

I didn't come to talk to you about Thomas. I've come to talk to you about Sister Beatrice.

Dammit. Why had the pinched-faced man from the diocese chosen that moment to interrupt?

Have you seen her, Eden? Do you know where she is?

What a waste of a morning. Bishop Munroe hadn't even known she was dead. Disappointment clutched at Eden as she fought for sleep.

In a courtroom, you only had so many opportunities to pose the correct question. If you phrased a statement wrong, or failed to ask something pertinent, you could kiss a winning verdict goodbye. That was what gnawed at her. She felt as though she'd asked Robert Munroe the wrong question.

Sighing, she closed her eyes and tried to force the matter out of her head. Easier said than done, it turned out, as she lay hopelessly awake. If only that man hadn't barged in when he had, or she hadn't let the bishop veer the conversation toward her aunt and mother. What if she'd brought up Sister Beatrice the second she walked in? What if she'd called her Celeste?

Celeste . . .

Eden lay there, the breath stalled in her chest. Seventeen years of repressed memories exploded like fireworks on the fourth of July.

She could barely make out Kevin's even breathing, so intense was the knocking of her heart. Her stomach rebelled as she bolted from the bed.

"Eden?" Kevin called after her.

She couldn't reply. She was too intent on finding the toilet before she lost the contents of her dinner. Slamming the door behind her, she dropped to her knees as tears flowed and she vomited.

The long-forgotten image of Father Munroe arguing and struggling with Sister Beatrice became seared into her brain. *Have you seen her, Eden? Do you know where she is?*

The bastard! He'd stood in the back of a cathedral and coolly and calculatingly lied to her. The fraud! He knew damned well Eden hadn't seen Sister Beatrice. Dear God, he'd killed her.

Her stomach empty, she continued to dry heave, her sobs equally uncontrollable.

"Eden." Kevin rapped softly. "Can I help? Can I come in?"

The caring she heard in those words brought further tears to her eyes. "Not yet," she said, humiliated, wiping her mouth with the back of her hand. "Please, Kevin, not yet."

She buried her head on her forearms, which rested against the rim. Amid this dark revelation, Kevin was her beacon. Robert Munroe had much to answer for. She would make him pay. He *would* suffer.

Sister Beatrice had once called Eden an angel in her midst. Another sob wrenched from her throat. She'd be an angel all right—an avenging one.

Chapter Twenty-Nine

IN HIS BOSS'S office, Kevin stood by helplessly as his commander pressed fingers to his wrinkled brow. It was the first sign that his recount of Eden's revelation had heaped additional stress on a man clearly in need of less, not more.

"Eden Moran's a reliable source, sir."

"You said she was nine years old, Detective."

"A nine-year-old with a quick mind, who grew up to be an officer of the court," Kevin reminded him.

Commander Benally glanced at Sal, who stood facing the damned window. He'd let Kevin do most of the talking, and now here Sal was pretending to focus on the goings on of the outside world.

"Detective Raez, care to comment?" Benally asked.

Sal turned from the window. "I've met Ms. Moran, sir. I agree with my partner. She's a competent witness."

"A church isn't exactly a clandestine setting," Benally continued. "I would expect a church to be precisely where we'd see a nun and a priest."

Kevin nodded. "But not in this case, sir. According to Eden, they were arguing inside St. Patrick's. She believes they were lovers."

"Can this case get anymore complicated?" Benally ran his hands over his face. "Did I tell you my mother wanted me to be a plumber?"

Kevin might have laughed if his boss had. But part of him thought the commander might not be joking. "What do you want us to do, sir?"

"Is Ms. Moran still on the premises?"

Sal looked to Kevin for confirmation. "She might be. Or she might have already left for work."

"If she is, get her back here. I'd like to talk to her. You two get over to the courthouse and see if you can find a judge who doesn't like his job and can't wait to be voted out of office."

As Kevin walked with his limping partner to the door, the Commander said, "Detectives?"

They turned.

"I don't have to tell you Robert Munroe will be surrounded by the best legal counsel money can buy. Go by the book on this one."

Chapter Thirty

AS ROBERT WALKED the diocesan grounds on Wednesday morning, the unkempt grass and tree-filled property all but disappeared. He supposed he needed to hire a new grounds keeper to replace Thomas, but his heart wasn't in it. How had his good work—his hopes and his dreams—come to this? Robert could still recall with vivid clarity the look on his college sweetheart's face the night he told her that marriage wasn't in his future, but the priesthood was.

He'd grown up a devout Catholic, and felt the Church's cries as it constantly lamented the decline in vocations. It was something his family prayed about over dinner. Even so, Robert was the last person among his three brothers and two sisters that his parents expected to have a calling.

But a calling he'd had. After graduating from Loyola and entering the seminary, he never thought twice about his decision. That was, until at a noonday Mass, when a recently ordained nun stood to lead the off-key children's choir that was constantly in flux. As her magnificent soprano voice filled the congregation, Robert, who'd been distributing communion, did something unheard of. He stopped to look back. After years of listening to Sister Agnes's warbling, he'd trained himself not to wince. Not many things could distract him when he was distributing the Eucharist.

But distract him she had.

He hadn't meant to follow up on his intense attraction. Nonetheless, he found himself visiting the school more often, just to catch a glimpse of her, dropping in periodically to where she taught Spanish and Latin, or where she volunteered her time to assist Sister Agnes, who ran the music program.

At first they were pulled together by their love of the Church. Eventually, they were pulled together by their love for each other. For months it didn't go beyond friendship. Then on one rainy afternoon they found themselves alone. From that moment on, Sister Beatrice ceased to exist, and Celeste Lescano had become his obsession.

"Bishop Munroe."

He whirled at the forceful use of his name. He'd been so engrossed in his sins from the past, he hadn't heard anyone approach. The injured detective from yesterday and Eden's Detective Dancer stood a few feet away. Unsmiling, they no doubt had more questions about Thomas. Robert lowered his head and tightened his grip. He'd cooperated with their every demand. From here on out, they could talk to his lawyers.

Apparently, taking a man's life had no ill effects on the recently suspended Dancer. An athletic type, who bore an intensity that made Robert uneasy, the detective hid his steely gaze behind mirrored sunglasses. Dressed in a plain navy shirt and jeans, he dressed more casually than his partner, though each displayed their badges and weapons with equal prominence.

Robert detested guns. They served only one purpose.

"Detectives," he said.

The man in the walking cast stepped forward. "We stopped by the administration, but it was locked. Any particular reason why?"

The question was harmless, so Robert answered, "Yesterday was a terrible shock for my staff and me. I insisted we take the day as a time for discernment to pray for Thomas's soul and the young woman he allegedly killed."

Dancer took over where his partner left off. "Allegedly. Interesting you should say that. We have a witness who agrees. She's made an allegation against you."

Robert's heart pounded harder. "*She?* What kind of allegation?"

"We'll need you to come with us," the Hispanic detective said, removing shackles from his belt. "We have a warrant. Bishop Robert Munroe, you're under arrest for the murder of Celeste Lescano, also known as Sister Beatrice of the Convent of Saint Ursula."

Chapter Thirty-One

GROCERIES IN HAND, Eden set the cloth bags on the counter and reached for her ringing cell. On a day that should have been one of the lowest of her life, something positive had occurred. She couldn't wait to tell the caller. "Hi, there," she said.

"Hi, there?" Kevin said in astounded voice. "I've been calling all afternoon, and that's what you have to say to me?'"

"How about I miss you?"

"Why do you sound so chipper? I stopped by your office. Where have you been?"

"At Mesa General," she replied unable to hide her excitement. "Mr. Lucero came out of his coma."

"He called you?"

"His daughter did. She said he practically woke up calling my name, he was so worried. I had no choice but to rush over so he could see I was okay."

"Does he remember the attack?"

"He does. It happened just as you suspected. He saw Thomas trying to break into my unit. When he ran, Mr. Lucero tried to stop him."

"Crazy fool."

"That's Mr. Lucero. What can I say, he thinks he's Clint Eastwood and his cat's General MacArthur. He's moving in with his daughter until his arm heals, and then he's coming back here, with the General, of course."

"Of course."

Eden slipped off her heels, propped her feet on the coffee table and crossed her ankles. "I like your boss. Is he always that quiet?"

"When he has something to say, you know it. Benally obviously believed your story. We made an arrest."

She took a deep breath and exhaled slowly. Her life would never be the same. Not only had she accused a bishop of murder, she'd accused her parents' best friend. This time she *had* checked her voice mail. She was surprised she didn't have more messages, or that one wasn't waiting for her when she got home.

"Did he admit it?"

"No. His overpriced defense lawyer showed up. Sal and I grilled that guy like he was a tuna, and every time Munroe started to speak, his five hundred-dollar-an-hour mouthpiece spoke for him."

She released her hair from its clip and rubbed her right temple. At the word *defense*, there was no mistaking Kevin's animosity. How odd they'd joined forces on this one. "A lot of directives not to answer?"

"How perceptive of you, Counselor. Munroe didn't spend one minute behind bars, and I doubt he ever will. At his arraignment, the judge practically apologized for the inconvenience. For a capital murder case, the amount of bail posted was ridiculous, and naturally the press was all over it."

Angry tears filled Eden's eyes. "I should have known this would happen."

There was a substantial pause in their conversation. Surely Kevin had to realize she was as upset as he was.

"Can I take you to dinner?" he asked.

His mention of food reminded her she had groceries thawing on the counter. "Why don't you come here? Feel like stir fry?"

"Perfect. I've got a couple of stops to make, but I'll be there as soon as I can. How are you doing in the loft?"

"I've been so busy, I haven't had time to think about it."

"I'm here for you, Eden."

Fingers curling around the phone, she wondered if he had any idea how much that simple offer reassured her. All day, even though she'd known he was elsewhere, she'd thought of him, looked for him.

Threatening a well-respected bishop, facing the ire of her family . . . Eden felt like she'd slipped back in time and was facing their alienation all over again.

"When you come over . . .?" Eden asked.

"Yeah?"

"Plan on staying?"

He hesitated, so she backpedaled. "Only if you want to, of course."

"I want to, Eden."

She hung up, feeling a burn on her cheeks. *Plan on staying?* How did those words slip out of her mouth?

Where was the woman who'd thrown herself into creating her mosaic countertops and in painting these walls? Where was the independent thinker who resented not having enough alone time to do exactly as she pleased?

Clearly she was rushing things, and an inner voice warned her to slow down.

But when the downstairs buzzer rang thirty minutes later, she told the invisible busybody to get lost. The fact Kevin had arrived early meant he'd foregone his appointments and was anxious to see her, too.

She'd changed into shorts and a T-shirt, unpacked the groceries, and was just about to add chicken to the wok. The accountants who leased the offices downstairs ordinarily didn't lock up until after seven, though often, like today, they surprised her. Drying her hands on a towel, she left the kitchen to buzz Kevin in. But the man standing on the threshold was hardly someone she'd invited.

"Bishop Munroe." Eden's hand flew to her chest. "What are you doing here? You *cannot* be here. You need to leave. Now."

The charismatic man she'd seen in the cathedral the day before yesterday, or at the wedding reception a week earlier, looked as though Father Time had carved years from his life. Though he was as handsome as ever, he appeared worn, beaten. Eden shrugged off the rush of guilt as her outrage took over. She couldn't worry what effect her accusation had had on him. A killer stood on her doorstep.

"Once the allegation was made, it didn't take long to figure out who was behind it. Only one person would spy on Sister Beatrice." Robert Munroe wore black, the only exception his clerical collar, and spoke with his usual authority. "I'll leave, Eden, but first you must give me a chance to explain."

"Why? So you can persuade me to recant?" She shook her head. "Not in this lifetime. I repeat. You *must* leave."

"Not until you listen to reason."

Her mind flashed back, fueling her impulse to slam the door in his face. "Words I seem to recall you said to Sister Beatrice all those years ago. I'm not about to make the same mistake."

His strength alarmed her as he grabbed the edge of the door. "It happened, Eden, exactly as you said. If you hear me out, I'll talk to the police. If you don't, your accusation ends with the grand jury." His slate-colored eyes bore into hers. "My lawyers tell me if I remain silent, that's where this will die. A young, traumatized witness, all the evidence pointing to Thomas, Celeste's death will go unavenged."

"So why are you here? You've won."

"Because I'm not the total bastard you think I am. Something's not right, and I swear to you at the feet of my Lord, I did not do this terrible thing. I, too, want justice."

Imagining Kevin's outrage, Eden nevertheless did the unthinkable. She stepped back and let a murder suspect into her home. If he was caught, this would be a violation of the bishop's bail. She would face censure from her office, risk her job. Bishop Munroe would be arrested for harassing a witness, and this time his chances for a fair trial would be tainted beyond repair.

Years of discipline and legal training took a backseat. Eden disregarded it all. Lord help her if he'd come simply to kill her and dispose of her testimony. She had to know. When it came to Sister Beatrice, Eden thought with her heart.

She stood away from him near the fireplace, ready to seize the brass poker should she need it. He sat on her sofa and poured out his argument with Sister Beatrice—details Eden had painfully and only recently recalled. Head hung, hands clasped, he didn't break down, but his account of his love affair with her mentor was weighted in sorrow.

His bizarre recollection aligning with hers, he rebutted her questions with alacrity. Second by second, his words thawed her heart, and her hatred of him lessened.

She pictured herself in front of a jury, visualizing how she would convince them of his innocence. Never in a million years would a panel of his peers buy his testimony.

Why, then, did she?

Robert Munroe possessed oratory skills second to none. He made a living plying people with words. He could also be playing her for the world's biggest fool.

When he concluded his tale, he glanced up, eyes swimming. "And now you know as much as I do. All these years, Eden, I swear to you, I thought she was alive."

It choked her to talk, and her resolve buckled.

Her heart tripped as she glanced at her watch. Kevin was due to arrive any second. She needed to think. More importantly, she had to avoid an altercation between them.

"Do you in any way believe me, Eden?"

"I don't know what I believe. It's not like men in your position have a good track record."

A smile lightened his bone-weary face. "While my spiritual side takes umbrage, my mortal side sees your point."

She opened the door and repeated what she'd said earlier, although with less heat, "I'll talk to Kevin. Please, leave."

It turned out she would have no time for quiet contemplation. Kevin stood on her doorstep. "You'll talk to me about what?" His astonished look then transformed into out-and-out fury as he took in the entire scene. "You let him into your *home?*"

"Will you give me a chance to explain?" Her words sounded ridiculous even to her ears.

"Tell it to the judge." He charged into Eden's living room, withdrawing cuffs from his belt. "Robert Munroe, you're under arrest for witness tampering."

Stunned, she watched as he restrained the bishop and called for a squad car to transport him to jail. As Kevin led him away, Eden was like a madwoman on speed, following him down the hallway and stairs, trying to make him stop and listen to what she had to say.

Knowing Kevin was a one-hundred-ninety- pound girder, who would turn only if he allowed it, she grabbed his arm. "Kevin! Would you wait? Please, wait. Three seconds. Give me three seconds."

He stopped on the porch, never once loosening his grip on his silent and unresisting prisoner. "You're on the clock."

She'd never seen Kevin look at anyone with such hostility. "I know what you're thinking, and you're right. I never should have let him in. But I did, and what he says makes sense. When the Angelus chimed, Kevin, I left. I *left*."

"What the hell is an Angelus, and what are you saying?"

"He claims Sister Beatrice woke up. She regained consciousness. The bishop . . . he was afraid to move her, so he went for help." Eden's gaze went from the bishop's to Kevin's pitiless face. "When he returned she was gone. That's why all these years . . . That's why he asked me if I'd seen her or knew where she was. Why would he say that if he'd killed her?"

Her lungs ran out of oxygen at the same time a patrol car swung to the curb. Why was it you could never get a cop in an emergency, but when you didn't want one, he showed up? Her shoulders slumped. "Please, Kevin. Do you see what I mean?"

"The only thing I see is that you're a bleeding heart defense lawyer, and I should have trusted my judgment. You flip decisions like you toss up a coin. He's guilty, he's not." Kevin narrowed a gaze full of vitriol as the patrolman strode up the walk. "I risked my badge for you. No more. This has to go through the system. He's got his own squadron of lawyers. You're not one of them. You're a witness, stay out of it."

Desperate, Eden watched in disbelief as Kevin handed the high-ranking clergyman over to the patrolman. "He's got lawyers schooled in contract law and civil litigation," she argued when Kevin turned to scowl at her again. "He'll need a criminal attorney."

"And it can't and won't be you," Kevin said raising his voice.

"You have to know this isn't a typical case to me," she shouted back. "Ordinarily, I'd go by the book."

"Ordinarily." He scoffed. "What was I thinking? You're just like all the rest. You go by the book only if it serves your purpose. I repeat. I will not break the law for you."

His words, his tone, they struck her like bullets. He hadn't said it, but he had just compared her to his stepfather. This wasn't the man who'd held her, made love to her, talked her down from the ledges. It was as though everything they'd been through meant nothing.

Kevin hadn't held back and neither could she. "All right," she said. "You're so convinced I'm just like him. Maybe I should see for myself."

"What the hell does that mean?"

"It means Bishop Munroe will need the best criminal attorney available. The best one I know to hire is J.T. Garland."

Chapter Thirty-Two

KEVIN STOOD with Sal outside Interrogation as the two watched their commander sit at a table in the interview room with the bishop. Neither Kevin nor Sal said a word. What more was there to say? Kevin had screwed up, and even though his longtime partner had every right to say "I told you so," he seemed to recognize the subject of Eden Moran was taboo.

The best one I know to hire is J.T. Garland.

Damn her. Kevin squeezed his hand into a fist. How could Eden do this to him? After all the lines he'd crossed, the risks he'd taken to see her safe, to help her remember, she'd pointedly ignored the fact that as an accusing witness she could have no contact with a suspect. And then to throw it in his face, referencing his stepdad? Kevin thought she cared about him. Why in the hell hadn't she called the moment Munroe showed up on her doorstep?

Kevin knew why. Because despite his better judgment, she was no better than J.T. These clowns worked the system. If it suited their purpose to respect the law, they did so, but they had absolutely no problem circumventing it.

Benally exited Interrogation, shaking his head. "All right, as much as I've advised against it, Bishop Munroe has waived his right to counsel. I read him his rights *again,* and he knows he's being recorded." The commander focused first on Sal and then Kevin. "If he does a bait and switch on us, end the interview and call his lawyer. We don't need him playing martyr one moment and suing us the next."

Their nods of understanding were followed by Benally saying, "Dancer?"

"Sir?"

"You were right to bring him in."

Kevin nodded.

"But regarding your public defender playing witness, don't let her shenanigans hang you out to dry."

As stress worked its way through Kevin's neck and shoulders, he replied, "I don't plan to, sir."

The commander paused before walking away. "Munroe claims he waived counsel because of her. Crazy. Eden Moran botches our case, then persuades him to come forward? Whose side is this woman on?"

Sal caught Kevin's gaze before entering the room. "I know what side. Do you?"

Inside Interrogation, the bishop recounted what Eden said to the letter. Kevin wasn't surprised that Sal, a practicing Catholic, treated the bishop with respect, while Kevin silently cringed and took a chair.

"You realize why Detective Dancer arrested you, don't you, Bishop Munroe?"

"Certainly."

"That, as a condition of your bail, you were to have no contact with Eden Moran?"

"Yes, and I believe that's precisely what I did."

Smartass, Kevin thought. The guy was as collected as if he was discussing his preference for argyle socks.

"Do you want to go to jail, Bishop?" Sal asked.

Sobering, Munroe said, "I had no choice. My attorneys were hired to quash this. Like you, Detectives, I answer to someone. Cardinal Anderson has instructed me to keep silent and let my legal team handle this."

"So you willfully went against the Cardinal?" Sal frowned. "Why?"

"Because you don't have all the facts. Nor do you have all the evidence to get to the truth of this case without my help."

Kevin leaned forward, scowling. "So, out of the goodness of your heart, you've decided to help us convict you. How thoughtful."

The corners of Munroe's mouth turned upward. "Yes and no. As you can see, I have my human frailties, too. The truth is, I loved Celeste, and was willing to leave the priesthood for her. I'd gone to the church that day to ask her to marry me. When I found her beside herself, I admit I handled it badly and things went horribly wrong. But while I'm not perfect, I categorically deny I'm a killer."

"You claim she woke up," Sal said. "What happened afterward?"

The calm façade he'd been projecting faded a bit. "I was elated and terrified at the same time. I'd always heard not to move an injured person, so I ran for help. It was the lunch hour, and I couldn't find a single member of my staff. I started to go to the school, and then had the sense to return to my office instead and call for an ambulance."

"What do you mean 'had the sense'? Even if it was the lunch hour, if you'd found a teacher on the premises," Kevin argued, "you could have phoned for emergency services from there. Why would you waste valuable time?"

"My staff would have handled the matter with discretion. There were students, lay teachers, possibly parents to contend with. I was thinking of Celeste—her honor, her reputation."

"You weren't worried about *your* reputation?" Kevin lifted a brow.

"Not at that point, most certainly not. The woman I loved was in jeopardy. I told the ambulance to come to the church and ran back to her." He glanced between Kevin and Sal. "When I returned, she was gone." Munroe's face went gray. "I searched for her. I went to the convent and finally to the school. I talked to Sister Joseph Marie. I called the hospital, the bus stations, I drove to the airport, but she'd literally vanished."

Kevin rose from the table. Facing the two-way mirror, where the commander and DA were watching from the other side, Kevin gave a slight you-can't-possibly-buy-this shake of his head. But they were law enforcement professionals, who'd dealt with the best liars in the business. Eden had a history with Munroe. If she had heard this smooth-talking man's sob story, no wonder she was well on her way to recanting.

He turned toward the table, where suspects and prisoners had scratched initials or burned cigarettes into the wood. "Is there anyone who can verify your story, Bishop?"

"The school principal, Sister Joseph Marie," he said. "And possibly my business manager, Marshall Knight."

"He's been with you a while," Kevin commented.

"He has."

"Do you like women, Bishop?" Kevin asked conversationally.

Munroe tilted his head and gave a small smile. "I'm fond of many."

Edging sarcasm into his voice, Kevin said, "I'll bet you are. The night of Meghan Moran's wedding, it was obvious that women are fond of you. How did it feel when one wasn't? When Celeste Lescano rejected you—told you she was leaving?"

The bishop wrapped his hand around a near-empty glass of water and said tonelessly, "I was disappointed, angry."

"If you'd truly planned to ask her to marry you, why not do it the moment you saw her and avoid the whole argument? You're story's not adding up, Bishop Munroe."

Sal glanced up from scribbling his notes. No doubt the Catholic in him disapproved of Kevin's badgering, while the cop inside Sal wondered, too.

"If you knew how many times I wished I'd done just that," the bishop said. "I'd never seen her so angry. All I can say is, she wasn't herself."

Kevin had heard enough of this shit. He stood, forcing the man accustomed to being in charge to look up. "Know what I think?" Kevin said drawing his lips into a sneer. "I think you *were* worried about your reputation. I think you had no intention of marrying her, and that's what your argument was about.

"When she hit her head, maybe she still was alive. That's when you knew you were in trouble, right?"

"No."

Kevin circled the table and raised his voice. "You left, not to call an ambulance but to get a weapon. A knife."

"I did not."

"No? Then maybe it was to find your little buddy Reuben Sharpe. You know, your twisted *pervert friend*, to help you get rid of the body." Kevin glared, placing his hands flat on the table. He wanted to rattle this guy, force his confession so bad he could taste it.

"Is that what happened? Is that why Sharpe was so devoted to you? You kept him around all these years because you owed him. He was, after all, very useful." Firing one question after another, Kevin continued, "Is that why he came after Eden, attacked her neighbor? Did you *order* him to go after her?"

Looking from one cop to the other, the bishop shook his head. "You couldn't be more wrong. Why do you think I'm here talking to you without my lawyers? You've got it *all wrong*."

Sal sent Kevin a silent message that he'd take it from there. Unhappily, Kevin stepped back, folded his arms and leaned against the wall.

"All right, Bishop," Sal said, using a softer tone. "We're listening. Tell us where we're off base."

"I didn't kill Celeste," Munroe said definitively. "And neither did Thomas. I'd stake everything I've ever worked for on that statement. Yes, Thomas snapped, and I take full responsibility for not recognizing he was suffering. I was too consumed with Church business to know what was going through his troubled mind."

Kevin balked. "I'll tell you what was—"

"Kev." Sal sent him a warning glance. "Hear the man out."

The bishop shook his head. "Thomas Timms was not a sex offender. He wasn't before he went to prison and he wasn't afterward."

"I hate to call a man in your profession a liar, Bishop, but Sharpe's prison record says differently," Kevin countered, this time in a more civilized tone. "Did you know about the identity switch?"

For the first time, Munroe flushed. Reaching for the pitcher of ice water on the table, he poured a glass and drained the contents. At last, he said, "Reuben Sharpe became Thomas Timms after I came up with the idea and made the arrangements."

Kevin lowered himself to his chair. With a quick nod, he transferred the interrogation once more to his partner.

The consummate good cop to Kevin's bad, Sal said, "Assuming a false identity and aiding in its commission is a felony, Bishop Munroe. Why would you do that?"

Munroe's powerful persona seemed to fade and his gaze appeared far away. Unsmiling, he answered, "Because Reuben Sharpe deserved a fresh start. Because he spent ten long years in prison for a crime I know he didn't commit."

"You know?" Kevin challenged. "A judge and a jury said differently. How do you *know*?"

The bishop continued to control his emotions and hold his head high. He stared at the blasted wall and then went quiet.

"If he was innocent, why not pursue it through legal channels?" Kevin persisted.

"It wasn't an option."

Kevin scoffed. "You have an answer for everything. Know how much sense this makes?"

"Kev." Sal held up a palm.

Kevin looked from his partner to the clergyman as the two shared a private glance. Suddenly Kevin felt as if somebody had thrown a bag over his head and he'd missed a key piece of information. "I'm into secrets as well as the next guy. Somebody want to include me?"

Sal ignored him and leaned forward. "Bishop Munroe," he said softly. "Did you learn something about Sharpe's innocence in the confessional?"

A look of relief seemed to come over Munroe. He glanced at his watch. "I'd like to talk to my lawyers now. I think we've had a productive session." And then his jaw hardened and his eyes went cold. "If Celeste's killer is still out there, I know where he'll spend his eternity. What I want now is for him to pay for his crime in this life."

Chapter Thirty-Three

TWO WEEKS LATER, remarkably, Eden was still employed by the Albuquerque Public Defender's Office. She sat, drumming her fingers over a lengthy brief, staring at her lovely brick-wall view. She still hadn't heard from Kevin. She'd been reprimanded on her unethical behavior by her managing supervisor, and her mother and father were barely, just barely, speaking to her.

Her Aunt Caroline had sent a funny pick-me-up note every day, and Meghan was due back from her extended honeymoon that evening. Thank God!

She would have loved to know what had gone on during the bishop's interrogation, but it wasn't to be. As a witness to the case, the only way Eden had learned any details was from the *Albuquerque Journal*, blogs, or the whispers around the water cooler. It was inconceivable how people spouted their opinions without firsthand understanding. Some claimed Robert Munroe was a living, breathing saint, while others called him a pedophile of the worst order. Eden had never come close to suggesting that, but when it came to an ordained clergyman, the gossips fed off of other scandals around the world.

One blog, however, called him a womanizer, and on that Eden couldn't be sure. After all, Sister Beatrice had asked him about the numbers of women he'd seduced. She'd obviously suspected something.

The District Attorney, as she'd feared, hadn't bought the bishop's story that someone else had killed Sister Beatrice. And now that Bishop Munroe had come forward in such a nonconventional manner, the DA was touting him as a charlatan who'd invented the sad, moving story to gain sympathy within Albuquerque's predominantly Catholic population.

Eden released her hair out of its twist and knotted it up again, then buried her head in her hands.

Kevin. She'd give anything if he'd call, even swing by to yell at her. It might be a clue that he still gave a damn. As it stood right now, it appeared he was determined to erase her from his life as he would a bad debt.

Kevin was right, the Church would surround the bishop with the best counsel money could buy. Why had she made that remark about Kevin's stepfather? It was thoughtless and beneath her.

Where before she'd been included in the investigation, now she felt ostracized and useless. Although there was plenty of work on her desk, she didn't have a court appearance until tomorrow. It would be prudent to shove all these meandering thoughts from her mind and concentrate on her job while she still had one. But an ability to focus wasn't happening.

She opened her desk drawer and removed a yellow legal pad where she'd written the names the bishop had mentioned during his heartfelt confession. Maybe the DA was right; maybe Munroe was an exceedingly good liar. Maybe he was a womanizer hiding behind his clerical collar, and like Kevin had said, she a bleeding-heart defense lawyer who changed her mind at the flip of a coin.

Depression dragged her down as Eden studied the names. Two in particular made her shudder. These two, she'd learned, didn't live in Albuquerque anymore. Her research said they'd retired to Santa Fe.

Eden tore off the sheet and stuffed it in her briefcase. She was suddenly in the mood for a drive. She could catch up on work tonight. It wasn't like she'd be sleeping.

Chapter Thirty-Four

KEVIN HAD NEVER ended a relationship badly before; maybe that's why he couldn't get Eden out of his head. He stared at the phone on his desk, tempted to stuff it in his drawer. A few times he'd picked it up to call her just to make sure she was okay. Each time he'd come to his senses. Not only were things over between them, but since the interrogation, things had seemed strained between him and Sal. If anyone had told him Sister Beatrice's case would strain *that* relationship, Kevin would have laughed outright. But that's apparently what had happened. Sal had become increasingly withdrawn, and although Kevin knew his partner had his back, an undercurrent of tension existed between them.

So this morning, when Sal waltzed into the division free of his walking cast and tossed Kevin a breakfast burrito, he literally felt the pressure lift from between his shoulder blades.

"You're a free man," Kevin said.

"Damn straight. I feel like I've had a cannon ball removed from around my ankle. I got you one with sausage."

"Thanks." Sal would only eat bacon. He lived on Diet Pepsi, while Kevin refused to go near anything labeled *diet*. Funny what you learned about a guy when you worked side by side for five years.

"You got the list of the delinquents we need to go after?" Sal asked.

Kevin printed off a list of gangbangers who were suspects in the security-guard copper-theft murder and slid it toward his partner. "Everything okay at home?"

"S'right." Sal glanced up from reading the printout. "Why do you ask?"

"You've been quiet."

Sal unwrapped his burrito. "I reckon the Sister Bea thing finally got to me."

"You think the DA is wrong about Munroe?"

"It's not my job to think after a case goes to trial. Let the grand jury sort it out."

"You think I handled the interview wrong?"

"You handled it like a cop." Sal shook his head. "This is my problem. I'll deal."

Kevin glanced around. Fortunately, the nearby desks were vacant, the other detectives in the large division too preoccupied with their own caseloads to be concerned with this conversation. "Out with it. You really think you're onto something with this confessional crap?"

Sal's mouth split into a half-smile. "Yeah. I think I'm onto something with this *confessional crap.*"

Kevin leaned back in his chair and threaded his fingers behind his head. "Munroe has affairs, has no problem taking a dead man's identity and giving it to an ex-con, but then refuses to give us any other details. The DA was spot-on to seek an indictment, in my opinion."

"What can I say? You're entitled to your opinion. But in this instance I gotta go with Munroe."

"Why?"

"It's personal. It goes way back to a faith issue, and you wouldn't understand."

"Sal." Kevin lowered his arms and shifted in his chair. "We don't have to agree, but I gotta know what's in your gut. We're partners. This confessional stuff is new to me. If I screw up, I talk to the big Man direct. I can't imagine how talking to a corrupt priest is going to get me into heaven. So, explain it to me."

Shrugging, Sal took a bite of his burrito. He chewed his meal, seeming to think about it. "It doesn't make a whole lot of sense to you because you weren't raised in the Church, and you never knew Father Benitez and my Uncle Louie."

Kevin held back a smile. This was the *tall-taled* partner he knew and loved. He sat forward, ready to take it all in. "No. Tell me about Father Benitez and Uncle Louie."

"Uncle Louie," Sal said. "Best damned diesel mechanic in the state of New Mexico. On the weekends, he never left the house without a beer in his hand, except for Sunday Mass. And on Friday nights, he and his buddies played poker for hours. One of the regulars—Father Benitez."

Drawn into the story, Kevin enjoyed Sal's animation. Although by the way he waved the burrito around Kevin worried it might land on a neighboring cop's desk as Sal spoke.

"As a kid, I got to watch these old farts tell their lies, smoke their cigarettes, drink their beers, and hurl cuss words I still don't use to this day, and Father Benitez was right along with 'em.

"Then I became a cop," Sal said, sobering. "I was a young rookie, and one day I stopped by and saw Louie pull up to the house in his old beater. He'd been drinking and driving. I told him the next time I saw him with an open container in a vehicle, I was going to do a breathalyzer, and if he was over the limit, I'd run him in."

"Ah, man," Kevin said. "How'd he take that?"

Sal shook his head. "How do you think he took it? He called me a *diablo desgraciado* and told me to get off his property. We didn't speak of it again, but things between us at family functions were tense from then on."

"Did it ever get better?"

"Louie got lung cancer twelve years ago. I went to see him near the end to make amends, tell him I was sorry for my disrespect, even though inwardly I felt I was right for doing my duty. My Aunt Gala was crying and told me Father Benitez was with Louie in the bedroom, hearing his confession and giving him last rites."

Kevin watched his partner's Adam's apple bob up and down. "When Father Benitez came out, he was crying, too, and Louie had passed. He hugged my aunt. By this time, I'd lost it and went out to the front porch. Father Benitez came out and sat by me. Know what he did?"

"What?" Kevin asked.

"He handed me a beer."

Nodding, Kevin shared a small grin with his partner.

"I wondered if my uncle had forgiven me, and Father Benitez said of course he had, it was just one of those things. But that wasn't good enough. I wanted to know if Louie'd mentioned me, specifically, in his confession. And even though I was crying my eyes out, and that priest knew how much it would have relieved my conscience to know, he stood up and said, 'God bless you, Salvatore,'" and walked away.

"Why I tell you this, Kev, is because when it comes to confession, this is probably *the* most serious job these guys do. It's their link to the Almighty, and most won't cross it. That's why I recognized what the bishop was going through the other day. It was like seeing Father Benitez all over again."

Glad that Sal trusted him with such a personal story, Kevin said, "Learn something new every day. And after witnessing what went on between you and the bishop, your explanation makes sense. Appreciate it, partner."

"Any addresses to go with that list of names?"

"Coming right up." Kevin breathed easier. Now that his relationship with Eden was in the tank, the last thing he wanted was to jeopardize his and Sal's special friendship. "I've located some relatives known to harbor these guys."

The two rose in unison.

"Good," Sal said. "Let's see if we can't shake up their world."

Chapter Thirty-Five

SANTA FE. Eden loved New Mexico's capital. The Hispanic and Indian culture, the preservation of its history, the museums, the architecture, the *food*—these facets brought tourism and the wealthy to the city, and nostalgia to Eden's soul. When she was little, before the incident in St. Patrick's, her mother had taken her to Loretto Chapel, with its miraculous staircase built without a single nail. They'd visited the opera, too. Eden had gone home and played the music she'd heard on that grand stage for days afterward.

But now she was here for a less-than-pleasant reason. Her GPS device took her straight to a two-story adobe home in downtown Santa Fe. Several sisters from the Ursuline order had chosen to live out their remaining days here. In particular, Sister Joseph Marie and Sister Agnes.

Behind her sunglasses, Eden raised her eyes to the car's ceiling. If anyone told her she'd be looking up Sister Agnes again, she would have suggested they have their medication adjusted.

But here she was.

At the door, Eden was greeted by the tiniest woman she'd ever seen. Hispanic, with a large wood cross around her miniature neck, the woman's snow white hair brought out the bronze of her skin and the shimmer in her incredible dark eyes. Dressed in a simple white blouse and tan slacks, she greeted Eden with fluttering hands and a thick Hispanic accent. "Ms. Moran, when I told Sister Joseph Marie you were coming, she got so excited. She doesn't get many former students, you know."

The place smelled familiar and homey. In the background, Eden detected the scent of candle wax and simmering pinto beans. "I hope she remembers me," Eden said, entering a small but spotless living room, complete with lacy doilies and religious icons.

"I do, Eden, I do," Sister Joseph Marie said as she entered the room.

Eden turned to catch herself staring. To a third-grader being expelled by the woman, the nun had appeared huge. Today, she had to look down to see the chubby woman with short gray hair and bifocals. Wearing attire much like the sister who'd shown her in, Sister Joseph Marie and her direct blue gaze welcomed Eden. "*Que bonita*, eh, Sister Henry?"

"*Sí*, Joseph," the elfin woman said. "Lemonade, tea, me?" She giggled.

A smile spread over Eden's face at Sister Henry's attempt to be funny and the casual use of their names. "Iced tea would be wonderful, Sister Henry."

A short time later, iced tea in hand, Sister Joseph Marie led Eden to the sofa. Sinking down onto a soft cushion, Eden explained why she'd come and Sister Joseph Marie's happy smile faded.

"We heard about Beatrice a short time ago. So, so sad. We've said novenas for her soul." Sr. Joseph Marie sighed. "I owe you an apology, Eden."

Eden folded both hands around her glass. "How's that, Sister?"

The old nun shook her head. "That first day in my office . . . If I'd known you'd been sneaking away to see Beatrice, I might have made the connection. Instead, when we saw your uniform torn and your knee scraped . . . Well, unfortunately, we jumped to another conclusion. If I'd asked you if you'd been to see Sister Beatrice instead of asking you about strangers, things might have turned out quite differently."

"You can't look backward, Sister," Eden said, even though her throat clogged at the woman's obvious truth. "All we can do is move forward."

"In any case, I'll always blame myself for my lack of perception. I know you loved her, Eden, and I'm so sorry for your loss."

Eden continued to stare. This was the woman she'd thought hated her? After hearing what had gone through her head in those days, Eden could easily forgive her. She could also scratch her off any possible suspect list. Sister Joseph Marie was so *nice*.

Eden showed Sister her badge, explaining her position with the Albuquerque Public Defender's Office. And, because she was already in enough trouble, she emphasized she had no official capacity to come here. It was a long shot that Sister Joseph Marie would confide in her, and an even longer shot that Sister Agnes would even agree to see her.

Still, Eden had to try. "I deal with sensitive information every day, Sister. It's my job to respect confidences. Under any other circumstance, I would never ask you to break yours. I'm asking you and Sister Agnes to talk to me, knowing that anything you tell me, I will give to the police, and to the police only, in an attempt to catch Sister Beatrice's killer."

Studying Eden over her bifocals, Sister Joseph Marie grew thoughtful. "When Henry said you were coming, I knew why. If it will help apprehend Beatrice's killer, I'll answer your questions. As for Agnes," the former principal said, shaking her head, "I'm sorry. I for one feel she would love to see you. But she's not here. Sister's in frail health and requires more care than we can give. She's in Kentucky in a nursing home."

"I see," Eden said, swallowing hard and averting her gaze. She was disappointed, of course, but as uncharitable as it seemed, it was only because she couldn't gauge the old nun's responses in person. Working with the only source she had, Eden asked the woman sitting before her, "Did you know Sister Beatrice well?"

"Well enough," Sister Joseph Marie said. "As her supervisor, I had several sessions with her, and she often sought me for counsel." The old nun's pensive look returned as she folded her hands. "Beatrice felt out of her element at St. Patrick's. Undervalued. Lost. She had grand plans for children, but felt her talents were stymied at the same time."

"Why is that?"

"You know yourself that she loved to teach music, but then we had Sister Agnes."

Eden glanced sideways and bit back sarcasm. "I know."

"I told Beatrice she could teach the new students coming into St. Patrick's. But out of consideration for Agnes, I insisted she stick to the curriculum we'd hired her for. I asked Beatrice that she refrain from, for lack of a better word, *stealing* Agnes's current students away. My compromise was unsuccessful."

Eden knew much of what Sister was saying. Still, it helped to know her memories were correct. "Do you remember Father Munroe?"

The woman didn't miss a beat. "Oh, yes. Father Munroe was a constant around the school and parish. A very good pastor, devoted to his parishioners and the education of our children."

A practiced statement, Eden thought. "I hate to be indelicate, but it's been discovered that Sister Beatrice and Father Munroe had an affair." Eden placed her glass on the coffee table and leaned forward. "I'd like you to think back. Did you ever see any evidence of it?"

"I did. Why do you think I counseled her?" Sister Joseph Marie sighed. "Beatrice fell in love, Eden. She was involved in a terrible struggle between honoring her vows and being with the man she loved."

Eden frowned. "How did you handle that?"

"I don't know what you mean."

Uncertain how to phrase such a sensitive question, particularly to a nun, Eden did her best. "Do you kick them out, send them to their rooms? What do you do when a sister violates her oath?"

"Do we give them twenty lashes, you mean?" A small smile crossed Sister's face, and she shook her head. "We give them guidance, Eden. We're not a prison. And anyone who looked at Beatrice could see she'd make a fine wife and mother. I suggested she pray and let her conscience guide her. I never quite understood the decision she made."

Eden's heart rammed against her rib cage. "What decision?"

"She'd decided to leave the Ursuline order. She felt sure that Father Munroe was having the same struggle, too. Being in his presence was too tempting, she said. Beatrice claimed he'd hinted at marriage, and she felt awful about being the reason he might leave the priesthood. She thought if she returned home to Chicago—that's where she was from—it would give him the time and distance he needed. Help him make a choice he could live with."

Remembering the angry woman in the church, Eden whispered almost to herself, "She felt the same about him. Why do you think she changed her mind?"

"I wondered, too. The night before she left," Sister Joseph Marie said, "Beatrice came to me. She told me she was leaving the order, but that she and Father Munroe were through. She wanted nothing more to do with him, but that she could no longer be a nun."

This was it, the key that would unlock her myriad questions. Eden held her breath as she formed her next question. "Did she say why she'd reached that decision?"

"She would not. And believe me, it wasn't because I didn't press her. Beatrice was devastated. And that, my dear, is as much as I can tell you."

Eden didn't think her spirit could sink any lower. "Did you tell any of this to the police?"

"I'd been on a Mediterranean cruise with my brother and his family, then later traveled to Baton Rouge. The New Mexico winters are hard on these old bones, and I only learned they'd been trying to contact me when I returned."

A nun on a cruise? That visual took getting used to. One thing was clear; these ladies had more fun than a lowly public defender. "Did Sister Beatrice have any enemies?"

Sister Joseph Marie's lips formed the disapproving line that Eden remembered as a child. "I don't think enemy is a good choice of word. A few were displeased with her, yes."

"Because of Sister Agnes?" Eden asked.

"That and, remember, Eden, Beatrice was violating her vows," Sister Joseph Marie reminded her. "A secret such as Beatrice's wasn't easily contained."

Eden tasted bile. "Sister, this is important. I'm looking at all this through, I admit, a jaundiced viewpoint. I remember Sister Agnes and Sister Beatrice arguing. I was there. Was there anyone else who disliked Sister Beatrice as much?"

Sister Joseph Marie hesitated. "No, Eden. As awful as it sounds, Agnes hated her. She was jealous."

At the next question that came to mind, Eden threaded her fingers tightly. "Do you think Sister Agnes could have been capable of murder?"

Straightening, Sister Joseph Marie remained silent for nearly a full minute. Eden was prepared to press her again when she finally said, "I would like to think no. Unfortunately, some of the other sisters and I witnessed the most astounding occurrence between them. One day after school, when we returned to the convent, we found them . . ." Sister Joseph Marie turned the color of the red glass candle on the table beside her. "The other sisters and I were simply shocked—how is it you young people say it?—they *came to blows?*"

Stunned, Eden rose and thanked Sister Joseph Marie for her time.

Unable to glean much more from their conversation, Eden strode out of the Ursuline retirement home, reeling. *They came to blows?* It was imperative that the police interview Sister Joseph Marie and get Sister Agnes's account as well.

Eden slid behind the wheel of the Honda and fastened her seatbelt. If this had been two weeks prior, she knew precisely who she would call. She picked up her cell phone and scrolled down to Kevin's number on her speed dial. What did it say about her that she'd rather hop a plane to Kentucky then press send? Pride was a dangerous thing.

Driving the speed limit never occurred to her. She mashed down on the gas pedal and headed toward Albuquerque.

Chapter Thirty-Six

AFTER HOURS of footwork on the security guard's murder, Sal went to physical therapy and home to rest, while Kevin returned to the District. Fresh out of the cast, Sal's ankle was weak. They'd done a lot of canvassing of rundown neighborhoods, trying to coax gang members' relatives to open up and turn police on to possible suspects.

Deadly business these young men were into. One grandma was so afraid of her grandson she begged Kevin and Sal to go away. But they had managed a couple of leads, so the day held promise. One thing was certain. Conducting a present-day investigation was child's play compared to working a cold case.

Kevin's phone rang the moment he returned to his desk. It was Officer Montano, the cop he'd seen a few minutes earlier working the front desk. "Uh . . . Detective, there's a woman here to see you. Says it's extremely important and insists you're the only person she'll talk to."

"Okay." At the cop's low, secretive voice, Kevin hesitated. "Something buggin' you, Montano?"

"Who me? Nah," he continued in that hushed tone. "Why should I care if a cute little thing with a newborn waltzes in and will only talk to you?"

Rolling his eyes, Kevin said, "Send her up."

A Hispanic woman carrying her pink bundle of joy walked toward him. She looked familiar, and he could have sworn he'd seen her before. He stood, met another detective's waggling eyebrows, and resisted giving him the finger. What? Did they think the kid was his?

He positioned a chair for her to sit next to his desk.

Every dick in the division gave his guest and her package his undivided attention as she headed his way. Even Commander Benally raised his gaze from beyond his glass partition. After she left, guilty or not, Kevin was going to catch holy hell.

He held back a grin for the benefit of his civilian guest. He'd be doing the same if the situation was reversed on any one of them. Cops. They were brothers. Jokers one minute, ready to risk it all the next.

"Ma'am?" Extending his arm toward the chair, he studied her pretty face. Oh yeah, he'd seen her before, but where? Enormous, fear-filled eyes stared back at him. "Detective Dancer, you don't know me."

Not that he'd thought otherwise, but as long as she agreed, that worked fine with him. "How can I help you?"

"A few weeks ago you were at my husband's trial. Do you remember?"

Kevin had sat in only on a couple of trials recently, one in which he was called to testify and . . . He snapped his fingers. "You were sitting next to me at—"

"Manuel Aguirre's trial. He's my husband."

"Ah, got it." Remembering the pregnant woman, Kevin held his arms out indicating the size of her stomach at the time. "You were out to here."

"Yes." She smiled, the fear in her soft brown eyes lessening for a moment.

"Mind if I have a look at her?" Kevin asked.

She held the baby in the crook of her arm and pulled back the blanket.

"She's a doll," he said. "Congratulations."

"Thank you. Her name is Carmen. And my name is Lupe. The day of the trial when you sat by me, I saw your badge. I wondered why you were there." Her expression went from frightened to pleading. "Manuel. He was innocent."

Yeah, yeah, yeah. As if he needed a reminder of Eden right now. How could he ever forget her staunch defense of Aguirre, her nervous tendency to play with her hair, the antic with the tattoo, and the beauty and passion that had attracted him to her in the first place? Hell. Why did Aguirre's wife have to show up now? Had she brought along a shaker of salt to pour in his wounds, too?

"A jury agreed, ma'am. How can I help you?"

Her gaze darted around the room. She whispered, "Is it safe to talk?"

"It's safe, Lupe. But if you like, we could go into an interview room for privacy."

Eyes widening, she shook her head no. "Just keep my secret, *please*."

"I would if I knew it. Are you and Manuel having problems?"

"No, no." She pulled at one of the tassels of the baby blanket. "But I think Manny, while doing his painting jobs, may have given the gang members who hurt that man a way to commit those burglaries . . . without knowing it."

Kevin ground his teeth. Sure he had. And here Eden had gotten the guy off scot free. Schooling his expression, he encouraged the young mom to continue. "How could he not know, Lupe?"

"Yesterday afternoon when I got home, he was still at work. Manuel, his work comes in spurts so he works long hours whenever he can. My mother, she was babysitting while I was at the doctor, so I didn't think anything of it when I see my brother's car out front. It's just my mom raising my brother and sisters. Anyway, my brother . . ." Lupe closed her eyes. "He doesn't listen to nobody no more. He's in a gang."

At the all-too-familiar story, Kevin nodded. Gangs were epidemic among Albuquerque's young male population.

"When I get inside my house, my mother, she's upset, you know? My brother has brought his *boys* with him." Lupe flashed an angry gaze. "He calls them his boys. They are upstairs in Manny's and my bedroom. I run upstairs. There are four of them. Such disrespect. Touching everything, lying on our bed. And then I find out what they're really there for. My brother is reading off my husband's painting jobs from the calendar and one of them is writing it down."

For the first time, Kevin picked up a pen. Damn, the woman was right. Manuel hadn't cased the houses. He'd simply inadvertently given the bad guys the means, motive and opportunity.

"When I yell at them to get out of my bedroom, my brother, he shoves me. He tells me if I love my baby, I will keep my mouth shut." Lupe shuddered as she hugged Carmen close. "Mr. Dancer, if Manny finds out my brother threatened our baby, this time he will go to jail, and this time he will be guilty." Chewing her bottom lip, Lupe appeared to be doing her damndest not to cry.

"Does your husband know you're here?"

She shook her head rapidly. "Manny would be so angry. He's offered to hire my brother, but he never shows up."

"You saw my badge, but how did you know my name, and why ask for me?"

"Ms. Moran, she brought me a gift when Carmen was born." Lupe smiled and her cheeks turned the shade of the baby blanket. "I saw the two of you together the day of the trial. You looked so cute together, so I asked about you. She told me you were a cop. She thought you were a good one." Lupe's smile faded. "In my neighborhood, you don't run into many good cops."

Kevin nodded. "I appreciate you taking this risk to come see me, Lupe. I admit I'm as guilty as the next cop of having a closed mind. You taught me something here today."

As Lupe smiled back at him, Kevin realized he should probably thank Eden for showing such faith in him, too. If he ever ran into her again, he would. Suddenly he found the idea of never seeing her again dismal. He shook away the intrusive thought and got back to business. Here came the hard part—asking Lupe if she'd be willing to testify against a family member. "What gang is your brother in?"

She paused, seeming to recognize the inherent risk she was taking. She studied her daughter's small face. "He's a member of the *Ciclónes*."

A ray of sunshine peeked out from this gloomy tale. The *Ciclónes* were one of the gangs accused in the security guard's murder. "And your brother's name?"

Glancing around the room, she whispered, "Richito Florez. His boys call him Richie."

Kevin suppressed his excitement at this gift of a witness. He didn't even have to refer to the computer printout. His small world just got smaller. Today, when any of the frightened neighbors *would* talk to police, Florez headed the list of suspects.

"I can help you, Lupe. But I need you to come forward. And to do that we'll have to keep you, Manuel and your daughter safe. Will you talk to my boss?"

"You can keep us safe? You swear?"

"The only way I can do that is if I get your brother and his gang off the street. I know how painful this is for you." Kevin paused and tried for a reassuring smile. "How about it? Will you talk to my commander?"

She studied her infant daughter's face again and returned a swift nod.

By seven that night, Lupe, Manuel and the baby had been transferred to a safe house, and Sal had returned to work. A warrant was underway, and cops, SWAT and an arrest plan were in formation.

Lupe Aguirre had guts. *You can keep us safe? You swear?* What an enormous task to have on Kevin's conscience.

Anytime Kevin's team risked their necks to go into a gang-infested neighborhood, adrenaline spread through his body. Tonight's operation was no different. Antsy, he didn't even mind the additional weight of the Kevlar vest as he paced the squad room, listening to his commander's and sergeant's directives.

"My client is innocent," Eden had said. It hadn't been the first time he'd been forced to recognize the woman had amazing instincts. He ordered Eden out of his head and tuned back in to his sergeant.

Chapter Thirty-Seven

AFTER LEAVING urgent voice mails on Kevin's voice mail with no response, Eden swung by her office. Hours of work awaited her, thanks to her trip to Santa Fe. *Might as well make up for lost time.* Her logical side understood he'd ended things between them. Even so, her emotional side wondered how a man could go from caring one minute to loathing the next.

Had her actions been so wrong?

Really Eden, you have to ask? He'd been nothing but supportive of her, ignoring protocol, working with her to recall her past. He'd even saved her life with great risk to his career. What had she expected him to do when he'd discovered she let the murder suspect into her home—one *she'd* accused in the first place? Shrug his shoulders and say, "Oh, well, Eden, that's okay?"

A major revelation hit her at the same time she pulled into her office parking space. She'd pushed him too far with her remark about hiring his stepfather. That biting comment had sent Kevin over the edge.

Whatever he thought of her, she had it coming and more. She switched off the ignition. Eden had no choice but to respect his decision not to see her, but she'd been clear in her voice mails that she'd learned further information about Sister Beatrice. By tomorrow, if Eden hadn't heard from him, she'd take the information she'd learned from Sister Joseph Marie to his commander. She took the stairs instead of the elevator. Knowing how Kevin felt about her hurt. Badly. She wanted to hate him right back. She couldn't. She'd fallen in love with him.

KEVIN TOSSED his keys on the unvarnished table near the door, emptied his pockets, and removed his shoulder holster and gun, his badge and his cell. Depositing them in the left-hand drawer, he slumped in fatigue. The clock read almost eleven. After taking Richito Florez and two of his gang members into custody, it hadn't taken much to finagle Florez into boasting he'd been the one to pull the trigger on the security guard.

Now the coward who'd terrorized his sister and family was behind bars and bawling for his lawyer.

Lupe and her family were safe. *For now.*

Through it all, Kevin had thought of Eden and her unflappable belief in her client. While if it had been Kevin on that jury, Manuel Aguirre would have been serving time, innocent of the charges.

Ready to turn in and block out his narrow-minded stupidity, he saw that his phone log contained messages. At both recognizable numbers in such close proximity, his gut twisted. Had she done it? Hired his stepdad to represent Munroe? Was J.T. calling to gloat? Eden calling to justify her decision? She might have impeccable instincts, but involving J.T. in Kevin's case was something he would never be able to put aside.

Still, he was through trying to read minds. What's more, he owed his mother a return phone call. He pressed resend to his stepdad's number, ready to voice violent opposition if he'd decided to represent Munroe.

Over the years, their hostility for each other had been whittled away to forced civility.

"Hey, J.T.," Kevin said. "I saw that you called. It's kind of late so I worried."

"That makes two of us," Garland snapped. "This suspension business—you left your Mother and me hanging."

He had. Kevin had left them with a terse *everything's under control.* "Sorry about that. It's been crazy around here," he said. "I've been returned to active duty, but the investigation's ongoing."

"You know," Kevin's stepfather said, "if you run into legal problems, I'm here for you, don't you?"

"You'd represent a *cop*?"

There was dead silence before J.T. replied, "I'd be honored to represent my *son*." Another moment passed before J.T. added, "It occurred to me that while we'll never see eye to eye on your chosen profession, that doesn't mean I'm not proud of you."

Kevin swallowed hard, the events of the past warring with this frank admission.

"I said some things I'll regret forever," J.T. said. "It was my dream for you and Josh to come into the practice and work alongside me. When he died in that rollover, wrong or right, I transferred that ambition to you." Garland let out a sigh. "And, yeah, I still blame the cops. When you wanted to go into law enforcement like Will, my disappointment got the better of me."

The cell shook in Kevin's hand. The night he'd been accepted into the academy, J.T. had called William Dancer, Kevin's biological father, a blue collar lackey, not worthy of Kevin's mother. Then he'd proceeded to call Kevin an ungrateful lout. He'd made the callous remarks at the dinner table in front of Kevin's mom and his younger brothers. His brother Evan, barely in his teens at the time, had gotten into the melee. Not having a clue what he was talking about, he'd sided with Garland.

Kevin's mom had been devastated as she'd tried to calm both sides of her blended family.

Kevin had stormed out of the house that night, from then on the proverbial outsider.

That real-life nightmare had happened several years ago, but it still felt like yesterday. J.T. had lost his son, and he had made sure something in Kevin died as well. "My dad was a good man, J.T. He made a difference. He saved lives."

"You don't think I know that? Just look at his son."

It choked Kevin to talk, and J.T., always the better with words, went on, "I have no doubt that you're a good cop, but you'd have made an outstanding lawyer. Evan and Andy are salivating over that corner office, but as the eldest, I've reserved it for you. Just say the word."

For the first time in years, Kevin smiled at a conversation he was having with his stepfather. "As hard as that is to turn down, I'm good."

J.T.'s voice cracked. "Josh would have made a great lawyer, don't you think, Kevin?"

Lowering his head, Kevin pinched the bridge of his nose. He missed his best friend and brother, but J.T. missed his son. J.T. had eased Kevin's inner turmoil, how could he not try to ease some of his pain? "Josh would have made a *helluva* lawyer, Dad."

Chapter Thirty-Eight

EDEN STAYED so late at the Public Defender's Office, she outlasted the janitor. She familiarized herself with her cases scheduled for the next-day's court docket, and when she thought she might be able to sleep, she drove to the loft. She was adapting to being alone again. Or maybe it was because Thomas was dead, Mr. Lucero was alive, and she too tired to think about the last horrific few weeks.

At the time she'd purchased the loft, she hadn't considered that the unattached carport in the back of the building would be a drawback. Now, however, she was hyperaware of the distance she had to walk and the late night hour. Parking next to Mr. Lucero's ancient Impala, she removed her pepper spray and keys and walked fast, nearly stumbling when she caught sight of the silhouette near her front door.

With her heart thudding out of her chest, she fixed disbelieving eyes on him and pressed a hand to her mouth.

Kevin.

He sat under the porch light with his back propped against the side of the building, arms crossed and long legs in front of him.

Talk about a case of déjà vu. Blowing out a breath of relief, she moved quietly up the walk, and just as she'd done before, sat on the step below him. What are you doing here, Kevin?"

"Waiting for you." He opened his eyes. "Don't you ever come home? Where have you been?"

"At work."

"That far behind?"

"Something like that." She forced a smile.

He rose from the steps and stared down at her. Extending his hand, he pulled her up to meet him. "I want to talk to you."

She met his gaze and swallowed hard. Oh, God. She wanted that, too. But he was probably here because of the mysterious voice mails she'd left. She could tell him about Sister Joseph Marie's statement later. Imagining the verbal battle about to take place, she went on the defensive. "I want you to know, Kevin, I understand your anger. I should have never invited the Bishop in. No matter what, I should have insisted he talk to you. And I never would have called your stepdad. *Never.* To make that insensitive remark . . ." She shook her head. "Who knows why I said it? Call it desperation, or a stupid attempt at vengeance. But knowing how you feel about him, I simply wouldn't have—"

"I know."

A first for Eden, words failed her. At last she replied with, "What do you mean, you *know*?"

"I know you were spouting off, and you wouldn't have called him."

"How do you know?"

His smile slid into that half grin she thought she might never see again. Tracing a finger over her cheek, he said, "I know because when I talked to J.T. tonight, he said he'd never heard of you."

"Well." Eden folded her arms. "How flattering is that?"

"While it might be bad for your ego, Counselor, it was the best news I'd heard in a long time."

"You asked if I'd called him about the bishop?"

"I did. But not before we hashed out a few other things. We came to an understanding tonight."

"Meaning?"

"It means that while we despise each other's career choices, we're still family."

Family. What a nice sounding word. "That's great, Kevin. I'm happy for you." And she was, truly. But something down deep in her was jealous that he was on the verge of recovering something that had gone missing in her life. "Mind if I ask where this leaves us?"

"I thought that if I could come to a truce with the likes of J.T. Garland, maybe there was hope for you and me."

She wanted that so much her chest ached. "I'm open to terms," she said softly.

He leaned forward and stared into her eyes. "How about I agree not to practice law and you agree not to interfere in police business?"

"And if my business and yours overlap, which they're bound to?"

"Then we talk." He nearly growled the words. "We decide how to handle it. Together."

Still on tenuous ground with him, she held back a smile. His compromise sounded ideal. Still, if things worked out between them, there would be times their careers would be in direct opposition to each other's. It was inevitable, and he had to know it. He arrested the bad guys. She defended their right to due process. But as she studied Kevin's set jaw and jutting chin, his dimples belied the harsh look he tried to convey. "All I can promise is to do my best. Can you live with that?"

"If I ask to come upstairs with you, will you put away the pepper spray?"

"Will you put away the gun?"

"What if I begged and said I missed you?"

Eden's heart gave a little tug as he bent his head to kiss her. When they pulled apart, he took her keys and opened the building's front door.

"So when you told Garland a bishop had been accused of murder," she said. "Did you inadvertently pique his interest?"

"He'd already read the papers. He was definitely interested, but lucky for me, he's wrapped up in other things." Kevin held the door for her as she entered the tiny foyer and moved toward the stairs. "He's representing Senator Ashworth in his latest call-girl scandal."

Eden gasped. "Another one?"

"What can I say? J.T. got him off twice. Why not go for a hat trick?"

"Incredible," she said, laughing. "He really does go for the highest bidder. So, knowing you, I suppose you think the Senator's guilty?"

Kevin shook his head at her. "Don't start, Moran."

She brought Kevin's head down for another kiss. Then, winking at him, she said, "I'm glad we declared a truce."

"Back atcha." He undid the top button of her blouse, then the next one. "You know, daylight's not too far away."

"I know," Eden said. "What do you say we wait up for it?"

Chapter Thirty-Nine

SEVERAL DAYS AFTER the police invaded the diocese with search warrants, Janice hid the latest *Albuquerque Journal* from the Bishop. She couldn't bear for him to see the cruel words. The phone calls from major networks and national syndications were all demanding comments. Some had the gall to show up uninvited and were stationed with cameras beyond the property line. The job she loved, the mission she'd respected, had been compromised. Imagine anyone thinking that Robert Munroe could stab a woman to death.

Marshall stormed into her office and shut the door, to her horror, carrying another newspaper. "Have you seen this?" He tossed *The Los Angeles Times* on her desk. She had no time to worry about where he'd gotten it, though. The headline glared up at her.

Bishop accused of ancient murder.

"I've read a similar version, she replied, growing lightheaded.

"Well? Any suggestions?"

"Besides doing what the cardinal has already told us to do?" she asked icily.

Marshall strode to the window and shoved his hands into the pockets of his cheap polyester pants. "The police interviewed me, you know."

Janice felt her heart jolt. Evidently, Detective Raez *had* listened when she'd mentioned his longstanding relationship with the bishop. Marshall couldn't kill anybody. He had too much fun tormenting people while they were alive. But at the thought of Detective Raez making Marshall's life difficult, she wanted to hiss, 'Yes!'" Instead, she said, "What would they want with you?"

"I remember that day," he said, snidely. "I was there. The school furnace was on the fritz, and Thomas and I had spent the morning trying to fix it. Damn thing was costing the parish a fortune. The way Tom could fix anything back then was almost magical. Who knew he'd turn into such a loon?"

Janice wanted to toss out an insulting barb about compassion, but if his comments would protect the bishop, she would listen to the business manager *ad nauseum*. "How on earth can you be sure it was *that* day?"

"I remember because Bob rushed back from his retreat. He'd said he had an emergency. I offered to handle it, but he said he had it under control."

It irked her no end when he called the bishop Bob—particularly when he never did so to the bishop's face. Janice narrowed her gaze. Her stomach roiled as she brought her hand to her throat. "Did you see anyone else near the church that day?"

"I might have," he said, like a kid withholding a juicy secret from a playmate. "It's still a bit fuzzy. But I remember because Bob was upset . . . he kept taking off without explanation." Marshall turned from the window and stared at her. "But don't worry, I have an excellent memory. It'll come back to me."

Chapter Forty

KEVIN DISCONNECTED a call from Eden and glanced across his desk to see Sal frowning.

"What was that all about?" he asked.

Kevin cleared his throat and tried to get back to the case file. "That was Eden."

"I gathered. So what's making you nervous?"

"Who said I was nervous?"

Sal returned one of those looks he gave a suspect after cornering him during an interview. "You asked for an address. I'd guess right about now, she wants you to meet her parents, doesn't she?"

"I've already met her parents. Now she wants me to have dinner with them—hence the address."

"Ah," Sal said, dragging it out.

"What 'Ah'?" Kevin held out his hands.

"Just what it says, 'ah.' Dinner with the parents. It means Eden's got plans for you. She's bringing you in for the test run."

Leaning back in his chair, Kevin rolled his eyes. "In this case, it's more like she wants me along for protection."

"Why would she need protection?"

"It's a command performance. Her sister and new husband will be there. Her mother wants to do the family thing."

Sal nodded and replied a simple, "Ah."

Kevin glared at the man across from him and twisted his mouth into a thin line.

"You gonna tell her about Kentucky?" Sal asked.

Kentucky. There his partner went being a mind reader again. Kevin had already booked his flight. After he and Eden finally went to bed, their pillow talk had surrounded—what else?—Sister Beatrice. Eden had told him about her visit with her former elementary school principal, and the alleged altercation between the dead nun and the school's music teacher. He'd taken the information to Commander Benally, who, because of the soon-to-convene grand jury, had ordered the partners to check it out. Kevin had drawn the shorter straw, hence the trip to Kentucky.

"You don't think I should tell her?" he asked.

"She took it upon herself to go see her old principal. What's to keep her from booking a flight to see Sister Agnes?"

"She already admitted she screwed up with the bishop. I can't stop her from talking to people she knows, but I can tell her that Sister Agnes, like Munroe, is now part of the official investigation. I want to interview this woman without Eden there."

"Eden doesn't like her?"

Kevin shook his head. "Let's just say I don't see Eden crossing the street to save the old woman from being hit by a bus. She has a new suspect in Sister Beatrice's murder."

Sal lowered his head and started reading again.

"That's crazy, right?" Kevin asked.

Sal didn't look up.

"Sal?" Kevin said.

His partner shrugged.

Chapter Forty-One

KEVIN KISSED Eden at the front door of her parents' high desert estate and thought about the similarities they shared with his own folks. They had money and weren't afraid to show it. No doubt, they'd bought the exclusive property for its views. Golden light sparkled from floor-to-ceiling windows, decorative cement encased a long circular driveway, and wrought iron fencing surrounded the property's Southwestern terrain.

Eden slid her arm through his and sent him a grateful look. "Thank you."

"Is Meg here?" Kevin asked.

"Not yet." Eden's voice held a hint of desperation. "I was the first to arrive." She led him into a foyer filled with as many stylish amenities as the outside. Not many in his current circle of friends displayed a rock waterfall in their entryway.

Edward Moran emerged from the back of the house, drink in hand. "Kevin. The man of the hour. Glad you could make it." Eden's father gripped his hand. "We haven't had a chance to thank you in person for all you've done for our daughter."

"I'm just glad I was there." Kevin paused, looking first to Eden and then to her old man. He might not have a better opportunity, so he asked, "Do you remember Thomas Timms, sir?"

"Can't say that I ever met him, no. Joanna seems to remember him, though. But then she was around that school way more than I was back then." Edward slapped him on the back. "Let's you and I go into the den."

Kevin walked beside Eden's dad while she winked and then did one of the fastest disappearing acts he'd ever seen in his life.

The den, as Edward had called it, was more of a grand-sized media room with leather sectionals throughout, a surround sound system, two big screen TVs and wall-to-wall bookshelves. The outside led to an ornately designed flagstone patio, complete with a pitted fireplace and a lagoon-style swimming pool.

"Beautiful place," Kevin said, stopping at several black-and-white photos of Eden and Meghan, as well as an oil portrait of Edward and Joanna. This portrait looks recent," Kevin added.

"Thirtieth wedding anniversary," Edward explained.

"Matrimonial bliss, right, Edward?" Joanna entered the room. "Detective Dancer," she said coolly. "My daughter's hero."

Like her husband had, she clasped Kevin's hand. Her smile appeared painted on, as though she'd had one too many Botox injections. Kevin tried to look past Eden's accounts of her mother to form his own impressions. But even if Eden hadn't influenced him, he most likely would have labeled Joanna one icy bitch.

Eden came into the room carrying two beers. Handing one to Kevin, she told the group, "Meg and Steve are on their way."

Dinner went well enough. It was as though everyone had reached an unsaid arrangement to stick to neutral topics. The honeymooners regaled the group with their island adventures, while Edward controlled the remainder of the evening with stories of his antique automobile collection. Finally, Eden hijacked the conversation by talking of Kevin's love affair with hot air balloons, and soon Meg and Steve were begging Kevin to take them all up.

After dessert, Edward invited Kevin to see his car collection, an invitation he jumped at.

A separate garage housed five classic black Model Ts, all built before the 1920s. Kevin estimated Edward had a fortune, not only in the cars, but in the slate floor, track lighting and security alone. The wealthy CPA picked up a chamois and polished a bumper.

"I appreciate you not bringing up the bishop in front of my wife," Edward said without preamble.

"Not a problem," Kevin replied. "Although you both should know you'll most likely go before the grand jury at some point."

He nodded. "She sees Robert through some pretty rosy glasses, I must admit."

"And you, Mr. Moran?"

"Call me Ed. I see Robert as a man. A decent one, but he's just a man."

"One who's capable of murder?"

A muscle in Edward's jaw jumped. "I think anyone is capable of murder if driven far enough."

"Were you surprised to learn Eden was a witness in the church all those years ago?"

He looked up. "Shocked. Shocked! But, you know, now that we do, so much makes sense. Her acting out, her refusal to go to Mass. Our good little girl turning into the very devil. Running away, bed wetting, disrupting class. Kevin, you have no idea how difficult she was."

Fighting the urge to call Eden's father a fucking idiot, he said, "And you never sought therapy for her?"

"Joanna sought help through the Church. Discipline and prayer proved about as effective as swatting a B-1 fighter with a newspaper." Edward clenched his jaw and rubbed harder on the bumper. "I suppose I wasn't much of a father. I had a company to run and Joanna was already a firm disciplinarian. I thought . . ." He shook his head. "I thought she controlled it about as well as anyone could."

"You were okay with letting your wife ship off your daughter to live with her sister?"

Edward tossed the cloth to a workbench and nailed Kevin with a hard gaze. "You look like a man who came from a pretty smooth home life. I suggest you try not to judge us unless you've been there."

Maybe he should pull up a chair and compare notes. "Just trying to get the facts. Eden says that Sister Beatrice accused Robert Munroe of affairs. Any comment?"

Perhaps in a sign that the conversation was over, Eden's father walked to the security pad. He started to key in the alarm code, then hesitated. Turning to Kevin, he said, "Now that the bishop's been accused, I'm sure the police will leave no stone unturned." He sighed. "I might as well get this over with and tell you, rather than explain it to a stranger who might not be as discreet. I told you the truth when I said we shipped Eden off to Caroline because our little girl had become incorrigible. But the main reason was because Joanna and I had separated."

Kevin didn't even inhale while waiting for Edward to explain. When he failed to expound, Kevin asked, "Any particular reason why?"

"Lord, I wished I'd kept my mouth shut back then. I was a jealous fool. But, remember, I thought Joanna and I were over. I told my wife I was through competing with Robert Munroe."

HOLDING HANDS with Kevin, Eden walked him to his Jeep. "Well, that went better than I expected."

"I thought so, too. Meg plays a mean piano," Kevin said.

"She does."

Leaning against his vehicle, he brought Eden with him. "I'd love to hear you play sometime."

"Taking sides with my mom?"

"Did I say a word when she asked?"

"That part of my life is over, Kevin. I don't play anymore. Please don't pressure me."

He tilted her chin upward. "Wouldn't think of it. I'm satisfied with what I've got."

"Are you?"

He loved the catch in her voice. Smiling, down at her, he said, "I am."

"Will I see you tomorrow?"

He kissed her lightly and played with a strand of her hair. "I'm going out of town for the day."

"Really? Where?"

Kevin stared into her eyes and debated lying. But Eden Moran had been hoodwinked enough in life, so he said, "I'm going to Kentucky, Eden. Benally wants me to talk to Sister Agnes."

"I see."

Did she? Fully? Her voice was so devoid of emotion, it scared him. "You know I have to go alone, right?"

"Don't worry," she said, frowning. "I have no plans to stow away in your suitcase."

He blew out a heavy breath. "I wouldn't put it past you."

She stepped away from him with a worried glance. "What do you plan to say to her?"

After everything they'd been through, it still amazed him how much she wanted to do his job. "Gee, Eden, I don't know. I'll think of something."

She ignored his sarcasm, undeterred. "Are you going to accuse her of murder?"

"Maybe not in those words," he said, using a little more heat than he'd intended. "But I am going to ask her why she and Sister Beatrice fought with one another."

"*Okay.*"

"What do you mean, okay?"

She lifted her hands. "I just wanted to make sure you brought it up."

"Maybe I *should* put you in my suitcase. You obviously don't trust me."

Stepping close again, Eden wrapped her arms around his waist and leaned her head against his chest. "I trust you. I just wish I could be there to see her mean, rotten, evil face."

"*Eden.*"

"Sorry," she muttered against him. "Will you call me the minute you're through?"

"I'll do better than that." The interview he'd been anticipating couldn't be over soon enough. "When I'm done, I'll come straight to your doorstep." He kissed her long and deep.

Chapter Forty-Two

FROM EVERY indication since he'd arrived at Our Lady of the Bluegrass Retirement Home, Sister Agnes was going to be a pain in the ass. Kevin glanced at his watch and paced the wood floor of a former living room converted to a reception area. Everything had gone like clockwork until he'd arrived. His five-hour flight had landed early, a taxi had swung to the curb the second he stepped out of Louisville's International concourse, and the humidity had been less than he'd remembered. The whole trip had been perfect. Blue skies, an abundance of green vegetation, light traffic. Perfect.

Even the administrator, Danielle Kennedy, had greeted him with businesslike efficiency when he showed his badge and confirmed he'd been the Albuquerque cop who'd contacted her yesterday. But that was twenty minutes ago, and now he needed to call out a search party to locate Ms. Kennedy.

An old-timer tottered by with help from his walker. "Nice day for a run, don't you think?" The sweatband wrapped around his forehead gave Kevin a moment's pause, until a ponytailed brunette—garbed in workout gear, and clearly an actual runner—appeared from the hallway. She smiled at Kevin and then to the resident said, "Ready, Father?"

The ancient athlete turned his walker in her direction. "Let's do it. Get that door for me, will ya?"

Then, like everyone else in the place, they left Kevin alone.

Danielle finally reappeared from wherever she'd been hiding. "Detective Dancer. I'm so sorry. Who knew that Sister Agnes receiving guests would be such a production?" She shook her head. "She refuses to have a man in her bedroom, so I had to arrange for a member of my staff to bring her to my office."

The three-hour window to catch the first flight home was rapidly closing. Kevin added inanely, "Can't be too careful, I guess."

"Or paranoid," the attractive middle-aged blonde responded. "I even told Sister I'd stay in the room."

"It's fine. I'm looking forward to meeting her."

He might have spoken too soon. Just then, an orderly rolled a wheelchair into the room containing a black and white form. The form—lump for lack of a better word—sat clutching a Bible to her breast.

He attempted to smile, even as he searched for a face underneath her veil. But when she raised her head, his smile froze in place. It wasn't that she was grotesque, exactly, but he sure wouldn't be asking for references to her dentist.

Kevin offered her his hand and gagged on the scent of mothballs.

"Sister Agnes, I'm Detective Dancer from the Albuquerque Police Department. I appreciate you taking time to see me. Did Ms. Kennedy tell you why I'm here?"

Staring up at him through amazingly clear eyes and, displaying her George Washington-like wooden teeth, she said, "Well, you didn't leave me much choice, did you? What would the cops want with me?"

"Information, ma'am. Mind if I sit down?"

She pointed to a chair near Danielle's desk. It was a good five feet across the room. "You may sit over there."

He picked up the chair and brought it close, much to her pinched-face displeasure. "So neither of us has to yell," he said, removing pad and pen from his shirt pocket. "I understand we have something in common. We've both lived in Albuquerque. I've lived there for around ten years now. How about you?"

She watched him warily. "Forty."

"So you're familiar with St. Patrick's School?"

"I'm old, not senile."

Danielle Kennedy, who stood by the door, raised her eyes to the ceiling.

"I'll treat you with respect," Kevin said. "But I'll ask you to do the same for me, Sister. Now, about St. Patrick's?"

"Of course, I remember St. Patrick's," she said with a sneer.

"One of your fellow sisters died around the same time you were there. Sister Beatrice, do you remember her?"

The old woman stiffened. "We read the papers, watch TV. I know about the bishop's arrest and the trouble he's in."

"Good. Then we should be able to get down to business. Bishop Munroe has admitted that he had an affair with Sister Beatrice. Does that surprise you?"

"When you get to be as old as me, you'll find nothing surprises you anymore. You wasted a trip, Detective. I'm not going to speak ill of the bishop, and where I come from, we don't speak ill of the dead."

Summoning patience, Kevin lowered his head. Where he came from, you weren't disrespectful to little old ladies, particularly ones as old as Sister Agnes. But in her case, he might make an exception. Further, he was determined not to have made this trip for nothing.

"Sister, have you ever heard the term 'obstruction of justice'?"

"I've heard of it."

"I'm involved in a capital murder case, and my flight leaves at five o'clock. That gives you less than three hours to talk to me. In one of the biggest bluffs of his career, Kevin added, "If you don't, I'm going to read you your rights and personally escort you to the Louisville Police Station."

Her teeth clacked as she turned an outraged face to Danielle. "Will you listen to this disrespectful young pup? I'm a member of the order—"

"Sister Agnes." Danielle Kennedy stepped away from the door and approached the old nun's wheelchair. "I want my office back. I have work to do. I've catered to you all I plan to today, helping you get your habit out of that trunk and then ironing it. The detective needs answers. And I'm here to tell you that if you don't help him, and he *does* take you to jail, I'm going to take my sweet time about bailing you out. Now, what's it going to be?"

Outnumbered, the old nun glared between the two. "Your behavior is shameful. Both of you. What do you want to know?"

"When you learned that Bishop Munroe was accused of Sister Beatrice's murder, did that surprise you?"

"No."

"Why not?"

She lifted an impatient hand. "Because by the time Beatrice seduced him, there was talk he was about to be made monsignor. He was not going to abandon that prestigious honor or leave the Church for a woman. Quite frankly, with so many willing women, he didn't have to. As I said before, *Beatrice seduced him.*"

Sister Agnes reminded Kevin of a chained dog fighting to break its leash. She wanted to talk, it was just a matter of time. He'd heard the whispered suspicions about the bishop before. The point was, if Robert Munroe was innocent, why were there so many? "Do you have any proof of this, Sister?"

"You want proof? I met the other woman."

Her impulse to talk must've been greater than her need to act wounded.

"Want to tell me about it?" he asked.

The leash finally snapped. "Bishop Munroe might have been a priest, but women fell all over him. He was a ladies' man. If you think Beatrice was the only one, you're *crazy.*"

"Why do you say that?"

"Father Munroe and Sister Beatrice played a mean-spirited trick on me. Ruined the music program I'd worked months on. After that, I was out to prove to all those who thought she hung the moon that she was exactly what I thought she was—a faithless little liar. The day after my failed recital, I followed them past the school grounds. And what do you know? I wasn't the only one watching."

The hair rose on the back of his arms. "Who else was there, Sister?"

"Some woman. Pretty little thing, too. Standing off to one side, behind an old cottonwood. She wasn't happy I'd intruded. Until I told her I wasn't fond of the pair she was watching either. That's when she told me she was in love with Robert Munroe, and she couldn't believe what she was seeing."

"I don't understand," Kevin said. "What was she witnessing? A man and a woman taking a walk?"

"A priest and a nun taking a walk, Detective. There is a difference."

Gripping his pen, Kevin had high hopes he'd stumbled on something significant. "Did you get this woman's name? Could you describe her?"

"She wore a scarf and dark glasses, but she wouldn't say, although I asked her. All she mentioned was she was a volunteer for St. Patrick's and that Father Munroe had seen her through some very dark times."

Could be something or nothing. A priest's entire job was to see people through very dark times. Kevin's thoughts wound back to last night's conversation with Edward Moran. "Could the woman have been a mother of a student at St. Patrick's?"

"Anything's possible. She wasn't a parent of one of my students, if that's what you mean. This woman was a stranger to me."

Working to keep the frustration out of his voice, Kevin asked, "Was she in her twenties, thirties?"

"She was young. Around Beatrice's age. Father Munroe liked 'em young."

"You said she was wearing a scarf. Did you see the color of her hair? Did she have a birth mark, an accent? Was there anything unusual about her that you can remember?"

"She was wearing a wedding ring." The old nun cackled. "Oh, that Father Munroe, he might have been the devil's playmate, but he was cagey about it. He only got involved with women who were unattainable. That's why I know he wasn't interested in Beatrice. When he discovered she was willing to leave the convent for him, that's when he knew he had a problem. Do your research, Detective. This is nothing new."

"Did you know any of the bishop's staff at St. Patrick's?"

"A few of them."

"Do you remember Thomas Timms?"

"I remember Thomas fondly," she said.

Another monumental surprise, Kevin thought. As much as he didn't like the vitriolic woman in front of him, he might have hit the jackpot. "Why is that, Sister?"

"I was Thomas's catechism instructor. I was also his sponsor into the Catholic Church."

"What can you tell me about him?"

"Polite, pious." She glared at him. "Manners."

"Yes, ma'am," Kevin said, doing his best rendition of Sergeant Friday on Dragnet. "Did you ever doubt his sanity?"

"Who? Thomas?" She jutted her lower lip. "Never. He did everything around that school. Kept things spotless. If it was broken, he fixed it. You'd go to empty a trashcan and find Thomas had already gotten there. He was a gift from above if there ever was. Know what I found him doing once?"

"What's that?"

"Tuning my piano. He could play, too."

"Sounds like you two were close."

"Not close. Respectful. That's what we were. We were respectful of one another."

"How was he toward Father Munroe?"

Her furrowed brow added yet another wrinkle. "I'd say with Father Munroe, he was attentive. Almost like he couldn't do enough for him. Does that make sense?"

Unfortunately, for a bishop hiding a sexual predator's identity and proclaiming his innocence, it did. "Did you ever see Thomas interact with Sister Beatrice?"

"What does that mean?"

Kevin shrugged. "Just trying to create a picture in my head. You said he was polite. Was he polite toward Sister Beatrice?"

"I can't imagine he wasn't."

"How about you, Sister Agnes? How did you feel about Sister Beatrice?"

The old woman flashed a nervous look to Danielle, which Kevin found interesting. Was she cursing her decision to have the administrator present? "We got along all right."

Danielle folded her arms and lifted an eyebrow, which caused Sister Agnes to retreat further into her wheelchair. "All right. We argued. We didn't like each other. She belonged in a convent about as much as I belonged on the Matterhorn."

"Why is that?"

"Why?" Sister Agnes threw up her hands as though Kevin were brain dead to pursue this line of questioning. "Beatrice wasn't pretty. She was beautiful. Even in her habit, people noticed her—particularly men. There's a reason we dress like this, Detective. We're not supposed to be noticed."

It isn't working, Kevin thought. "Sister Agnes, it's been reported that you and Sister Beatrice had an argument that turned physical. Is that true?"

"Who told you that?" Again she looked at Danielle, who was pursing her lips and tilting her head. Sister Agnes turned back to Kevin. "Oh, all right. It was over my students. But she started it. She wanted to take them from me. Beatrice was jealous because Joseph Marie wouldn't assign Beatrice her own students."

"You both taught music?" Kevin asked.

"*I* taught music," Sister Agnes said caustically. "She simply wanted to. I'd earned my degree in music performance and composition. Hers was in primary education and French, while I will admit she had a *slight* musical background and a pleasant enough voice."

"So you were the more experienced?" Kevin said.

"Infinitely."

"Did you fight with Sister Beatrice over Eden Moran?"

"Who?" The old nun's eyes narrowed.

"Eden Moran. Wasn't Eden one of your students?" Kevin asked.

"Never heard of her."

Again Danielle stepped forward. "Sister Agnes, this is extraordinary, even for you. I've heard you mention that name several times since you've been here."

"I wish you'd mind your own business," the old nun told the administrator. "All right. I taught the ungrateful wretch. What has she got to do with any of this?"

"Everything, if that's what drove you and Sister Beatrice to violence."

"It was one time, and she deserved everything I dished out." Sister Agnes did her best to curl her arthritic fingers into a fist and slammed it down on the arm of her wheelchair. "Ruining my music program. You don't take the gift Eden Moran had and give in to her childish whims. You cultivate it, develop it. You practice."

The administrator sent Kevin a worried glance, and he nodded, grateful he was asking these questions in her residence and not police headquarters. "The bishop claims he didn't kill Sister Beatrice, Sister Agnes. You realize, don't you, that we have to clear anyone who had a motive?"

"Well, of course. Wait a minute." The old woman put a hand to her breast. "You think *I* killed Beatrice? Danielle, will you listen to this reprobate?"

The nursing home administrator returned to the door, folded her arms and shook her head slowly.

When Danielle didn't support her, Sister Agnes drew herself up and waved her Bible. "The fifth commandment says, 'Thou shalt not kill.' Danielle, take me back to my room!"

Flustered, the administrator moved away from the wall.

Kevin held up a hand to stave off Danielle's approach. "Sorry, Lady, we're not done yet."

Chapter Forty-Three

"KNOCK, KNOCK. May I come in?"

Eden glanced up from her case file to see the last person she'd ever expect in her office doorway. "Mom? Wow. This is unexpected. What are you doing here?"

"I'd love to say I was just in the neighborhood, but the truth is I was hoping to take you to lunch."

Swallowing her surprise, Eden rose from her chair. "You want to take *me* to lunch?"

"If you have time."

"I really don't. I'm sorry." She rounded the desk. "I'm due at the courthouse in thirty minutes. Is something wrong?"

"Do you mind if I shut this door?" her mother asked.

"Of course not. Would you like something to drink?"

"No. Thank you."

Eden was used to sharing hostile moments with her mom, but never awkward ones. If there was anything the two of them were good at, it was bandying words. Not in this instance. Glancing at everything, appearing as if she wanted to touch something, then deciding not to, Joanna appeared full of nervous energy. Who was this woman, and what had happened to Eden's mother?

There wasn't room in her office for a visitor's chair, so she pointed to her own. "Mom, please. Sit down."

"All right." Joanna rounded the desk, again peering around the office, finally settling her gaze on Eden's brick-walled window. "Oh, Eden, that's awful."

Okay, this was better. No one had abducted her mom. "I know. But I'm low man on the totem pole here. Why do you think I'm so humble?"

"Perhaps your father could find you something to do at his office."

"I'm a lawyer, Mother, not an accountant." Propping her hip against her desk, Eden glanced at her watch. "What do you want to talk about?"

Lowering her head, her mother pretended to flick a piece of nonexistent lint off her jacket. As if it would dare.

"Mom?"

"I didn't know," she began. "Eden. I was a ghastly mother to you, and

I've come to apologize. One minute you were begging me to switch teachers, then you just stopped. I didn't ask why because . . ." Joanna shook her head. "In a way, I thought I was protecting you. The truth was, Sister Agnes made dreadful accusations against Sister Beatrice. Quite frankly, when you stopped talking about her, I was relieved."

Squeezing her eyes closed, Eden bowed her head. When she glanced up again, she said, "I'm trying to let all of this go. But the more I learn about Sister Agnes, the more I'm certain that if there's a hell, the devil has reserved the hottest place in it for her."

"I would love to lay all the blame on her doorstep, but I can't," Joanna said. "My volunteer work, your father's job." She sighed. "The truth is, Edward and I were considering divorce at the time. Unfortunately, you, my love, were a casualty."

"*Divorce?*" Eden didn't even try to hide her shock. With the exception of her, everyone else in her family had seemed so *perfect.* "I can't believe it. Did Meg know?"

"I'm sure she suspected. I hoped it was all in the past, and I never intended you or your sister to find out. But your father told Detective Dancer last night. I can see things are becoming serious between you two. I wanted you to hear it from me."

Eden placed a hand over her churning stomach. Kevin hadn't said a word, nor would she expect him to. He was investigating the case, and Joanna and Edward were Eden's parents. She was also certain he wouldn't let the comment lie. He would be bound to pursue it as part of the investigation. She had no choice but to ask the question he would. "Did the divorce have anything to do with Bishop Munroe?"

"Eden, please," Joanna begged.

Her tiny office began to spin. If Joanna had been intimate with the bishop, then Eden had been dead wrong about everything. What's more, Kevin had already tossed her mom into the murder suspect category—and rightfully so. "Mother," she demanded. "Did you *sleep* with Bishop Munroe?"

When Joanna didn't answer, Eden lowered herself to her mom's eye level. Grasping the arms of her chair, she swiveled the chair and forced Joanna to meet her gaze. "If you've ever told me the truth about anything, you better be honest with me now."

"No," her mother said finally. "I never slept with Robert. But based on what he's going through now, I have no choice but to defend him." Joanna squeezed her eyes closed and lowered her head. When she looked up again, tears welled in her eyes. "It wasn't because I didn't offer, Eden. He said 'no.'"

The air that had been trapped in Eden's lungs whooshed out. Sick and numb from this revelation, she rose and used her desk for support. "You know what the police will be thinking, don't you?"

Tears streamed from her mother's eyes. "I do."

Eden hardened her voice along with her heart. "Did you kill Sister Beatrice, Mom?"

"I swear to you, Eden. I did not."

Chapter Forty-Four

IT TOOK A FEW minutes to calm Sister Agnes down, and Danielle Kennedy was none too pleased. She claimed the old nun had a heart condition and ordered a staffer to take her up to her room. Danielle was *not* going to be the indirect cause of a massive coronary.

No. That role fell to Kevin, he assured her. He'd be as gentle as he could, but he was not going home without answers. So forty-five minutes later, Danielle allowed him to enter the nun's second-floor bedroom, but not before giving the old woman a sedative.

Sister Agnes sat in a chair staring out the window, the Cathedral of the Assumption in the distance.

Her back to Kevin, she seemed to gather as much authority as she could muster. "I didn't kill her."

He kept his distance this time, taking in the fair-sized quarters in the refurbished Victorian. Two twin beds made up the room, the one closest to her unmade, the one opposite looking like it would pass military inspection.

"You said she wanted your music students." He spoke quietly, knowing of no other way to draw her out but this one. "You had so few, you couldn't share?"

"She . . . wanted Eden."

Kevin eased beside her to study her face.

The old woman lowered her head. "Beatrice said I was bad for Eden, claimed I was crushing her spirit." Shaking her head, Sister Agnes went on. "Imagine, everything I'd done for that child and that . . . that woman could say such a hurtful thing to me."

It was Kevin's turn to look down.

"Do you know how she is?" Sister Agnes asked.

Unsure how strong her meds were, or how stable the old nun was while on them, he clarified, "You're talking about Eden?"

"Of course," she snarled. "You really are a young fool, aren't you?"

So much for misplaced compassion. Kevin bit back a smile at the same time she raised head to look at him. "Whatever happened to her?" she asked.

"She lives in Albuquerque now. She became a lawyer. She works for the public defender's office."

A hint of something close to a smile lit Sister Agnes's pale lips. Her eyes drew into slits, as though trying to picture Eden. "Does she still have all that hair?"

At the image of Eden towel-drying her hair, her nervous habit of pinning it up then taking it down, he smiled. "It's long, yes."

Staring back at the cathedral, the old nun said, "Beatrice loved it, you know. Praised that child to no end about her looks. Too bad, too. All it did was make her vain. 'Play the piano your way, Eden. You don't have to read the music,'" Sister Agnes mocked. Then she sighed. "All I ever wanted was for her to learn discipline. I assume she's pretty? She was a pretty little girl."

Suddenly, he felt very sorry for this bitter old woman. "She's pretty, Sister."

She arched a bushy gray brow, then faced him fully. "She's caught your eye, has she? I suppose you think she's some kind of genius the way she plays that piano."

"I wouldn't know. She doesn't play anymore."

"*No.*" Sister Agnes virtually threw herself back in her chair. Her already reedy voice trembled. "She no longer plays? I don't believe it. I've never seen a child with such God-given talent. Damn Beatrice and her interfering ways. I told her to leave Eden alone—"

"Detective Dancer." Danielle came to his side and with pleading in her eyes whispered, "Are you almost through?"

Was he? He honestly didn't know. Was he looking at a lonely, miserable old soul or a jealousy-stricken killer? He pulled out his business card at the same time he saw the red and gold braided border of her bookmark. He'd seen one like it recently, and adrenaline flooded his system. He lowered himself to the old woman's eye level. "Sister Agnes, your bookmark, do you mind if I have a look at it?"

She opened her Bible and removed the holy card he'd committed to memory. Unlike the flimsy ones the police had in evidence, this one was laminated. Aiming a flaming sword toward heaven, the Angel Gabriel stood before the cloud-covered golden gates, fearless and righteous. The card, captioned *The Messenger,* was the same one he and Eden had researched on the Internet, identical to the five that had been found in Thomas's apartment.

"Isn't it beautiful?" Sister Agnes said. "I'd give you one, but I don't have any more."

He stared down at the card. "You had more of these, Sister?"

"Oh, yes. I purchased twenty-five of them, intending to give to my students many years ago."

"Do you remember giving one to Thomas?" Kevin asked.

"Of course I do. I gave him one when he came into the Church. I told him the card applied to him particularly. I called him God's messenger."

She smiled. "Thomas cried, it meant so much to him."

Then her smile vanished. She glanced hesitantly at Danielle, who was shaking her head. "I know, I know. You and all the other old coots around here think I'm crazy."

"Not crazy, Sister, more like confused," Danielle said.

Sister Agnes wasn't the only one. Kevin looked from one woman to the other.

"I'm sorry, Detective," the administrator said. "The subject of her missing holy cards has been something of a debate around here. She's insistent that somebody stole her holy cards." Danielle smiled. "Can you imagine? Somebody stealing holy cards?

"Yeah," Kevin said, mulling over the possibility. "How ironic would that be?"

Chapter Forty-Five

QUAGMIRE. That was too sedate a word to describe Sister Beatrice's murder investigation. Eden paced the loft, occasionally crossing to the full-length window that faced her street, willing Kevin to appear. Even Alicia Keys singing in the background couldn't ease her spirit. Her stomach was a giant-sized tea bag steeped in acid.

Hand on her belly, Eden continued to walk. Kevin had the nerve to sound upbeat when he phoned from the airport. What had happened to leave him 99.9 percent sure that Sister Agnes had nothing to do with the murder? And who had he been referring to when he mentioned a mystery woman in scarf and glasses? And why hadn't he seemed particularly open to talking about it?

Probably because he'd developed a new suspect in the case—Eden's mother. Eden, herself, was having a hard time accepting Joanna at her word. She pictured the expressions of the grand jury's faces when they learned of her parents' separation, due in large part to Joanna's attraction to a priest, at the same time he'd been accused of murdering his lover.

Eden's stomach nosedived yet again.

Kevin had a duty to advise his commander of this newfound information. Eden also had no doubt that if Bishop Munroe had any clout with his attorneys, he would have quashed the information.

That was the problem. In a case of this magnitude, he didn't. Cardinal Anderson ran the minions here, and his mission was to protect the Church. If she were representing Robert Munroe, she would leap at a chance to take this red herring before the grand jury. It went to reasonable doubt, and that was all a good lawyer needed to set his client free, and to tear her mother's reputation to shreds in both the local and national spotlights.

What had Kevin been about to say when they called his flight? She'd pleaded with him to tell her, but all he left her with was dead air.

Yes. Quagmire. Definitely. Eden squeezed her eyes shut and fought not to panic. But panic was what one did in circumstances like these. The grand jury was set to convene on Monday—*four days away*. Her instincts were failing her. Someone close to her bore the label of murderer, and she could not recognize his face.

"SEVEN TEXT MESSAGES?" Kevin crossed Eden's threshold a little after eleven.

She held the door open for him, her face hidden behind a mass of disheveled blond hair.

"What?" She shoved her hair out of her eyes. "I should have sent more?" Fixing a sleep-deprived gaze on him, she said, "I don't know if you know this about me, but I hate waiting."

"Really? I'd never suspected." He leaned forward to kiss her. The woman he taken to bed two nights before held the folds of her silk wrap protectively. In her current mood, it probably wasn't a good idea to remind her that he already knew and admired what she hid beneath the short silk robe.

He walked her backwards toward the couch, pressed her down onto the supple white leather, then removed his sports coat and tossed it over the arm. Then, slumping onto it, he leaned his head back and recounted the extraordinarily long day that had begun at four that morning.

She listened quietly and shifted to a cross-legged position, while he shook away how much he wanted to make love to her. With ZZ Top's *Legs* beating inside his head, he told her instead what she wanted to know.

"The woman in the scarf and glasses?" Kevin asked, when he'd given her a complete account. "Any idea who she might be?"

"Besides two thousand parishioners or my mother?" Eden crossed her arms and arched a brow.

Kevin lifted his head from the back of the sofa. *Shit.* He should have found a way to bring up her mom. "Who told you?"

"She did, so you can relax. She came to my office today, informed me about your chat with my dad." Eden grimaced. "It was the strangest conversation I've ever had with her. She apologized, Kevin. Told me they'd almost divorced, said she'd been consumed with appearances, volunteering, her social status . . ."

Kevin sat up. "What did you just say?"

"What part?"

"The volunteer business."

"She volunteered," Eden said frowning. "Is that important?"

"Probably not . . . I don't . . . think." He slumped forward, folding his hands.

"Kevin?"

"Sister Agnes mentioned the woman in the scarf and dark glasses was a volunteer, that's all."

"Well, just so you know, many parishioners donate their services, and we're talking seventeen years ago. Good luck following up on that one. So you asked Sister Agnes if the volunteer could have been my mother?"

"What do you think?"

"I think you're a cop. Of course you did." Eden sighed and rose from the couch. "Mom categorically denies anything happened between her and the bishop."

Kevin nodded. "I'm just sorry you had to learn about it at all. I suppose it would've been worse if it came out at the grand jury and you hadn't been notified."

"True. That doesn't mean I'm not freaking out all the same. Joanna Moran may have been a lousy mom, but she's the only one I've got, and I'm not out to see her destroyed."

Kevin watched Eden move back and forth, getting a glimpse of how she stayed so slim when she ate anything that wasn't nailed down. Undoubtedly, while he'd been crammed into an aisle seat of a 737, she'd walked the entire time.

She stopped and pivoted in his direction. "What did you think of Sister Agnes?"

"I didn't join her fan club, if that's what you're asking. But a murderer, she's not. I don't think she had it in her to kill Sister Beatrice."

When Eden opened her mouth to argue, he reached for his jacket, removed the laminated holy card from the coat's lining and handed it to her.

Her eyes went wide. "Where did you get this?"

"From your former music teacher. Sister Agnes claims she bought twenty-five to give to her students."

"She never gave one to me," Eden said, sounding remarkably like a sulking five-year-old. She ran a finger over the image. "Except for the plastic coating, it appears identical to the one we saw on the Internet."

"I think so, too. Identical also to the five we have locked up in evidence—the cards we took from Thomas's apartment. Sister Agnes claims she gave him one, not five."

Eden placed a hand on her hip. "Sister Agnes had to be sixty when she taught me, Kevin. What is she now? Eighty?"

"She's old, not senile," he said, repeating Sister Agnes's words. "Besides, she didn't make this up for my benefit. It's been a point of contention at the nursing home. The other residents have been giving her a hard time, because, as they put it, who would steal holy cards?"

He'd had seven hours dealing with layovers and in a plane to reason things through. All this other crap worthy of a soap opera only muddied the water. When it came to police work, you went with the suspect who had means, motive and opportunity. No matter how much Eden and Sal believed Munroe's version, the bishop still fit the bill.

Kevin patted the seat next to him. "Come sit with me. We need to talk."

Warily, Eden joined him on the couch.

"You can breathe easier about your mom. I don't believe she's our killer, and as much as you want it to be Sister Agnes, she didn't do it either." Kevin took the card from Eden's hand. "I know you think I'm a judgmental hard-ass, and I'm being unfair. I also want you to know I've heard every word you and Sal have said. But whether it was from panic or rage, my gut tells me Munroe did this. The way I see it, he used his influence with Thomas to persuade him to get rid of the body. It would also explain Thomas's departure from reality. Devout guy, forced to do something repugnant to him? As for the additional holy cards in his apartment, I believe Munroe sent them over the years as a reminder for the old handyman to keep quiet."

The room filled with an intense silence as Eden lowered her head, wrapped an arm around her middle and pressed her free hand to her throat. Finally, she said, "Number one, I don't think you're a hard-ass. I think you're trying to solve this case. But while everything you say is a nice way to connect the dots, you're still speculating. And that's dangerous, because when I'm called to the witness stand, my testimony will corroborate your thinking." She released a sigh. Then, changing positions, she clasped her hands. "When I'm called to represent a client, I get a tremendous sense of his guilt or his innocence. He can be sitting there crying his eyes out, saying he didn't do it, and I just know that he did."

"You're claiming to be psychic now?" Kevin asked.

"Not at all. More like intuitive. I know when they're telling the truth, and I know when they're not. In this case, my intuition tells me to believe the bishop."

Kevin narrowed his gaze. "Just like you knew Manuel Aguirre wasn't lying when you represented him?"

"Yes," she said, folding her arms and staring back at Kevin, ready to defend her position further. "*Exactly* like Manuel Aguirre."

"What if I told you, you were right?"

Still wearing a look of suspicion, Eden said, "I'd wonder what made you change your mind."

"Lupe came to see me. She let me in on the fact that her brother and his little gang of cutthroats were the ones who set up her husband."

"And you never told me?" Eden slapped her thigh.

"Sorry. It slipped my mind. We were involved in some great makeup sex and I wasn't exactly into talking." Before she could lash out again, Kevin grabbed her. A distracting kiss later, he pulled away, only to realize by Eden's arched brow his attempt to change the subject hadn't worked. "Okay. I'm willing to go with the fact you have great instincts. But

Munroe . . ." Kevin shook his head. "Eden. This guy would be out of a job if he wasn't convincing."

The woman beside him was like an old-time alarm clock winding up. Before she leapt from the couch and started her damned pacing again, he took hold of her legs and set them in his lap.

"What do you think you're doing?"

"Giving you a foot massage."

She angled her head. "I don't know about this. It feels like you're trying to win me over to your way of thinking. I'll have you know, I'm not that easy."

"Or maybe I'm just a nice guy, trying to help you de-stress." Kevin pushed hard on the arch of her foot and applied circular motions with his thumb. Slowly, she leaned back and relaxed until she let out a moan nothing short of orgasmic. "Oooh, you don't fight fair."

"Stop over-thinking things and enjoy."

She closed her eyes, until the rise and fall of her breasts told him she was giving in. Too bad he couldn't follow his own advice. He wanted an end to this case as badly as she did, with the real killer prosecuted and behind bars. He thought it was Munroe, Eden didn't. Surely she had to see how much evidence they had against him.

Moving on to knead the ball of her foot, he stared between her and the holy card on the coffee table. Just as she felt her instinct was right on, he was equally certain the missing cards were integral to this case.

And then there was this volunteer business.

She was right. Seventeen years meant there would be a helluva lot of parishioners to contend with. Talk about searching for a grain of sand in an hour glass.

Go ahead. Torture me," Eden said, eyes closed and smiling. "You'll never get me to change my mind."

"What if I stop?"

"I'll cry like a baby."

At least she was honest. If anyone was dedicated to bringing this case to a close, it was Eden. "Still in the mood to do my job for me?"

Propping her weight on her elbows, she opened one eye. "Is the pope Catholic? What do you have in mind?"

"How does your day look tomorrow?"

Both eyes open now, Eden said, "Packed in the a.m. In the afternoon, not so bad. Why?"

"I wonder what would happen if you talked to your ol' buddy Father Slater."

"Not that I don't want to, but why?"

"Because of all people, he knows the importance of volunteers." Kevin winked at her. "Congratulations, Ms. Moran. You're about to become one."

Chapter Forty-Six

"THE FILES are stored where?" Shortly after lunch, the next afternoon, Eden stood in Father Slater's office, her offer to help Kevin suddenly wavering.

"They're stored in the basement of St. Patrick's." The parish priest sighed. "Perhaps Detective Dancer sent the wrong person on this particular errand?"

"Ya think?" Eden's shoulders slumped. The fates had to be clinking their glasses together on this one.

Father Slater's round face flushed. "And I'm sorry to give you further bad news, but who knows if they even go back seventeen years." Rising, he reached into his trouser pocket to remove a thick ring of keys. "Although I've never known any of my predecessors to throw away anything, or for that matter, microfiche, scan or digitize anything either," he said, revealing a broad grin. "When I think of all that storage in the basement, I get the urge to grab a cold rag and an aspirin and lie down."

Eden smiled, appreciating his humor, though it hardly made her task any easier.

He headed for the door. "We might as well get started."

"*We?*" she asked.

"I have a few hours. If it will help prove the Bishop's innocence, it's the least I can do."

Her heart gave a hopeful squeeze. "Do you think he's innocent, Father?"

The ordinarily direct man avoided her gaze. "I want to, Eden, very much."

They left the rectory to walk across the blacktop, her nemesis standing formidable in the distance. St. Patrick's truly was a beautiful church. With a stone masonry façade, the stained glass windows set off its austere mushroom coloring to twinkle in the New Mexico sunlight. A warm breeze lifted Eden's wilting hair. She pulled a band free to repair her sagging ponytail.

Regretting that she'd been too impatient to stop by the loft to change, she did her best to keep up, but in a tight skirt and heels, it wasn't easy.

When she descended the stairs into the basement, it was worse than she thought. Decades of dust-layered old boxes stacked as high as the ceiling caused her to sneeze repeatedly.

Father Slater cranked open three small cellar windows and shoved boxes aside.

The term "long shot" played through Eden's head as she perused the long rectangular room. When it came to sacramental records or employment, the priest had said they could access these instantly and electronically. Items like age-old newsletters, bulletins and volunteer lists, however, were an entirely different matter.

Draping her blazer over a folding chair, she kicked off her shoes. If she was going to work in this hell-hole, she'd damned well get comfortable.

The good news was that some wonderful soul had had the presence of mind to label the boxes from year to year. Together, she and Father Slater combed through containers and separated the ones that went back as far as ninety-two.

An hour later, they dropped into chairs and exchanged hopeless expressions. They were ready to open box number one.

KEVIN TRIED EDEN'S cell, checked his voice mail, then examined his pager and frowned. If he didn't get an update from her in the next few minutes, it would be an hour or more before he could do so again. He was about to go into his third session with Dr. Olivia Jones, the Albuquerque Police Department shrink. When it came to their meetings, she made it clear that Kevin was on her time and on no one else's. He rode the elevator to the third floor, strode down the hallway toward her office and found the petite black woman sitting behind her desk. From what he could tell, Dr. Jones was good at her job. And because he planned to keep his for many years to come, Kevin had no choice but to answer her questions.

She greeted him, "Detective Dancer, welcome back."

He closed the door and collapsed into a comfortable high-back chair. "Doctor Jones."

"How'd last week go?" she asked. "Any problems?"

"None," he replied.

"You're sleeping all right?" she went on.

"I'm fine, Doctor. I don't seem to be suffering from post-traumatic stress, if that's what you're asking."

Clasping her hands together, she rested her chin on them and smiled. "I do believe you're adjusting quite well, but why don't you let me be the judge of that."

Duly chastised, Kevin nodded. Her preliminary questions were about to go deeper, and he steeled himself. Six weeks of ordered therapy sessions seemed a small price to pay to keep his badge. Reuben Sharpe, aka Thomas Timms, hadn't been so lucky. He'd been duped most of his adult life, wrongfully imprisoned for ten years, and then used as a pawn. Learning all of this, Kevin felt bad for the guy. But Eden was alive today because Kevin had pulled the trigger.

Let's get this over with.

"I want to go back to that evening in Mesa General's chapel," Dr. Jones began. "What went through your mind when you knew you were about to fire your service revolver?"

Kevin sighed, closed his eyes, and recounted his story.

WITH EVERY CONTAINER she waded through, Eden flipped faster. She'd only run across one computer printout that contained volunteer names, but in perusing them she realized she had no clue what she was looking for. She placed the printout in a stack for Kevin and Sal to decipher in greater detail and moved on to box five. This one, too, had a few more printouts, but nothing stood out, and her pile loomed larger.

She glanced at Father Slater. If he was tired of helping her, he didn't show it, as he skimmed file after file without complaint. Then, standing, he stretched and reached for another box.

"I'm feeling guilty about taking up all your time," Eden said. "Should I go get you something to drink?"

He pulled out a thick sheaf of papers. "Later perhaps. We're making progress."

Myriad boxes remained unopened behind him. *We are?*

Next to him, Eden looked like a slacker, so she went back to work. A while later, he began to hum, and soon she did the same, engaging in a game of *name that tune.*

At least their silly guessing game passed the time. So when it was his turn, and he didn't come up with another song, she glanced his way. He stared at the printout in front of him, his lips puckered, his narrowed gaze glued to the page.

"Father Slater?"

He turned toward her and paled. "I do believe, Eden, we've found our connection."

Chapter Forty-Seven

JANICE SLAMMED the side drawer to Marshall Knight's desk, looking for any shred of evidence to take to Cardinal Anderson to make him rethink his ghastly decision. Until the grand jury handed down an indictment, or found no cause to go to trial, the Church had removed the bishop as head of the diocese. Bishop Munroe had taken the news with his typical dignified calm, while Janice and the other staff members around the conference table had wanted to throttle the snowy-haired cardinal.

Although, the cardinal had made an important point about the media. Before the bishop was even convicted, the networks and newspapers were trying Robert Munroe in the press. In addition to skirting the diocese's perimeter, investigative journalists were attempting to schedule interviews for any crust of *nothing* they could find.

It *was* in the bishop's best interests as well as the Church's until this nasty business blew over to have him step down.

But to leave Marshall in charge until Monsignor Winger could tie up his affairs at St. Gabriel's and run the diocese? Janice slammed the third drawer, then tugged off the silk scarf from around her neck. Sweating, she blotted her face and her brow.

What the church officials saw in the balding, ill-tempered Marshall Knight, in his faded shirts and polyester pants, she couldn't fathom. During her volunteer days at St. Patrick's, she'd heard the rumor he'd been married once, but that his wife had run off.

Janice curled her lip. Who could blame her? Poor thing probably wanted him to update his wardrobe, or asked him for money.

Checking her watch to ensure she had plenty of time before Marshall returned from lunch, Janice scanned the walls. Several were framed certificates of appreciation from Catholic charities. She'd nearly passed out when someone compared Marshall to a modern day John the Baptist, claiming he earned so little but gave unselfishly to others.

Janice had never even seen Marshall smile. She was sick to death of his acerbic behavior, knowing he was pious to the clergy's face, while behind their backs, he pointed out any perceived incompetence.

She knew the truth. He loathed them all.

That is, until the bishop's setback. Then the smirk that seemed permanently affixed to Marshall's mouth had become an all-out grin. Twice she'd even caught him whistling. *Whistling!*

So far her calls to the bishop had gone unanswered. She desperately wanted his advice. If he was stepping down permanently, and Janice was expected to report to Marshall, she had no choice but to resign.

His hated voice carried from down the hall. Disappointed, yet certain he kept nothing she could use against him, Janice slipped out of his office and into her own across the hall. When he rapped on her door, she turned, proud of her feigned nonchalance.

"Did you make the deposit?" He asked the question as though his new rise in power should have her jumping to attention.

She picked up the envelope he'd left on her desk. "This one? The one you so *courteously* scrawled and underlined three times 'bank'?"

"You'll forgive me, if with all the pressures these people are putting on me, I forgo the pleasantries. I'm a busy man."

Janice picked up the deposit, along with her purse, and strode to the door. "That's all right, Marshall. I've never known you to exhibit any pleasantries in the first place."

Outside the admin building, she smiled for the first time in hours. She was absolutely through being civil to the business manager. It was going to destroy her to leave The Diocese of New Mexico. A victim of abuse, she'd worked long and hard to rise to this position, something Robert Munroe had been instrumental in helping her achieve. She owed everything to the man who'd helped her heal, and not a thing to anyone else.

Her throat tightened as she spied the cathedral to the south of the property, the stable of garages behind it and the small garage apartment housed above. She couldn't walk by any of it without thinking of Thomas. She whispered a prayer for mercy upon his poor soul and trudged up the hill to the employee parking lot.

Placing the deposit on her passenger seat, Janice started her Mini Cooper and began to back up, but quickly applied the brakes. Parked in its standard spot under a Russian olive tree, Marshall's run-down yellow Mercury beckoned like an invitation.

He didn't keep anything in his office. What, if anything, did he keep in his car?

Seconds later, she was standing beside the driver's side door, sweating profusely. The door was locked, but like most people who survived the Albuquerque clime, he kept a window ajar. Janice surveyed the parking lot and chewed on her lower lip. Being found entering his personal vehicle was entirely different than being discovered in his office. There, she could make up an excuse. But his car?

She was determined to discredit him, if it was the last thing she did.

Janice slipped her fingers through the old fashioned wing window and finagled her fingers downward. Releasing the lock, she sighed in relief and almost laughed out loud at the image of a bishop's executive assistant breaking into a car.

But in the next moment, Janice wasn't laughing. And the seriousness of what she'd stumbled upon made her heart lurch. In a brown paper bag on the floorboard, Marshall had several random travel brochures—St. Tropez, Goa, Cairo. Even if he worked in the private sector, trips to these tourist hot spots cost thousands of dollars.

Still, what did flyers prove; that he planned to take a dream vacation? That was no crime, and he could certainly explain it away. Needing more, Janice popped the trunk. Nothing but an old tire iron and three containers or motor oil sat in his trunk. But on closer inspection, there was a bump in the gray felt lining. Janice ran her hand over it and pulled up the old coarse fabric. Underneath the lining were several South American properties for sale and his passport. Excitement coursed through her and she wanted to squeal with relief. And then she saw the stack of holy cards. She picked one up. Studying it, she recalled Sister Agnes's dismay over misplacing them, and Marshall's phony concern that he hoped she found them.

Suddenly, Janice became aware she wasn't dealing with miserly pond scum. She was dealing with someone in cahoots with Satan. Careful not to lose the card, she raised her arms to shut the trunk when a hand shot out to stop her.

"Find what you were looking for?"

Her heart rammed against her rib cage. Janice gasped and hid the holy card behind her back. "Marshall. I . . . You must have left your trunk open. I stopped to close it for you."

"Always thinking of others. How kind of you."

She blinked rapidly, confused by his sneering sarcasm. Until he held out her scarf, the one she'd carelessly left in his office.

At her major blunder, her hand flew to her throat. "Marshall. I . . . I can . . . let me . . ."

He never allowed her another word. The blow he delivered knocked her off balance, making escape an impossibility. As he wound the material around her throat the irony hit her. He would use her own scarf against her to end her life. It was almost a relief when the world went black and Janice no longer fought him to breathe.

Chapter Forty-Eight

"JANICE CHARLES?" Eden asked, glancing over Father Slater's shoulder. "Why does that name sound familiar?"

"She's the bishop's executive assistant," the priest replied. "And just look at all the volunteer hours she logged in. No wonder the diocese hired her."

Suddenly the name registered, and she remembered Sal's disgust with the woman. "She's the one who failed to tell the police about the bishop's ordination and kept them in the dark for weeks." Eden took the printouts from the priest and read through them. "Her primary duties at that time were preparing the flower arrangements and cleaning the church."

"She certainly had access," Father Slater said.

"I should say. Overly protective of the bishop, and she's been with him for years. And as Kevin pointed out, we need someone with motive and opportunity," Eden added. "Well, there ya go."

"You think she might have—"

"I do. More importantly, I think Kevin and Sal will think so, too." Eden grabbed her purse and withdrew her cell. "Dammit. Kevin called and I missed him."

Father Slater frowned. "I'm sure the reception down here is lousy."

"No, I'm getting a signal." She pushed resend. The call went straight to voice mail. "He must still be in his meeting. Dammit," she said again, and then winced. "Sorry, Father."

"You damned well should be." He smiled and arched his back as he stretched. "I'll walk you to your car. From there you can try Detective Dancer again."

Nodding, she lowered her head.

"Eden," he soothed. "This is progress. Janice Charles has moved high on the suspect list."

"I agree," Eden said, rising. She slid on her shoes and looped her jacket over her arm. "Do you know her, Father?"

"I've seen her, of course. But I can't say that we've ever been formally introduced. Why do you ask?"

"I've forgotten—rather, blocked so much. I wonder if I'd recognize her."

"Many years have passed," the priest said. "People change."

"You're right." Dust had accumulated on her blazer, and Eden brushed it off. "Thank you, Father. You saved me hours of work. But now I have hours of work ahead of me someplace else."

"Glad to have been of service."

They walked up the basement steps and through the church's atrium. Outside, Eden enjoyed the fresh air while she waited for St. Patrick's pastor to lock up. He pocketed his keys and glanced over his shoulder at her.

At the worry she saw in his gaze, tears sprang to her eyes.

"I wish I could do something to help, Eden. But know one thing. Detectives Dancer and Raez are committed to solving this case."

"They absolutely are." She lifted her chin. "I'm okay from here, Father. See you soon—"

"You're thinking if you saw this woman, it might trigger more of your memories, aren't you?"

"What?" Eden laughed. "They teach mind reading in the seminary?"

"Far from it. It's acquired, compliments of on-the-job training."

She swallowed hard. "Sister Beatrice meant everything to me, and I blocked her. I'm wondering what else I've blocked. Kevin told me once he thought I was the key to this investigation. I denied it, but now I believe with my whole heart that he's right."

The priest grew quiet. Eventually, he glanced at his watch. "I have a friend in Adoption Services—Penny Gibson—who works at the diocese. I pay her a visit every now and then to catch up on some of the children we've placed."

"Okay?"

"No one would think twice if we use Penny as an excuse and *happened* to *run into* Janice."

Eden gasped. "Really? You'd do that for me?"

"I don't see how the police could object to a simple passerby. They ask people to assist in lineups all the time, after all."

"They do at that." Nevertheless, Eden hesitated. The night she and Kevin reconciled, she'd made him a promise. He wouldn't practice law and she wouldn't interfere in a police investigation. She had every intention of keeping her word. Even so, two days ago in the park, Kevin himself had encouraged Eden to focus on remembering. She was still haunted by that little girl on the swings. Would Janice Charles trigger the entire puzzle?

Hugging the very generous priest, Eden said, "You're on. I'll drive."

He laughed and shook his head. "I imagine you would. But I'm due at a parish function this evening so I'll need my car. Plus, I should stop by the office and check in. I've been gone quite some time. How about I meet you at the diocese in, say, thirty minutes?"

"Thirty minutes. I owe you, Father."

"Indeed you do. And the first thing you can do to repay me is to call Detective Dancer and let him know what we're up to."

"I'll call him the moment I'm in my car."

"Good enough." Father Slater sobered. "Eden, if you get there before me, do not approach Janice, or try to question her. She may be our murderer. Our objective is to look—see if she triggers a memory. When you get there, pick up a magazine. Tell the staff you're waiting for me. Is that clear?"

"Perfectly," Eden said, smiling. "Don't worry, Father. I'm not interested in taking down a killer, only identifying one."

Chapter Forty-Nine

FOR SUCH A TINY woman, Dr. Jones packed a wallop. Kevin left the shrink's office feeling like he'd been sacked by a 350-pound lineman. He'd tried to stay in the moment, while shutting down mentally, but her questions had been grueling, and she had a way of digging deep.

They tackled issues he hadn't faced in years: what had gone through his five-year-old mind when he learned his dad had been killed in the line of duty; how he felt when his mother remarried; J.T's numerous attempts to adopt him, followed each time by Kevin's adamant refusal; and, of course, Josh. What was it like to have his best friend become his stepbrother, and then watch his rebellion and later his death tear a family apart?

Kevin had lashed out only once at the stoic Dr. Jones. Although, sometimes, once was all it took.

Hell. What kind of report would she write? Did she see him as a cop with the ability to deal, or one whose background made him likely to snap?

Jerry Reece, a homicide cop who sat one row over, slapped Kevin on the back on his way to his desk. There would be little said about where Kevin had been for the past hour. No cop on the force wanted to face the department psychologist for the reasons Kevin had. Reece's gesture, plain and simple, had been one to show solidarity.

"Heard where you've been, Kev." Denise, the department's longtime secretary, headed his way. "How would you like some good news for a change?"

"I don't know if my heart could stand it. Try me."

"Cox called from the lab. He claims he's either a miracle worker, or it must be divine intervention, but he pulled a print other than Reuben Sharpe's from those holy cards."

At that surprise, Kevin's heart did rev up a notch. Initially, Cox had insisted he'd had no success, but at Kevin's constant cajoling, he'd gone back over the cards one more time.

The secretary grinned. "I wish you could see your face. Cox said it's a partial, so not to get your hopes up."

Kevin thanked her and picked up the phone. In a division the size of—and as busy as—this one, he didn't often call in special favors, but with Robert Munroe facing the grand jury in three days, this case had extenuating circumstances. If the print was the bishop's, well, it pretty much sealed his fate. If the print matched someone else's, Eden and her intuition would be very happy.

Kevin left Cox a message, asking him to give the holy card match top priority. Kevin hung up just as Sal returned to his desk.

His partner sank into his chair and narrowed his gaze. "I was about to ask how the session went, but I guess there's no need. Maybe I should go. What's with the face? You look happier than a lone customer in a strip club."

Kevin tossed the file his way and sat in his chair. "The shrink didn't make me happy. We caught a partial on one of the holy cards."

"It's because I'm living right," Sal said, giving Kevin a thumb's up.

Grinning, Kevin held his phone to his ear to review messages. As he listened to Eden's breathless explanation of what she and Father Slater had uncovered in St. Patrick's basement, he underwent another round of elation. That was, until he heard what they planned to do with said information. He shot to his feet. "No way."

Sal looked up. "What?"

"Eden. She and Slater discovered something. They're headed to the diocese."

"Did she say what they found?" Sal asked.

Kevin adjusted his shoulder holster and checked his weapon. "She indicated it had something to do with Janice Charles."

"Want some company?" Sal asked.

"I thought you'd never ask." Kevin paused and raised his gaze to the ceiling. "How does she do it, Sal?"

"What's that?"

"Con people into going along with her lamebrain ideas."

Sal lifted a brow. "Well, I don't know, Kev. You'd be better qualified to answer that than me."

Chapter Fifty

EDEN LOVED her smartphone, with its GPS device that told her precisely which street to take. Getting lost when she was this close to staring Sister Beatrice's killer in the eye wasn't an option. Nor was getting a ticket, she observed, noting the speedometer. Easing up on the gas, she settled for watching her knuckles turn white on the steering wheel.

Father Slater's discovery had to bear some sort of significance. If not, why wouldn't Janice Charles have mentioned that she'd been a volunteer at St. Patrick's all those years ago? Still, Eden reiterated her number one goal was to look—not approach. Piece of cake if Janice triggered no memory. The hard part came if Eden recalled something significant. No matter what she remembered, Eden visualized keeping calm and her emotions in check.

The top of the cathedral came into view, and she swung her Honda onto the property. The second she stepped into the diocese's reception area, however, she knew something was off. For a place supposedly known for its faith, hope and charity, it seemed more in line with a complaint department. Three executive-types stood at the young receptionist's counter, voicing their displeasure over some occurrence, while the young woman behind it did her best to assuage their tempers.

Unobtrusively, Eden moved to a waiting room chair and reached for a magazine while naturally homing in on the conversation.

"If this meeting was so critical," the ringleader said, "why isn't he here? This is the height of rudeness, and if the diocese wants my help or my *money*, this is a poor way to get it."

Flipping through pages, Eden felt waves of sympathy for the gangly young woman being bullied by these men. The poor girl, whose nameplate read Lindsey Abercrombie, was still wearing braces, for crying out loud.

"I'm sorry, Doctor," she said, displaying her hands. "I don't understand. Mr. Knight's never late. All I can say is, when I see him, I'll let him know how unhappy you are."

The man behind the physician wasn't any more appeased. "When you do see him again, tell him I have a business to run. Damned shame what's happened to the bishop. It's affecting this entire organization."

"Tell him to hire a competent staff while he's at it," said the disgruntled MD.

That's all it took for Eden to see red. As the uncharitable man strode by, she lifted a reproachful eyebrow. "She doesn't deserve that comment or your tone of voice. I'll bet you've never kept a patient waiting."

The older man blustered. "And you are?"

"Me? Oh, I'm nobody," Eden said, returning to her reading material. "You're the only one who matters here."

She braced for his backlash, but the two who followed suddenly distanced themselves and averted their gazes. The doctor turned, obviously wanting support. When there was none, he shot a hateful glare at Eden and walked out the door.

When they were alone, Eden rose from the chair and offered the girl a conciliatory smile. "Tough day?"

The young woman's pent-up breath lifted the bangs on her forehead. "The worst. Please tell me you're not here to see Marshall Knight."

"That I can do. I'm waiting for Father Slater. He asked me to meet him here." Eden glanced around the room, which was filled with statues of patron saints and decades of diocesan history. "I take it he hasn't arrived?"

"Father George? I haven't seen him yet."

"I might be a little early. Mind if I use the ladies' room?"

Lindsey smiled. "Straight down that hall and to your right."

Eden found the bathroom immediately, but kept on going, bypassing several departments until she reached the end of a long hall. The bishop's office stood at the end of the corridor. The rooms on either side, however, housed Marshall Knight, the diocesan business manager, and across from Knight, the bishop's executive assistant—and Eden's quarry—Janice Charles.

Eden peered first into Marshall's office, then, holding her breath, peeked into Janice's. As Lindsey had indicated, both were empty. Eden scanned Janice's walls for a picture of the woman. But while murder might have been one of her sins, vanity didn't appear to be one of her vices.

Shoulders slumped, Eden returned to the reception area to find a smiling Lindsey had recovered from her verbal assault.

On the phone, she said to a caller, "Would you like her voice mail? . . . No, ma'am, she went to the bank . . . She shouldn't be gone long . . . No problem . . . I'll transfer you."

Lindsey disconnected and glanced up. "Your name must be Eden. Father George called while you were in the bathroom. Said he had a small crisis but he's on his way."

Wanting to kick something, Eden settled for an eye roll. This cloak-and-dagger stuff was definitely meant for the cops. What had started out as a simple ID was taking more time than she'd anticipated. And now Janice was nowhere to be found and Eden monopolizing too much of

Father Slater's valuable time.

"Thanks. You weren't by any chance talking about Janice Charles?" Eden asked.

"I was." Lindsey tilted her head. "Do you know Janice?"

"Used to. Thought I'd say hello while I'm here. As I said, it's been years," Eden hedged. And then a simple solution occurred to her. "You wouldn't have a picture of Janice, would you?"

Lindsey reached below her counter and came away with a gloss-covered booklet, which read *Diocese of New Mexico Staff Directory*. She flipped a couple of pages and turned the publication toward Eden. "Janice Charles, right here."

Excitement coursed through Eden, but as she studied Janice's face, it fizzled rapidly. Janice Charles was an attractive, otherwise average-looking, middle-aged brunette. Father Slater had been right about the passage of time. Still, nothing about the woman's photo led Eden to believe she'd ever known Janice before.

That didn't mean she didn't have something to do with Sister Beatrice's murder, it simply meant Eden didn't know her.

Giving in to a well-deserved sigh, she thumbed the pages to Marshall Knight's photo. He turned out to be the pinch-faced man who'd interrupted Eden and the bishop in the cathedral the day after the shooting. Focused then only on the bishop and why he'd protected a predator, she had paid limited attention to an employee butting in.

She trained her gaze on Knight's harsh features; her first thought he might lessen the effect with a smile. But in the next moment, gooseflesh rose on her skin.

Vaguely aware of Lindsey asking if she was okay, Eden's mind traveled back seventeen years. To a little girl in a ripped skirt and a bloody knee, who, because she'd heard voices, had squeezed into a cranny beside St. Patrick's front doors.

The voices turned out to be the school's creepy, always-staring janitor and the old grump who took up the collection.

Marshall Knight. He'd been the one walking with Thomas. Eden tasted bile. She slid the book across the counter to Lindsey. "He's the old grump," she murmured. "He was there that day."

"I'm sorry. What? Who's the old grump?"

Eden crossed the lobby. She collapsed in a chair and dug through her purse for her phone to call Kevin. She never pushed send. The doors to the admin building opened, and along with his partner and Father Slater, Kevin walked in.

Chapter Fifty-One

INSIDE A DIOCESAN conference room, Kevin leaned against the wall, and listened to an agitated Eden and a more rational Father Slater defend their actions in coming to the diocese.

On the opposite side of the room, Sal sat at the conference table. Typically, as he was known to do, he withheld comment and took it all in.

Explaining what they'd found in St. Patrick's basement, Eden might as well have been addressing a jury. She walked while she talked. "All right. I admit Father and I both agreed Janice looks good for this murder. Even so, Knight was at the church that day. Now *him*, I saw."

"Maybe so," Kevin countered. "But you said it yourself, you came here to confront Janice."

Eden circled the table. "Not to confront. I wanted *one* look at her. That's all. And you certainly can't dismiss the strange fact that nobody knows where she is, or where Marshall's gotten off to, for that matter."

"Yeah, and while it's strange to disappear for a couple of hours, Eden, it's not criminal," Kevin said. "Will you listen to yourself? You're all over the place."

She huffed and returned to her chair. Propping her elbows on the table, she ran her fingers through her hair. Kevin waited for her to do her thing. But before doing so, she made eye contact with him and stubbornly dropped her hands.

All right, Nick and Nora," Kevin said. "As of now, Janice Charles and Marshall Knight are high on our suspect list. I promise you, we'll talk to them. You did good work, and we're grateful for your help, but we'll take it from here."

"And if you can't find them?" Eden asked. "What happens then?"

Kevin reached for her handbag, gave it to Eden, along with a meaningful look. He stepped close and lowered his voice. "What happens next is you go back to the job you get paid for, and I'll call you tonight."

Father Slater cleared his throat. "It was my idea to come to the diocese, Detectives. If you're upset with anyone, that someone is me."

"Nobody's upset," Sal replied at last. "Like Kevin said, you saved us hours of digging and sped up this investigation."

Yanking her purse up on her shoulder, Eden rose from the chair.

"C'mon, Father," she said, guiding the priest to the door. "We know when we're not wanted." She walked out without a look back.

Kevin closed the door behind the two cohorts and pinched the bridge of his nose. "I'm going to catch holy hell tonight."

A few seconds later, Lindsey poked her head in. "Detective Raez? Mr. Padilla, president of Citizen's Bank, returning your call."

Sal picked up the conference room phone. "Mr. Padilla. Appreciate the fast response. What have you got for us?"

Sal hung up a moment later, frowning. "No deposits or withdrawals made today to any of the diocesan checking or savings accounts." He clutched the back of a chair. "You think Janice found out Eden and Father Slater were on to her, took the money and ran?"

"It's a good theory. We can link her to St. Patrick's seventeen years ago. But Knight was also there back then." Kevin dropped into a chair. He picked up a pen and twirled it between his fingers. Taking his eyes off the pen, he met Sal's gaze. "Could they be in this together?"

"Not unless she's an incredible actress," Sal said. "I interviewed her. She hates the guy."

Kevin called Dispatch and requested patrol to do a welfare check on both Janice Charles' and Marshall Knight's residences, then launched from the chair. "Let's have a look at her office and then the place where she parks."

According to the receptionist, employees weren't allowed to park in the visitor's section. To enter and leave the building, the staff generally took the shortcut through the admin's back door. From there Kevin and Sal climbed a hill, which led to the employees' cars.

Sal growled as he trudged up an incline. "Man, I ditched my crutches too soon. Seriously, haven't these people ever heard of the Americans with Disabilities Act?"

"We'll leave 'em a note," Kevin said.

At four p.m., upon cresting the hill, Kevin noted that only six cars remained.

"Well, what have we here?" Sal said. "Lindsey said Janice drives a turquoise-colored MINI Cooper. Check this out."

The two walked over. Locked, and as pristine as they'd found her office, the vehicle looked like its owner had secured it with plans to return. So the question was, where was Janice and why hadn't she made the deposit?

"We'll have to call a locksmith," Sal said.

Kevin nodded. "She has to be with Knight." He scanned the area, particularly the spot Lindsey claimed was the business manager's coveted parking space. She also mentioned Knight drove a yellow clunker. Lindsey had guessed a Ford.

If you didn't count two missing employees, nothing about the area screamed suspicious. Lindsey made a competent witness, though. Clunker was right. In Knight's space, oil deposits had soaked into the decaying asphalt.

Prepared to call for a locksmith, Kevin paused when a gust of wind snared a crumpled piece of paper. The breeze carried it away from the Russian olive tree near Knight's space. From a distance, it looked like a simple piece of trash. Although, as Kevin approached, the glimmers of red and gold piqued his interest. Feeling a jump-start to his pulse, he bent to retrieve it. He beckoned to Sal, who limped over.

"What is it?"

Kevin smoothed out the rumpled paper.

Pushing his shades on top of his head, Sal mused, "Okay. Two people vanish who were at the same parish at the same time the nun disappeared. And now this little beauty miraculously appears. Unless you believe in hell freezing over, I can't call this a coincidence, can you?"

"Not a chance." In Kevin's palm he held one of Sister Agnes's long-lost Angel Gabriel holy cards. "Besides, hell can't freeze over. It's right here in Albuquerque."

Chapter Fifty-Two

LONG MINUTES after Father Slater drove off, Eden sat in her Honda with the air conditioning on high, trying to cool off both mentally and physically. It wasn't working. *Go back to the job you get paid for, Eden.* Easy for Kevin to say. How could he ask her to stay out of something so absolutely vital to her well-being? Worse, to simply pat her on the head and add Janice Charles and Marshall Knight to the suspect list.

Eden pounded the steering wheel and glanced between Kevin's Jeep and the admin building. If she were honest, she'd admit she was waiting for him and Sal to exit the building so they could fill her in on what they'd found.

Now wasn't *that* an efficient use of her time. They could be inside thirty minutes or several hours. Accepting her fate, she withdrew her phone and texted Kevin to call her no matter what time he got home. Then she put the car in reverse, looked over her shoulder and saw trouble.

Eden slammed on her brakes. *What a dipshit!* A photographer had entered the grounds.

She switched off the ignition, removed keys, phone, and, because she was angry enough to threaten somebody, her pepper spray. She left the car, regretting once again she'd worn these friggin' high heels. Traversing the lot where he stood taking pictures of the apartment over the diocesan garages—and the place where Thomas had spent his last tortured years—Eden wanted to douse the creep in pepper spray so he'd suffer, too.

"Hey," she called. "What part of the posted signs, *Unauthorized personnel will be prosecuted* do you not understand?"

The jackass, with his very expensive-looking telephoto lens, continued snapping images, barely looking at her. "Freedom of the press, sweetheart."

"Reporters have no more access than average citizens, *honey*," she said, grabbing his arm and spinning the shaggy-haired blond to look at her. "There are police all over this place." She held up her phone. "And I'm about to call one."

He snapped a picture of her. "Thanks for the warning."

Leaving Eden shaking her head, he jogged off between the cathedral and the garages and took a sharp right away from the fence he must have climbed over. Her simmering anger exploded. She stalked after him to make sure he got off the property.

She turned the corner and her peripheral vision caught movement by the side door to the garage. *Unbelievable.* Eden ground her teeth and barged through the door. Thomas's apartment, as well as the entire area beneath it, was still categorized a crime scene. The only reason the police had removed the crime scene tape was out of respect for the parishioners who attended daily Mass. Mr. Overly Ambitious had not only trespassed, now he was breaking and entering.

"Hey, this place is off li—" Pain exploded in Eden's head and her legs crumpled beneath her.

Chapter Fifty-Three

AFTER FINDING a monumental clue like Sister Agnes's holy card, Kevin and Sal returned to the admin building and immediately sequestered the remaining employees in their offices. A night of interviews ahead of them, Kevin requested patrol cars to be stationed at both parking lots. He also had Dispatch run Marshall Knight's plates and put out an all-points bulletin for the Diocese of New Mexico business manager and the bishop's executive assistant, Janice Charles.

It wasn't a guess that Eden would be frantic by now. He excused himself to let her know what was happening. When she didn't answer, he gathered she was pissed beyond belief. Until her text popped up that said *Call me no matter what time you get home.*

Kevin ran a hand over the back of his neck. Maybe there was hope for them yet. She'd kept his trip to Kentucky in stride, after all—at least as well as could be expected for Eden. Time for her to get a grip and understand that police work didn't produce instantaneous results.

The bishop's receptionist had turned into an amazing helper, providing coffee and soft drinks to employees, who after a long day at work preferred to be elsewhere. She handed Kevin a cup and he took it gratefully. He stepped outside to stretch his legs and spotted Eden's Honda in the visitor's center.

What was she still doing here?

Taking back the *hope for them yet* thought, he tossed the coffee, strode to Eden's car, and found it empty. He continued on to the police cruiser several feet away. "That Honda, has it been here since you arrived?"

The cop leaned forward, looked out his window and narrowed his gaze. "Yes, sir."

"Have you seen a blonde, good-looking, five-six, five-seven, red skirt and jacket?"

"I think I'd remember someone like that, and no, sir."

"Damn it." Kevin scoured the vast property and its numerous structures, then jogged back to the admin. Locating Lindsey in the hallway, he asked, "Do you have Father Slater's number?"

Eyes wide, she nodded and headed back to the reception area.

"Call him," Kevin said following. "See if he and Eden Moran are together."

Lindsey made the call. She hung up shaking her head.

Kevin's world stopped. His rational thoughts turned to dust. He bounded down the hallway, nearly colliding with Sal and an employee leaving his office.

"Eden," Kevin said. "Her car's out front—empty. Cop says it's been there since his arrival."

Sal glanced at his watch. "That's almost an hour ago." To Lindsey, Sal said, "Get the remaining names and send these people home, and get us keys to all the buildings on the premises."

"Right away," Lindsey said.

"No. Wait." Kevin whipped out his phone. "Let's get the officers surveilling the exterior to see the staff to their cars and do a search of their vehicles."

"And if someone screams illegal search?" Sal asked.

"If that happens, I want their names. I couldn't care less if they have weed in their car. Three people have gone missing from this place. We have more than enough probable cause."

By five o'clock, with only three hours of daylight remaining, Kevin was painfully aware of the time. Lindsey stubbornly refused to go home. She argued something about Eden coming to her rescue today, and Lindsey, along with three other co-workers, wanted to stay and help search.

Kevin breathed deeply. Eden. Always taking it upon herself to save the day. And sometimes she did. If he weren't ready to kill her, he'd be damned impressed.

Cell phones in hand, law enforcement and volunteers spread out and went to work.

Wiping sweat from his brow, Kevin left the cathedral, tamping down his panic and praying for good news, when his phone rang.

"The stalls beneath Reuben Sharpe's apartment. Get over here."

Kevin sprinted in that direction.

Sal had opened all four garage doors, letting in daylight but otherwise displaying an empty setting.

"What?" Kevin held out his hands.

Squatting in the stall closest to the west wall, Sal tugged off a polyester glove and ran a finger over the cement floor. "Motor oil." He rubbed it between his fingers. "Recent. Bishop Munroe's been staying in his Albuquerque residence since the cardinal asked him to step down."

"Marshall Knight," Kevin said.

"Marshall Knight," Sal agreed.

Chapter Fifty-Four

EDEN SWAM in and out of consciousness, aware of several things. The back of her head felt like it had connected with a brick, her neck was twisted in an unnatural position, and whatever she was riding in was moving one moment and stopping abruptly the next. She also was in a hot, fume-ridden environment, trapped against something hard.

All this before she even opened her eyes.

And when she did, it was as though she were wearing an execution hood. Surrounded in pitch black, she let out a gasp and a horrified squeak as she recalled the seconds before she'd passed out.

No. Not passed out. Knocked out. The photographer. She'd been chasing him. Had he lain in wait, grabbed her and tossed her into his car? That made absolutely no sense.

How long had she been unconscious, and why couldn't she change positions?

Shifting as much as the tight conditions allowed, Eden finally freed her hands. They were numb from her body weight, and she flexed them to restore the blood flow.

The car pitched forward and her already strained neck rebelled. Her abductor obviously hit a rut.

Where was he taking her? Should she cry out? Yell her head off? Her throat burned as she tried to swallow.

Kevin. She'd been trying to call him. Had he received her text—assumed everything was all right? Dear God. Nobody knew where she was.

Her car. It was parked at the diocese. Surely he'd discovered it by now.

From the way the car pitched and stopped, they appeared to be stuck in traffic. She could scream, but would passengers in surrounding cars even hear her? In this heat, they'd most likely have their windows up and their air conditioners on. *Shit, shit, shit!*

Trapped in a trunk gave a body time to think. For one thing, she was far too curious—far too confrontational for her own good. Applied to every case she'd ever tried. Had been since she'd gone to say goodbye to Sister Beatrice and snuck into St. Patrick's. But the fates would teach her a lesson: Those dreaded traits would likely get her killed.

No matter what, she had no choice. If she stayed silent she was going to be raped or die anyway. That was all the incentive she needed. Eden drew air into her lungs and prepared to scream her head off.

That's when she heard it. Ringing. Really? Her kidnapper had let her keep her cell phone? This had to be some kind of nightmare. Either that or these fumes were making her delirious.

Chapter Fifty-Five

MARSHALL KNIGHT didn't stand a chance if he planned to leave Albuquerque, Kevin thought as he sped south on Alameda. It was mid-week, on the tail end of rush hour. Traffic was already backed up, and every available police cruiser was on high alert. The Air 1 helicopter had been utilized, and the Public Information officer had notified the media. Already, civilians were aiding cops via their smartphones. Knight's beat up Mercury had been spotted on Coors Boulevard. Unfortunately, people had reported a lone driver, which didn't bode well for Eden, and in that regard, Kevin had serious concerns for Janice Charles. The two-to-three lane road would hamper his escape all the way, particularly when he reached Paseo del Norte, home to The Plaza and the Cottonwood Mall, a huge commercially developed area and the city's perpetual bottleneck.

If this were any other case, Kevin would be punching the air and giving his partner a high five. But this wasn't any other case; Knight had Eden, and the moment Kevin realized that, his usual objectivity had flown out the window.

There was no point in speculating how Knight had gotten his hands on her in broad daylight in the diocesan parking lot, or what he might have already done. All Kevin knew was that Eden hadn't come all this way to end up on a slab in the morgue. He knew this as instinctively as he knew how to breathe.

Still, he'd been optimistic before . . .

Kevin felt like he'd been toppled off a cliff and was hurtling downward. He gripped the steering wheel and focused on the only thing he could, easing through bumper-to-bumper, stagnant traffic.

Sal was doing an impressive job of multi-tasking. Directing Kevin from his side of the CJ-7, talking between his squawking hand-held radio and cell, he said, "Rio Rancho cops are with us, Kev. They're standing by with spike belts. Knight's probably trying to make it to Bernalillo and the Santa Ana Indian Reservation." Sal shook his head. "We'll get him."

Kevin's bumper nearly rammed the BMW in front of him. It didn't alleviate the situation that concrete construction barriers and traffic cones in the middle of the median added to the chaos.

Blocking out what Eden must be going through, he concentrated on the times they'd made love. He focused on her smiling, laughing—even arguing. He'd argue with her twenty-four/seven if he could get her back in one piece. Far better than to consider the alternative.

Before he rammed the car ahead of him for ignoring his lights and sirens, Kevin veered onto the shoulder. "To hell with this," he said, and then mashed down on the accelerator.

Chapter Fifty-Six

CHEWING HER LIP furiously, Eden struggled to listen, to figure out what she was hearing. Had her abductor left a cell phone in the trunk? Not very bright of him if he had. She'd take what she could get, however. Eden infinitely preferred a stupid kidnapper than one with smarts. She reached out to whatever lay next to her and felt material. She ran her hand over a large swath and finally found the nerve to wrap her hand around it. That's when she realized she was touching an arm. She choked down nausea and croaked, "Hello?"

Not that Eden had expected an answer, but that did nothing to calm her stomach. Another "Oh God," escaped as her will to live outweighed her horror. If this body had a cell phone on its person, Eden had to find it before the bastard behind the wheel figured out that she'd found a lifeline. Ignoring the fact she was very likely touching something dead, Eden ran her hands over the corpse. Sweat poured from her tangled hair and brow, and by the time Eden located a bulge in the fabric, it had stopped ringing.

The silence, however, suited her fine. She could only hope the driver hadn't heard the four Westminster chimes. She slipped her hand into the victim's pocket and located the phone. When she flipped it open, the trunk filled with a sliver of light. In that moment, she was relieved she'd asked Lindsey for a picture of Janice. At the sightless eyes that stared back at Eden and the red and blue silk scarf wrapped around the woman's throat, Eden slapped a palm over her mouth to stifle her scream.

If there was a bright side to this macabre situation, at least she knew who planned to kill her. She wasn't trapped in the trunk of a trespassing photographer; her abductor had to be Marshall Knight.

A few seconds later, after her breath had returned to her lungs and her heart had settled down, she located the phone's last caller. She wanted to call Kevin, but she'd programmed his number into her phone and her panicking mind would not cooperate. If Robert Munroe did have anything to do with Sister Beatrice's murder, Eden would know shortly.

I know when they're telling the truth, and I know when they're not. In this case, my gut tells me to believe the bishop.

Ready to put her instincts to the test, she pressed redial. When the caller answered, she kept her voice low. "Bishop Munroe," she said hoarsely." It's Eden. Oh my God, Bishop, please, help me."

Chapter Fifty-Seven

KEVIN FLINCHED when his cell phone rang. Concentrating on the road he traveled on next to wall-to-wall Albuquerque traffic, he cursed that he hadn't programmed his Bluetooth. The last thing he wanted to do was answer the phone. He chucked the phone to Sal, who caught it in an impressive show of coordination. Although his partner wasn't happy about the delegation, he already had his hands full with the radio and his own cell phone. The exasperated look he gave Kevin said, "You want me to walk on water, too?"

Tucking the radio between his knees, Sal answered, "Raez."

Kevin glanced sideways to see his partner's eyes widen. "Bishop Munroe?"

Kevin lay on the horn as a motorcycle tried to swerve onto the shoulder even as his partner gave him the A-OK sign. "Call her back, and whatever you do, stay on the phone with her . . . No. She doesn't need to talk. We can only hope the phone's a newer model. It'll include a GPS device . . . Yeah . . . God bless you, too, Bishop."

It took everything Kevin had not to rip the wheel out of the steering column. "*What? What?*"

"Bishop Munroe. He heard from Eden."

The relief Kevin felt was short-lived once Sal added, "She's in the trunk of Knight's car. Unfortunately, with Janice Charles' corpse. The bishop was returning a call from Janice. Eden heard it ring and answered." Sal frowned. "She's scared but so far unharmed."

Dispatch chose that moment to pipe through the hand-held unit. "Suspect spotted leaving Coors Road Bypass. Now entering Cottonwood Mall near the Dillard's location."

Now they were getting somewhere. The mall, already in view, was three minutes away. Kevin didn't dare get his hopes up. Not yet. But with so many resources aware of Knight's location, how the hell could they miss him?

Chapter Fifty-Eight

WITH BISHOP MUNROE on the other end, Eden held the phone close, and as he'd advised, did her best to stay quiet. She wasn't imagining the noxious exhaust fumes she was breathing in. As for the corpse she was leaning against, whether real or imagined, poor Janice's body was creeping her out. Eden's nausea was less now that the phone let in a fraction of light, but with the engine running, the muffled sounds of horns blaring around her, and Marshall's stop-and-go pace, she could hear very little of the outside world. She also thought he might have the radio on. If the police had solicited the public as they were prone to do in cases like this, he knew that the police were on to him.

Did that help or hurt her? With no way to know for sure, Eden suspected that as long as Marshall was stuck in traffic, she was safe.

She hated it when she thought too soon. He picked up speed. Eden's heart threatened to ram out of her chest. Had he somehow broken free from the jam? Could he lose the police, perhaps hide under an underpass or in a residential area? No matter how much she needed to stay quiet, Eden had to take a chance. "Bishop Munroe, she whispered. "I'm hanging up now. I have to talk to Kevin." She winced as she heard his panicked objections, then ended the call. She dialed 9-1-1 and furtively asked the operator to patch her through to Kevin's cell phone.

Sal answered on the first ring. "Raez."

"Hi," she croaked. "I guess by now you know that I'm in kind of a tight spot."

"So we heard. Hang on, here's someone who wants to talk to you."

"You okay?"

At the sound of Kevin's voice, she lowered her head and stubbornly refused to cry. "I'm okay now that I can hear you," she whispered. "And for the record, I'm really not in the mood for you to say, 'I told you so.'"

"Wouldn't think of it. Not now anyway. I'll save that for later. And there will be a later. Do you hear me? I'm coming to get you."

"Sounds good to me." She swallowed painfully. "The reason I called is he's picked up speed. What if you lose him?"

"No way. I'm right behind you. We're also tracking you by phone. So stay with me. Can you do me a favor and stay calm?"

"Okay," she said softly, becoming aware that the car she was trapped in was slowing one minute speeding up the next.

"Eden." Kevin's voice was urgent. "Is there anything in the trunk you can use for a weapon?"

"Not exactly, Kevin. I'm in the trunk with a corpse."

"You found the phone. See if you can't locate something to defend yourself."

"I was kind of hoping that would be you," she whispered, unable to hide her fear and exasperation. "Hang on a sec." Flinching, she strained to reach beneath Janice's body. After a great deal of groping and maneuvering, she encountered solid metal. Eden wrapped her fingers around something long and cylindrical and tugged. When she drew it near, she shone the cell phone's light over it and gulped in semi-relief. "I found a tire iron."

"Good girl. If Knight opens that trunk before we can stop him, you may need it. Be ready."

"So far, I don't think that's going to happen. Oh, crap, Kevin, what's he doing? I feel like we're racing the circuit."

"He's somewhere in Cottonwood Mall. Probably negotiating around parked cars."

The fright that had taken up residence in her chest wasn't anywhere close to what she felt a few seconds later when the car stopped and her kidnapper killed the engine.

"We've stopped," Eden squeaked. Hearing Knight's footsteps round the car and close in on her, she dropped the phone. Pitched back into darkness, she clutched the tire iron.

He popped the trunk.

Light flooded the compartment, but she had no opportunity for her eyes to adjust. The moment he raised the lid, he used her pepper spray against her and came at her with a knife. Instinct had Eden burying her face against Janice's clothing for protection, but in the next instant, Knight grabbed her by her hair.

Be ready. Never had Eden been so grateful for such sound advice. Throat clogging, eyes watering, she strained against his brutality, held her breath and came up swinging.

The tire iron connected with mass. Eden was rewarded with a satisfying thud, the kind a baseball player must know when he knocks the ball out of the park. The knife clattered and her pepper spray went sailing. Clutching his hand, Knight's eyes wild with rage, he emitted a garbled oath and an agonized wail.

When she thought he might attack a second time, Eden raised the tire iron to strike again.

But by then, sirens were closing in on them and the killer ran.

Chapter Fifty-Nine

WITH CUSTOMERS grabbing their children and packages and scrambling away from the lights and piercing sirens, Kevin and Sal rounded the department store's parking lot. Each saw Eden at the same time, along with the fleeing man.

Knight had parked close to a building under construction with a nearby dumpster. There was no mistaking how the bastard had planned to dispose of the evidence from the trunk.

Rage had Kevin sprinting in Knight's direction, and though the wiry man must've been fueled by adrenaline, he was no match for Kevin's size or speed. He grabbed the miserable scum by the collar and flung him against a parked car. And with Knight begging for mercy and citing his hand injury, Kevin cuffed him. Then, because there was no way in hell he was blowing this case, he read the suspect his rights. After that, Kevin didn't say another word. He couldn't. He didn't trust himself to speak.

Immediately after, police cruisers and emergency vehicles converged on the premises. Turning Knight over none too gently to two uniformed patrol officers, and wading through a curious crowd and TV crews, he went in search of Eden. Freed from the trunk, she sat on the curb with Sal, who'd already retrieved eye wash, a bottle of water and a blanket to cover her shoulders. No doubt, his partner and his humorous way with words were already at work, helping to dispel her trauma. When she saw Kevin, she was both laughing and crying.

Kevin went down on one knee. Eden stared back at him through red-rimmed eyes. Her hair was matted, her cheeks stained with motor oil, her camisole and skirt soiled and shredded beyond repair. His throat clogged as he asked, "Still after my job?"

His comment brought on a new barrage of tears. "Your job sucks. From here on out, I'm retired."

He raised her hand to his lips. "Now I really do believe in miracles."

She swiped at her cheeks, smudging the oil on her face even further.

"Does this mean I can see you later?" he said.

"Do you have to ask?" she said, laughing. "Your place or mine?"

"Mine. Although it may be a long night. Securing the scene and then coaxing a full confession out of Knight, it'll take a while. Oh, by the way, I'll pay for your new window."

She frowned. "What window?"

"The one I smashed in the diocese parking lot when we were trying to locate you. I also have your purse. It's in my Jeep. You'll need it for the E.R."

"That won't be necessary. I don't need the E.R.," she said, wincing even as she touched the back of her head and her hand came away with flecks of dried blood. "Look, it's already stopped," she began when he shot her a glare.

"I think I'll go to the E.R.," she amended quickly. "My favorite place, the E.R."

"Great, I'll have someone drive you there and then to your place. I'll meet you there as soon as I'm free."

Though suddenly it occurred to Kevin she wasn't listening. He turned to see what had absorbed her attention. Bishop Munroe and Father Slater headed their way. At the sight of the uniformed cop who tried to halt their progress, Kevin thought the rotund Slater just might deck him.

Slater rushed to Eden. "I knew better than to leave you at the diocese without me."

Shaking his head, Kevin glanced between the two and acknowledged the bishop who stood somberly in the background. "I'd like to have seen you try to stop her, Father."

Eden flashed a chagrined expression at Kevin, who winked. Then she reached for the priest's outstretched hand. "You're a hero, Father. Without your knowledge of St. Patrick's history, we might never have solved this case."

Kevin watched some interesting dynamics going on as Eden's gaze left Slater's to settle on Robert Munroe. As the bishop tiredly waved off reporters, the dynamic individual Kevin had met at the reception was gone. No doubt a murder accusation and an affront to his reputation had taken their toll.

Munroe finally entered their inner circle, and Kevin knew a moment's regret. In large part, by doing his job, he'd been instrumental in the high-powered man's fall from grace.

Eden came to her feet and wrapped her arms around him. The bishop, in turn, clung to her. "Marshall? All this time, it was Marshall? Celeste, Eden? Why Celeste?"

Her gaze connected with Kevin's. "Ideally, Bishop, Detective Dancer will have those answers for us very soon."

Kevin returned a swift nod.

The bishop pulled free of Eden's grasp. Focusing on Kevin, his jaw hardened as a spark of his former self returned. "Janice?"

Kevin reluctantly let his gaze wander to where cops had cordoned off Marshall Knight's yellow Mercury. Techs were already whisking a gurney, with a black body bag, toward an ambulance with flashing lights. "I'll take you to her, sir."

"I'd appreciate that." The bishop's eyes misted. "Marshall has much to answer for."

A pretty Hispanic reporter, followed by other members of the media, shoved a microphone in his face. "Bishop Munroe, does this absolve you of the murder accusation? Would you care to—"

Father Slater, with his palms outstretched, was at the bishop's side in an instant. "Bishop Munroe has no comments at this time."

Afterward, Kevin walked Eden to a patrol car, where he'd arranged for an officer to take her to the hospital and then home. Father Slater was still in the crush of things, helping police keep onlookers at bay, and for the first time all day, Kevin laughed. He pictured Slater at his next family reunion in Boston, regaling his cop relatives of how he and his priestly connections had brought a cold case to a close.

"See you two at Mass?" Slater called over his shoulder.

Eden glanced at Kevin and grinned. "You never know, Father."

Kevin took hold of her elbow. "Does he know I'm not Catholic?"

"I don't think it matters," Eden replied. "He's kind of like a cop, he has quotas to fill. Come to my place as soon as you can?"

Opening the door to the squad car for her, Kevin said, "At the speed of light."

Chapter Sixty

KEVIN'S PROMISE to arrive at Eden's loft "at the speed of light" came several hours later. Marshall Knight's interrogation and subsequent confession had not been rendered easily, and an intense grilling session had ensued among the suspect, his defense lawyer, the Bernallio County District Attorney's office and the Albuquerque PD.

Eden buzzed him in and Kevin climbed the stairs to her loft. Given their respective professions, these midnight sessions could well become the norm. Still, this particular late night had been well worth it. For Kevin and Sal, it brought closure and inordinate satisfaction after months of hard work. And he could only guess what it had done for the lady he'd come to see.

Eden opened the door for him, looking much better than the last time he'd seen her. She'd pulled her hair into a tight pony tail, scrubbed her face and applied make up. Her T-shirt and jeans hugged every curve.

Assessing her from head to toe, Kevin asked, "What did the doctor say?"

She pulled the door shut and smiled up at him. "He said other than a slight concussion, I have cement where my brain should be."

"And for that he gets to bill you? I could have told you all that for free."

Eden walked into his open arms. "Oh, yeah? What medical school did you graduate from?"

Kevin held her. Close. It was late and he probably did so longer than necessary, but damn, he'd almost lost her today. All through his interview, between wanting to strangle Marshall Knight with his bare hands and wanting to tie up all the loose ends, the what-ifs had played through his head. Eden very well could have joined Sister Beatrice and Janice, if the twisted bastard had found a way out of the city.

It had taken him seconds to fall in love with Eden Moran; he suspected it would take him a lifetime to get over her. He breathed in her scent and rubbed his hands up and down her arms, relishing her smooth, soft skin.

But if a woman's look could kill a mood, it was Eden's. "Who's representing him?" she asked.

Kevin stared back at her. Naturally, the person Knight had chosen for a defense attorney would be foremost on her mind. Perhaps this would go a long way in creating empathy for each other's careers. By joining the ranks of victim, she now had an understanding of what went through a cop's brain every time a lawyer showed up to defend the bad guy. Was there any way Marshall Knight could get off and not pay for his crimes?

"Brian Sandell," Kevin told her.

She raised an eyebrow. "He's good."

"Not good enough. When the DA told Knight he intended to see him in prison for two murders and twenty years of embezzlement, the lowlife didn't even flinch. But when the prosecutor added *where* he planned to see him rot out his remaining days—in the New Mexico State Pen's Level VI facility—Sandell finally lost his smug look and relented. He described just a few of the atrocities that had happened at the last prison riot and advised his client to spill his guts. That little turd wouldn't last two weeks in that maximum security facility."

"So he admitted everything?" She drew her hands into fists and squeezed her eyes shut.

"We think so, although on a hunch, we're still trying to locate his ex-wife."

Her pretty face formed a harsh mask. "Too bad the state legislature voted down the death penalty. Ordinarily, I'm on their side, but Marshall Knight can't get to hell quick enough for me."

Kevin released her.

"I've waited forever to hear this, Kevin. Please don't try to protect me. Keep going."

He took her hand in his as he led her to her couch. "Before Sister Beatrice came to St. Patrick's, Marshall Knight had a nice little siphoning job going on. With three offertories on weekends, various fundraising drives and special collections, he was acquiring his nest egg. He was careful, even to the point of making staffers count the money together when he'd already taken his cut. What a joke," Kevin added. "No one suspected him, because he'd enacted all these holier-than-thou policies and procedures to prevent the very thing he was successfully carrying out.

"He saw what was going on between Munroe and Sister Beatrice and had accepted he was going to have to abandon that particular gold mine. Munroe showed all the signs of a man determined to leave the priesthood. Whoever replaced him would likely bring his own staff from his former parish, or might not be as trusting as Munroe, and Knight wasn't willing to risk jail.

"So the day of the argument, when Sister Beatrice fell and hit her head, Knight claimed it was just dumb luck that he'd found her."

Eden winced and buried her head in her hands. "His words, Eden. Still want me to go on?"

She nodded, but as she swiped the tears from her face, Kevin faltered.

"Marshall Knight had gone into the church to see what had his boss in a panic. When he saw her lying there in the center aisle, he thought she was dead—that Father Munroe had killed her. Instead of checking for a pulse, all Knight thought of was himself. With the nun out of the picture, Father Munroe had no reason to leave the Church.

"So he carried the body to the storage shed in the garden behind St. Patrick's, locked it and waited. When the cops and emergency services responded to Munroe's summons, they left empty-handed. Knight went back to dispose of the body and that's when he heard her moan."

Eden pressed a hand to her mouth and lowered her head.

"Eden?"

She shook her head. "I'm okay."

Kevin gulped down a painful swallow and continued. "By then Knight had gone too far to let her walk away. If she woke, she'd expose him. The garden shears in the shed were within reach . . ."

Kevin stopped talking. If one could give a visible description of pain, it was etched on Eden's face. He pulled her against him and held her while she cried.

Her sobs finally lessened. She wiped her tears from her face. "And Thomas? How was he involved?"

"Knight needed someone to clean up the evidence, and Thomas was the logical patsy. Knight told the handyman that Father Munroe had lost control, flown into a rage and killed Sister Beatrice. After everything the priest had done to offer Thomas a new life, it was up to Thomas to save him. Thomas went along, albeit reluctantly.

Gritting her teeth, Eden said, "The pieces just fell into place for that . . . that bastard."

"What's scary is how close he came to getting away with it."

"Did you ask him about the holy cards?" Eden asked.

Kevin released a deep breath. "Knight had seen Thomas's emotional response when Sister Agnes gave him the first one. Sensing a way he could keep the janitor in line, he broke into the music room and stole them from her piano bench. Every so often, he'd drop one where Thomas was working as a reminder to keep quiet. Little by little, as Thomas slipped from reality and started spending less time working and more time on his knees, Marshall became worried.

"By this time he was skimming money from all the parishes in the diocese, not just St. Patrick's. The last thing he needed was for Thomas to confess to the bishop how he'd gotten rid of the body. So he started making late night calls, calling himself the *Messenger*, telling Thomas that God had forgiven him and that it was His will that Robert Munroe never know what had happened."

"Did Marshall tell Thomas to attack me?"

"By the time you came on the scene, Thomas was already mentally gone. Knight said it had become Thomas's mission in life to carry out the bishop's every whim, asked for or perceived. Knight surmised that Thomas must have seen you near the church that day. As long as you stayed away from Albuquerque, you were safe," Kevin said shrugging. "When you moved back, that's when Thomas went after you."

Eden stood. Straightening her shoulders and lifting her head, she seemed to reclaim some of her strength. She walked to the loft's window, peered out for a while and then faced him. "And Janice? Father Slater and I were so sure she had something to do with all of this."

"So did Sal," Kevin reminded her. "She didn't, Eden. Janice Charles was exactly what she seemed—devoted, possibly even in love with Robert Munroe, but that's as far as it went. She was married at a young age to a man who abused her. One night, when Janice's husband landed her in the hospital, her parents called Father Munroe. He became Janice's confidant and confessor. It appears she never forgot his kindness."

Evidently, he'd answered all of Eden's questions for now, because she grew quiet. Knowing of nothing else to say that would ease her torment, he rose from the couch and entered the kitchen, leaving her alone with her thoughts. She didn't speak for some time "Does the bishop know all of this now?"

Kevin returned to the living room. "Yeah. He came to the precinct tonight and demanded to see the man he'd trusted for so many years. The bishop was heartbroken, to say the least. He considered Marshall Knight a friend. I'll spare you the ugly details, but even facing life in prison, Knight stayed an offensive, unrepentant piece of slime. Munroe left despondent and angry."

"I'm so sorry to make you go through all of this twice, but you can't know how relieved I am to know." Eden hugged herself tightly. "Do you think we can talk about something else, please?"

He'd been about to suggest the same thing. Walking to where she stood, Kevin said, "Great idea. We could talk about us."

Surprise registered on her face as she glanced up at him. "Us? After what I put you through? You're not mad at me?"

"Furious," he said. I was hoping you'd stay at my place for a few days. If you do, I'll show you how much."

KEVIN'S INVITATION for her to stay with him were the most beautiful words Eden had ever heard. He followed her down to the bed, showering her with gentle kisses as though she were made of porcelain and might shatter at any second.

She was hardly fragile. She was a survivor, of both her childhood trauma and of this unfortunate tragedy. She was also rock solid, capable and ready to deal. "I won't break, Dancer," she said, smiling.

His dark eyes sparkled as though he were happy to oblige. He lowered his mouth to hers, but before kissing her, he whispered, "You had me out of my mind."

He soon had her arching toward him and demanding more. In Kevin's arms she was mindless, entrenched in him and the infinite pleasure he provided. She massaged the back of his short-cropped head, his firm shoulders and powerful torso. Her nails dug into the muscles of his biceps and his lower back and settled on his taut behind. He was like a magnificent machine, a composition of looks, charm and superior fitness, and she was hopelessly in love with the entire package.

His eyes never left hers, nor did she break his gaze. This was too important, this kinetic energy sizzling between them. The thought that earlier that day she might have breathed her last was all the impetus she needed to free her of inhibition. She wanted to be with him in this moment and celebrate life and all that was destined to happen between them.

Later, after they'd engaged in the ultimate physical connection, Kevin wrapped her in his arms and smiled at her as though he were privy to something she wasn't.

"What?" she asked.

"I was just trying to figure out how best to tell you that I'm in love with you."

"Really?" She placed a hand on her heart. "You are?"

"Well, yeah, Eden," he said, frowning. "I am. How about you? How do you feel?"

She tilted her head as though she even had to consider the idea. At the uncertainty that spread on his face, she held back a smile. Finally, she said, "I'd guess I was from the moment I met you."

His eyes sparkled. "Damn, I'm good."

"That doesn't mean I knew it." She laughed and sent a playful slug to his shoulder. "One has to analyze these things."

Grabbing his arm as though she could possibly have hurt him, he said, "Oh, I don't know about that. I pretty much knew."

She tugged the sheet over her breasts. "All right, hot shot, when did you decide you loved me?"

"Probably when you took a bite of that ridiculous hot dog and smeared mustard all over your face. Or maybe it was when I caught you in your office banging your head against the desk."

"Ah, so the fact remains, you weren't sure either. And how charming of you to list all of my foibles."

He stared at the ceiling. "I can't believe we're having this conversation."

"Well, we are." She frowned. "What conversation?"

"About when we knew we were in love. You just do, Eden." Dropping his gaze, he pulled the sheet down, exposing her breasts. "You leave yourself vulnerable." He traced a finger over her collar bone, then her shoulder, while she thrilled to his touch. "You fall in love with the whole person. You don't rest when they're in trouble, and you can't wait to hear from them at night."

"Kind of like what's happening between us?"

"Exactly what's been happening between us."

"Ah," she said. "Thanks for the explanation."

He cupped the back of her head and drew her close for another kiss. When she snuggled against him, Kevin rested a muscular arm over his forehead and chuckled. "All I can say is, this is going to be interesting."

Chapter Sixty-One

TWO WEEKS AFTER Marshall Knight's arrest, Eden walked down a hilly knoll to meet the bishop. Wearing a sleeveless black dress and flat sandals, she carried a single white Easter lily, her broken heart matching her somber attire.

Robert Munroe was clad also in black, with the exception of his clerical collar. He'd been offered reinstatement as the Bishop of the Diocese of New Mexico after being cleared of all charges against him regarding Sister Beatrice, also known as Celeste Lescano. A reinstatement he'd turned down, to the entire city's shock, although he'd done so with much love and gratitude for the Church and his diocese.

Garbed in priestly vestments, Father Slater gave a quiet service over Sister Beatrice's grave, while the bishop bowed his graying head and remained stiff, as though facing the inevitable final goodbye. Eden placed her hand at the crook of his elbow, noting his grief was thick, while hers, thanks to her young age at the time and the trauma she'd suffered, was fractured. Though, one could argue, she'd been no less affected. The one thing she knew with certainty was that the woman they were honoring had been loved, and she had been taken from them much too early and in the cruelest of ways.

For the first time in seventeen years, Eden lowered her head to pray, while her heart and mind tried to grasp the fleeting memories of which she'd been robbed. The few that remained would have to last her a lifetime.

A gentle breeze ruffled the hem of her dress as she caressed the feather soft petals of the lily in her hand.

"You wrote this, Eden? Truly? All by yourself?"

"Yes, Sister, I did. Really."

"I believe you. It's also very, very good. It seems we have an angel in our midst."

Eden swiped at her tears and lowered herself to her knees. Placing the lily on the plain utilitarian marker, she whispered, "You were the angel, Sister. I'm so sorry I had to forget you. I hope you'll forgive me, but I just can't play anymore." A sob tore from her throat.

Father Slater, who hadn't known Sister Beatrice, stood off in the distance. It was Bishop Munroe who helped Eden to her feet. His smile was sadly gentle as he said, "There's nothing to forgive, Eden. You were a little girl whose mind coped in the only way it knew how. If there's any forgiveness to be granted, it should be from all of us, begging it of you. I ask that of you now."

Her throat threatened to close as she nodded.

"I can understand you not wanting to play, and of course, the decision has to be yours." Then, although his eyes remained red-rimmed, his smile seemed genuine, as though he were drawing upon a fond memory. "Celeste loved all the children of St. Patrick's. I suppose that's no secret to you?"

Eden nodded. "I know she did."

"But if she had a favorite, it had to be you. I can't tell you how often she talked about one of your surprise escapes from Sister Agnes, your tremendous gift and how she looked forward to hearing you play. And with all that hair constantly in your eyes, she called you her little ragamuffin."

Tucking a strand behind her ear, Eden smiled through her tears.

"She wouldn't be able to call you that now, Eden. The shorter style is becoming."

She brushed away a new onset of tears. It had taken iron nerves to keep that appointment and ask the stylist for the popular bob cut. She'd thought about cutting it forever. After all, she was an adult now with an impossible schedule. Still, something had always held her back. As she sat in the chair, she realized that cutting the long hair that Sister Beatrice had admired was Eden's first step to letting her go. "It is easier," she admitted.

"I can see you're making great strides in putting your life back together," he said. "Might I ask one question? Won't you *try* to play again?"

With an adamant shake of her head, Eden said, "I'd think of her every time I'd sat down."

"And that's a bad thing?"

"I forced myself to learn how she died, Bishop. I'm doing my best to deal."

"I understand. So it isn't that you don't love playing?"

"*Love playing?*" She scoffed at him. "When I was little, there was nothing more I'd rather do. It came so easy to me."

"It probably still does," the bishop replied.

"I'm afraid." Eden lowered her head. "What if I no longer can?"

"I think you underestimate yourself, Eden. What's more, I believe you will play again, when you decide to."

The man was grieving, and she certainly didn't want to argue the point at a time like this. Nevertheless, she raised a skeptical brow.

"Believe it or not," he said smiling, "now that you've unlocked those memories, the hard part's over. I think a time will come when you say the name Sister Beatrice and the pain won't be so intense. And when you do, you'll be ready. Eden, don't shackle her memory or imprison yourself by saying you won't. Honor her memory and free your spirit by saying you will."

"You're quite eloquent, Bishop, and I appreciate all that you've said. I'll keep it in mind."

"That's all I can ask, isn't it?"

"What time does your plane leave?" Eden asked.

"Father George will drive me to the airport as soon as we're through here."

Eden lowered her head. Looking up at him again, she frowned. "You've decided to become a teacher?"

The bishop laughed. "Don't look so surprised. I used to be quite good at it. My first stint is a hundred-year-old monastery in the Pacific Northwest. Who knows, I may eventually travel abroad. I need this time to clear my head, to re-evaluate the decisions I've made."

"Will you leave the priesthood?"

He shook his head. "Never."

There was much conviction in his statement, and Eden widened her gaze.

"They say you have one soul mate in life, Eden, and Celeste was mine. Without her, I simply have no reason to leave the Church, and I still feel I can make a vital contribution."

Of all the questions Eden had asked, she still hadn't stressed one important point. Knowing of no tactful way of saying what was on her mind, she just blurted, "The day she died, she was angry with you. She thought you'd been with other women. Why would she think that?"

Bishop Munroe's eyes took on a faraway sheen as he seemed to relive the past. Sighing, he said, "I don't think a day has gone by that I haven't asked myself the same question. You and I have the same nemesis, I'm afraid."

"Sister Agnes?"

"Dear, wonderful Sister Agnes." The bishop actually laughed. "She needs our prayers and our pity, Eden, not our hatred. Hate's easy. But it can eat you alive. Don't let it."

He glanced at his watch and then down at the grave. "I need to be going. I hate to be rude, but do you think you can give me a private moment with my beloved?"

"Of course, and I don't think you could be rude if you tried." Again, Eden was overcome by another wave of sadness at how torn this man must have been all those years ago. She hugged him and then received his blessing. Along with his prayers, he'd given her much to think about. Would there come a day when she'd be able to think of Sister Beatrice without her memory piercing Eden's heart as well?

Somehow she doubted it.

Eden climbed the grassy hill, looking directly into the sun. It made the silhouette standing at the top difficult to see. She didn't need to see his face to recognize the tall, muscular form that was Kevin Dancer. At the sight of the man, with his arms at his side, his legs slightly apart, Eden's melancholy turned a corner. She strolled away from unhappiness into his waiting arms.

Epilogue

SIX MONTHS LATER, a nervous Eden arrived for a Sunday afternoon barbecue at the home of her parents. She had a particular reason to be jittery today. Kevin was coming and bringing *his* parents. Things were entirely serious between them now, as evidenced by the diamond ring on her left hand. She suspected this little soiree had been arranged to get his mom and stepdad's final seal of approval.

As for *her* mom and dad, it wasn't a problem. She already knew they adored Kevin, sometimes, more so than her. As she placed a fruit salad on the table, she smiled. The September afternoon was still warm, and the chlorine-scented blue water inviting. She suspected that later, with very little coaxing, she could persuade Kevin to join her in a swim.

Her dad, complete in chef's hat, stepped out on the patio to fire up the grill. "You're mother's asking for you. Stop by the den and put on some music for our guests, will you?"

"Sure, Dad. What kind?"

"Oh, I don't know. Whatever kind of music people in Ohio listen to. And find out what's keeping your sister and Steve. And don't let her give you any of her morning sickness nonsense, for crying out loud, it's afternoon."

"Yes, Dad," Eden said, drawing out her sentence.

She stopped by the den and waded through her parents' elaborate collection of CDs. She selected a mix of classical, jazz, country and rock, having no idea what J.T. and Connie Garland liked to listen to. But before she turned on their sound system and the speakers that would pipe music throughout the house, she glanced into her mother's immaculate living room and the rarely played Steinway that at one time had been a major part of her life.

Thanks to Kevin, and constant gatherings with her once-estranged family, Eden was happier than ever. Every so often she recalled the bishop's promise, *there'll come a time when the pain's not as intense.* She took a deep breath, realizing for the first time that thoughts of Sister Beatrice didn't leave an ache in the pit of her stomach.

The first CD Eden loaded into the system was one she'd heard several times. *What a Difference You've Made in my Life* was sung and played magnificently by a blind country singer named Ronnie Milsap. She'd always loved the lyrics and awe-inspiring tune, and placing it first seemed apropos, given her love for Kevin Dancer.

It was also the powerful memory of the tune she'd written that propelled her in the direction of the abandoned Steinway. At one time she could have sat on the bench, pressed down on the keys, and the music would pour from her fingers.

Part of her rationalized it wasn't only Sister Beatrice's memory that was holding her back, but the thought that she'd stayed away so long, that her gift of playing the piano by ear had been taken away.

Unfortunately, there was only one way to find out.

She walked into the gold- and brown-accented living room, with the polished black Steinway, then closed the beveled double-glass doors. If she could no longer play, there was no reason to embarrass herself. And if she couldn't, well, that settled that. She'd have no choice but to accept it as fate.

Her palms were damp as she sat at the piano. She wiped them on her slacks and let her mind focus on the heart-warming melody she'd loved. She lifted one hand to the black and white keys and pressed the first note. It was exactly correct, so she pressed another, and then the next. When she'd figured out the sequence to her right hand, she incorporated the chords of the left. Then something like magic hummed through her body. Eden took a deep breath, and set her heart free.

And as the combined notes and chords brought the song to life, she saw Sister Beatrice in her mind's eye. The woman she would love forever was smiling. Tears welling, Eden smiled back.

Acknowledgements

Dear Readers:

Deadly Recall brought to mind so many memories of my Catholic school days, but know that with any writer, the muse elaborates and speeds us in a direction all its own, and nothing in this novel has any basis in fact. I am grateful to so many who gave me guidance on this book, particularly my sister Maria Gravina and my friend Kathleen Irene Paterka. To Jean Willett, Robin Searle, Misty Evans, and Allegra Gray, to Rose Colored Ink, my Colorado Springs critique group and to my online Mystery Critique Group, thank you for your invaluable comments and suggestions. To the members of Crimescenewriters, and my editor Pat Van Wie, what would I do without you? To my daughter Audra, my son David, my husband Les, and my mom, Irma, always my first reader, thank you for your encouragement. And to all the teachers out there who give guidance to a child, know that people like my protagonist Eden really do exist and they never forget you.

About the Author

Donnell Ann Bell is as at home in nonfiction as she is in fiction. She has worked for a weekly business publication and a monthly parenting magazine, but prefers her fictional writing compared to writing about stock portfolios or treating diaper rash. She has a background in court reporting, has worked with kids and engineers, and has volunteered for law enforcement and other organizations.

Raised in New Mexico's Land of Enchantment, Donnell has called the state of Colorado home for the past twenty-four years.